one sweet holiday

LUCY DAY

Blue Crow Books

Publisher's Cataloging-in-Publication Data
Day, Lucy 1978-.
One Sweet Holiday: Jasmine Falls Love Stories/ Lucy Day.
p.____ cm.____
ISBN 978-1-947834-74-3 (Pbk) | ISBN 978-1-947834-73-6 (eBook)
1. Women—Fiction. 2. Love—Fiction. I. Title.
813'.6—dc23

Blue Crow Books

Published by Blue Crow Books
an imprint of Blue Crow Publishing, LLC
Chapel Hill, NC
www.bluecrowpublishing.com
Cover Design and Cover Illustration by Lauren Faulkenberry

Also by Lucy Day

The Almost Lovebirds

Almost Definitely Never

for all of you out there who ever
feel that you aren't enough…
You are.

Chapter One

GWEN

I thought I could survive an hour in Brenda's bridal boutique. But I was wrong.

My sister Victoria holds an emerald-green gown up to my face and says, "This one brings out your eyes," and I feel a sting deep in my ribcage.

For the first half-hour, I did all right. Victoria led me through the boutique, pulling one dress after another from the rack, sliding her fingers along the fabric as she held them up for me to see. My little sister, thankfully, is no Bridezilla. Her wedding is fifteen days away, and she's exactly as she always is: sweet, calm, and unsinkable.

I'm the one who can barely breathe.

"How about this one?" she says, holding up a garnet-colored sheath. Behind her, Brenda, the owner, is helping another young woman try on a wedding dress with hints of antique lace and beading. My stomach twists into a knot at the sight. The woman, red-haired and lithe with bouncy curls, spins by a bank of mirrors, studying the dress from every angle.

"Sure," I choke out, "I like it." *Keep it together,* I tell myself. *You can handle trying on a few dresses. You've been through worse.*

Like when Mark cheated on me the week before our wedding. That was much, much worse. It was a year and a half ago, but sometimes it feels like yesterday.

Such as today, for example. I can still picture his face when he told me—the way his brow furrowed and his nose twitched like he was about to sneeze. He didn't even *apologize* for cheating. He just said, "This isn't right. I don't think I'm in love with you anymore." He said it so matter-of-factly, with such ease, like he was just telling me his bank balance or suggesting which restaurant we visit.

I don't think I'm in love with you anymore. As if those words excused his horrible behavior and the fact that he'd just split the world in two.

He said some other things, too—like I was a workaholic, I didn't make enough time for him, I didn't know how to have fun anymore. But what hurt the most was the *I'm not in love with you anymore.* That was the part that snuck up on me and left me completely blindsided.

How did he go from loving me to not loving me in the span of one evening? One dinner? One nanosecond? We were together for three years, and suddenly he was tossing clothes into a duffle bag and saying he'd go stay with a friend.

He left me completely dumbfounded, my mouth hanging open wide enough to catch flies. He kept talking as he packed, while I stood there thinking, *I should say something. I should try to stop him.* But I chose not to argue with him. Because how do you argue with *I don't think I love you anymore?*

When you want to keep your last shred of dignity, you don't.

So I said nothing because silence was better than any words I could put together in that moment.

Later, I came up with plenty of words. Enough to tell him that the wedding was off, and I'd be sending him invoices for everything that couldn't be refunded.

"First I thought shades of red or green because it'll be close to Christmas," Victoria says, leading me to the next rack. "But then I thought navy or black would work, too. I don't want my wedding to look like a holiday party."

Her mouth is still moving, and there are definitely words coming out, but in the last thirty seconds, the store has shrunk to the size of a coat closet. The pain behind my ribs is spreading like I've been stung by a furious hornet. I swallow hard and take a deep breath, but it does nothing to help me. Everything hurts, right down to my bones.

Brenda appears out of nowhere, dressed in a cute floral dress, her graying hair in two braids that make her look far younger than her sixty years. With a wide smile, she scoops the dresses out of Victoria's arms and says to me, "I'll start a room for you, honey. I just got a few new ones in that might work for you, too." Brenda hurries to the back, like she's afraid I'll jinx the gowns if they're around me for too long. She's owned this place forever and has tailored dresses for every woman in Jasmine Falls.

Including my dress for the wedding I never had.

"Are you okay?" Victoria says. "You look pale."

"I'm fine." I'm a brick house. A fortress, even. This is not my sister's problem and I want to keep it that way.

She arches a brow. Four years younger than me, Victoria's my opposite in almost every way. Petite and slender, she's dainty like a wood sprite, with a heart-shaped face and cute upturned nose that make her look perpetually earnest. Her dark blond hair falls in perfect ringlets, defying the South Carolina humidity with ease. She always moves quickly, zipping around like a hummingbird, making me feel like I'm moving in slow motion.

Sometimes she makes me feel like my whole life is going in slow motion. She's always so sure of what she wants and has a solid plan to get there. I'm the total opposite, fumbling my way toward goals that sometimes feel impossible. Victoria's always on a fast track, in the passing lane—and I'm on a dirt road full of potholes that meanders through the woods.

I tower above her at just under six feet, heavier by at least fifty pounds. I like my curvy frame, but next to Victoria, I feel like a giant with my wide shoulders and thick thighs. My hair, brighter blond, is cut just above my shoulders so it won't hang all limp and frizzy. When I remember to have it cut regularly, I can tame it into loose beach waves. I need it to be as low-maintenance as possible, and easy to pull out of my face when working at the cafe.

We have the same bright blue eyes (just like Dad), and the same generous hips (just like Mom). Every other part of us is just as different as two people can be. But we have each other's back, always. So when Victoria asked me to be her maid of honor, I said yes without a minute's hesitation. When she told me her wedding would be in mid-December, in the busiest part of my year when things are completely nuts at the cafe, I said *No problem*. And baking her cake for her? Absolutely.

She's been dreaming of a fairy tale wedding forever, and I'm here to make sure she gets exactly what she wants. She and her fiancé Theo have dated since college and she had a wedding Pinterest board going before she even met him.

Victoria narrows her eyes at me. "You're a terrible liar."

I wince at that knot in my chest again. "I'll be okay." Everyone in Jasmine Falls knows that we called off the wedding. We had zero chance of keeping that disaster out of the rumor mill, especially since the invitations had already gone out. Everyone knows that I left him, but only Victoria and Theo know why. And no one knows how much being in this shop makes me wish the ground would open up and drag me down to the center of the earth.

Well. Victoria might have an inkling.

This feeling isn't all because of Mark, not really. The worst part of that whole fiasco was that I'd felt like what we had was solid. He didn't make my heart do cartwheels, but he was practical, responsible, and down-to-earth. He liked to cook, he kept a tidy house, and he saved part of every paycheck for retirement. With him, I felt safe—until he yanked the rug out from under me.

I've always wondered what it would be like to have a partner who makes my heart do cartwheels. But I decided at some point that safe was an okay trade-off for that. And then *safe* blew up in my face, and now I don't know what I should be looking for anymore.

Maybe I shouldn't be looking at all.

Thirty is probably too early to give up on happy-ever-after, but I'm starting to think that a cartwheeling-heart kind of love might not be in the cards for me. And today's just another reminder that everyone around me seems to find their perfect match—so why can't I?

The problem must be me.

"I've got a room all ready for you!" Brenda chirps. She's extra perky today as if she's trying to erase the fact that I already went through this whole process when I bought my dress here—the dress I later sold online because an altered dress can't be returned.

Victoria gives me a skeptical look as we head towards the dressing room. Truly, she can read me like a book. It's super irritating—especially when I'm trying to convince her that I'm fine, and there's no need for everyone to be concerned about how I'm coping through all of the wedding preparations.

It's not true, but I'd like it to be.

The last thing I want is pity, and I certainly don't want everyone tiptoeing around me during my sister's special time. Mom thinks I'm so fragile that I'll have a meltdown just by watching my sister get married a year after my engagement turned into a dumpster fire. Mom underestimates me in a lot of ways, but this cuts deeper.

To make matters worse, Mark will be at the wedding, too. Victoria lobbied hard to remove him from the guest list, but Theo insisted that he be invited. "He's an asset," Theo told Vic, "A good connection that will pay off big-time." Victoria apologized to me about a million times because even though I told her it was no big deal, she knew I was just saying that so she wouldn't feel guilty about giving in to Theo.

Did I feel blindsided by my fiancé? Sure. Am I going to fall apart watching my sister get married? No.

Too bad the rest of my family doesn't have such confidence in me.

Inside the dressing room, I take a deep breath and shove all those thoughts of cartwheeling hearts way down deep. Down with the hurt and the anger, down in that place that's now twisting in on itself and threatening to cut off air to my lungs. I bury that all as deep as I can as I strip out of my jeans and sweater and pull the first dress from the hanger.

"So, I forgot to tell you," Victoria says from behind the dressing room door. "Theo's friend Logan is coming in today. He's going to stay at the lake house until after Christmas." The lake house is Victoria's, which is right next to mine. She lives with Theo now, in a big Georgian house in the historic district that he bought as a foreclosure and has been renovating ever since. Like Victoria, Theo's also in real estate—but he toes some ethical lines in a way that makes me wish that he and Vic worked for different firms. He's her opposite in a lot of ways, too.

"Really?" I say. "What's an out-of-towner going to do in Jasmine Falls for a whole month?"

"He said he wanted to get away for a while," she says. "He's from Scotland."

"And he's coming here for the wedding? Must be some friend."

"Yeah, Theo met him when he did his semester abroad at St. Andrews. Sounds like they've stayed in touch."

I shimmy my hips to get into the dress, bouncing a little on my toes.

"Theo offered to let him stay the week of the wedding," Victoria says, "but then Logan insisted on paying us for the whole month, as a rental. Sounds like he wants to avoid his family around the holidays."

"That's fair," I say, squirming my way into the top half of the dress. If I could avoid my family at Christmas, I totally would. I love my sister, but our mother is like a Gucci-wearing grenade. A die-hard Southern socialite, she loves throwing big parties and decorating like her life depends on it. Everything in her life must be perfect—and that's where she and I run into trouble. Victoria might fit well into the daughter-shaped mold my mother created for us back when we were born, but I've given up on trying to meet Elaine Griffin's outrageous expectations. That doesn't mean she's given up on trying to make me fit them, though. Our mother is a fixer. A problem-solver. When she looks at Victoria (crushing it in her real-estate firm at twenty-seven, about to marry a guy Mom adores), she gets giddy with pride. When she looks at me (staring down thirty-one, a canceller of weddings and owner of a cafe that she deems "tacky"), she sees an unending list of things that need fixing.

And let me say for the record: I'm exhausted by her attempts to fix me. Lately, she's forced her matchmaking skills on me and has been setting me up with every man in town that she deems capable of providing me with "stability and security" (her words, not mine), which means they are way older than me and completely boring in every way.

The setups just show that my mother doesn't want to know

me at all. I don't have a long list of expectations for my dreamboat future partner—he just needs to be respectful, kind, and passionate. And he needs to make my heart turn cartwheels.

Those traits are not on my mother's list. She doesn't know why I left Mark, but she was furious when I canceled the wedding. And of course, she saw it as another of my failures.

Christmas makes everything worse because the end of the year is when Mom not only throws big boastful parties for her friends but takes inventory of all the parts of her family that need adjustments and overhauls. Every year, I make the top of her list. Victoria's the tough one—she's got this endless confidence that allows her to stand up to Mom and still manage to be on speaking terms with her. But for me, talking to my mother about my feelings, and how she makes a sport of stomping on them, only makes the rift between us wider.

With a groan, I wiggle into the next dress—a skin-tight dark-green satin one that reminds me of Miss Scarlet in *Clue*. Victoria should be the center of everyone's attention for this entire month —not me. But I know my family. They'll be laser-focused on me during this time, speculating about how I'm holding up. I couldn't be happier for my sister. I just wish everyone believed that enough to let me be.

The dress is a little too small, but I tug the zipper up anyway because I know Vic loves the dark green satin. It gets stuck halfway, though, and even as I lean sideways and arch my back, I can't contort myself enough to zip it all the way.

"He's a bazillionaire, but it sounds like he wants to go into hermit mode," Victoria says, still talking about this Logan guy. "You probably won't even know he's there."

Stifling a groan, I imagine some trust-fund playboy doofus living next door to me for a whole month, doing god-knows-what late into the night that will no doubt shatter the quiet I'll need to survive this month of extra work. Wedding prep aside,

December is the busiest month for the cafe, and I have other plans, too—like taking this winter to get my life in order and get my goals aligned with my purpose. I've been taking more special orders and learning some cake sculpting techniques that could make for a powerful revenue stream—but that kind of planning takes uninterrupted quiet time.

Theo and Victoria rent out the house as a vacation home for part of the year, except for the weeks they use it themselves. They're both so busy that they rarely come up anymore, so I've grown accustomed to it being rented through the summer and fall. Most of the renters are quiet, but now and then somebody shows up and wants to go totally wild, and it feels like I'm in the midst of a party on the last night before the world ends.

"How on earth does Theo know a bazillionaire wannabe hermit?" I say, picturing the handful of billionaires I know from social media posts and monologues in late-night comedy shows. None of them seem like the sort of people who would hang out with Theo Thomas. Or the kind of people who would come visit Jasmine Falls for a month. Or the people I want to have living next to me, even for a short time.

"His family's in banking or something," she says, still waiting patiently on the other side of the door. "He hadn't reached billionaire hermit status when they were in college together. Theo told me that he sold an app for a ton of money after college and has been doing his own thing ever since."

I sigh, thinking of a stuffy, spoiled, buttoned-up guy with an ego the size of a planet, and the zipper creeps up one more inch.

When I finally step out of the dressing room, Victoria lets out a squeal of approval.

"Help," I say, turning around. "I'm trapped."

She tugs the zipper up as far as it will go as I suck in my belly. This one is too tight to successfully breathe in (and forget about sitting down), but before I can say that, I glance up in time to see something that stops my heart.

The bell over the front door chimes just as my ex-fiancé Mark steps inside. His eyes go straight to the woman in the white gown, who's now giggling as he leans in to give her a quick kiss.

That pain behind my ribs sparks to life again and my throat seals shut. Before I can fully process the scene, I dive back into the dressing room, feeling like the whole building has tipped onto its side. I'd heard that Mark was seeing someone else, not from Jasmine Falls—but engaged? Already? Seeing him with this woman yanks me back through time to the day he left, and the crushing feeling is back, stronger and more ferocious than ever. The feeling that safe and solid is just an illusion.

"Off!" I gasp, reaching behind my neck and fumbling for the zipper. "Please, Vic, get this off!"

Victoria, eyes wide, slams the dressing room door closed and yanks the zipper down like this dress is on fire. My knees wobble and I sink down to the floor in a puddle, and she's right there next to me, her tiny body like an anchor, precisely where I need it to be.

"It's all right," she says, one hand on my back, moving in big slow circles. "I'm so sorry, Gwen. We can go."

"No," I pant. "I'll be okay." If I say it enough times, it might become true. I stretch out on the floor as much as I can, the dress pooling around me as my feet poke out from under the door.

"Stop being so stubborn," she says, her voice like a warm breeze. "Screw dresses. Let's go get ice cream instead. We can sneak out the back. Unless you want me to run out the front and tackle him to the ground, which I would absolutely do."

"I know you want to mark my dress off your to-do list," I wheeze. "Just give me a couple of minutes. Plus, it's forty degrees out."

"So what? There's no temperature threshold for enjoying ice

cream. And there will always be dresses, as long as Brenda has breath in her body."

"Everything okay in there?" Brenda's voice comes from behind the door. Her taupe kitten heels are pointed just slightly toward each other in that way that means she's poised to jump in and sweep up the pieces of whatever has fallen apart just beyond her line of sight. With my feet sticking out from under the door I probably look like the wicked witch when that house fell on her. But we aren't the first women to have this kind of meltdown in her dressing room, and we sure as heck won't be the last.

"We're good!" Victoria chirps. She lifts a brow and I nod, confirming that yes, we are good, and my lungs are working again. I pull my knees in toward my chest, heaving in a big breath that reminds me I am still alive and this is not the end of the world.

"Ugh. I wish I could un-invite him," Vic says, frowning.

"It's okay," I tell her because it has to be. In a town this small, I can't avoid Mark entirely. Even though I'd really, *really* like to.

"You get dressed," she whispers. "I'll handle Brenda."

Victoria springs to her feet and slips out the door, her voice a calm lilt as she tells Brenda how she just loves those new dresses she set aside, and she's certain we'll find my perfect one.

But deep down I know the truth: I couldn't be farther from perfect if I tried.

And holding it together when I finally see Victoria in her big white dress might be a whole lot harder than I thought.

Chapter Two

GWEN

When Victoria drops me at my house, it's a little after four in the afternoon. The sun will sink soon, right over the lake, and I'll be waiting for it with a glass of wine on the porch. This is one of my favorite parts of the day—and I have my Grandma June to thank for it. This was her house, and when she died last year, she left it to me. The house next door was her sister Bernice's, which she left to Victoria. Both were built back in the 1940s, in a cute Cape Cod style with newly added decks and open floor plans. Victoria completely remodeled the inside of hers, but I've done little to change mine, aside from stripping wallpaper and painting the rooms a pale dove gray that gives everything a boho-cabin vibe. It's not huge, but it's big enough for me. My house and Victoria's are close together, separated by a row of boxwoods that give just enough privacy without making you feel you're a world apart.

As I step inside, I shake my head and try to let go of all these thoughts about Mark. It's not like I haven't seen him around since our split, because in a town this small, it's impossible to avoid anyone forever. Still, seeing him in the grocery store or at the gas station isn't the same as seeing him steal a kiss from his new fiancée.

But I realize should be grateful. Mark's bombshell made me realize that I wasn't totally in love with him, either. And that was the scariest part of all—I'd been going through the motions, convinced that what we had was what I wanted, and what I was supposed to want.

But I was wrong on all counts.

Safe is necessary. Solid is important. But I need cartwheels, too.

In my bedroom, I hang the garment bag I've been carrying on my closet door. While I was recovering in the dressing room, Victoria and Brenda packed some dresses for me to try at home. Peeking out of the top of the bag is a note:

So sorry about before. I think you'll like these. I'll call you later.
—V.

Curious to see what they selected, I unzip the bag and find six dresses—two that we pulled from the rack and four more that Brenda must have set aside for Victoria to see. As badly as I want to strip out of my clothes and into my pajamas right now, I have to do this one thing for Vic first. She wants to check this dress off her to-do list so she can move on to the other details. So I take the bag into the bedroom and text her.

Hi, I type. **Trying on dresses now.**

Oh super! Vic writes. **Thank you! Are you doing okay? If you want company, I'll bring wine and we can binge-watch the bake-off show.**

All good. The lump forms again as I pull the first navy dress from the bag. Why does wedding stuff have to make me such a wreck? I should be able to breathe, buy a dress, and help my sister without having a panic attack.

Send me pics of any contenders, she writes. **I'm grabbing a few things at the store, so I can swing by and break any ties!**

Will do, I answer, though I just want the rest of this evening to myself. I'm peopled out and desperate to unwind without having to think about anyone else's feelings.

The first navy one is a bust—so tight in the hips that sitting is impossible. The garnet fit-and-flare has a sweetheart neckline and about ten pounds of beading—but it's a solid maybe if it were a little bigger. After trying on another red one that's a full size too small, I text Victoria in a huff.

Why can't Brenda get it through her head that I'm a 16? I write. **There's no way I'm wearing something so tight my boobs pop out.**

Maybe it's those awesome skinny jeans you wore today, she replies. **You know how Brenda is. She thinks she can guess the fit of every dress in that shop, regardless of the size you tell her.**

Brenda might need new glasses, I answer.

I can always grab more this week, she types. **We'll find the right one. Don't stress.**

I groan, wishing this one task could be easy.

Staring down my reflection in the full-length mirror, I narrow my eyes. I can do this. I can go to her wedding and not think about Mark. I can be happy for her without being sad about what I lost.

Feeling hopeful, I squeeze into the second navy dress, another fitted style with some serious sparkle. I have to wiggle to get it over my hips, but at least it has a little stretch. I manage to get it halfway zipped when there's a knock at the door.

"Geez, Vic," I mutter. "At least give me time to get through them all." With the top half of the bodice unzipped, the front of the dress is gaping open, but I stumble through the living room anyway, forced to take tiny steps because the dress isn't as stretchy as I'd thought.

Not a contender.

"I thought you meant later," I say, flinging the door open. "I haven't gotten through them yet and I think I pulled a muscle getting out of the last one."

And then I gasp, clawing at the front of the dress that's almost definitely showing my lacy bra.

Standing on my steps is the most gorgeous man I've ever seen. His hand is raised to knock again, his lips parted in surprise. He's a good five inches taller than me, broad-shouldered with unruly reddish hair and intense blue-green eyes that make me think of glaciers. His eyes drift down the length of the dress and then dart back up to my face before his full bottom lip quirks in surprise.

"Hi," he says, "Are you Gwen, I hope?"

Holding the dress up to cover myself, I croak, "Yes, that's me." How is it that this day can still get worse?

"I'm Logan Fyfe," he says, and to his credit, manages to keep his gaze firmly fixed on my face, as if I haven't just nearly flashed him. "I'm a friend of Theo's. Staying in the house next door." His voice is all gravelly and rough, with a brogue that could melt me right into these floorboards. His smile, though, is warm and friendly. "So sorry to bother you, but I've just arrived and can't seem to find the key. Theo said you might have a spare."

I blink at him for what feels like a full minute, taking in the slim-cut dark jeans, the green cable-knit sweater with sleeves pushed to his elbows, a hint of a tattoo swirling along his forearm, peeking out of the sleeve. Close to my age, he has tiny wrinkles at the corners of his eyes, and just a hint of beard stubble that makes him look right at home in the woods.

This man is going to be my neighbor for the next month? I

open my mouth to answer and he pulls his phone from his pocket. "Text from Theo," he says, holding the screen out toward me. "Promise I'm not a serial killer or some such thing."

I glance at the screen and read enough to see that indeed, Theo sent him here. Theo, who is apparently too busy to bring him a spare key and solve this problem himself. I swallow hard, wishing that Logan had knocked on my door just a few minutes earlier when I was wearing the sparkly red dress that managed to zip all the way. I feel like a mess, and I'm so tired of feeling that way.

"I do have one," I say, opening the door wider. "It might take me a minute to find it. Come on in."

As Logan smiles and follows me inside, I realize with horror that half of my back is exposed. As I round the kitchen island, I give one more valiant tug at the zipper near the base of my spine, but it's impossible to grab it at the right angle to pull it up. Changing out of this dress isn't an option because I'm not about to leave this man in my kitchen while I go down the hall to pry myself out of it. Plus, I know it'll take some serious effort to get it over my hips again—in the length of time it took to squeeze myself out of all this satin, I could tell him the entire history of Jasmine Falls. So instead I shuffle over to the island where I keep things like spare keys and rummage through the drawer with one hand while holding up the neck of the dress with the other.

From the other side of the island, Logan says, "You need a hand there, darling?"

His voice is a deep rumble, smooth as velvet. It sends a shiver straight down my shoulders and I can't help but imagine how that voice might sound right against my ear.

Mercy, Gwen. Get it together.

When I glance up at him, he steps closer and motions toward the back of the dress. He doesn't seem to notice that my heart stopped when he said *darling*. "May I?" he says. His tone is completely nonchalant as if this sort of thing happens to him all the time.

A man as gorgeous as this one, though—he probably handles a lot of dress zippers.

Mortified to be caught this way, and tired from battling the dress, I turn my back to him and sigh. "Thank you. It seems to be stuck." This can't get any more embarrassing, so why not let him put me out of my misery?

His finger trails slowly along my spine as he eases the zipper up. Forcing all the air from my lungs, I pray to whatever higher power might be witnessing this debacle that the zipper will go all the way—and try to ignore the delightful tingling that his finger leaves along my skin. For a moment, I savor this feeling of someone offering to help me when I most need it, even in this minuscule way. Asking for help isn't something I do. Ever. I'm supposed to be able to take care of myself, after all—and that includes dress-shopping, holding myself together for my sister, and yes, even managing antagonistic zippers.

"There," he says. "Now you have use of both your hands." His breath tickles my neck and I will my knees not to buckle.

When I turn around, he gives me a boyish smile—the kind he might give to a little old lady after he helps her step up onto a curb—and I feel equal parts relief and humiliation. His eyes meet mine and I'm struck by how kind they look—and how they seem to shift from blue to green depending on the light. He blinks at me for a moment, obviously unaffected by the last few moments, and says, "You think you have that key?"

"Key," I blurt. "Yes. Right." I turn back to the drawer and shove pencils, batteries, and screwdrivers aside for what feels like an hour until I locate the keychain with the chickadee on it that holds Victoria's spare key. "Here we go," I say.

He holds out his hand and I frown, the key hovering just above his large palm. "The lock sticks sometimes," I say. "And you have to jiggle the handle just right, and if you don't get inside fast enough, the alarm goes off. You have the code, right?"

"Code?" he says, pulling his phone from his pocket again. Victoria usually remembers to turn the alarm off when guests are coming, but not always.

"I'll just go over and show you," I say. "If the alarm goes off, then the sheriff shows up, and then the busybody neighbors have more fodder for the rumor mill. And believe me, they'll have a field day with you."

He lifts a brow. "And why's that?"

"Seriously? Have you seen you?" I wave my hand in a circle to indicate all of him, from his carefully tousled hair and roguish grin to his expensive-looking chukka-style shoes. "A handsome mysterious stranger who shows up in a fancy car like that one?" I gesture behind him, toward the zippy Mercedes coupe in the driveway. "They'll think you're James Bond or a billionaire vampire and they'll discuss it for weeks."

His laugh is a deep rumble that makes the back of my neck tingle in the most delightful way. I can't believe I just said all that out loud—this dress must have cut off all blood flow to my brain.

"So my plan to go incognito has failed," he says as if he has no idea that he's pure sin wrapped in denim and cashmere. "But to be fair, that was the last car on the lot that wasn't either a monstrous SUV or a roller skate." His eyes glitter with amusement.

"Good luck doing anything incognito in a town this small," I say, leading him out the door. I'm barefoot, but that hardly seems important right now, and going back inside to wrestle my way into shoes isn't appealing. "Let's see if we can do this without landing above the fold in tomorrow's paper."

Before he can argue, I shuffle across the porch, still taking my awkward tiny steps. There's no way I can wear this dress through the entire ceremony because the bottom half is so tight it might as well be a mermaid tail. I love my curves, but I'm still self-conscious in clothes that are so clingy they leave nothing to the imagination. And this dress makes me feel like every inch of me is on display.

"I'm sure I can manage," he says, watching me like he thinks I might tip over. "I don't want to make you late for—" his voice trails off as he nods towards the dress. "Whatever I'm keeping you from."

"You're not keeping me from anything," I say, hiking the skirt up to my knees so I can make it down the porch steps. "Except for the cardio that comes with squeezing in and out of a bunch of dresses that might as well be painted on." Something flares in his eyes and there's that teasing smirk again.

"Thought you might be getting ready for a big event," he says, offering his arm as we cross the thick grass between the houses. I loop my hand in the crook of his arm when we cross the rise where the ground is uneven from mole runs. His bicep feels solid under my hand, and I wonder for a moment if his whole body is corded in muscle like that. As soon as we're back on level grass, I pull my hand away.

"The wedding," I say. "My homework tonight was to find the right dress." Homework, because I couldn't hold myself together long enough to try on a few dresses in a store I've been inside a hundred times.

"Ah," he says. "How's that going?"

Hopelessly disastrous. And now epically mortifying.

"Let's just say this day hasn't been my finest."

His lip lifts with a hint of a smile. "For what it's worth, that one's quite lovely. Assuming you don't need to move very much."

"Moving is optional. Unless I need to make a fast getaway."

"I can help you with that, should the need arise," he says.

"It's the least I can do to repay you for helping me to unlock the door."

"I'll hold you to that, Bond." I'm left wondering if he means carry me over his shoulder or plunk me down in his very fast car. Or maybe both.

"I certainly hope so."

And just like that, I feel a fraction more at ease. When have I ever felt so comfortably awkward with a man who can also leave me breathless?

When we get to his porch, I'm babbling about restaurants he might try and telling him where to find the nearest grocery, because apparently I go into tour guide mode when I'm feeling comfortably awkward. I tug the skirt a little higher so I can make it up the steps and I don't miss the way Logan's eyes follow the hem of the dress. He holds one arm out behind me as if he fears I might trip, and I say another silent prayer that I make it through this day without doing a faceplant. Slipping the key into the lock of the front door, I show Logan how to jiggle the fussy lock to make it turn. Once inside, I flip the light switch and…nothing.

Annoyed, I shuffle across the living room to the kitchen and flip the other bank of switches.

Still nothing. The house is completely dark.

"Guess the next thing you need to see is the breakers," I tell Logan. "We had a storm a couple of nights ago that probably tripped them. I lost power for a little while, too. It happens now and then."

He follows me into the back hall, where the breaker box is located.

"Here," he says, holding his phone out towards the box. "Flashlight app."

"Well, aren't you the boy scout," I say, flipping all the breakers, just for good measure.

"Highly debatable," he says in that rumbling brogue.

"Have to navigate lots of dark houses, do you, Bond?"

"Now and then," he says. "I like to be prepared for anything."

When I turn all the breakers back, I hear the beep of the stove and the hum of a fan starting up. A light flicks on in one of the bedrooms off the hall and everything seems just as it should.

"That did it," I say. "You should be all set now. Until the next storm, anyway."

His deadly smirk is back. We're stuffed into the small hallway together, so close that I can see a tiny scar on his left eyebrow that makes him look like he could throw a good punch if it was warranted. Logan and his very muscular frame seem to take up all the space around me that isn't occupied by shimmering satin. It's not a bad feeling, being so close to him, and I have the irrational urge to move closer.

"Thank you, Gwen," he says, his voice friendly and smooth. "I'll try not to trouble you again."

"It's not," I say. "I mean, trouble me anytime." A blush is rising in my cheeks—what on earth is wrong with me? My voice sounds all raspy and breathless, and why can I not form sentences that don't sound ridiculous? I should leave, right now, before my brain completely short-circuits. I move to squeeze past him, but he does the same, and I walk right into his solid chest. I inhale his woodsy scent and slide my hands over his sweater because it's so very soft—and I shouldn't be doing either of those things. His hand has landed on my hip and I'm standing on his foot. It feels like being struck by lightning.

"Sorry," I say.

At the same time, he says, "My fault."

He backs against the wall as I peel myself from his body and head back to the living room as if he didn't just knock me completely sideways.

"Well, you know where to find me if you need anything and can't get a hold of Theo," I say, my heart pounding in my ears.

He rakes a hand through his hair as if he felt that bolt of lightning, too. Those blue-green eyes bore into mine as he says, "Maybe I can repay the favor sometime."

My brain goes straight to the kinds of favors it should definitely not be thinking about, and I make a beeline for the front door as fast as my tiny steps will take me. I push aside all thoughts of his broody gaze and his roguish smile because this man is a billionaire playboy and there's no way I'm his type. And even if I were, these are dangerous waters and I am definitely out of my depth. What I need is to go back home, get into my pajamas, and not think anymore about the hard line of his jaw, those perfectly chiseled forearms, or that gravelly voice that's raised goosebumps on my arms no fewer than three times.

Nope. Not going to think about any of those things. Not today, Satan.

"Have a good night," I say, flinching at the way my voice has suddenly risen an entire octave.

"You too, Gwen." His voice rumbles in a way that vibrates along my skin, but I'm not going to think about that either.

When I glance back over my shoulder, he's leaning against the doorframe, one hand resting on his hip, drawing my eyes to his muscular forearm and the tattoo that peeks out of his sleeve.

I definitely don't need to think about how far that tattoo might reach and how those planes of muscle might feel under my fingers. And I definitely am not going to think about how my name sounds on his lips, made rounder by that delicious brogue that makes me tingly all over.

Not even for one more minute.

Chapter Three

LOGAN

My phone buzzes with another incoming call from my brother Rory, and for a second I seriously consider chucking it into the lake.

He's been calling and texting all day, and if I answer he's going to needle me and try to suss out where I am and probably lay on a boatload of guilt in his annoying passive-aggressive way. Rory's the most predictable of my siblings, and usually, there's a certain amount of comfort in that fact. But not today.

It's nearly seven in the evening, which makes it almost midnight where he is, home in Edinburgh. After being here a few short hours, I've managed to unpack my things and get settled in the house—well, that's a lie. My clothes are arranged in the closet and I've figured out the wi-fi situation and made myself a cup of decent tea. But settled? No. I'm still feeling completely unmoored, and that feeling has only been magnified by my brief interaction with Gwen, the woman next door who has clearly been placed here to completely unravel me.

This trip was supposed to comprise three parts: One, avoid my family and their ridiculous behavior until the end of the year when I have to deliver a decision I'd rather give them via carrier pigeon. Two, toast my old mate Theo and his new bride and celebrate like a normal human who isn't running from a problem that seems to grow bigger every day. Three, give myself some space to consider what I want to do with my new life after I send that pigeon across the ocean and remove myself from the Fyfe empire for good.

Not one of those parts included meeting a woman who already has me tied up in knots and devising ways that I might casually bump into her again without seeming like an incompetent lunatic.

Because only a lunatic would practically beg to get his hands on a woman's zipper within five minutes of meeting her.

I just couldn't help myself. She looked so flustered, so mortified to be caught off-guard—as if she had anything to be embarrassed about. I just needed to remove the obstacle that was making her feel awkward—it's a habit ingrained in me, removing obstacles like that. I'm good at fixing things. But the words were out of my mouth before the logical part of my brain could stop them, and then she was standing just a breath away and whispering a thank-you that was so filled with relief it made my ears tingle.

I zipped so carefully, determined not to pinch her skin and also prove that this was just a friendly favor, helping someone escape a vulnerable moment, and that I was not in fact, a handsy weirdo.

At first, I was annoyed when I walked up onto this porch only to discover that the lockbox by the door didn't hold the house key. But that feeling quickly dissipated after spending five minutes with Gwen Griffin. When she walked me over here, I crossed the yard like a man in a trance, so engrossed in the sway of her lovely hips that I could barely focus on the words she was saying—which mostly had to do with restaurants I might enjoy and where I might find a good beer. I wasn't interested in either of those things but was instead focused on Gwen's long legs and luscious curves—and the delightful lilt in her voice. The walk to the house was entirely too short, and I felt a momentary thrill as the lights refused to come on and Gwen decided to lead me through the dark to search for the breakers.

Part of me hoped she wouldn't solve the problem so quickly. Because after the day I've had—or the last hundred, to be honest—it was a relief to have an easy conversation with someone who didn't want a single thing from me.

As we stood crowded in the hallway, the switches flipping under her fingers, one thought pushed all others right out of my brain: this was the most interesting woman I'd encountered in a long time. Something about her drew me in close as if she were a magnet—and though that made absolutely no sense to me, I wanted to know why.

My phone rings again. Rory's name flashes on the screen and I see a string of missed texts from him, too. He's never going to stop, because he got the Fyfe gene for stubbornness—same as me.

He's caught in the middle, though, just like always. And he wants this problem solved as much as I do. Rory and I see eye-to-eye on most things: how to handle our mother, when to drink Macallan over Balvenie, and when and how to rock a tan suit. But with our current situation, we're at an impasse.

With a groan, I answer the call.

"Did you not see my texts?" Rory says. "I've been trying to reach you all day."

"Have you?" I search the kitchen cabinets, hoping that Victoria and Theo might have a nice whisky stashed away in case of trying circumstances like this one.

Rory snorts, and I know he's rolling his eyes as he mutters a curse under his breath. "Where are you, anyway?"

"Away." It comes out shorter than intended, but I don't

apologize. I didn't tell anyone in my family that I was coming here for the wedding—or the whole month, to be more precise. I've kept the Fyfes on a need-to-know basis for a long time now, and my life's much easier that way. The urge to micro-manage runs deep in my family, and I've spent most of my adult life trying to break that habit. The other Fyfes, however, have not.

"Funny," he says, his voice sharp. "Grandad's about to have a coronary."

"Hope Cait's around to put him back together, then."

"You're hilarious."

Rory's been working for our grandfather, a shrewd real estate developer, for years. He's the obvious heir to all things Fyfe because he actually has an interest in growing the company and isn't appalled by their way of gobbling up land and turning it into useless things like luxury golf courses and condos that are used three months out of the year. To be fair, Rory has ideas about transforming Fyfe into a more progressive and less ethically gray company—he's always been the most optimistic of us. He's thirty-one, but Grandad still thinks of him as a kid and believes I'm better suited to run the company. My sister Cait is off the hook because she chose another worthy profession—she's a cardiologist, and at thirty-seven is the youngest in her hospital. She's already won an impressive number of awards for her research and service to the community. The Fyfe clan doesn't know how to do anything but excel. It's exhausting being around so many people who chase perfection.

As the middle kid, I often slipped beneath the radar—especially after I took a gap year and went to work for a non-profit based in New Zealand that specialized in doing ocean cleanup. (All those stories about floating islands made of plastic? One hundred percent true.) It was about as far as I could physically travel on the globe—almost precisely halfway around the world from my family and all of their expectations.

Still, it hadn't been far enough.

You'd think that by now, at age thirty-five, I'd be confident telling my family how I feel about their expectations of me. But you'd be wrong. Every time I've tried to tell them that I'm not interested in stepping in for my grandfather, it's started an epic feud. They think loyalty means doing whatever they demand, without question. So while Rory's the obvious choice to take the reins, Grandad's trying to bully me into taking over when he retires next year. He sees me as the charming fixer who can solve all the company's problems and maintain the empire, and now he's trying to force my hand using every weapon he can.

His current ultimatum: come back and run the company, or he sells the country home that my family dearly loves—and forces my mother to move out. It's a cruel way to tighten the screws because he knows that to me, the estate is just bricks and timber. But to my mother, it's a sanctuary, the place that holds memories of my father—and Da's the one thing she's sentimental about. It would break her heart to leave, even though she'd never show it. She might be a hard woman, but only because Grandad made her that way.

But that's David Fyfe in a nutshell. Keen on power and wealth above all else.

The thing is, I have no interest in being the new CEO of Fyfe Industries, and never have. It only took me one summer of working with my surly, elitist grandfather to realize that the Fyfe business wasn't for me. So I teamed up with a friend of mine and sold an app that gave us a big chunk of seed money. Together, we invested in some start-ups that grew even bigger than what we'd expected. I had a good eye for fledgling businesses and had a way of fixing problems, and I used that skill to make some hay.

My family calls my investments pedantic—a whisky distillery, a few software apps, and a cyber security company. These are not sectors they deem worthy of my attention, but they're investments that brought in surprisingly good returns and did exactly what I wanted: they made me enough money to stand on my own, independent of my family.

I don't need the Fyfe fortune, and I never will.

Ma and Grandad don't understand that, though, because they think they can hold the fortune, and this company, over my head and make me cave. No matter how much they have, they always want more—and they think I'm the same.

Rory's on speakerphone, still going on about how I'm ruining the holidays, and I'm hearing about every third word he says, thinking instead of the way Gwen seemed so flustered when I offered to help with her zipper and how heavenly her skin felt against my fingertip. And the way she'd laid her hand on my chest when we collided in the hallway, sending a wave of heat rolling through me all the way to my toes. I'd expected to hole up in this house until I came up with a solution, but already I'm itching for an excuse to see Gwen again.

It's an urge I haven't felt in ages.

"How are Ma and Grandad?" I ask him.

"Planning your funeral. How do you feel about a pyre?"

"It'd be fitting, considering Grandad's archaic business tactics." He spent decades bullying competitors into submission, and now he has the mistaken impression he can use that tactic on me.

"When are you coming back to end this little standoff?" Rory says.

"Sometime after New Year's," I say.

A string of curses fills the air and I hold the phone away until it stops. That gives me time to check the cupboards under the kitchen island, where I find two bottles of wine and a half-empty bottle of bourbon.

That will have to do. I pour two fingers of bourbon into a

glass as Rory continues his tirade and make a mental note to leave the newlyweds a top-shelf whisky when I leave.

"You about done?" I say, stepping into the bedroom that faces the lake. The walls are painted a pale blue, and I imagine waking each morning to soft light and chirping birds. When Theo first invited me to the wedding, I was surprised because we hadn't talked in ages. We'd been in classes together at St. Andrew's, but did we really have the kind of relationship that warranted wedding invitations? I'd always found him arrogant and a little too eager, to be honest, but maybe I'd misjudged him. First I'd considered sending a nice gift, but then he offered to let me stay in this lake house for a week. When I googled this town, I instantly decided it was exactly the kind of place where I could lie low and retreat until I figured out how to resolve this ticking time bomb with my family—so I asked to rent it through the end of the year. Based on Rory's colorful swearing, coming here was the right call.

"Are ye trying to wreck Christmas?" Rory cries. "If Da were alive, he'd—"

"Finish that sentence and I'll never speak to you again," I growl.

There's a beat of silence. He knows I never joke about Da.

"Where the heck are you?" he says, quieter now. "Just come home."

"I'm not going to be harassed all through the holidays." I keep my voice even, because I'm done letting the Fyfes get under my skin. "I said I'd give them my answer by Christmas, and that's what I intend to do." I take a sip of the bourbon—it's a smooth one that I'll enjoy more when I don't feel like my brother is trying to give me an ulcer. "I'm trying to come up with a solution that serves all of us. And I can't do that if they're needling me all hours of the day."

Rory sighs. He's always been sympathetic, even though I

know he feels overlooked and undervalued. Rory did exactly what our parents wanted him to, pretty much his whole life. The worst thing he ever did, to date, was drink Da's eighty-year-old scotch while they were away on vacation and then hide it by filling the bottle with water. That was when he was fifteen. Since then, he's played by all the Fyfe rules. He has a lot of solid ideas for growth, he takes just enough risk to reap staggering rewards, and he has enough empathy to not be a cutthroat jerk. If anyone could turn Fyfe into a humane practice, it'd be Rory. He'd be the ideal heir to the empire.

I, on the other hand, would not. While I'd never turn my back on my family, I can't be the fixer they want me to be. I won't solve their problems anymore, and I won't spend my life trying to redeem the company and atone for all its sins.

Rory, though—he's big on redemption.

"He's not going to settle for anyone but you," Rory says.

I let out a heavy sigh. "I could murder the whole PR team for planting that idea in their heads."

A few years ago, my grandfather hired someone who caused a scandal that boiled down to embezzlement and a mistress. If it wasn't for a top-notch, million-dollar PR team, that sordid story would have sent the company into a death spiral. The team suggested that a fresh face could shepherd a new era and sense of trust and fed my family a solution: me. And Grandad agreed.

There's just one problem. I don't want the job.

That's not reason enough for my family, though. They've tried every tactic to make me come to heel: family loyalty, shame, and guilt. The Fyfes are used to getting what they want, by any means necessary. Grandad's even threatened to write me out of the will—ridiculous, considering I don't need a cent from him. But that's how David Fyfe operates: under the assumption that everyone can be bought.

Rory grunts. "Still, it's juvenile to just run away to Istanbul or wherever you've gone."

I smile at that, Rory thinking he's sly enough to make me tell him where I am. "The air here will clear my head."

"Aye, so you figured a week in Sweden would help with that, did you?"

I sip my bourbon, savoring the burn. "Aye, so I did."

Theo inviting me to the wedding was the perfect excuse to get away. Deep down, my family wants the best for me, but they have some very specific ideas about what "best" means. Some days, those ideas make me want to fake my own death. Coming here for a month felt like a reasonable compromise.

Walking away from the family business means leaving behind my family's legacy, but it also means freedom. The question is, how much sacrifice is my freedom worth?

"You're impossible," Rory says. "And you're breaking Ma's heart."

"Oh please. There's a chunk of coal where her heart should be, and we both know it." My mother, Maisie Fyfe, looks sweet on the outside, with her perfect white bob and her ice-blue eyes. But underneath the makeup and the Hermes threads, that woman is pure honey badger. She'll stop at nothing to get what she wants, and right now what she wants is grandchildren—specifically mine, brought to her via Eileen Finlay, the woman she's decided is my perfect match.

That's just one more thing she'll lay into me about if I darken her door.

"She'll be livid if you miss Christmas," Rory says.

"She should have considered that before she pulled that stunt with Eileen."

Rory groans. "Not this again."

"It's not exactly a minor infraction," I growl.

Eileen Finlay and I dated until a few months ago, and she's a decent person—just not the one I want as my partner. Her family's just as old and powerful as mine, and she doesn't care for their outdated viewpoints, either. She likes having a trust fund and living on a giant estate, though, and has no intention of leaving that life behind. We dated because my mother decided that Eileen was both a complement to our family and a sizable financial addition. But I finally broke it off when I realized that I didn't love Eileen, and never would. And to be fair, she didn't love me, either. She loved the idea of me, which is a different thing entirely.

Ma didn't take the breakup well. She's hopeful that I'll just surrender to her will like a fox that's been chased from one end of the countryside to the other, winded and bedraggled and resigned to its fate.

"Rory, she went ring shopping for me. Just last month she told Eileen that they needed to start planning the wedding— even though I never proposed."

Rory sighs. "She loves that gal."

"No, she loves the idea of a power couple." I grit my teeth, wishing he could just see this for what it was—a desperate plan to control me as I hurtled out of her orbit with my financial freedom.

"She does this because she loves you," Rory says, "Deep down, under her layers of Burberry and barbed wire."

He'd feel differently if Ma's attention was so laser-focused on him.

"Wrong," I snap. "She does this because she's a control freak. Ma needs to understand that this behavior is not okay."

"It would be nice to discuss this face to face," he says. "Tell me where you are, and I'll meet you."

He'd do it, too. Rory would nick the company jet and be here in a blink.

"Look," I tell him. "I've got to go. I have somewhere to be."

"Just consider coming home for Christmas," Rory says. "Okay?"

"Enjoy the holiday," I say, and end the call before he can argue any further.

Exasperated, I walk out onto the deck of the house, willing myself not to howl into the night like I've become completely unhinged. This would be so much easier if I could cut myself off and leave them forever. But they're my family, and I can't stand by and do nothing while Grandad turns us all against each other. It's my duty to at least try to fix that much. It's what my father would have done.

The lake beyond is still as a mirror. Above, the moon hangs full and bright, casting a blue-tinted glow over the water. Bone-tired, I stretch out on a deck chair and close my eyes for a moment, trying to push aside that conversation with Rory and will my heart to go back to its normal rhythm. When I finally feel my body relax, my stomach rumbles, reminding me I never got around to supper. *Just a few minutes more,* I think, taking in the chilly breeze, the splash of a fish. As the birds call from the nearby trees, I let my mind wander, not at all surprised when it drifts back to Gwen and the delicate curve of her neck, her full lips as she gave me a teasing smile.

If my dad were still alive, he'd tell me to fall in line and do what the family needs. He'd tell me it's my duty to fix what's broken because that's the way it's always been. *We all have skills,* he used to say. *Yours is fixing things. And family comes before all else.*

But it's that kind of blind dedication that put him into an early grave. He'd had a heart attack at fifty-one, no doubt from the stress of working for Grandad and being held to impossible standards. Later, Grandad had told everyone that he'd had a weak heart—a phrase that he'd chosen carefully to take one last jab at my father for at least attempting to dedicate a fraction of his life to his children instead of the company.

Staring out over the lake, one thought rises above all the others—one that I've tried to tamp down for a long while now.

I'm not sure I want to fix my family anymore, because maybe they deserve what's coming.

Chapter Four

GWEN

"True confession," I say to Dan, whom I've known for precisely three and a half minutes. "I hate the holidays. Don't get me wrong: there are lots of things I love about winter. Like cozy fires, the first snowfall, gingerbread cookies with immaculate icing, and big mugs of cocoa with tiny marshmallows. Those are the parts I look forward to. But the rest of it, no thank you."

"Um, okay." Dan clenches his jaw and checks his watch as if hoping it might teleport him someplace else. With his deep brown eyes and wavy blond hair, he reminds me of a Ken doll. He's drawn a big smiley face on his name tag with a sharpie and that should have been my first clue that this would go sideways.

"Let me guess," I say, feeling like I've just crushed a butterfly. "You love Christmas." It's December the second, and he's wearing one of those Nordic-style sweaters with frolicking reindeer and festive snowflakes that would likely win over any woman in this town who has a soft spot for the holidays.

That woman is not me.

"Well, it *is* the most wonderful time of the year," Dan says with a boyish smile. Bless his heart, he still thinks this ship isn't sinking.

"Not in my family. Did you ever watch *The Jerry Springer Show*? Because we make that look like NPR." My parents might look fancy, but it's not uncommon for the sheriff to get a phone call when they start screaming at each other at top volume. And holiday stress dials them up to eleven. A few years ago, they started spending the week of Christmas on a cruise ship, and that's worked out best for everyone.

His mouth falls open and his eyebrows furrow in what looks like barely restrained horror. I am such a delight today.

Good job, butterfly crusher. You are officially a Grinch-Scrooge mashup, and because of that, you will die alone in your lake house, surrounded by all the other feral animals.

"Time!" Sharon yells. She's in charge of this speed-dating disaster. As she gleefully rings her tinkly bell, she tells us all to switch partners. Sharon, in her thirties and newly married, teaches kindergarten when she isn't playing matchmaker, which explains both her sugar-sweet tone and her ability to herd cats.

"Nice to meet you," I say to Dan, because I'm not completely feral, but he shoots over to the next table like he's been fired from a cannon.

Good grief. I haven't gotten one bit better at flirting. I feel a little sorry for Dan—but only for a moment, because his next date is wearing an elf hat, and when he shakes her hand, he lights up like a Christmas tree. He'll think she's a holiday miracle after meeting me, and I feel my job here is done.

"Hi there," the next guy says, extending his hand. He has a roundish face, an impossibly bright smile, and dark hair that's sculpted like a dollop of meringue. His faded tee shirt and jeans make him look like a teenager, but he's easily in his late twenties. "I'm Elliot," he says, and he seems bored already.

"Gwen," I say, shaking his hand and trying to mentally

wipe my slate clean. I'm 0-9 so far this evening. There's no way any of my dates will be clamoring to see me again. No matter how hard I try to be sociable and polite, I just feel awkward in these situations that call for small talk and icebreakers. It all feels so orchestrated, the opposite of me. I do it, though, because my friend Fiona suggested that putting myself out there was a good way to move past the Mark disaster. Somewhere deep down, a little part of me is still hoping for cartwheels.

Elliot's eyes rake quickly down my body and back up to my face. He gives me a wolfish smile that makes me want to roll my eyes.

"So what do you do, Gwen?" he asks as he sits across from me.

He's the tenth man to ask me that tonight. I want to say I'm a dog groomer, or a librarian, or a park ranger—just because I'm so tired of answering the same question the same way. Does no one around here ask interesting questions anymore?

And yes, I realize that I could ask the interesting icebreaker question—like *if you could live anywhere in the world for a month, where would it be?* But in my experience, most men here plow right into their monologue before my ass hits the chair. And sometimes that tells me all I need to know about them.

"I own a cafe," I tell him. "I'm a baker."

"Neat," he says.

When it becomes evident he has no other thoughts about that, I open my mouth to ask him where he'd like to live in the world, but he's clearly one of those people who takes every beat of silence to pivot back to themselves.

"I'm between ventures myself," he says. "I'm starting a YouTube channel and building my brand."

Oh no.

He pulls out his phone and starts scrolling, and someone

please put me out of my misery. Sharon really needs a no-phones rule, but that would likely end in a revolt.

I sip my apple cider, now as lukewarm as my feelings about being here tonight. My eyes glaze over as Elliot scrolls through his channel, showing me lots of videos that appear to be about his dog and his wardrobe, which is a cross between hipster and vacationing octogenarian. Eliot can rock a floral shirt though—I'll give him that. Mostly, I'm watching the clock on his phone and waiting for Sharon's bell to split the air again and free me from this agony—but then out of nowhere, my brain conjures an image of Logan standing on my doorstep, his eyes locking on mine as he gave me a lopsided smirk that had just a hint of bad-boy charm. I didn't mind the way his eyes swept over my body, half admiration and half wonder. It was…reverent.

Stop, I scold myself. *He's the definition of off-limits. Here for a hot minute and so far out of your league, he's like a twinkling star.*

My brain refuses to accept that answer, instead choosing to remind me of his angular jaw, his enticing beard stubble, and that heavenly accent of his that makes the tiny hairs on my neck tingle. Now I'm imagining him whispering all sorts of delicious words into my ear and it's suddenly too warm in here.

"Isn't that awesome?" Elliot asks, grinning at his screen.

"Yep," I say, still thinking of Logan and his lethal smirk. "Awesome."

This is only my third night of speed dating, but tonight is my last hurrah because it's not my scene and I know when to cut my losses. Jasmine Falls is a hard place to be single. Everyone knows your business in a town this small, and most people have shaped you into a mold that's hard to break out of because they've known you forever.

That's why tonight's gentlemen are all from Liberty Hill, a neighboring town. Importing strangers was the only way Sharon could make her speed-dating venture last more than six weeks because most of us already know each other around here. Sharon no doubt has a map full of pins in her home office, a spreadsheet that has a list of towns she can target next.

Fridays used to be movie night, but Victoria's been prodding me to get out and date again, and I started to think maybe she was right. It was time. And then she got engaged, and then everyone gave me those raised brows full of worry, and the solution became clear: speed dating.

It seemed like a good idea at the time—it was a way to throw myself into the dating pool again with little effort. When Vic's wedding came around, I needed a date for a whole other reason. The last thing I want is for everyone to be focused on me at Victoria's wedding, feeling sorry for me and wondering if it's hard for me to be there. If I have a date, they won't pity me because they'll see that I've moved on. Their focus will be on my sister, where it should be.

If my date has to be someone like Elliot or Dan, just for one evening, I can manage. I just need to create an illusion. For someone who sculpts lifelike flowers from frosting and slips vegetables into desserts, an illusion should be a piece of cake.

So to speak.

"Grumpy Cat made a fortune," Elliot says, his eyes widening. "I think my dog Spinach can be even bigger—we just need to monetize the channel and get in front of the right people. Look, here he is skateboarding!"

I knock back the rest of my cider, wishing it was the hard kind. I put on a nice green sweater dress for tonight and took the time to style my hair with some fancy spray that promised to give me "beach waves." I even put on volumizing mascara and lipstick that would stay on after a thousand sips of cider.

"Time!" Sharon calls, ringing her bell. "That does it for tonight, everybody! I'll compile your surveys and be in touch when I have your matches!"

After a polite *Nice to meet you*, I slip away from the table while Elliot waves to Carly Bennett, who was once the head of the debate team and now works for the mayor. She's wearing the heck out of a red mini dress with a motorcycle jacket and has her dark hair piled in a loose bun. She probably thinks skateboarding dogs are awesome. She probably kills it at speed dating events like this one. She probably doesn't scare guys off by talking about how she hates the most beloved holiday of the year.

She probably isn't leaving here with zero matches and going home alone on a Friday night.

Once outside, I text my best friend Fiona, who recently moved back to town. She always wants a run-down of the speed dates, partly because she's secretly hoping some mysterious stranger will swoop in and make me have honest-to-goodness stars in my eyes.

She's probably curled up on the couch with her hottie fiancé, but she'll call me later if I don't get in touch because she also wants to know I got home safe. And honestly, I'm desperate to have a conversation with someone who isn't trying to size me up in five minutes.

Please don't ever let me do this again, I type. **You have my permission to smack me with a pillow the next time I bring it up.**

Went well, did it? She writes back.

They should serve alcohol at these things. Otherwise, it's just abject cruelty.

So no potential dates? Fiona's on my team all the way, but she's found her dreamboat fella, and she's completely forgotten what awkward dating was like before him.

I'm so bad at dating, I type. **The actual worst.**

Not the worst, she replies.

In one hour, I met ten guys, and there wasn't even a hint of a spark. By now, I should have found a spark somewhere, because I feel like I've dated every eligible guy in a fifty-mile radius who is not a serial killer.

Well, that might not be accurate. A couple of them were iffy.

I'm done dating, I write. **It's just going to be me and my dog. I'm okay with that.**

Gonna have to get a dog, then.

Get me one for Christmas. The fluffier the better.

Want to come over and help me with this Shiraz? she types. **We can discuss the best dog breeds for you.**

We're overdue for girl time, but for some reason, tonight's strike-out hit me harder than usual. **I'm beat,** I type. **Just going to go home and crawl into a hole. Raincheck?**

Sure, she answers. **But if you watch the last *Bridgerton* without me, we're going to have words.**

I would never, I answer.

THE LIGHTS ARE STILL on at the lake house next door. It's almost nine, and I'm desperate to curl up with a nice cheese plate and stream a goofy TV show before going to bed. Most nights I have trouble sleeping—mainly because it's so hard to shut my brain off and stop overthinking. Every night when my head hits the pillow, my brain decides that it needs to replay every gaffe from that day, resolve all awkward interactions and devise witty comebacks that I can file away for later use, go over all of my to-do items for the next day, and then consider how things might go awry and cook up some back-up plans. Generally, a few episodes of my favorite baking show will silence that part of my brain long enough for me to fall asleep.

Generally.

Once inside, I quickly change into a long-sleeved tee shirt

and pajama pants and pour myself a glass of wine. My fridge is like a wasteland because I put off grocery shopping again, but there's a frozen pizza that I can spice up with the last of the veggies. I've just unearthed a package of mushrooms when a knock on the door startles me and I fight back a groan.

Victoria. I forgot to call her back about the dresses, and she has to return them ASAP. I sigh, wishing I could just stop my brain from feeling like a hurricane of endless to-do items and focus on one task at a time.

When I open the door, I drop the mushrooms and the package bounces at my feet. Logan's standing on the porch. His hands are shoved into his pockets, his hair tousled as if he just rolled out of bed. He's changed into a rust-red flannel shirt that seems tailor-made for his body.

It's a really good look for him.

He bends down and picks up the mushrooms and hands them to me, as though such a thing weren't at all unusual. "Hi, there," he says in that rumbling voice that I've decided will send a shiver over my skin every time I hear it. He glances down at my pajamas and gives me a lopsided smile.

"Hi," I say. "Everything okay at the house?" I try to keep my voice cool, even though I'm acutely aware of the fact that I'm wearing my goofiest pajama pants, the ones with dachshunds and cupcakes, and I just tossed baby portabellas at the hottest guy I've ever met.

"Do you know a good place for dinner?" he says. "I shut my eyes for a minute, and now it's hours later and I'm starved." His eyes rest on mine, all sleepy and hopeful, and *mercy*—Logan's clearly one of those men who looks incredible even first thing in the morning. "I was going to head to town and grab a bite. Care to join me?"

Something flutters in my chest and I try hard not to picture him lounging in bed with tousled pillow hair and delectable day-old beard stubble. My poor overworked brain is going to have a field day cataloging all of these details later when I'm trying to fall asleep.

"You won't find anything good open at this hour," I say. "The town rolls up early this time of year."

"Oh." He frowns, raking a hand through his hair. "Didn't think about that."

"Perils of a tourist town," I say. "But I was about to throw a pizza in the oven. You're welcome to have some."

"I don't want to put you out," he says, but his arched brow indicates that he's not eager to leave. And lord help me, I'm not eager for him to leave, either.

Chapter Five

GWEN

I open the door wider. "Come on in. It's not fancy, but it's better than a gas station hot dog. That's about all you'll find this time of night, and I wouldn't wish those on my mortal enemies."

He smiles as he steps inside and I catch the scent of something manly, like leather and cedar that makes me lean in a little closer. If someone hasn't made a candle with this scent, they're missing out on serious bank.

"Och, thank you," he says, holding my gaze. "You're a saint."

"It'd be criminal to let James Bond starve."

He smirks, still giving nothing away. I can't help myself—teasing those little half-smiles from him is too much fun.

He leans against the counter as I set out another wine glass. "Would the soccer—er, football—star like some wine?" I ask him, nodding towards the open bottle.

He snorts at my ridiculous guess about his profession and pours himself a glass while I dig through the fridge, searching for anything to put on the pizza. I usually buy simple frozen ones—cheese only—and then add my own veggies. It's almost real cooking.

"Got everything you need at the house?" I ask him. "Except for the obvious, I mean."

"Aye, it's grand." He pulls a knife from the block and starts to chop the mushrooms he rescued. His hands are large, his fingers nimble, and he moves with a slow, easy grace.

"You just gave yourself away," I say, unwrapping the pizza. "Celebrity chef."

His eyes rest on mine as he moves on to a pepper. "Leave room for a little mystery, Gwen Griffin." He gives me the sort of devastating wink that only a guy like him gets away with, and my mouth goes dry.

"Oh god, you're an influencer, aren't you?" I give him an exasperated sigh. "I knew it."

"Can't say I've ever been accused of being a good influence." He gives me an evil grin and I'm melting inside.

"Are you ever going to tell me what it is you do?" I ask him.

He stares at me through long lashes. "Why would I? Your guesses are so much more fun."

"So, more of a Bond villain, then."

Another tantalizing smile. "How'd the rest of your day go?"

"Torturous. My friends think I'm hopeless and talked me into speed dating. I don't recommend it. Zero stars."

He rests the knife on the counter and arches a brow. "Och, no," he says, his tone deepening. "Those two words should never go together. Some things you should take your time with." His big hands rest on the counter and my brain's on fire, thinking of other things those hands might do, oh-so-slowly.

Stop, I think. *You just met this man. Stop thinking about his big hands and his chiseled forearms, and all of his other perfectly put-together parts.*

"But it's great in theory," I say, sprinkling the sliced veggies on the pizza. "You have five minutes to talk and get all of your awkwardness right out on the table from the start. You have your first impression, usually a silly icebreaker question that can actually tell you a lot about a person, and then a chance for any red flags to pop up. You get to see if you have those instant butterflies, or if it's a total mismatch. In the long run, it saves you a lot of time."

"So this is a productivity thing," he says, crossing his arms over his chest. "Mere efficiency." His teasing stare puts me oddly at ease.

"I'm just saying, think of how much time you could waste on a bunch of first dates—when in the first few minutes you have a pretty solid feeling that it's not going to work. And of course, we want to be polite, so we don't end the date after just a few minutes. We have that coffee or sandwich and suffer through it even though we know we'll never see that person again because that's what polite people do. Haven't you been on dates like that, where every minute after the first five was excruciating and just drawing out the inevitable?"

"Did you meet anyone interesting?" he says, his eyes turning stormy as if that thought is unsettling.

"Interesting, maybe. Interested in me? No."

"I find that hard to believe."

I laugh, reaching for my wine. "It's true, though. I have the scorecards to prove it."

"Scorecards? That's positively barbaric."

"We're a little obsessed with scoring and winning over here if you haven't noticed. We have endless reality shows to prove it."

He snorts. "I'd wager you collected skewed data tonight. You can't discern true interest based on a quickie date. You need a proper date to determine how you feel about someone."

"Speed date," I correct. "And actually, I've gotten pretty good at determining a lot in the course of five minutes."

He leans his hip against the counter, his brow lifted in a way that implies all kinds of mischief and I wonder exactly what he means by *proper*. "So where would I land on your speed date?" he says. "Did I pass the five-minute test?"

"I'm still here, aren't I?"

He lifts a brow. "I'd have to be pretty awful to drive you from your own house."

"You could never. I'd shove you right out the door."

He grins and my heart does a barrel-roll. "I do not doubt that," he says, his voice dropping an octave. He rolls up his sleeves, slowly revealing those chiseled forearms that draw my gaze like a magnet. It's the most glorious thing that's ever happened in this kitchen.

From this distance, I can see a little more of the tattoo that curls around his arm. It looks like black and gray leaves with bold outlines and intricate shading, a style that reminds me of woodcut prints. I'm dying to know how far it goes up his arm, if it spreads over his broad shoulder and onto the well-defined muscles of his back.

I didn't realize I had a weakness for forearms and tattoos until this moment. He smirks when he catches me looking, and his gaze drops to my lips.

I feel like a bunny staring up a wolf. But I think I like this wolf.

"So what do you consider a proper date?" I ask him, dying to know what Logan Fyfe does when he turns the charm up to eleven.

He rubs his fingers over his scruffy chin, and the faint scratching sound makes me imagine how that stubble would feel scraping against my neck, my shoulder blade. A shiver runs all the way down to my toes, and I am in so much trouble.

Mercy. I haven't felt this weak in the knees around a guy in… well, ever. Just my luck it would happen with one who's merely passing through town.

"Dinner's a lovely start." He turns toward me and leans closer, his hand lingering on the counter between us. "Then a nice walk in a garden, someplace quiet and calm where we can hear each other talk. Someplace where you can see the moon and stars overhead, where there are no distractions. A quiet place, only for us, where it feels safe to reveal as much as we want to each other."

The deep rumble of his voice and the matter-of-fact way he says these wildly romantic things is enough to make my knees buckle.

"That sounds better than literally every date I've been on."

His eyes lock on mine. "Is that so?"

I shrug. "Between the speed dating and my mother trying to set me up with the most boring men alive, I haven't had the best luck lately."

His brow lifts and his jaw tenses as if I've poked a wound. "Aye, I know a thing or two about matchmaking mothers."

"Aren't they the best? It makes me wonder what, exactly, my mom thinks of when she sees me, and how, precisely, she imagines me fitting with men like—" I shudder at the thought of how determined Elaine Griffin is. "Never mind. That's a rabbit hole we need not venture down."

He laughs then, a deep rumbling sound that makes my skin hum all over. "I'll drink to that," he says, clinking his wine glass against mine. "Nothing like a meddling mother to make you rethink all of your life choices."

And now I want to know about all of his life choices and how they led him to me.

The timer chimes and I grab the hot pads from the counter and pull the pizza from the oven.

Logan smiles, revealing lethal dimples. "So what do you do for fun around here?" He makes *fun* sound absolutely sinful.

He arches a brow and I wonder what Logan Fyfe does for fun. That single thought has my belly filling with butterflies, because whatever he does on a date is probably thrilling. Unlike what I usually do here.

Stop, I tell myself. *You just met this man. He's a total stranger.*

"Depends on whether you like touristy things," I say. "People here go bonkers during the holidays—hay rides, tree-lighting, contra dances—you name it. If you can dress it up for Christmas, they do it. The town gets decked out to wazoo with twinkling lights and sparkly garland, and you'll feel like you're in a Hallmark movie. Plus there's the Congaree National Park, and there are lots of places to go hiking and whatnot, if that's more your style."

Instead of tromping around in our local swamp, however, I picture him doing Scottish outdoorsy things like pheasant-hunting and caber-tossing, and wonder if kilt-wearing is the common practice I'd like it to be. This man looks perfectly at home in a casual flannel and broken-in jeans, like a walking advertisement for the rugged outdoors. It's just one more way that he seems to be my opposite. My friends Fiona, a wildlife painter, and Sadie, a former park ranger, insisted I go camping with them once, and they regretted it the instant a spider crawled across my face in the night and I screamed so loud and so repeatedly that the rangers came to make sure no one had been eaten by a bear.

He smiles. "Sounds like a great place to spend a month."

After slicing the pizza, I serve it up on a couple of plates. "If you like Christmas, you're in for a whole lot of wholesome small-town fun. For the entire month of December, it feels like we're all trapped inside a snow globe. Minus the snow, of course, because that never happens here."

"You never have snow?" he says, his voice so sad it's like I've just told him we also have no chocolate, no dancing, and no kissing.

"It hardly ever gets cold enough. Usually, we need the AC at Christmas."

"Hmm," he says. "I might not have packed appropriately."

"You might be spending Christmas in your skivvies," I say, teasing.

He arches that brow again, and my cheeks turn hot as lava as I imagine precisely what he might look like under those finely tailored clothes. Why does this man short-circuit my brain so that it goes straight to the inappropriate place? Like imagining all of his hard muscle and chiseled lines, and where that tattoo ends.

Totally inappropriate. And delicious.

I take a long drink from my ice water and fight the urge to hold the cold glass against my cheek. His lip quirks like he's reading my mind.

Lordy.

I think of frozen lakes, icicles, anything cold enough to soothe this fire that's spread over my skin. "Just once, I want to spend a winter someplace where the snow's up to my knees," I tell him. "I want to go sledding and make snow angels, and catch snowflakes on my tongue. And have a real snowball fight."

He smiles as if he's picturing me doing all of those things.

A wave of longing washes over me. "I'd planned to do all the winter things this year," I explain. "I found this great little bed and breakfast in Vermont, back in the summer, when it was a thousand degrees and I was daydreaming about a winter vacation."

"So why not go?" he asks.

I shrug. "I've been wanting to expand my cafe. Seems like it'd be smarter to put that money into my business rather than into a week in the mountains."

He nods, sipping his wine. "Don't you think you should also

invest in yourself, though? Give yourself the things that you need to grow and thrive?"

I'm struck dumb by the question. He makes it sound so obvious, so easy—isn't that exactly what he's doing here in Jasmine Falls? I almost blurt, *I don't have piles of money to spare, unlike you.* But I bite my tongue because for some reason, I don't want to draw attention to that difference between us. From what Victoria told me, he has enough money to do whatever he wants in this life. Taking time for himself is no sacrifice.

"If you let yourself thrive," he goes on, "then you give your business a better chance of thriving, too."

It's probably the smartest thing anyone's set to me in years, but it still stings knowing I can't just snap my fingers and make it happen.

"Maybe next year," I say, taking a bite of pizza. "This winter's too busy. Between the wedding and all the extra orders I took on, I can't leave for a week." Eager to change the subject, I say, "What are you going to do in Jasmine Falls for a whole month?"

"This will be the first time I've spent the holiday away from home in a long, long time," he says, and there's a note of sadness in his voice.

"You're close to your family?"

He takes a big bite of pizza and nods. "I used to be." Instantly I wonder why Logan Fyfe would high-tail it to another continent during the holidays. Not that I wouldn't do the same if given the chance. I love my family, but they're a lot to handle. And this month already has my mother's drama dialed up to eleven. Victoria told me he wanted a vacation, but I get the sense it's more than that.

"If I can be nosy for a minute," I say, "of all the places you could go around Christmas, why here? Why not like, Iceland? Or

Finland? Or some gorgeous island in the Caribbean? Because if I had my choice, I'd be just about anywhere but here."

He gives me a small shrug. "Fair question. I just wanted to go somewhere I hadn't been before. When Theo told me about his wedding, it was an easy choice. I like small towns, and I like remote."

"Well, mission accomplished, sir. The only way you get more remote around here is to venture into the Congaree swamp."

He smiles, reaching for another slice of pizza. Something in his eyes, though, hints that there's some hurt behind his decision.

"Are you sure you're not a fugitive?" I say, teasing him with my hardest stare.

He laughs, and the tension falls away. "Pretty sure. Though my family might argue with that one."

I like his easy smile, and his soothing tone. He feels like someone I can just relax and be myself around, and I don't find people like that too often.

"It's nice you were able to take so much time off," I say. "Victoria said you were an investor. But if I'm being honest, you don't seem like the stuffy investor type. I just assumed that was your cover."

He laughs again, reaching for his wine. "I'm more of an angel investor. A silent partner."

"Is that code for mafia boss?" I say.

"I know," he says with a shrug. "Not nearly as alluring as a Bond villain. Though my family probably thinks of me that way now."

"Because you blew up their castle and made off with their diamonds?"

"Something like that." He gives me a crooked smile that feels like a sucker punch. "It's a bit of a sore subject right now. My family's not used to being told no, and I've been doing a lot of that lately."

Across from us on the counter, my phone buzzes with a text. I ignore it and say, "Sorry. That's none of my business."

"It's okay," he says, his eyes resting on mine again. They're like pools of deep blue water, tempting me to come closer. His voice deepens like I've hit a sore spot and he says, "My grandfather would really like for me to take over the family business when he retires."

"And you?"

"Really would not."

My phone buzzes again, and then over and over with text messages, and I consider tossing it out a window.

Logan nods toward the phone and says, "You need to get that?"

"One second," I mutter. "Let me make sure nothing is on fire." When I grab the phone from the other end of the kitchen island, I see six text messages from my mother, telling me about some guy she thought would make a great date for the wedding. And suggesting that she create a profile for me on a new dating app she discovered. And sending me photos of three men she thinks are "great matches."

This is my life now. At nearly ten p.m. on a Friday, my mother is trolling hookup sites, searching for her potential son-in-law. I swallow the ball of fury that's forming in my throat and take a deep breath.

"Everything okay?" he says.

"My relentless mother is all fired up to find me a date for the wedding and is threatening to use a dating app. She's done everything except take out an ad in the classifieds." I type out a quick response to her—**NO DATING APPS. NO. Good night, Mother**—and put the phone face-down on the counter.

"Does anyone even do classifieds anymore?"

"She'd rent a billboard on I-95 if there were any available," I grumble.

He smirks, and my phone buzzes with another text.

She's pleading her case, so I hurriedly dictate a voice text: **CEASE AND DESIST OR I WILL WEAR A HALLOWEEN COSTUME TO YOUR FANCY HOLIDAY PARTY AND TELL EVERYONE THERE THAT I'VE QUIT BAKING TO MAKE ADULT FILMS.**

That should do it.

Logan barks out a laugh.

"Got to nip that in the bud so we don't fall into a full-on crisis," I explain. "She thinks she'll be better at finding me a date than I am."

"Sounds like your mother and mine have the same playbook," he says.

One more buzz and I glare at the phone. **There's no need to be crass,** she types.

An idea so preposterous enters my head that I feel heat rising in my cheeks. Now I'm thinking of introducing Logan to her as my co-star and that's not a scenario that needs to be playing in my head right now.

"Why's your ma so hot to get you a date?" Logan says, fixing those big blue-green eyes on me again. A zip of electric current goes straight down my spine, but I manage to hold his gaze.

I bite my lip, wishing the next part wasn't so true. "It's her way of making sure that I'm okay at the wedding. If having a date gets everyone to stop focusing on me, then that's great—I just don't want my mom playing matchmaker."

He cocks his head to the side. "Are you not happy about them getting married?"

"Oh god, no. Nothing like that." I refill our glasses, feeling myself flush again. "I'm happy because Victoria's happy." I have to choose the words carefully because while Theo's not my favorite person in the world, he's who my sister has chosen to be with—and that's what matters. I sip my wine and turn back to Logan. "My family won't say it outright, but I can see it on their faces. They're all worried that I'm going to be a wreck and have some kind of meltdown at the ceremony."

His eyes are full of concern. "Why would they think that?"

The truth feels like a giant rock resting on my shoulders, one that I can't seem to shake no matter what I do. "Because I was supposed to get married last year," I tell him. "And then I called it off a week before the wedding."

"Oh," he says. It feels like an eternity passes. I expect his face to fall, for it to morph into a look of pity the way it always does with everyone else.

But it doesn't. Logan simply looks at me with curiosity, like he wants me to go on. Who is this guy? And why is he sitting here talking to me over frozen pizza? He seems so likable, so down to earth—it's easy to forget that he's, as Victoria said, a bazillionaire.

"The short version is that he was cheating. I found out, end of story."

Logan mutters something in Gaelic, scowling.

"Do I want to know what that means?" I ask.

He lifts a brow and bites his lip, and now I very much want to bite that full lip. "Loosely translates to your fella being a donkey's arse."

I shrug. "Accurate. Took me a while to see it, though." I narrow my eyes at him. "But only Victoria knows about that part. My family thinks I just changed my mind."

"Your secret's safe with me." His voice has a protective edge to it that makes me feel warm all over.

"They act like I'm some fragile flower, and I hate it. But it's easier to have them just think I course-corrected than to have them know the humiliating truth." My stomach churns at the thought of my mother and all of her pointed remarks—the ones that make me feel like I'll never live up to her expectations. "But now they think I can't separate my own failed relationship from my sister's wonderful one."

I choke on the word wonderful, and Logan raises a brow.

"I'm sorry," he says, his voice tender. "That sounds really hard."

I shrug. "Getting married would have been a mistake, and what happened was for the best, even though it hurt. I keep telling them all that I'm fine, but I can see the worry in their faces. I wish they'd just take me at my word and forget about Mark."

"They should," he says. "Clearly this Mark was an eejit and a million miles away from good enough for you."

I smile at that, and Logan gives me a heated look that makes my insides melt.

"I just want the day to be about Victoria and Theo, you know? Not me."

"Victoria's lucky to have you," he says. "Anyone would be."

Heat blooms in my chest.

"I should probably get to bed," I tell him. "I've got to open the cafe in the morning and the early crowd is brutal when they're waiting to be caffeinated. It's like a bunch of bears coming out of hibernation."

"Of course," he says. His lip curves with a hint of a smile, and part of me wishes I could have this kind of easy conversation all the time. "I'll be off, then."

He stands, and when I climb off the stool, I trip over the leg and stumble right into him, my hands landing on his chest. He catches my arm and drops one hand onto my waist to steady me and a zing of electricity rushes straight down to my toes. In my bare feet, I barely come to his shoulder—he's a mountain of a man, but somehow doesn't take up all the space in the room.

When I look up at him, he gives me a warm smile and I try desperately not to stare at his sexy stubbled jaw and imagine how it would feel scraping along the soft column of my neck. His gaze drops to my lips, and he looks like he wants to kiss me.

Nope. Off-limits, Gwen. Out of your league.

"Thanks," I murmur, prying my hands from his solid chest.

"Any time," he says, his voice so gravelly and deep it nearly stops my heart.

Mercy. Mom's not going to find any man like this on her dating app.

Willing my heart to get back to a normal rhythm, I step out of his grasp and head for the front door.

"Thanks for dinner," he says, stepping out onto the porch. His tone is casual as if he didn't just come within an inch of setting my kitchen ablaze. "I'll see you around, Gwen. Hopefully sooner than later." When he turns and walks out into the night, I say a silent prayer that he will—even though it feels like I'm playing with fire.

Chapter Six

LOGAN

This trip is not at all what I expected. Four weeks at a secluded lake house was supposed to give me space. Solitude. Time when I wouldn't have to interact with anyone and could be alone with my thoughts and finally figure out how to deal with this nightmare with my family. As frustrating as it is to analyze the Fyfe family and all of their expectations for me, I know I need to sit with all of those thoughts long enough—with no distractions—to plan a course of action that won't leave me stuck in a job I despise and leave us all resenting each other until the end of time.

But instead of some grand plan to save my family from a complete meltdown, I've been thinking all morning about Gwen and her soft curves and her addictive laugh, and how when she tripped last night and stumbled into my arms, she leaned into me like a plant bending towards the sunlight. It usually takes me a while to warm up to people, and I rarely talk about things like feelings with anyone. Laying all that truth bare feels like giving up a weakness. In my experience, people who want to know about your weaknesses are usually angling for a way to use them against you.

Being with Gwen last night was different, though. She seemed genuinely interested in the real me—not the version featured in annual reports and financial news. I can't even remember the last time I had a conversation that felt so real.

Before I know it, I'm driving into town convinced that I need coffee.

When I walk into the door of the Sentient Bean, I'm struck by how cozy and inviting it is. *Homey* doesn't do it justice, because this place is like wrapping yourself in a warm blanket and snuggling up by the fireplace. Most of the walls are painted a pale gray, except for the wall behind the coffee bar, which is a soft blue-green like ocean mist. The decor is both modern and a bit rustic, with tables and chairs made of dark reclaimed wood and steel. In one corner are two blue-patterned upholstered chairs with a bookcase behind them, set up like a reading nook. It's a little before nine, and half the tables are filled—locals, I'm guessing, after what Gwen told me about this being the lull between tourist seasons.

Every head turns toward me as the bell on the door rings, as if to remind me that I can't easily fly under the radar in a town this small. Everyone knows each other here, and I'm easily marked as an outsider. I give a friendly nod to the locals, who smile in return, and then I head toward the counter.

There's no sign of Gwen, but two baristas are working behind the coffee bar. To their left, behind the register, is a pair of chest-high swinging doors that must lead into the kitchen. Just as I approach the counter, there's a crash from the kitchen, followed by a yelp.

One of the baristas—a young woman with bright red hair— peeks over the top of the swinging door and calls back into the kitchen. "You okay back there?"

"Yeah, fine," Gwen calls from behind the swinging doors. "All limbs still attached."

When the barista turns toward me, she smiles and says, "Hi there, what can I get you?" The name tag on her apron reads *Maggie*.

"Aye, hello," I say, eyeing the scones. Extra large. Very American. "I actually came by to see Gwen."

Her eyes widen, just slightly. A few feet away, the espresso machine whines, and the second barista, a twenty-something Black guy with closely cropped hair and epic eyebrows, smiles as he steams some milk.

"Oh," Maggie says, giving me a long look. "Let me see if she's available."

There's another crash from behind her, another shout of, "Sweet baby cheeses!"

Maggie grins and ducks into the kitchen. Browsing the pastries, I step closer to the register and can just barely make out the conversation behind the swinging doors.

"Who is it?" Gwen says. "I'm up to my ears here."

"Don't know, but he's super hot."

I bite back a grin as the bell over the front door rings and another customer walks in, a lady with a platinum bob who waves to the other barista and calls, "Hi, Sam!"

Sam grins and says, "Mornin', Paula Sue. The usual for you?"

The kitchen door swings open again as Maggie darts through carrying a tray of muffins. Gwen's right behind her, a tiny smile on her face as she holds the door partway open, as if inviting me into a secret room.

I like making her smile.

"Hi, Logan," Gwen says. She glances around the cafe as if looking for someone, and then motions for me to follow her as if she's in the middle of a covert operation. "Come on back."

"Everything okay?" I ask. The kitchen area is bigger than I imagined, newly remodeled with stainless appliances and work tables. Two of the walls are lined with bakers' racks, the shelves filled with baking ingredients. One work table is covered with an array of muffins and cupcakes and the other is dusted in flour and piled with dishes.

"Kinda crazy today, to be honest," she says. "I had an emergency order come in this morning and it's going to be all I can do to get it out by closing."

Today Gwen's wearing a green button-down shirt and jeans, a bright floral apron cinched around her waist. Her hair's pulled back into a short ponytail under a bright pink chef's cap. One blond curl has slipped out by her ear, and I resist the urge to tuck it back into place.

I've never fancied myself one of those insta-love people, but Gwen's so utterly adorable and warm that I just want to soak her up like sunshine on a winter day. There's just something about her that makes me relaxed, curious, and desperate to learn everything about her.

I can't remember the last time I felt that way about someone —especially after knowing them for less than twenty-four hours.

"A cupcake emergency?" I say, glancing around.

She scoffs, planting a hand on her hip. "Emergency in the sense that Mr. Jacobson forgot to order the cupcakes for his wife's birthday party, which is tonight. He conveniently remembered over his morning coffee when she asked him to pick up her dress at the cleaners. So now I have until five today to finish a hundred cupcakes with peonies—that's her favorite flower—on top."

"You know there's an expression that says 'your lack of planning doesn't constitute my emergency.'"

She rolls her eyes like she knows I'm right. "I know, I know. But when it's the fire chief and he doesn't complain about the outrageous rush fee, it's hard to say no."

"Nice of you to take that on at the last minute. But I'm glad there's a practical upside for you."

She sighs, leaning against the counter and rolling her neck in a small circle until there's an audible pop. I imagine how tight her shoulders would feel under my hands, and how much I'd enjoy teasing out all those knots with my fingers. Gwen strikes me as a person who takes care of everyone else's needs before her own. The urge to do something for her—anything to relieve a burden—is overwhelming.

"I was really hoping for a quiet day today to catch up on other things, but here we are," she says. "Maggie's got to leave early this afternoon and I've got a hundred peonies to make out of buttercream. Meanwhile, my website crashed sometime late yesterday and no one's able to order anything online, and I don't have time to fix it, so lord knows how much money we're losing over that. No one wants to order over the phone anymore, so they'll just go across town to the grocery store. And it hurts my heart to think of them getting sub-par baked goods made from fake eggs and vegetable oil just because my 'buy' button doesn't work."

The words come out in a rush, and she leans down on the counter, taking a deep breath as if just thinking about those tasks is exhausting.

"Let me help you," I say.

She arches a brow. "Are you volunteering to spend the day wrangling my ornery espresso machine? Because, while I admire your confidence, there's a ninety percent chance you won't come out of that alive. Sometimes I'm convinced there's a gremlin living inside it, and to lose a good guy like you to that beastly thing would be a crime."

"You think I'm a good guy?" My heart hammers against my ribs, and honestly, this woman could ask me to do anything and I'd say yes. I don't know what's come over me. It's possible the jet lag has put me into some kind of waking coma, but all I know is that I want to find a way to spend more time with Gwen and keep making her smile like I'm the most brilliant thing she's laid eyes on.

A faint blush colors her cheeks and spreads down to her lovely collarbones. "Aren't you?" she says, lifting a brow.

"Aye, most of the time. Or at least, I try to be."

She purses her lips as if she's considering exactly what that means and oh, how I'd love to show her.

I lean closer, suddenly intoxicated by the scent of vanilla and lavender and fighting the unwavering urge to kiss her and see if she tastes as sweet as I imagine. She needs help, and it's clear she hates to ask for it. Lucky for her, I have nothing but time. And the growing urge to show this woman how much good she deserves.

"I'd make a crap barista," I tell her. "But I can fix your website." Apparently, I'm on fire to solve any problem that isn't mine. And honestly, the idea of staying here all day with her—or at least until I fix the site—sounds like the best possible way I could spend my day.

The ticking Fyfe family bomb will just have to wait.

Gwen's big blue eyes widen like she's won the lottery. "Seriously?"

"Sure. I did web design years ago. Still do it for friends now and then." It's been a while since I worked on a site, but hers likely isn't too complicated.

"I usually do it myself, but I only know the basics," she says. "I can handle about half an hour before my eye starts to twitch and I fantasize about putting the laptop in the microwave."

"Yeah, that's not the best solution."

She gives me an evil smirk. "But it might be the most cathartic."

"Show me," I say. The relief in her eyes makes my heart squeeze. I'm about to build her the best website she's ever seen.

"I'll pay you, of course," she says. "You just tell me a number.

Literally, any number of dollars is better than the number of hours I'll stare at the screen cursing like a maniac."

"Absolutely not."

She puts her hand on her perfectly rounded hip and fixes her bright blue eyes on mine. It's an adorably stern I-mean-business face, and that pouty lip of hers is going to be the end of me. "Logan." The way her voice drops as she says my name makes the back of my neck tingle in the best way. Suddenly I'm thinking of a very different scenario in which she might use that tone with me and that image will be etched in my brain forever.

"Okay, I see what's happening," I tell her. "You don't like asking for help, and you don't like feeling indebted to someone. I get it." I love that she's so fiercely independent, but I know the road to burnout well, and I like her enough to keep her as far from it as I can.

She blinks at me, her lips parted like she wants to argue. But she can't, because I'm right. And she knows it.

"You offered me dinner when I was ravenous and jet-lagged. How about you let me do something for you now?"

"This kind of work you're offering to do is not equivalent to frozen pizza." She gives me a saucy look that dares me to cross her.

"You underestimate the value of your company."

A faint blush touches her cheeks as her lips part, and something in my heart lights up like a sparkler.

"And also," I say, crossing my arms—because I can mean business too—"why must we think in equivalencies? And how about you trust me to tell you how I'd prefer to be paid?"

She purses her lips. "It seems unbalanced."

I nod, conceding her point because I can tell that she struggles to find balance every day. It's clear from the tension in her shoulders and the long hours she's mentioned in passing. Finding balance between the things you want to do and the things you feel responsible for is one of the hardest skills to learn in this life—and she wants to control balance in any place that she can.

I understand that all too well.

"How about coffee and breakfast until I leave?" I ask her. "That's something I'd really, *really* like."

That earns me a hint of a smile. "I guess I should wait to see your work until I barter away a few weeks of breakfast."

"Aye, so you should."

She lifts a brow and then seems content to call this a win. This woman does not like asking for help, and it seems she's not too keen on accepting it, either. Pity that, because I'm starting to envision lots of ways I could help her relax and unwind.

A few weeks here suddenly seems like not much time at all.

TWO HOURS LATER, Gwen has nearly a hundred unfrosted cupcakes resting on the counter and the last batch in the oven. With a few design tweaks and a little coding, I not only have her site working again but have the whole ordering system more streamlined. When the final changes are live, I call her over to take a look and make sure the navigation is what she wants.

After clicking through a few pages, she says, "Amazing. I never would have thought to do that."

"This should make ordering much easier to track," I tell her. "Each order will auto-populate to your calendar, and add the customer to your mailing list. If you want, I can set it up so that they get a series of emails that tell them about specials and offer them a discount on their next order. It's a great way to keep people engaged with your new products."

Her lips part and she blinks at me as she says, "I really can't thank you enough."

I shrug, like it's nothing. "You're welcome."

"I could barely manage the basic fixes, and it would have taken me about a million years to get around to it, with everything else going on." She swipes her hand over her forehead, leaving a smudge of flour that I'm tempted to brush away with my fingers. The back door's open to let some cool air inside, but the room is still hot as blazes from all the baking.

Well. Mostly from the baking.

"Happy to help," I say, trying hard not to focus on the way her apron accentuates all of her delightful curves.

A timer buzzes and she grabs her oven mitts and pulls the last two trays of cupcakes from the oven. They're perfectly golden brown, but she studies them for a brief moment, leaning down so her ear is next to them.

When she catches me staring, she says, "You can hear when they're done enough."

"Is this the part where you tell me they speak to you?" I tease.

"Sort of. It's mostly steam escaping." She places them on the counter and looks at the clock hanging above us. "As soon as these cool I can start the icing."

"How about we get out of here for a minute?" I say, desperate for a little cool air, but also sensing she could use a break. "Grab an iced coffee and take a walk with me?"

Her brow furrows and I know she's calculating how much time she'll have left if she spends even half an hour on herself.

"Just a quick one," I urge. "Recharge a little?"

She considers that and then unties her apron and flicks it over her head. "A short one," she says, grabbing a sweater from one of the racks. She slips into the walk-in fridge and fills two travel mugs with cold-brew coffee. "It's the secret stash," she tells me. "Half-caff, so I don't buzz around like a hummingbird all night."

She hands me a mug and I hold the back door open for her. "Come on, cupcake whisperer. Everyone needs some downtime. That's how the good ideas get in."

Her grateful smile makes my heart flutter, and I am completely under this woman's spell.

When we're a few steps down the block, she says, "So what are you doing on your second day in Jasmine Falls? Aside from saving my website from complete devastation." She has one of those sweet lilting accents that makes everything sound alluring, and part of me wishes that her website would crash once more so I can fix it all over again for her.

She smirks, and I love how one corner of her lips always lifts a little higher.

Manners, I tell myself. Stop staring at her lips, her long legs, and the way the buttons on her shirt strain ever so slightly around the swell of her breasts. I do love button-down shirts, specifically taking my time undoing each button to reveal all the gorgeousness beneath—but I definitely shouldn't be thinking about that right now.

I have to focus on walking. Coffee. Not buttons, not what lies beneath them.

"Not sure," I tell her. "I'm just trying to unwind and take things as they come." It's not a total lie—I've been a walking tangle of knots since this whole take-charge-of-the-company idea was hurled into my lap. Now I'm realizing that it's insane to think I can sit in a lake house all day and try to think myself out of that situation. I can't hole up like a hermit, and I might need to take my own advice here—some distraction might allow for the creative solution to shine through.

She smiles and says, "Sounds like my kind of holiday. I wish I could turn my brain off for a while and take things as they come."

Something tells me that would be very hard for her to do.

Gwen doesn't seem distracted, exactly—preoccupied is a better word. It's obvious that she's driven and has a lot of things on her mind. She's a problem-solver. It's also obvious that she puts a lot of other people's needs before her own and rarely carves out enough time for herself.

I used to be that way, too.

Turning the corner, we come to the town square, which is full of elaborate decorations with reindeer, just like Gwen said it would be. The grassy area has been made into a tableau that includes a runway, a couple of wind socks, and hand-painted wooden signs.

"North Pole Flight School?" I chuckle, reading the biggest sign.

Gwen smiles. "Did I mention this town loves Christmas?" She points to another sign that includes a "pre-flight checklist" for the deer.

"It's pretty adorable," I say. "And elaborate."

"It started a few years ago," she says. "Grady Catoe brought in a bunch of those big plastic deer that people use for hunting targets and then gave them giant reindeer antlers and harnesses with sleigh bells. People went nuts over it, and now every year they add something new." She nods toward a deer with a bright red nose. "Obviously they had to bring Rudolph."

She sips her coffee, watching me take in the whole scene. Near the back of the field, at the end of the runway, a huge round hay bale is set up with the back end of a deer poking out, as if he crash-landed.

"This must be so different than what you're used to," she says.

"Aye, we like our sparkly lights, too. They're just more often torches and fireballs."

She snorts, and I say, "You think I'm joking? Look up the Fireballs Festival sometime. A bunch of people parading with torches and swinging fireballs around. The story goes that the parade purges all the unwanted things from the old year and makes way for what you want in the new year. What do your wee reindeer do?"

Gwen smiles and whispers, "They're magical reindeer."

"Well of course they are."

"Elf on the shelf has nothing on us," she says. "As we get closer to Christmas, the deer magically change positions overnight. You know, as their lessons progress. Sometimes it gets a little out of hand."

"Elf on the what?"

She rolls her eyes. "It's too American to even explain."

"You say that like you're not a fan." I give her a playful nudge. "Are you secretly a Scrooge?"

She flashes a wicked smirk. "Bah-humbug. You got me."

"What's turned you against Christmas, love?" I'm teasing, but when her eyes flick to mine, I see the briefest flash of pain and instantly want to kick myself.

"Thirty years with the other Griffins," she says, her tone matter-of-fact.

I nod, curious, but not wanting to press her.

"At my house, Christmas always means arguing, and rushing around, and trying to keep up this impossible image of perfection," she says. "And of course, a big heaping dose of guilt. 'Tis the season when my mother hounds me about not being married yet and giving her a bunch of grandchildren—in her super passive-aggressive way—and reminds me that another year has passed and she's not getting any younger, and surely my ovaries will shrivel if I don't hurry up and find myself a husband. It's a time when she takes inventory of all of my sister's successes and all of my failures, and reminds me of all the ways that I can never live up to her standards." She bites her lip. "She thinks my cafe is a joke, and she thinks my dreams are silly. I could have the most successful business in the world, and she'd still find a flaw."

She sighs and tucks a loose lock of hair behind her ear. She looks so vulnerable for a moment that I want to wrap her in a hug.

But that would be totally inappropriate, and probably touching her would set me on fire. I shove my empty hand into my jeans pocket, just to stifle the urge. Words don't seem to be enough to fix this problem, but I try some anyway. "I'm sorry," I tell her. "That sounds really unpleasant."

"Severe understatement," she says with a snort. "I used to love Christmas because my Grandma June did. She and her sister, my Aunt Bernice, had these warm, cozy gatherings where we'd pretend to camp outside with our blankets and cocoa. After they died, though, the only get-togethers were the stuffy parties that my mom likes to throw—a bunch of frenemies getting together to one-up each other with stories about their exotic travels and their perfect children. It's all so fake. It makes me dread the holidays now." With a small shrug, she says, "My solution is to bury myself in work. And this year I took on way more than I should have—special orders for holiday parties, and helping Victoria with the wedding, and now it feels like this month will never end."

She lets out a sigh so heavy, it seems she pulled it from the core of the earth.

"My family can be a lot to handle too," I tell her. "I get it."

"Is that why you're here?" she says. "I mean, aside from the fact that we have the amazing Reindeer Flight School, which is reason enough for anyone to cross an ocean." She gives me a teasing smirk, and just like that, she's buried the hurt that welled up for a moment, and is back to focusing on me. I want to wrap her in my arms and tell her to let all of those feelings out —the ones she tries too hard to hide because keeping them buried inside will just make your heart explode one day like a grenade.

And I don't want that for her.

"Aye, I needed a break from them," I say. "From a lot of things." Was it cowardly to leave the country to avoid having hard conversations with my family? Probably. Was it necessary to maintain my sanity? Absolutely.

"I'd hoped to hide from my family this year," Gwen says. "My excuse was going to be work—being overwhelmed with new clients and special orders, and short-staffed. But then Victoria had to go and get married, and now I have to see everyone twice as much as I would at any other Christmas." She rolls her eyes again, but it's obvious she's mad about her sister and would do anything for her. Even if it means making herself uncomfortable. I see my old self in her at that moment—the version of me who felt like he had to be completely selfless to be a good person. But I learned that too much selflessness just leaves you feeling burned out and used. It was hard for me to find the balance, but I learned that to be of service to others like I want, I have to look out for myself and my needs, too. And sometimes that means saying no. And fleeing the country.

"I'm a little ashamed to admit that I'm thirty-five and hiding from my family," I confess. "But this year they left me no choice. I couldn't handle being at my folks' while everyone brawls over the family business."

"Well, good luck to them trying to find you here," she says, teasing. "You're in the middle of nowhere now."

"My family can find me anywhere if they look hard enough. I'm just hoping they'll respect my wishes and give me the space I need."

"You mean James Bond can't disappear?" she says.

I shrug. "My brother's resourceful. But this time I paid the pilot enough to lose the flight data."

Gwen snort-laughs, and then seems to realize I'm serious. "I should get back," she says, clearing her throat. "Those cupcakes aren't going to ice themselves."

"What are you doing later?"

"After the emergency cupcakes?" She stares up at the sky as if her to-do list is written somewhere in the clouds. "Have to pick a bridesmaid dress, meet Victoria to look at flowers, drop off a cookie delivery to the senior center, answer the one hundred texts from my mother that I've been ignoring, and then…crash?"

"You do a lot for other people," I say, studying her bright blue eyes. Framed by thick lashes, they look almost stormy in the sunlight.

She shrugs like it's not a difficult task. But I know how hard it is to juggle all those people and their expectations. I know how exhausting it is to run a business and manage your family's needs at the same time. She puts on a bold face, but I can tell from the hard set of her shoulders and the wistful look in her eyes that she's feeling strained.

"There's a lot to take care of," she says at last, and the finality of her tone tugs at the corners of my heart. Something tells me she doesn't reveal these parts of her to just anyone—so what's special about me?

"So tell me, love," I say, brushing that stray lock of hair out of her eyes. "Who takes care of you?"

She blinks at me, biting her lip in the most inviting way. Something flickers in her eyes—hurt? Relief? Panic?—and in an instant, I've gone one step too far.

Chapter Seven

GWEN

Logan hardly says a word on the walk back to the cafe, and I don't either. These are the longest three blocks in the history of the world.

Who takes care of you?

It seems like an easy, innocent question on the surface. But the moment the words left his lips, all I could think of was how I've been wanting that for so long and never admitting it to myself. The truth is, I *do* want someone to take care of me. Not because I want to be coddled or kept or any of those other words that make this desire seem needy or demanding—it's not a question of having someone wait on me hand and foot and meet my every evolving need. But when I'm exhausted from work, tired from juggling all the things and feeling like I can't make one more decision, even about where to order take-out—I long for someone to lift the burden, if only for an evening.

So yes, I'd like someone to care for me. Specifically, I'd like someone to *want* to care for me.

I'd love to have a partner someday who cooks me dinner, decides to vacuum without my hints, or brings me my favorite comfort food when I'm feeling sick. There are times when the world's coming at you at a hundred miles an hour, and the little daily tasks feel like death by a thousand paper cuts. On those days in particular, it would be great to have someone else take the reins for a minute—even if it's just to either make those small tasks disappear or run me an epic bubble bath where I can escape with a good book.

Mark wasn't interested in taking care of me. He claimed he couldn't cook, and he couldn't even be bothered to clean up after himself—if I plucked one wet towel from the floor, I'd picked up a thousand. It never occurred to him to do anything to lighten my daily load or give me a nice shoulder massage at the end of a long day. Being with him just brought truth to the adage that Victoria tells me all the time: *if you want something done, you have to do it yourself.*

Probably, that should have been the first indication that Mark wasn't the partner I needed. He made me feel like (1) he didn't see that I needed help, or (2) he didn't care enough about me to offer to make my life a little easier.

Logan, after knowing me for one day, volunteered to fix my website and then did even more than he promised. It's completely baffling to me and my brain is already analyzing this situation to pieces, trying hard to make sense of the gesture. It didn't seem like a big deal to him, but it's a very big deal to me. It feels a little like Bill Gates just sat down to streamline my business plan, and that irritating voice in the back of my mind keeps whispering, *Why's he so eager to help* you?

Maybe it was an innocent, friendly question—*Who cares for you?* But when he asked me, his brows had pinched with concern, and even though I said nothing, I was afraid he could see the answer as plainly as if it had been stamped on my forehead.

Because truthfully, I've never felt cared for in the way that he means. And for a moment, I let myself wonder exactly how he'd care for the person he valued most in the world.

And then I try to imagine what that would feel like, and that's a dangerous thought indeed.

When he leaves the cafe, I push that thought way down deep and turn my attention back to the peony cupcakes, where it belongs.

IF I EVER GET ENGAGED AGAIN, I'M just going to elope.

I don't ever want to have to make a thousand decisions regarding the thread count of a tablecloth or the species of daisy that's least likely to wilt. Victoria seems to thrive on these kinds of decisions because she enjoys making sure that everything is perfect, down to the last detail. Sometimes I enjoy details—like when I'm decorating a cake with lifelike flowers made of icing. But other kinds of details are completely overwhelming and make me feel like the room's closing in on me, sucking every molecule of oxygen out.

"Are you listening?" Vic says, tossing a pillow at my head. She stopped by my house to help me choose between the two dresses from Brenda's that I like the best. She's been going on and on about flower substitutions while I model the garnet dress —a pretty A-line with a full satin skirt that Brenda had set aside.

"Yes, completely," I tell her. It's a total lie because all afternoon my mind has been drifting back to Logan and his mischievous smirk. How he commandeered my laptop and fixed my website like some white-hat genius hacker. How last night he'd called Mark an *eejit* with zero hesitation and then dropped his hand to my waist as I'd stumbled over the leg of the stool.

And how delightful his hand had felt there, silencing all the noise in my brain and grounding me there, only with him.

And then how he'd asked so pointedly, *So who takes care of you?* Ever since that moment, I've been imagining all the ways that Logan might take care of me—and not one of them is unappealing.

"Gwen!" Vic says, waving her hand in front of my face. "You're like, out in the stratosphere. Are you okay?"

"Fine," I squeak, shoving aside those thoughts of Logan and his sturdy hands for the thousandth time. "I'm just distracted. Sorry." I wriggle out of the garnet dress and toss it onto the bed next to Vic. "Mom texted me last night, threatening to put my profile on a dating app, and I think she nearly broke me."

"Good grief," Vic huffs. "That woman needs a new hobby."

"She texted me this morning to suggest she ask her newly divorced dentist to be my date to your wedding."

She gags, rolling back onto my bed and burying her face in a pillow. "Sometimes I think we were delivered by the stork," she says, her voice muffled. "How did we come from that woman?"

Mom always needs a project to pour her energy into. She constantly complains about things that need fixing (whether it's the roof of her garage or the way her daughter decorates the café), but in truth, she's miserable if she doesn't have something to make over. She believes in miracles, and thinks she was meant to create them (she would have made a great TV host on a home makeover show). Her house is in a constant state of redecorating or remodeling, and she can't help but apply that critical, problem-solving eye to everyone around her, too.

Sometimes it's easy to overlook. Sometimes it makes me want to leave the country and move to an island with spotty cell service. The problem is that whenever I even hint to her that she's getting too involved, she acts offended and hurt, and won't speak to me for weeks. It's a ridiculous tactic, but it almost always makes me cave. It's easier to give in to her than to keep wasting my energy in a fight that truly has no winner.

I shimmy into a navy sheath dress that has a halter-style bodice and an appropriate amount of shimmer, my favorite of the bunch. "This one just needs to be taken up a little in the top," I say, tugging at the straps.

Vic gasps. "It's perfect! I love it."

"You sure you wouldn't rather have red or green?"

Vic grins so her dimples show. "Nope, it's you. Just as it is. Makes you look like a goddess."

I turn, checking out the back in the full-length mirror. "Okay, but—"

"No buts. It's perfect." Vic collapses on the bed. "You look amazing. And I'll talk to Mom and tell her to get off the hookup sites. I'll remind her that you're thirty, and a total dynamo, and you don't need her…expertise."

I groan. "I've got half a mind to just hire an escort. Or ask Jake from the hardware store. I think he's the only guy in town I haven't had a speed-date with, so who knows? Maybe it wouldn't be a disaster."

"Okay, first off, Jake from the hardware store is like forty-five and drives a truck that has duct tape on the bumper."

"He's nice, though. And funny."

She glares at me, chewing her lip. "He is often nice and occasionally funny. But not what you need."

I sigh and collapse on the bed next to her. "You're right. Jake would just make Mom fixate more on me, instead of on you." I cringe when Victoria makes a face. "I mean, focus on you in a good way, of course."

Vic frowns. "It's okay. I'm immune to her tactics."

That's true, and it makes me completely jealous. Victoria's always had enough confidence to stand up to our mother. She can strike this incredible balance that doesn't leave any hurt feelings in her wake. But I typically bottle up all of my frustration and rage and then explode in a way that leaves enough fallout to earn my mother's ire for years.

"I should probably just go with the escort," I mutter. "A mystery man that Mom would never see again."

"I can do you one better," she says, raising a brow. "Ask Logan."

All of the blood leaves my head in an instant as I picture Logan in a pale gray suit—or maybe dark blue—tailored to perfection to accentuate those lovely broad shoulders and muscular thighs. "Noooooo," I say, shaking my head. "No, no, no." The thought of him being all charming, pretending to be my date, standing so close to me that I can smell his woodsy scent and see the flecks of green in his eyes is enough to make my heart hammer against my ribs so hard that I'll surely die. I take another deep breath, trying to push that image way down deep. The last thing I need is to be swooning over a guy like Logan Fyfe, who's a million miles out of my league.

Victoria blinks at me, her gaze challenging. "Why not?"

My cheeks burn hot enough to grill toast so I turn away from her, fiddling with the skirt of the dress. *Because he's lethally hot. Because he makes my heart pound like a jackhammer.* "Because he's a total stranger."

She rolls her eyes with a snort. "Did you not just declare you'd hire an escort? That would also be a stranger."

"Not the same thing."

"It's perfect," she says, giving me an evil grin. "Think about it. He's only here for a few weeks, and then you never have to see him again. He's not from here, so you won't have the gossip train following you for the rest of your life. You show up with someone from town, and everyone's going to think you're an item, and then they'll ask you about it forever."

She's not wrong about that part. This town is full of expert storytellers. If the details you tell them aren't juicy enough, they'll make up their own. Before you know it, you're the hero in the story yanked from someone else's wildest dreams.

Unless of course, you're the villain. I don't especially want to be either.

Victoria shrugs like this is the easiest decision she's made all day. "You show up with Logan, and no one will worry about you for a second, because he's light-years from your last boyfriend."

"Gee, thanks."

She grabs my hand for emphasis. "You know what I mean. We both know you deserve—and will find—way better than Mark the blockhead. Logan's already going to the wedding, so just go together. Mom will get off your back, and you can just relax and have a good time." She smirks and nudges my ribs. "And Logan looks like he knows how to have a really good time."

My cheeks burn again as I consider how dead-on she is about that, too. I definitely do not need to be thinking of all the ways that Logan and I could have a good time together.

He's off-limits. Hard no. I'm not looking for a fling, and that's all he could be because this town is just a bump in the road for him. I won't be a roadside attraction.

"You know I'm right," she says, giving me a smug smile that dares me to argue.

"Still, though," I sigh, draping an arm over my face. "It's awkward. I feel weird asking him."

"Then don't," she says, but she can't possibly be giving up that easily.

When I turn, she has her phone in her hand, her fingers flying across the screen.

"What are you doing?" I shriek.

She types quickly, a grin spreading across her face. "Asking for a friend."

"Vic!" I cry, tackling her on the bed. "Don't you dare hit

send!"

"Too late. You're welcome."

I lunge for the phone and she tickles me, which is hardly fair because I can barely wriggle away from her in this form-fitting dress. I freeze, not wanting to rip a seam, and she holds her hands up in mock surrender.

"I hate you," I grumble.

"You love me like no other." Holding the phone above my head, she taps the screen with her finger and I lunge again.

She squeals and curls into a ball as I tickle her. For a moment we're teenagers again, flailing and hurling ourselves at each other on the bed, as if being tickled were the worst possible fate. Victoria screeches as she wriggles away from me and I collapse on my back, out of breath and grinning so hard my cheeks hurt.

"You're the worst." I poke at Victoria's ribs and she snort-laughs.

"Is it so wrong to ensure that both of us have a wild night after my wedding?" she says. "I don't think so."

"Your meddling is worse than Mom's."

"You take that back!" she cries in mock insult. "At least I'm hooking you up with a guy who's worth your time and young enough to chase you around the house."

I reach out to tickle her again and a knock on the door stops me cold.

Pausing gives her a window to escape, and with a victorious cry, she scrambles off the bed and hurries out the door and down the hall. Unfair, because I'm still trapped in a sheath dress that has me rolling around like a mermaid on the shore.

Once I pry myself up and get to the living room, I find Victoria standing next to the open front door. A puzzled-looking Logan stands in the doorway, his brow furrowed.

"I couldn't quite understand your texts," he says to Vic. " Figured I'd just come over and clarify."

"Vic," I whisper-shout, giving her my most stern look.

She winks at me, in full-on meddling wood sprite mode.

"Something about knitting and an armoire?" Logan says, scratching his stubbled jaw as he stares at his phone.

"Stupid autocorrect," Vic says, shoving her phone into the pocket of her jeans. "I was trying to say knight in shining armor. We need a favor."

"My sister is drunk on wine samples and out of her mind," I tell him. "Don't listen to her."

Logan turns to me and his eyes drift down to my feet and back up again—appreciative but respectful. A muscle in his jaw flexes and a little zing of electricity shoots straight down my spine to my toes. I decide right then that this dress will go back to the boutique over my dead body.

"Hi, there," he says to me, his voice gravelly. "I feel severely underdressed. Again."

"Come in already," Victoria says, pulling him inside. "We need your help."

"Vic," I growl. "For the love of—"

"So what's this favor, then?" Logan says, his gaze still fixed on me. He crosses his arms over his broad chest, the button-up shirt straining over his biceps in a tantalizing way.

Mercy. Does this man have any clothes that weren't tailor-made to showcase all the muscle beneath them? That kind of fit should be criminal.

"Gwen needs a date for our wedding," she tells him, ignoring my face-melting glare. "Our mom is driving her crazy trying to fix her up with the most boring men on earth, and I love her too much to see her suffer that way. Would you be her date?"

Logan's eyes flick to my sister and then back to me. A hundred years pass as my heart bangs against my ribs. His lip curves in a hint of a smile as he says, "Aye. It'd be my pleasure."

My cheeks blaze hot enough to burn this house to cinders.

I'm flooded with a sense of—relief? Glee? Terror? Because *he said yes.*

"Full disclosure, it might be more than one date," Vic says, as if this is just as ordinary as scheduling an appointment for a haircut. "There's the rehearsal before and the holiday party after."

"You don't have to do all that," I tell him, feeling that familiar knot of anxiety forming in my chest. The last thing I want is for Logan to pity me, or to feel obligated to be my date. The thought of that is way worse than the pain of failure after speed dating. It's that feeling that tells me I'll never find someone who loves me because of all my quirks and flaws, and not despite them.

"He does if he's your date," Vic says to me. "It has to look real. You know how Mom is." Then she turns to Logan. "It'll be a blast. Gwen's the coolest person you're going to meet here." She shrugs as if this is a done deal. "Plus, despite all her faults, our mom throws a killer Christmas party. And she breaks out the top-shelf booze and makes specialty cocktails that you definitely don't want to miss."

I stare hopelessly at Logan, trying to read his expression. His jaw's tight and his eyebrows are pinched together. Is that pity? Sympathy? Ugh.

"This is too much," I mutter, feeling like the wind's been knocked out of me. "I'll just ask Jake from the hardware store."

"No!" she shouts.

At the same time, Logan growls, "Nay."

I'm still processing that growl when he turns, pinning me with his roguish smile and stormy eyes. "I'll be your date, darling. However many times you need."

Mercy. The way he says, *Darling.* I'm not usually one for endearments, but coming from his mouth the word sounds like part hymn and part dare. It's somehow both devilish and sweet. And one hundred percent delicious promise.

Victoria smirks at me in that way that means *See there. Told you.*

Sometimes I hate my sister for being such a genius.

"See?" she says, triumphant. "Problem solved. I keep telling you, babe—you just need to ask for what you need. If Logan's your date, then you get to focus on your business without constant interruptions from Mom." She gives Logan a saucy wink. "And Logan, you get like a million good karma points, and get to hang out with my amazing big sister—and you don't die of boredom at the most wonderful time of the year."

Logan purses his lips, flicking his gaze back to me. Is he regretting his offer yet?

"Okay, I've got to run," Vic says, no doubt satisfied that her plan came together. She flits into the bedroom and leaves me locked in a heated gaze with Logan, wondering if this might actually work.

He gives me a shrug that seems to say *Relax, this will be fun,* and then Victoria's back with a heap of dresses in her arms. "I'll take these back to Brenda," she says. "Actually, would you ride over there with me now? Theo wants to change the cake flavor, and I'd love to get your thoughts on that so I don't lie away agonizing over it all night."

"Sure." I try to stop myself from staring at Logan like he's just saved me from a burning building and tell myself it's just a friendly favor—nothing more. He opens the door for Victoria and she pushes through under a pile of satin and tulle.

"Brenda closes in a few minutes," she hollers back to me.

"Can we talk later?" Logan asks, stepping out onto the porch. "You can tell me more about these other events and what to expect."

"Of course," I reply, but I don't know what to expect anymore. Is he just being friendly, or is he interested in something more? And which do I want it to be?

Chapter Eight

LOGAN

I have a problem. A gorgeous, sassy, bright-eyed problem that has stolen every bit of my attention.

Ever since last night, when I agreed to be her date, I haven't stopped thinking about Gwen. All day I've been trying to focus on the bigger problem at hand—the implosion of my family's business and legacy—but I'm failing. Big time.

So far, I'm coming up with no solution to my family's dilemma. My grandfather's demands are clear: I'm his only choice to run the company. But working there is the last thing I want and not an option. Rory would be great at this job, and he wants it. We just need to find a way to make Grandad see that Rory is the right choice. If we can make the stubborn old badger think it was his idea, then even better.

My phone chimes with a text, but I ignore it. I'm too busy thinking about my new problem, which is how I want to spend every moment of my time with Gwen.

I should just shove my phone in the freezer because my family is relentless, and every time the phone rings with a message or a missed call, I feel a twinge in my gut. Guilt, because I feel like I'm going to let them down. Aggravation, because I can't find a way to fix this problem. Resentment, because I'd rather be doing other things with my time.

And that's when I start thinking of Gwen again—more precisely, all the ways that I could be learning everything that makes her laugh her musical laugh, and everything that makes her give me that saucy smile that makes my heart pound in my throat. Whenever she's near me, it feels like there's an invisible thread drawing us closer together. Being with her is like taking off dark sunglasses and realizing the world is so much brighter than I'd believed. It doesn't make sense that someone I've just met could make me feel so comfortable and off-kilter at the same time, but somehow she does both. And I don't want it to stop.

I drag my hands through my hair as if that might make this tangle of thoughts any easier to navigate, but of course, it doesn't. It only makes me imagine how her fingers would feel there instead, and that's another problem entirely.

Annoyed, I strip out of my clothes and take a shower, hoping that some pounding hot water might shake something loose in my brain and drive all the distracting feelings away. They've been building up since this morning, and now I feel like I might implode.

But the shower does nothing to help me. Because under the spray of hot water, all I can think about is Gwen in that gorgeous dress she had on last night, the one that accentuated every luscious curve in her body and made me ache to trace those curves with my fingertips and my tongue.

I'm no closer to solving either of my problems.

When the water turns cool, I shut off the shower and head back into the kitchen to try calming myself with bourbon instead. My phone chimes again with a text, and I give in and take a look. It's not going to be anyone I'm interested in talking to because Gwen doesn't have my number (a problem to rectify immediately) and hers is the only voice I want to hear right now. Scrolling makes me cringe because the missed calls and texts are endless—a firehose of needs from Rory, interspersed with his goofy attempts to guess my location. He'd be able to track me if I didn't have an app that uses a VPN that I'm beta-testing for a friend. So far, it's a ten out of ten, highly recommend it. I scroll through his texts, relieved to see that many are amusing instead of the typical Fyfe passive-aggressive.

How's Tuscany? Gorging yourself on pasta?

Is Iceland as great as they say? I know you have a soft spot for hot springs and volcanic lands.

Greece is amazing this time of year, isn't it?

They go on like this for a while, but then the most recent one stops me cold.

We have a situation. We need to talk as soon as you get this.

The timestamp is half an hour ago. For a moment my heart stops as I run through the catalog of emergencies that range from stroke to police arrest. With the powder keg that is my family, it could go either way.

I dial Rory and he picks up on the first ring.

"What's happened?" I ask him.

"Things have escalated," he says. His voice is ragged and strained like he's been shouting for hours. "Now Grandad's sworn to write us all out of his will unless you come aboard."

I snort. "That's ridiculous."

"It sure is," he says. "But his lawyer just left and the papers have been drawn up. All he has to do is sign."

"He's bluffing." As soon as I say the words, though, I know they aren't true. There's nothing Grandad won't try to get his way. This is a pitiful threat to turn my family against me. But he knows it's the most effective screw to tighten.

"I thought so too, until the lawyer came over," Rory grumbles. "He says you have until Christmas, and then he's signing."

I knock back the rest of the bourbon and pour another.

"Tell me where you are," Rory says. "I'll come get you, and then we can get hammered on the flight home and come up with a counteroffer. One that doesn't involve losing your soul in a devil's chess game."

My jaw clenches hard enough to crack a tooth. Of everyone in my family, Rory's the one who understands me the most. He's always on my side, but now we all stand to lose if I don't give in to Grandad's demands. And that's the root of this whole problem: Grandad's used to getting what he wants, by strong-arming everyone around him until they fall in line. He wields his fortune like a weapon, and this time it's like his finger's hovering over the nuclear button.

If he writes us all out of his will, then hundreds of millions will go wherever he chooses—but not to me, my siblings, my mom, or my nieces. We won't be destitute, because Rory's saved every penny like a dragon hoarding gold, and Cait's built her own multi-million-dollar medical practice. But the estate we stand to inherit could do a lot of good in the world—and I've already got some ideas of how to put that money to good use. Because lord knows, it's more than I could spend in ten lifetimes. And it'll take a lot of charitable work to balance out all the bad karma that Fyfe Enterprises has racked up with my grandfather in charge.

But the very thought that Grandad has done this, has used his own child and grandkids as collateral, makes me want to never bend.

It'd be easy to say no if it only affected me. And he knows that dragging all the other Fyfes into this standoff is the best chance he has to make me cave. I hate that he knows me that well. Even more, I hate that it's almost enough to make me give in to his demands.

"You have thoughts about a counteroffer?" I ask Rory.

"I'm working on it. He's not the only one with lawyers."

"Give me a couple of days."

"I wish you'd come back so we could put our heads together," he says. "And maybe you could talk some sense into him."

"I can't be there right now, Rory. Not like this." I let out a heavy sigh because there is no talking sense into the eldest Fyfe. "If I do, then it's just coming to heel. And I won't teach him that this is how to get what he wants from me."

"You know you're just as stubborn as he is," Rory mutters.

"You can't tell me you wouldn't do the same."

Before I can say anything else, he ends the call.

———

IT'S ALMOST dark when I see headlights in the driveway next door. These houses are on good-sized lots, but they're both situated close to the property line, only a few meters apart. From where I'm sitting on the deck, I can see the lights inside Gwen's house switch on, mapping her path from the front of the house to the kitchen. A couple of minutes later I hear the sliding glass door, and she's out on her deck holding a glass of wine. She stares out toward the lake for a full minute until she turns and notices me.

"Hi," she says with a wave. The side of her deck is just a stone's throw from mine. The surrounding bushes are bare this time of year, save for a few evergreens, so I imagine there's a bit more privacy in the summer. Tonight though, I can see her clearly enough to make out her easy smile.

"Evening," I say, waving back. "How was your day?"

"Long," she says. "I made about a million snowflake cookies and my hands might be permanently cramped."

"Don't you have little elves to help you?" I ask.

"I wish. You know how hard it is to find elves this time of year?" She smirks, leaning against the railing. "How about you, mister? Did you get out and soak up a little small-town fun after crushing all the villains?"

"Yep, I've seen it all. I can leave now."

She sips her wine and sits on the wide railing of the deck like she's inching closer to me. "I bet there's at least one hidden place you didn't find. Did you have tacos from Eduardo's food truck? Or get a slice of derby pie from Shelley's? Because if not, you haven't fully experienced this town and aren't allowed to leave and spread your slanderous tales of woe."

"Tacos and derby pie? That wasn't on the listicle I found for this town. I feel cheated."

She shrugs. "I suppose the neighborly thing would be to introduce you to all the best spots."

"Aye, we are going to be neighbors for a while, aren't we?" I smile at the thought.

"Promise not to have any wild bachelor yard parties and I'll show you our hidden gems."

I laugh, leaning closer to the side of the deck. Talking this way is like trying to whisper across the aisle in a movie theater. With each passing second it feels like that invisible thread is back, pulling us closer.

"Wild bachelor yard parties?" I tease. "Part of me is dying to see what that looks like around here."

"No all-night shenanigans allowed, no matter how good it is for your Instagram. I need my baking sleep," she says. "I'm like an old cat lady, asleep under a quilt by ten every night. I'm not too proud to admit it."

"You stalked my Instagram?" I grin, already imagining ways I might convince her to break her curfew. And then I try to remember what I've posted on my accounts lately—not much, and certainly nothing since I flew across the Atlantic a few days ago.

"Stalked is strong. Don't you do a little investigating when someone moves in next to you?" she says.

"Aye, fair point."

"Your family's kind of a big deal," she says. "It's more than a little intimidating."

I sip my drink, wondering just how deep she dug. My grandfather built that company—an impressive feat—but he did a lot of things that I'm not proud of and that I don't want people to associate me with. And an internet search isn't always discerning.

Hoping to steer us far away from this topic, I say, "You know, you could come over here and drink your wine. We don't have to shout over the hedges like we're under house arrest."

"Oh, you've been under house arrest, have you?" Her tone is teasing as she stands, and then she's walking down her steps and climbing mine, her bare feet whispering against the smooth floorboards.

"Not in the sense that you're thinking. But if my family could arrange to do that right now, they absolutely would."

She sits in the wicker chair next to me and sets the bottle of wine between us. "You want to get yourself a glass?"

I pull my empty tumbler from the floor by my feet and she pours.

"You know, you're not at all what I expected you to be like," she says. Her eyes are bright, pupils wide in the moonlight.

I bite back a smile. "What did you expect?"

She lifts a brow. "Honestly? A spoiled, entitled billionaire playboy who would be so obnoxious he'd make me want to shove him in the lake."

I laugh, nearly spitting out my wine.

"Victoria didn't tell me much about you beforehand. She might have used the words 'bazillionaire' and 'hermit.'"

"To be fair, she only knows me from what Theo might have told her."

"I'm sorry I expected you to be awful."

"It's okay. You wouldn't be the first. But for the record, I'm no bazillionaire."

She cocks her head to the side and fixes her big blue eyes on me. "What it is that you really do? Since you're not a Bond villain or a royal."

"I thought you googled me."

She purses her lips, which I've decided are very kissable. "There's a lot of misinformation out there in the world. I prefer to go straight to the source."

I hesitate because there's a ton of information out there about Fyfe Enterprises. And most of it isn't good. I don't agree with the way my grandfather does business. That image most people conjure up with they hear *land developer*—akin to a comic book villain, he embodies it pretty well. He's had people evicted, built condos in bird sanctuaries, and razed historic buildings to make way for mini-malls. And much, much, worse.

I've worked hard to distance myself from him and the family business for years, but Gwen doesn't know that. And I don't want her to associate me with anything she might read about my grandfather's misdeeds. Once people tie me to the things my family's done, it's hard to separate myself again.

"Well, the internet probably taught you more about my family than about me," I tell her. "The short version is that my grandfather has a business that I'd like to have nothing to do with. I knew that early on, so when I was at university I got together with a classmate who was creating an app. I was good at design, but he was the coding genius. I had access to more capital, so we were able to make a real go of it. We got very lucky and sold it after college."

"Wow. I never met anyone who did that."

I shrug. "Right skills, right time."

She smiles. "You made one of those matchmaking apps, didn't you? Tinder for billionaires?" She's teasing, and I'm relieved. Usually, when people figure out who I am, they either kiss up to me or throw their drink in my face. Or worse. The odds are about fifty-fifty back home, because most people hear Fyfe and think of my grandfather, and not what I'm doing on my own. But sometimes when I travel, I can be more invisible. Luckily, Gwen doesn't throw anything at my face and seems to be interested in me as a person. She laughs at some of my silly jokes, and she reminds me that I can still have real conversations with people who aren't just out to get something from me.

It's a relief to feel so comfortable around her. Safe enough to be myself. With only a couple of friends back home, I don't have many people I can trust to be their true selves around me. It's refreshing to not feel like I'm trying to peek behind a mask and I want to enjoy this feeling for as long as I can.

"Nope," I say. "Not matchmaking."

"Rideshare? Yacht-swapping?"

I laugh, sipping my wine. "I'm sorry. Yacht-swapping?"

"You know, like house-swapping for vacations. I don't know what billionaires do."

I shake my head. "Not a billionaire. And it was a meditation app called Centered."

Her jaw drops. "You're joking. I love that one."

"Balance changes everything," I tell her with a small shrug.

She studies me for a moment and I think I've accidentally hit a nerve.

"Now I invest in other fledgling companies. Green housing initiatives, the occasional software app, an artisanal whisky distillery that's pretty incredible." I shrug. "It's nice to be able to help new businesses get a leg up."

"Well, I think that's amazing," she says at last. "And now I feel like a real jerk for fantasizing about how I might make your month here absolutely miserable if you pulled that wild bachelor crap."

"You should," I tell her. "Especially after I've agreed to escort you to the wedding and save you from your mother's horrid setups."

"About that," she says. "Are you sure you're up for it? My family can be a lot. If you want to back out, I wouldn't hold it against you."

I watch her expression carefully. "Why would I want to back out?"

She lifts a brow. "Because you were ambushed by my sister? Because you agreed before you knew all the details? Because you didn't want to say no and embarrass me?" She squirms in her chair, and it makes me wonder if she's the one who wants out of this. After all, it was Victoria who asked me to go—not Gwen.

That thought pierces my heart like an arrow.

"Do I seem like the kind of man who says yes when he means no?" I ask her.

"You seem like the kind of man who likes to solve problems," she says, biting her lip.

"I want to be very clear," I tell her, setting my glass on the table. I lean forward and look her straight in the eye. "I'd be lucky to be your date, and I'd like nothing more than to escort you. But the last thing I want to do is make you feel uncomfortable. So let me ask you something I should have asked yesterday." I rest my forearms on my knees and go on. "Would you like to go to the wedding with me?"

She stares at me for what feels like a year. Then she smiles, and it's brighter than the moon hanging high above us.

"Yes," she says. "I'd like that very much."

Thank goodness that's settled, because I might have crumbled into dust if she'd said no. I lean back in my chair and let out a breath that seems to set my heart a little closer to its natural rhythm. "So tell me about the rest, love. Victoria said there were other events?"

"You're doing me a huge favor just by going to the wedding with me," she says. "You don't have to pretend to be my boyfriend."

"But what if I wanted to?"

She laughs. "Because you're already that bored in Jasmine Falls?"

"Because I don't like the idea of you being uncomfortable. If I can do something to help, I'd like to."

Gwen stares at me for a moment. "You mean that, don't you?"

"Also, I never miss a chance to put on my tux and have a top-shelf martini. Have to keep myself in top villain-fighting shape."

She taps a finger against her lip. "It would get Mom off my back if she thought we were serious." She's quiet for a moment and then frowns. "She's got some specific ideas about how I should live my life. My mom means well, deep down, but she thinks she knows everything I need. And she's determined to tell me all about it. On repeat."

I consider that for a moment. "Your mom and mine would get along great."

"This is the busiest time of year for me," she says. "I took on a bunch of special orders that I'm hoping will launch me into the event business. I've got to bring my A-game every day, and that's impossible to do when I'm so stressed and distracted over Mom and her antics." She shakes her head, clearly frustrated.

"Her heart's in the right place, but I've just hit my limit. And I'm done with the matchmaking."

"Here's a crazy idea," I offer. "Why don't you tell your mother what you want? Or more precisely, what you don't want."

She barks out a laugh. "If only it were that easy. Getting my mom to stop meddling is like trying to stop the sun from coming up."

"Then let's make it look real," I tell her. "I think we should go out a few times before the wedding to be extra convincing."

She narrows her eyes, skeptical. "Fake dating?"

I cringe at the word *fake* but give her a shrug. "Sure. Meanwhile, you can spend your time doing what you want—when you're not having a rollicking time with me, of course—and not waste all that energy fending off your mum and all of her…good intentions."

Gwen lifts a brow. "Why do you really want to do this?"

"I like you," I say, holding her gaze. "Isn't that reason enough?"

She catches her lip in her teeth and gives me a sly grin, and I've never wanted to kiss someone so badly in my life. "Okay, Lancelot. You can be my pretend boyfriend. As long as you accept payment in booze and finger foods." This woman, good lord. She delights in keeping me a little off-balance and I'm starting to love it.

"I wouldn't have it any other way, gorgeous."

"We'll see about that." She tugs on a lock of her hair and fixes those big blue eyes on me. The moonlight's making her skin glow and I can't stop studying the elegant line from her neck to her shoulder and imagining how it would feel under my tongue.

"But just remember," she says, "after you've met my mother and it feels like your soul's been raked over a cheese grater, that it was you who asked for this."

"I don't know what that means exactly, but now I'm very curious about your mother."

She gives me a hint of a smile and in this moment, I feel like I'd do anything she asked.

This woman is going to wreck me.

Chapter Nine

GWEN

This day is already kicking me in the teeth. First, I overslept. I never oversleep, and I never sleep through alarms. But this morning I did, because I spent most of the night flopping around like a fish out of water. And the worst part? It's purely Logan's fault.

Last night, when he suggested going on multiple dates, I felt the air whoosh right out of my lungs. He said the words so casually, as he traced his finger along the edge of his glass, and all I could think about was how those fingers might feel tracing a line from my shoulder blade down to my hip.

That's the image that lodged itself in my thoughts as I finally fell asleep. And that's the image that grew into a delicious dream about him, with lots of touching, that my traitorous brain didn't want to let go of this morning.

My brain's been scrambled ever since. So scrambled that I poured myself decaf when I got to the cafe and then tried to make myself an espresso shot using matcha. Maggie and Sam had looked at me like I'd finally gone around the bend. Mondays are always a struggle, but today is a doozy.

Last night's conversation is stuck on repeat because I can't decide if it's a great idea or a terrible one. I don't love the idea of lying to everyone around me, but I also don't love the idea of sitting alone at Victoria's wedding while everyone stares at me like they're waiting for me to fall to pieces. Logan pretending to be my date is one thing, but pretending to be my boyfriend is something else entirely.

I don't know what's come over me. I'm never as relaxed around people as I am with him. I'm the woman who always says something awkward during the date, whose brain is always burning a hole in my skull with all of its constant thoughts about what this person is thinking about me, how I might erase the tension, undo the awkward thing I just did, or otherwise over-analyzing every minute detail of my waking hours.

With Logan it's different. It's like he's cast some kind of spell to quiet the flurry of thoughts in my brain, like a superhero who can control the weather. Everything's quieter when he's around, and all it takes is one of his adorable smirks or the brush of his fingers against my arm. A tiny movement that might, in any other moment, seem too insignificant to notice.

But I notice. He's like a tonic. A balm.

Like a guy who'd create the most successful meditation app in the world.

I want more, and I probably shouldn't. He's fascinating and alluring in a way that no one else ever has been, but he's only here for a short while. The rational part of my brain tells me to keep my distance and not get attached. But the irrational thought that pops to the surface is this one: why not just enjoy the moment and see where it leads?

Last night when he looked at me, his gaze was smoldering.

I like you. Isn't that reason enough?

Suddenly pretending to *make things look real* seems like the surest way to make me combust. Logan doesn't strike me as the kind of guy who does anything halfway—so if there will be heated gazes and fiery touches in this charade, then I'm definitely in trouble. He's exactly the sort of guy I don't need to get attached to because it could never be real between us. Guys like Logan don't fall for women like me. And even if he did, he's leaving in a matter of days. That should make him doubly off-limits.

We can be friends, and nothing more. I can pretend we're dating for the sake of surviving the holiday, and I can will my heart to stop its annoying flip-flopping whenever he speaks to me in that tantalizing brogue. Or looks at me with his intense blue-green gaze. Or laughs that throaty laugh that sends a shiver over my arms. I can handle a little pretend-dating because this has absolutely no chance of being real.

Logan Fyfe might be one hundred percent charming, but he's also one hundred percent out of my league. A guy like him could have any woman he wanted—supermodels, CEOs, rock stars—so why would he want a baker from a tiny town in the middle of nowhere?

Frowning, I make myself one more espresso, because caffeine will definitely make this situation better.

After dodging Paula Sue, who's pleading with Maggie to add five dozen more cupcakes to her last-minute order, I grab today's delivery for Stonebury Elementary and head for the door. It's a snowman cake the size of a toddler, complete with a jaunty top hat and pretzel-stick arms.

"Hey," Sam says. "You need some help with that? I can go with you."

Like a reflex, I tell him, "I'm good." It's tricky to wrangle a cake this large by myself, but I can manage with my travel cart. It's a ten-minute drive to the school, and that's long enough for my coffee to kick in. If I roll the windows down and blast myself with cold December air, it'll wake my brain up just fine.

He holds the back door open for me and I load the giant

snowman cake into the back of my small SUV. There's no need for the big delivery van today since this is the only order going out before noon.

"You sure you don't want me to come along?" Sam says. "My sister's kids run circles around me and I always need back-up."

"I'll be fine," I tell him. We'd have to close for an hour if he came with me because no one else is here today. We do that on the slow days, but not during the holidays.

He grins. "Watch your back."

When I get to the school, I try to shove that dream of Logan way down deep. Because one shouldn't be thinking of a sexy shirtless Scotsman and his very kissable lips while entering a school full of children. Somehow, that just seems wrong.

I park right next to the front doors and then unload my collapsible cart and carefully place the cake on top. It's one of my favorite designs, even though it's a challenge to put together. Fully vertical, it's made from half-domes that are held together with dowels and magic, and covered in white vanilla frosting. Of course, Frosty has an edible hat and a carrot-shaped nose, plus some chocolate buttons for eyes. Dusting it in coconut flakes is what makes it look amazing—that and the edible glitter that the kids love.

When I get to the front doors, there are a couple of teacher's aides waiting to help me maneuver it down the hallway to Sharon's classroom. Christmas is three weeks away, but the kids are having a party today and dressing up like their favorite characters from holiday cartoons.

Sharon's classroom is just down the hallway from the main office, which means we aren't pushing the cart for long. She meets us at the door, dressed as an elf with striped stockings and a green felt hat. Inside the classroom, her assistant gathers the children and tells them they all have to be very quiet for a moment and close their eyes because a special delivery has come for them from the North Pole.

Okay even I have to admit, it's pretty dang cute.

When the kiddos are (mostly) covering their eyes, I push the cart into the classroom and move the cake onto a table that Sharon has set up by the window. After turning the snowman so he's facing the kids, I catch one little girl peeking through her hands. I give her a friendly wink and Sharon says, "Open your eyes!" in her sugary-sweet teacher voice.

And then the kids go bonkers.

There are squeals of delight and shouts of "Frosty!" and a wave of tiny bodies surge past me and toward the cake. They all stand around the table for a minute, looking at all the details, and all those hours getting the snow just right are totally worth it.

"Amazing," Sharon's assistant Judy tells me. "I've got to take some pictures before they dig in." Before I can blink, she's snapping photos with her phone, and this will look great on Instagram.

There's a distinct *whomp* from behind me, and I freeze, recognizing the horrible sound from my days of playing kickball: it's the sound of a tiny sneaker connecting with a rubber ball. Before I can react, Sharon whips her arm out in front of me and catches the ball with the reflex of a pitcher who snags a line drive before it takes his hair off.

"Sampson!" she hollers. "You know it's not ball time."

I turn to see a boy with wild red hair pursing his lips, crossing his little arms over his chest. He's wearing felt reindeer antlers, has a black dot painted on his nose, and looks like he came out of the womb stirring up trouble.

There's another whoosh of air from a second point in the room, and when I step backward, my foot connects with something that isn't the earth and shoots out from under me.

There's a shriek from behind me as I stumble to avoid stepping on a child and then I'm completely off-balance. The kids are everywhere and I know two things in an instant: one, I am definitely crashing to the ground, and two, if I land on a child then my karma will never recover and I can kiss this revenue stream goodbye—because being a little grinchy is one thing, but squashing a kid is another. My arms pinwheel by my sides as I try to course-correct, but it's too late. I trip over something that squeaks like a dog toy and then land bottom-first into what appears to be a gingerbread house made out of cardboard and plastic blocks.

The sound is like a hundred-year-old tree crashing into the earth.

Somehow I've landed in the most ungraceful way possible with my feet in the air. There's a throbbing in my back and my arm, and I pluck a tiny plastic sleigh from under the small of my back, where it feels like it's punctured a kidney.

"Oh my goodness!" Sharon says, coming to hover over me. "Gwen, are you all right?"

Sharon and Judy pull me to my feet and I'm too shocked to register exactly where all the pain is coming from. It's everywhere all at once, and it's probably ninety percent humiliation, anyway. The kids are laughing like little maniacs and I can't blame them because I'd probably laugh if I saw a grown woman flail around like Mr. Bean and flatten a gingerbread house with her ass, too. A wail pierces the air and one of the kids is pointing at the detritus around me as tears spring from her eyes, and I can only hope that the snowman cake will make up for this.

Because karma.

"She killed Rudolph!" a tiny voice yells, and I turn to see that yes, there is indeed a crushed cardboard reindeer in the Gwen-shaped crater, and in the last twenty seconds I've gone from being a heroine to the mean lady who destroyed Christmas with her backside.

Mercy. I'm getting nothing but coal this year.

Sharon helps me into the hallway and Judy rounds up the kids and tells them they can build a new, bigger gingerbread house after cake, yay! The sniffles subside as the door closes behind me and I say, "Sharon, I'm so sorry. I don't even know what happened."

"Are you all right?" she asks me, her eyes wide. "Do you need to see the nurse?"

I bite back a laugh because, really, the school nurse? I imagine getting a band-aid and a lollipop, even though I know that's not accurate at all. "I'll be okay," I tell her. My shoulder aches and my entire backside throbs, and I'm pretty sure my tailbone is bruised from the impact.

At least I didn't take out any kids when I fell. Probably, I should have taken Sam up on his offer to be my backup.

"You really did an amazing job," she says, and of course, she's talking about the cake and not my awful reverse-cannonball. "I can't thank you enough," she says, patting my arm. "I hope we can arrange something for Valentine's, too."

"Of course," I say, making a mental note to always bring a partner in the future, and make my way back to the parking lot.

The drive back to the bakery is excruciating. My brain's still rattling in my skull from the impact, and my right arm's hurting worse than before. As I hobble in through the back door, I consider taking the rest of the day off. Sam's here until four, and technically we could close early if he didn't want to work an extra couple of hours. But there's another cookie order waiting for me that I'd planned to do this afternoon, and there's no way I can push it to tomorrow morning. Fiona sometimes helps me with orders because she has a hidden talent for baking, but I don't want to bother her with four dozen reindeer cookies. This is the kind of job that I can do in my sleep—I just need to put the pain out of my mind and focus.

Cringing, I wash down a few ibuprofen with iced coffee. My back's feeling stiff and my wrist is starting to throb. It's probably sprained, but I can't think about that right now. I have gingerbread reindeer to make.

By the time I've mixed all the ingredients into the big stand mixer and chilled the dough, my arm is aching from my elbow to my fingertips. Sam comes into the back and catches me holding a package of frozen butter against it.

"Are you okay?" he asks. His brows pinch together in concern. I told him what happened when I first came back and, to his credit, he didn't laugh—he just said, "Kids, man. Can't turn your back for a second."

"Sure, I'm fine," I tell him, pulling the ball of chilled dough from the walk-in fridge. I set the dough on the counter, sprinkle enough flour to stop it from sticking, and begin to roll it out.

The pain that shoots up my arm is enough to make my knees buckle and bring tears to my eyes. I gasp and Sam's eyes go wide.

"Dude," he says. "You're not okay."

"I think my wrist is sprained," I tell him. "Would you roll this out for me?"

He pokes his head back out to check for customers and says, "Yeah, no problem."

"I'll watch the front. Just roll it out a quarter-inch thick."

I prop the swinging doors open so I can see the counter. It's not quite one o'clock, and there are only a couple of regulars sitting out front, working on their laptops. Since we don't serve lunch, we don't get a midday rush. We're busiest early in the morning and mid-afternoon.

When Sam's done rolling a slab, I grab my reindeer cookie cutter and squeeze as many into the dough as I can, using my left hand. I lift all the scraps, wincing a little, and pile them into a rough ball using my good hand. Then I use a spatula to move the eight reindeer onto the sheet pan. Sam rolls the remaining dough into a smooth ball and then we repeat the process.

"You should see a doctor," he says, no doubt noticing the grunts and hisses that come out of me every time I bend my wrist the slightest bit.

"First I have to get these baked and iced," I tell him.

"Did you take something for pain?" he says, rolling out more dough.

Then I remember: I have painkillers in my office, left over from last year when I threw my back out. Once we get all of the cookies placed on baking sheets, Sam goes back to handle the front of the cafe and I root through the desk in my office until I find the prescription bottle I'm looking for.

I take two of the pills and chase them with more coffee. They made me drowsy before, but I just need a couple more hours to finish the cookies, and then I can go home and slip into my pajamas and forget this day ever happened. Sam offers to help me pipe the icing because he's a good guy and is always willing to help—but as much as I love Sam, his piping skills are a B minus at best, and the client is persnickety enough that there's just no room for imperfection this time.

While the cookies are in the oven, I sit in my office chair with a bag of frozen berries pressed against my lower back while I scroll through my emails. Three new requests have come through the website since Logan fixed it. They're all cakes for holiday parties, due in the next two weeks. My phone pings with a text from Logan.

Hi, neighbor, he writes. **Hayrides, yay or nay?**

Hayrides? I reply.

For context, he writes, **I went out for lunch and a lady**

named Paula Sue invited me to a hayride. Is that something I should attend?

I laugh. If you're looking for wholesome small-town holiday fun, then yes. One hundred percent.

Want to come with me? He writes. I get the sense it's more fun with two. Also, maybe it'll get you in the Christmas spirit.

I'd love to, but I'm up to my ears in a cookie order and I'm already way behind.

Can I help? he asks.

I smile, loving that he always wants to help me.

Only if you have a time machine so I can erase this morning entirely, I type. That would help me get my last shred of pride back, too.

What happened this morning?

You'll probably see it in tomorrow's paper, I reply.

Okay, now I'm concerned.

I did an accidental cannonball into a gingerbread playhouse and made a kid cry, I type. I didn't know you could get brain damage from falling on your ass, but I swear I hear something rattling between my ears.

I can't tell if you're joking, he types.

My pride may never recover. I have the giant bruises to prove it.

I'm coming over right now, he writes.

Not necessary, Lancelot. I'm fine.

No response.

<hr>

"IT'S BROKEN," Logan says, holding my arm as gently as he would a kitten. His brows are furrowed with concern, and can I just say how sexy he looks when he's in broody problem-solving mode?

I just wish I wasn't the problem.

Now that my sleeve is pushed up past my elbow, I see the ugly bruising and swelling that spreads from my wrist up into my forearm. I should have looked earlier, but honestly, I was afraid of what I might find if I did. And this is way worse.

Logan's positioned his palm under mine, supporting my wrist with his long fingers. His hand is huge and warm, and when he bends my wrist the smallest bit, I feel that shooting pain again, like I've stuck my finger in a light socket.

Awesome.

"It's just a sprain," I wheeze, feeling more lightheaded now. The painkillers have turned the intense throbbing into mostly a dull ache, but they've also made all of my other limbs feel like noodles. I realize now that I forgot to eat today and was no doubt jacked up on adrenaline when I decided to take my painkillers, which are now feeling more like horse tranquilizers.

"I played enough rugby to know a broken arm when I see one," Logan drawls. "We need to get you to a doctor." He's patient—something else that is utterly endearing—but his brow lifts in that way that means this isn't up for debate anymore.

"Don't have time for that," I say, feeling like I have a mouth full of cotton. "Those reindeer aren't going to ice themselves."

He blinks at me like I've just spoken the dumbest words in the English language.

"It won't take long to finish them," I press. "It's only four dozen."

He fixes his big blue-green eyes on me, and I swear there's a storm cloud swirling in them. It'd be a little scary on anyone else, but on him, it's lethally hot.

"You need to take care of yourself first," he says, his tone commanding. "Cookies can wait."

"Cookies can't wait!" I cry, wincing as I jostle my injured arm. "Jane Silver will be here at nine a.m. sharp, expecting perfect gingerbread reindeer. And that's what I'm going to deliver."

"Isn't there anyone else that can do them?" he asks.

"No. Maggie's off today and she's the only other person who can pipe."

He sighs, raking his hands through his hair.

"Unless you're about to tell me that piping is one of your hidden superpowers," I tell him, "then I'm going to have to do this myself." It wouldn't be so bad if I hadn't shown Jane a design where the reindeer are wearing little scarves and have cute faces. Of course I had to go above and beyond, like always. Giving people more than they expect leads to repeat business, after all.

"I'm not sure I even know what that means," he says. "Piping?"

Wincing at the pain in my lower back, I stand up from the stool and limp back to the work table, where I managed to finish six cookies before Logan came by. Yes, it took me forever to do them, but they look good. I grab my piping bag and start on another one, determined to show him that this can be done. That I, through sheer willpower, can work through a little bodily pain. Piping with one hand is too difficult, but if I hold my right arm close to my body and don't bend my wrist, I can use it to brace my left hand and create smooth piped lines.

Biting my lip, I pipe the outline of the reindeer at a snail's pace. Even using my right hand only as a guide sends a bolt of pain zipping through my arm.

But I'm determined to make this work. *I will not be felled by a gingerbread house.* When I finally finish piping on the scarf and the face, I turn back to Logan. "See? That wasn't so bad. Only forty-one more to go."

"You're sweating," he says, his big arms crossed over his

chest. He's not buying this act for a second. "Why is it so hard for you to put yourself first, love?"

"This business lives and dies by repeat customers. If these aren't perfect, I lose business."

"That doesn't answer my question." His tone's all deep and commanding. I shouldn't like it as much as I do.

Frustrated, I pick up the piping bag and start on another cookie. There are a few extras in case I make mistakes, but only a few. Of course I can always bake more, but that's just more time I don't have. And at this rate, I'll already be here until midnight.

"You can't solve every problem all by your lonesome," he says, not unkindly. "Sometimes you have to be able to rely on other people, you know."

"This isn't that big a deal, Logan. It's just cookies." But even as I say the words, I know that's not entirely true. This isn't just about cute reindeer cookies. This is about delivering on my promises and being able to tackle anything that comes my way. I don't want to have to depend on other people to solve my problems.

"Would Maggie want to come in for extra hours?" he says. "How long would this take her?"

I shrug. "Maybe two or three."

"Then what's the harm in asking?"

"She asked for today off," I say. "I don't want to call her in."

"I'm not suggesting you throw her in the trunk of your car and force her down here against her will," he says, and the teasing smirk is back. "What I'm saying, love, is why don't you call her and ask her if she'd like the extra hours—the extra experience. You said she likes decorating, right?"

I nod. Maggie's always eager to do more decorating.

"So if she says yes, then great. Problem solved. If she says no, then we move on to another solution. But don't decide for her— give her a chance to decide."

I frown, frustrated by how he makes all of that sound so easy. Of course he would have sound logic, on top of everything else. At this point, I don't have the energy to argue anymore. I'm feeling light-headed again, the pain's coming back, and the thought of being here icing cookies all night makes me want to cry.

"Okay," I mutter. "You're right."

"What was that?" he says, cupping a hand over his ear. "I couldn't quite hear you, gorgeous."

I toss a tea towel at him with my good arm, but there's still an echo of pain. "I'll ask her."

"Good girl," he says with a smirk, and a little shiver runs along my spine.

On the way to the urgent care clinic, I text Maggie and she agrees to come over and finish the reindeer cookies. Logan convinced me to let Sam close up the cafe when his shift ends at three o'clock, and then he insisted on driving me to the clinic because he's determined to make sure I follow through on this appointment. He can certainly be bossy when he wants to be.

It's not entirely awful.

Logan also insists on coming into the exam room with me when we arrive. At first, I start to argue, but then he makes the very good point that he's not flooded with adrenaline and that two heads remember details better than one. Especially the medical kinds of details.

Once we're in the exam room, I'm glad I let him come inside. Dr. Jacobson is friendly but stern, going over the treatment plan as she points to the fracture in my X-ray. She's a Black woman in her mid-thirties, with a bright smile and gentle hands, and when she points to the films and talks about misalignment, I feel like she's talking about more than my wrist. Because yes, I know I take on too much, and I never ask for help, and I'm always trying to prove that my success isn't an illusion. But I also feel like if I drop just one of all these balls I'm juggling, everything I worked so hard to build will come crashing down.

When Dr. Jacobson's assistant comes toward me with a needle that looks like it's meant to be used on a horse, I feel a wave of nausea and see little white spots dancing in my periphery.

"Surely that's not necessary," I tell her, and my voice sounds like it's at the bottom of a well.

"You'll only feel a brief sting," Dr. Jacobson says, "but trust me, it's better than feeling that bone when it slides back into place."

I try to focus on her bright purple nails and not the size of that needle, but then the white spots get bigger and Logan's voice comes from somewhere a million miles away. The assistant rubs my wrist with alcohol and Dr. Jacobson says something in her soothing voice that makes me feel like maybe everything isn't so terrible. Then my vision gets all speckled like static on an old TV and I barely recognize my voice as I say, "Okay then, good night."

Chapter Ten

LOGAN

This day isn't going the way I expected. First I'd gone into town for an early lunch, bored and looking for a distraction. Rory had texted me half a dozen times, and I just wanted to find something—anything—to take my mind off the Fyfe problem that seemed to be growing hairier by the hour. Then I texted Gwen because I couldn't get her out of my mind. And when she mentioned falling, I couldn't tell if she was joking about being injured. She has a fondness for hyperbole that's endearing when it's not masking her hurt.

When I saw her arm, though, I knew it was serious. And then she flat-out refused to ask anyone for help. This woman, good grief. She behaves as if asking people for small favors is like demanding they bring her the moon. It's obvious to me that someone along the way made her feel like she was always a burden. I don't know who that person was, but a growing part of me wants to track them down and kick them in the shins for making her feel like she always has to do everything alone.

When we got to the clinic, the doctor took one look at her arm and confirmed what I'd seen the second I laid eyes on her. Gwen had frowned, listening as the doctor described how she'd position the wrist back and apply a splint. At the sight of the needle, Gwen's eyes had gone wide and the color drained from her face, and I'd seen that reaction enough times in my life to know what was coming next.

Her eyelids fluttered and she slumped against me, and I knew then, just as sure I was standing next to her, that I'd do any little task she needed. The next few weeks would be hard for her, and I didn't want her to feel like she had to do everything alone. That's an awful feeling, and she's too good of a person to feel that.

"It's a small fracture and a dislocation," Dr. Jacobson says, "but a splint might be all you need. If it doesn't heal properly, you could lose range of motion in your wrist, and we don't want that. So I'll have you come back in a few days to check in."

Gwen frowns. "No cast?" She's completely loopy from the pain meds now, holding on to my arm like I'm a pool noodle and she's in the deep end.

"Probably not, but I'll re-evaluate in a few days," Dr. Jacobson says, noting something in the chart. "I'll call in a prescription to your pharmacy for some pain meds."

"Thank you," Gwen says. I can see the gears turning in her brain—she's no doubt thinking of how she's going to get through the next few weeks.

"You shouldn't drive while taking them," the doctor cautions.

"Not a problem," I answer. "I'll drive her wherever she needs to go." I'll fetch her groceries, cook her meals, and do whatever she needs. Sitting in this office has made me overwhelmed with a need to protect her, even though we've only just met. I've seen what Gwen does for everyone around her. She's always looking out for the people she cares about, and it's time someone did the same for her.

And that someone is going to be me.

They continue to chat while Dr. Jacobson applies a splint and a sling, which she says Gwen should use for at least a week to restrict movement. Keeping my little tornado immobile, though—that's a tall order.

When we finally leave the office, I link Gwen's good arm in mine as we cross the parking lot to her car.

"You have really nice forearms," she says, as matter-of-factly as if she's discussing the weather. "Bet you hear that all the time, though."

"I don't, actually. But thank you."

She gasps, clutching her chest. "Of course you do! Are you kidding? Take me to the gun show, sir."

I bark out a laugh because now she's squeezing my bicep. "No," I say, "I really don't hear—"

"You should be an arm model," she says, her eyes widening. "You could make a fortune." She giggles then and says, "A second fortune."

After I get her seat belt buckled, I climb into the driver's side. "Wow, this car's just like mine," she says, looking around. "And I have that same air freshener." She pokes the paper flower hanging from the rearview mirror and her eyes go wide.

"This *is* your car, gorgeous. Someone blocked me in at the cafe, remember?"

"Omigod, the cafe," she says, leaning over and gripping my arm. "I have cookies to finish. We have to hurry. You can help me—anyone can make gingerbread!"

"It's all taken care of," I tell her, placing my hand over hers. "Maggie's doing them for you. All you need to do is go home and rest."

"You are ridiculously handsome," she blurts. "Like AI-generated movie-star hot." She rests her cheek against the car seat and stares at me with those big blue eyes that could convince me of anything.

"And you, sweetheart, are on some very strong drugs."

"Pssshhh," she says, waving her hand at me. "It's about time."

"You need anything while we're out?" I ask her. "Groceries? Dinner?"

"To the lake house!" she cries. "We can have a pizza party in our pajamas. Do you even have pajamas?" She shakes her head. "Doesn't matter. We can have a pizza party without pajamas."

"How's the arm?" I ask. "Still hurt?"

"I can't feel a thing," she purrs.

"That's probably for the best."

We stop by the pharmacy to pick up her prescription on the way back to her house. It's nearly six-thirty by the time I get her home, and as soon as we're in the door, she's clawing at the splint and complaining that it itches.

"Why don't we get you settled on the couch?" I say, gently steering her into the living room. She's still a bit wobbly on her feet and I don't want to leave her alone. "Have you eaten anything today?"

"Does coffee count?"

"Nope."

"I tasted the gingerbread dough and the icing to make sure it was ellible...I mean eligible. Er...edible." She giggles.

"That doesn't count, either." I grab some pillows from one end of the sofa and arrange them so she can sit with her arm propped up.

She bites her lip, thinking hard, and I try not to stare at her perfect mouth. "Then no," she says finally, her drawl more exaggerated. "I don't reckon I have."

"Then let me cook you dinner," I say, heading back toward the kitchen. "What sounds good to you?"

"Getting these pants off, ugh."

By the time I get back to her, she's fumbling with the button of her jeans with her left hand, sliding down onto her back on the couch. One shoe's been kicked across the room and the other is still on her foot.

"Whoa," I tell her, reaching for her uninjured hand.

"It's pajama time," she huffs as if my stopping her from stripping in the living room is a capital crime. She peels herself off the couch and I help her to her feet, and then she slips from my grasp and heads for her bedroom, kicking the other shoe off on her way.

"Can you manage?" I ask her, hoping to god the answer is yes because my heart might beat right out of my chest if I have to help her out of those skin-tight jeans.

She laughs and says, "You're not going to get into my pants that easily, Lancelot," and steps into the bedroom, leaving the door open.

Mercy.

In the kitchen, I search through the fridge and the freezer, looking for anything I might be able to cook for us. Take-away's not an option—I don't want to leave her to fetch it because she's just woozy enough to lose her balance and fall. The thought of coming back here only to find her sprawled on the floor with her other arm broken—or worse—is enough to make me want to camp out here all night. I'm considering sleeping on the couch when I hear a thud from inside the bedroom, followed by an exaggerated groan. I'm at the door in a flash, and Gwen's bent over the bed, her shirt halfway over her head. The brass lamp from the bedside table is lying on the floor right behind her feet.

At least she's still wearing pants. Mostly. Her jeans are unzipped and pulled low on her hips like she started to wriggle out of them and gave up.

"Hang on, love," I say. "Let me help you."

"Ugh," she says, pulling at the neck of her shirt. "Stupid splint. Stupid arm. Stupid kickball! Stupid Christmas!"

"I don't know what all of that means," I say, and try not to chuckle as she wriggles around like a kitten in a pillowcase. She curses when she jostles her hurt arm and then freezes, letting out an adorable little huff. It makes me want to wrap her up in a warm blanket and pull her against my chest, but probably that's a bad idea. Once I move the lamp back onto the table, I get her upright and rest one hand on her shoulder. The shirt's still covering her face, stuck because of the sling.

"Do you want this shirt off?" I ask her.

She sighs like she's exhausted. Her voice is muffled when she mumbles, "Yes, please. I seem to have made a critical error."

"Do you want me to help you take it off?" Even though it's a simple act, it's a line that I need clear permission to cross.

"Logan, if you don't get me untangled out of this thing, I'm going to cut it off with scissors."

"Okay," I say, biting back a laugh. Once I have her splinted arm out of the sleeve, I take off the sling and pull the shirt the rest of the way over her head.

"Why are your eyes closed?" she says.

"Do you need help getting another shirt on?"

She laughs, a musical sound that makes my heart swell. "Like you haven't seen me half-naked already. Afraid you'll fall in love with me if you open your eyes?"

I like this playful side of her. She's letting her guard down like she did when we had dinner that first night, and even though I know it's partly because she's had enough drugs to knock out a tiger, I like to think it's also because she knows she's safe with me.

"What if I am?" I say, keeping my eyes closed and my hands glued to my sides, so that they can't accidentally touch any part of her that she doesn't want me to touch.

Something soft smacks my cheek and I open my eyes,

startled. "Did you just hit me with a pillow? After I saved you from that merciless sweater?"

She's got her head through the neck of a short-sleeved tee shirt now, the rest of it draped over her chest, her right arm completely bare. "Help me with the arms," she says, "and try not to get all smitten." She's teasing, but it's a tall order because she has no idea how enchanting she is.

Keeping my eyes on hers, I slip her arms into the sleeves, only looking away when I have to focus on her splinted arm and move it oh-so-carefully. She sinks down onto the bed and says, "Super. Now pants."

Swallowing hard, I think of an ice-cold pool, a root canal, my fifth-grade teacher Mrs. Benning, who smelled like sardines and wore orthopedic shoes and hairy sweaters that looked like a mammoth hide—anything to take my mind off Gwen's shapely thighs and the way her jeans are undone and still clinging tight to her hips.

This woman is the definition of voluptuous, and she acts like she has no idea. And I really can't think about all of her lovely parts right now—or the fact that I'd like to spend an entire day showing her just how perfect she is.

With her good hand, she shoves the waistband down, but those jeans are so snug it'll take her all night to wriggle out of them. I'm likely to find her lying in the floor in the morning with one leg still stuck inside.

"SOS," she says, breathing hard. "I've never wanted to be in flannel so bad in my life. Can you just grab the ankles and give these a solid yank? I promise I'll cover any vital parts so you don't combust."

She's got no idea how close she is to the truth.

"Don't worry, love. I'll be fine." And I will be, because she needs help and I wouldn't dare cross a line she doesn't invite me to cross.

Kneeling on the floor, I do as she says, tugging the ankles of the jeans while she lifts her hips off the bed and shoves the waistband down. Would this be easier if I just made her stand and stripped them down to the floor? Yes. But that's not an option because that would mean sliding my hands down every inch of her thighs and my heart can't take that right now. So I gently tug as Gwen squirms this way and that, and—true to her word—when I finally have them off at her feet, she has a pillow covering her lap. I make the mistake of looking up at her face, and she looks like a goddess. Her wavy hair's tousled just so, and the overhead light is creating a halo of gold around her head. Her cheeks are flushed pink, her wide blue eyes sparkling, and I want to stay at her feet here for just a little while.

Or maybe forever.

"See," she says, giving me a heartbreaking smile. "You survived, Lancelot. And now I can breathe, and the world is all right again. You make an excellent knight in shining armor."

"You have pajama bottoms somewhere?" I ask, getting to my feet.

"Yep. I can manage from here." She pulls a pair of polka-dot flannel pants from under her pillow.

"Okay, then. I'm going to find dinner."

She grunts something that sounds like approval and I leave her there to resume my search of the kitchen. By the time she comes out again, I've got pasta cooking on the stovetop and garlic bread in the oven and my heart rate is almost back to normal.

"I took a chance on pesto," I tell her as she eases onto a stool at the kitchen island.

Her eyes light up. "How did you know that's my favorite food ever? You are an actual saint."

"Aye, I thought you might be a fan, based on the liter of pesto in the fridge."

She grins and my heart melts. "It's my favorite comfort food."

The timer goes off and I strain the penne pasta. With shock, I realize I want to know what all of her favorite things are.

When I set our places at the kitchen island, she groans with delight as she takes a big mouthful. That breathy groan is my new favorite sound.

"This is amazing," she says. "You're my hero, Lancelot." And that's when I know I'm completely lost in her because I want to hear those little giggles and groans of hers all the time.

And yeah, I want to be her hero.

"Happy to help," I tell her, and she hits me with a megawatt smile.

"You're so sweet," she says, resting her chin in her hand. "Tell me the truth, do you think I'm boring?"

"Of course not. Why would you ask me that?"

She sighs. "Mark told me I'm boring. That I work too much and never had time for him. That I don't know how to make time for fun stuff." She pokes at her pasta and says, "That's why he cheated on me. I'm a boring workaholic." This is the unfiltered Gwen, talking like a relief valve has set free those competing thoughts that are swirling around in her brain. Her brain seems like a busy place, and I know that feeling well.

"I find that highly unlikely," I say. "And this Mark person is obviously a dolt." My head feels hot and I suddenly want to track down this eejit Mark and tell him a thing or two.

She frowns, picking at her pasta. "Ranger Chris said the same thing, though. That I worked too much."

"Ranger Chris?"

"We went out a few times and then he tried to ghost me."

"Also a dolt." Part of me hates that she's had these experiences with men who are fools—but if she hadn't, she might not be sitting here with me.

She bites her lip. "What if they were right? What if I never get my happy-ever-after because I don't know how to balance all the things?" She lets out a sigh that cracks my heart in half. "What if I'm just not good at love?"

"I don't pretend to have all the answers," I tell her. "But what I can tell you is this. You are a gorgeous, creative, inspiring woman who deserves to find someone who makes you feel as amazing as you are. Every day." I lean in closer, placing my hand over hers. "And anyone who makes you feel less than that doesn't deserve one more second of your time."

She stares at me for a moment, speechless. "You're so kind," she says. Then she rests her head in her good hand and gives me a sleepy look. "So tell me your big secret. I told you mine."

"My secret?"

"Why are you avoiding your family?" she asks.

I breathe a heavy sigh. "They're pressuring me to do something I don't want to do. I hate what my grandfather's company has become, and I don't want any part of it." My chest tightens as I think about these truths that I so rarely say aloud. It feels safe to say it now though, here with her. "My father used to work for him, and a few years ago he had a massive heart attack and died. I think I've always blamed my grandfather, at least in part, because he was so hard on my dad." I swallow hard, wishing this anger would go away.

"I'm so sorry," Gwen says, her brows pinched together. "About your dad."

"Sometimes I think I despise my grandfather." My chest aches as the words come out. "I don't want to do anything to help him, and I certainly don't want to save his company."

She leans over and throws herself against me in a big hug. "I'm so sorry," she whispers, her lips against my neck. "So sorry."

"It's okay," I whisper. My hands slip around her back, holding her steady. "Or at least, it will be."

She slides back onto her stool and says, "You're a good man." She says it so matter-of-factly that it nearly cracks my heart in half. Then her eyelids flutter and she says, "I'm so tired, Lancelot."

"You should get some sleep while the pain meds are working," I tell her. She looks like she might topple over at any moment, so I help her down the hall to her bedroom. The room's big, with a wall of built-in bookcases and a picture window facing the lake. A desk and chair are right by the window, and there's a big impressionist-style painting of birds hanging over the queen-sized bed. It's cozy and lovely, just like Gwen.

"Easy," I say, as she collapses onto the bed.

"Hey, let's put a movie on," she says, her voice dreamy. "It always helps me fall asleep. What's your favorite movie? Mine's *The Princess Bride*."

"I like that one, too."

"Oooh, let's see if it's on anywhere," she says, reaching for the remote. There's a small flatscreen TV sitting on a dresser opposite the foot of the bed.

I help her under the covers and get her splinted arm propped on a pillow. She flips through the channels while I go get her a glass of water. When I get back, she's started the movie.

"Got everything you need?" I ask her, setting the water on the bedside table.

"Watch with me, Lancelot," she says, patting the bed next to her, and this is dangerous territory. As badly as I want to curl up next to her and smell that sweet vanilla-lavender scent that is all Gwen, I know I should leave—at least go out and sleep on the couch. I still don't want to leave her alone all night, but I'd planned to at least keep a wall between us.

"Come on," she coos. "Don't be a party pooper." She sticks her bottom lip out and I'm completely undone.

"Aye, just for a little while," I say and climb on top of the covers next to her, propped up on a couple of fluffy pillows.

"Yay, movie night!" she says, and snuggles up against me, resting her cheek against my chest. She fits so perfectly there, like we're two pieces cut from the same jigsaw puzzle.

I comb my fingers through her hair because I just can't help myself. How is it that I've found a woman like this in the most unlikely place, at the worst possible time? This town was supposed to be a temporary sanctuary—a place that took my mind off my family and let me lie low for a while. It wasn't supposed to give me something else complicated to think about. I didn't come here to catch feelings, but heat blooms in my chest when Gwen snuggles up against me, and three weeks with her doesn't feel like nearly enough time.

Now I just want to find more ways to spend time with her and learn everything she likes, everything she hates, and everything she dreams about. I could worry about what happens after, well…after.

She giggles at the movie and then her breaths turn deep and even. I keep watching as Wesley steers Princess Buttercup from one harrowing moment to the next, thinking I'll move out to the couch as soon as Gwen's sleeping deep enough that I won't wake her—even though I want to stay in this moment forever.

Here, in this cozy bed in a small town in the middle of nowhere, I feel like I actually belong—and I can't remember the last time I felt that way.

Chapter Eleven

GWEN

"Gwen, are you here?!" My sister's voice splits the air like a siren and it feels like a full minute before I realize that sunlight is streaming through the window, I'm tangled up with Logan, and my arm throbs like someone's pummeled it with a meat tenderizer.

Wait, back up.

I'm in bed with Logan. My pajama-clad leg is draped shamelessly over his thigh. My face is nestled in the crook of his shoulder and I can still smell that woodsy scent that is somehow even more intoxicating in the morning. Moving is the last thing I want to do right now.

Victoria hollers again from the hallway and I nudge his ribs. "Logan!" I whisper-yell. "Wake up!"

He grunts and his big hand gives my hip a firm squeeze. I can't even pause to appreciate how delightful that feels because my sister is five feet from the door and we're halfway under the covers.

"Logan!" I pull my leg out of his grasp and shake his shoulder. "You have to wake up."

He opens one eye and gives me a wolfish grin. It's so dang

sexy I could die, but I poke him again and say, "My sister's here."

His eye widens and the grin disappears as he seems to realize where he is. He grumbles a curse and tries to untangle himself from the sheets just as the door opens and my sister says, "Well hi, Gwennie." She gives me a dramatic pause as her gaze shifts to Logan. "And mister plus-one."

She's grinning like a cat as she takes in this whole ridiculous scene. Logan sits up and drags a hand through his hair, which is standing up in all directions in a way that makes me ache to run my fingers through it. (Is it soft like a rabbit's? I bet it is.) He's still fully dressed in his jeans and flannel from last night, but that doesn't make Victoria any less delighted.

"What are you doing here?" I ask her, wincing as I sit up straight.

"We waited for you for half an hour at the cafe," she says. "Remember we were going to look at new cake flavors?"

"Oh crap," I say, rubbing my eyes.

"Yes, and then I texted you like a thousand times, and called, and there was no answer." She steals another glance at Logan. "So naturally I came over to make sure you hadn't slipped in the shower or been kidnapped or something. But I see now that you might have had a little of both."

"Sorry," I say. "Had a bit of a day yesterday." When I glance at Logan, he gives me an innocent shrug. At that moment, a few key images from last night flash in my mind: like when he put me to bed and *I begged him to stay.*

"I can see that," she says, lifting a brow. "And also, Mom's right behind me."

"Did you find her?" My mom's voice fills the room before she enters, and I collapse back into the bed, grunting at the pain that shoots through my arm. I never should have given out a spare key.

My mom bursts into the room, her voice shrill. "Are you sick or something, Gwen? It's almost ten in the—oh." She stops when she sees Logan and her eye twitches in that way it does when she's supremely disappointed. Logan turns his attention to a shirt button that's undone and my mother turns back to me. "You could have at least texted to say you'd be late. I have another appointment at eleven. Victoria, I'll wait for you in the car." She frowns at me and then strides back out of the room, apparently satisfied that I'm not dead or dying.

Logan tracks her movements and his jaw tenses as if he has some thoughts about my mother's reaction.

"Mom, Logan. Logan, Mom," I say, after we all hear the screen door slam.

Victoria directs an epic eye-roll at our mother and then turns back to me. Mom's dramatics rarely get her riled up anymore, and I swear if my sister could bottle that immunity, I'd drink it like my favorite fizzy water.

"I should go," Logan tells me, straightening his shirt. "I'll check in on you later, okay?" He gives me a sweet half-smile as he squeezes my good shoulder, then nods to Victoria as he walks past her. "Victoria, always good to see you," he says.

"And you," she says, her voice bright. She gives him an appreciative look as he heads down the hallway, and I also take a moment to marvel at the way those jeans fit his perfectly chiseled backside.

Vic turns back to me, eyes glittering with amusement, and says, "What's with the sling?"

AN HOUR LATER, Victoria and I are sitting at my work table in the kitchen of the Sentient Bean. We're halfway through the four new cake flavors I've prepared for her to sample and looking at some new sketches I've done for the design. I'm trying hard not to be annoyed that Theo has, for a second time, talked Victoria out of a decision she made about the flavor. First, he said her choice was too weird (coconut with lime filling), and then it was too boring (vanilla with honey and buttercream). He can't be bothered to taste flavors and make a decision with her, but he's more than happy to criticize her choices after he says to her, *Can't you just handle this one detail without me?*

"Are you sure you'll be able to do the cake?" she asks, laser-focused on my arm. "It's not a big deal if you can't."

I know she means it, and she wouldn't hold it against me, but I don't want to back out. It's important to me to do something special for her big day.

"I'll be fine," I tell her. "It's not as bad as it looks." I slide the samples toward her. "See what you think of these combos."

She raises a brow like she doesn't believe me, but she knows I won't back down. "You going to tell me what happened with Logan?" she asks, her eyes twinkling. "Because I'm thrilled for you, and I also have questions."

I shrug. "We fell asleep watching a movie. No big deal."

"You two were tangled up like the yarn in the back of my closet," she says, taking a bite of the first cake. "You're a grown-ass woman, Gwen. You're allowed to have a man in your bed, and you don't have to pretend like it wasn't a thing. You're allowed to have fun, you know."

"I know, but it's not a thing. We're just friends." She's right, of course, but I don't know what this is with Logan, and talking about it just makes it seem more complicated. I've never been one for flings, and I don't want word getting around that that's what this is with him. That seems like an important point and one that I don't want any confusion over. My mother, after all, tends to gossip like everyone else in this town and all it will take is one boozy brunch for her to tell her group of friends about finding Logan in my bed this morning.

And if she's feeling the need to gripe about my poor life choices—as per usual—then that means big trouble. Her friends lay the sympathy on extra thick when Mom tells them about something I've done that she finds especially disappointing, and Mom eats that up like a cat with cream.

The night's a blur (thanks, painkillers), but I do recall Logan insisting on taking me to the doctor, helping me home, and cooking me dinner. He was a perfect gentleman, getting me everything I needed. And then I begged him to stay like some total lovesick fool, climbed on him like a puppy, and probably drooled on him as I slept.

Awesome.

He's probably already thinking of a way to get out of this whole situation and not look like a jerk. And my freezing up this morning didn't help, either. He practically did a walk of shame after my mom looked like she wanted to swat him with a rolled-up newspaper.

"It was very sweet, but it's just friendly," I tell her. "I was completely out of it last night, and he took care of me. Then he let me use him as a pillow. That's all."

When the words are out of my mouth, the thought sinks in: *he took care of me*. And I didn't realize how much I've been needing that.

She stares at me for a moment, then nods. "Yeah, that makes more sense."

"Wait. What?" I know I'm painting a dull picture, but she didn't have to give up on her saucy version of events that easily.

She shrugs. "You're not one for casual flings. And you two are complete opposites." She laughs and says, "You never go for guys like him."

I know she doesn't mean to hurt my feelings, but when she

says the words, what I hear is *You don't do fun things like that* and *Guys like Logan don't go for women like you.* I think of what Mark told me about being predictable and boring, making time for work and nothing else. I hate feeling like everyone thinks they know me so well when they're holding on to some version of me they've constructed in their heads.

That's probably why I blurt, "He's pretending to be my boyfriend for the next two weeks so Mom will get off my back. His idea."

Victoria stares at me for a moment and breaks into a wide grin. "Well played, sis." She takes a bite of the lavender-almond cake, her eyes glinting with approval. "Because now that's exactly what Mom thinks. She was talking my ear off the whole way back to her house, shocked that you were seeing someone, hurt because you hadn't told her, and miffed that she was wasting *all that time*—her words, not mine—making a dating profile for you. And so on."

I groan. Of course Mom would find a way to make this about her.

Victoria shrugs. "So I went to bat for you and told her that it was new, and you were nervous about him meeting her and Dad, and yada, yada. She also wanted to know everything about him, but all I told her was a name. And that he wasn't from here."

"Victoria, you didn't."

"What?" she says. "She asked me a million questions about him, and I gave her the bare minimum. She doesn't know he's just in town for the wedding, and she doesn't know any of Theo's friends, anyway. You're good."

"This isn't the way it was supposed to go." I tug at the tips of my hair. I'd planned to just be vague with Mom—tell her I had a date, a boyfriend if she pressed me—and she could call off her search. I never intended for her to meet Logan any sooner than she had to. "This gives her way too much time to fixate on him. We're so screwed."

"Disagree." She shakes her head, moving on to the next slice. "This worked out perfectly because she walked in and saw the whole scene herself—she never would have believed you were seeing someone if you'd just told her on the phone. She'd have thought you were lying, and you know it."

I let out another groan.

"So really, you should thank me for bursting in on your sexy time," Victoria says. "I totally saved your bacon."

"It was hardly sexy time," I tell her, rubbing my temple. "Fake boyfriend, remember?" But part of me wishes that it had been real, and that's how I know that Logan and I have to stay firmly planted in the friend zone. The last thing I need is to start having real feelings for a man I can't have. And waking up with him this morning, all snuggled against him? That felt way too real.

"Sure looked real to me. And to Mom." Victoria takes a bite of the chocolate mocha and moans with delight. "Holy palmettos, that's amazing—you really are gifted, sis. Anyway, you should take this win. If Mom thinks you're with Logan, then that makes your immediate problem go away. She won't be obsessed with finding you a date for the wedding, and she'll stop meddling. No more uploads to dating apps—hooray!" She nods towards the last slice. "If I were you, I wouldn't say a single word about today. Let her think y'all are head over heels for each other. And I'll do everything I can to get her to focus on the wedding plans instead of your mystery man."

I let out a heavy sigh. This is a terrible idea, but there's no going back now.

She takes another bite of cake and says, "He's gorgeous. Funny. Charming. I say enjoy the heck out of all that while you can."

I bristle at that last part because it sounds a lot like *You won't get a chance with a guy like this again.* I know she doesn't mean it as a jab, but it feels like one just the same.

"Have fun with him," she says. "You can start with Mom's drop-in next Saturday."

I scoff. "No way. I'm skipping."

She stares at me like I've declared I'm on the next shuttle to the moon. "But I need you as backup. I can't handle all of Mom's snooty friends all by myself." She stabs at another piece of cake. "You can't bail."

"Watch me."

"Gwen!"

I point to my sling. "This is my free pass."

Mom's drop-ins are the worst. She and her friends all have these fancy parties every year and try to one-up each other with the home decorating, the hors d'oeuvre, the sparkly dresses, and the string quartets they hire to play in their newly renovated gardens. It's a ridiculous charade. Ever since we were teenagers, Victoria and I have been dragged to these parties and ordered to flit around pretending to be cheerful and refilling the wine glasses. When we were younger, we stumbled around in heels and cocktail dresses and then climbed up into the backyard treehouse to finish off the wine at the end of the night. The only difference now is that Victoria doesn't mind them so much because Mom's proud of her and can't stop listing all of her accomplishments to her friends.

In all these years, I've never skipped the drop-in parties. Past Me did so because it was impossible to say no to my mother. But after several months with a good therapist, Present Me acknowledges that I was raised a bona fide people-pleaser and was scared to set boundaries with my mom.

But I'm learning to do better.

"What are you going to tell Mom?" she says, her eyes narrowing.

"That I do not wish to attend. No further explanation needed."

She groans, tasting the last square of cake. We're down to matcha and white chocolate raspberry, which I've been dying to make for an event. It's an amazing flavor combo, but it's like a red wedding dress—daring and definitely not for everyone.

"She'll have a fit," Victoria says. "And it's all I'll hear about the whole time."

"Why does she even want me there?" I know why she wants my sister there—she can brag on Victoria all night long and show her off like a prize pony. Victoria with her perfect body, her successful fiancé, and her super-impressive job at the most prominent real estate firms in the tri-county area. Mom could spend hours raving about Victoria to her friends, but she never talked about me—not when my cakes won blue ribbons at the state fair, not when the Bean was featured as one of the five best "hidden gems" of the Lowcountry in *Southern Living*, and not when Jasmine Falls voted me Best New Business last year. And even after all these years, she's never once asked me to bake anything for one of her fancy events.

Not even petit-fours. And anyone with two brain cells and a mixer can make those. Granted, baking anything for my perfectionist mother would be a total pain, but still—the fact that she's never even asked me shows just how little she thinks of my talent and my business.

"Sorry, Vic. It's a hard pass. You'll be fine."

She huffs in that way that means she'll try again later. "I love this one," she says, "but Theo hates raspberry." She licks the frosting from her fork, her eyes sparkling. "If you want to sell the boyfriend thing, you have to bring him to the party. And let's go with the chocolate and buttercream."

WHEN VICTORIA LEAVES, I go into my office and sink into the desk chair. My tailbone still hurts, and my back lights up with a shooting ache every time I sit or stand. The fall was evidently harder than I initially thought. And now this broken wrist has ruined everything. It was all I could do to get my injured arm into a sweater today, so baking with two hands feels impossible. And decorating? No way.

The only other bone I've ever broken is my foot—probably further evidence of my boring life—back when I was in high school. I tripped playing volleyball, bent my foot at an odd angle, and ended up with a cast for six weeks. If this wrist takes six weeks to heal, then I can forget about filling all of these holiday orders I've taken.

And Victoria's four-tier wedding cake? Yeah, that's going to take a Christmas miracle.

Scrolling through the calendar on my laptop is making me want to close up the shop and never come back. I think back to what Logan told me about delegating and realize that he's right: that's the only way to fill these orders. Fiona helps me out some days, and Maggie's itching to learn more. To survive the holidays, I'm going to have to lean on them both. I have to ask for help, even though that nagging voice in my head still whispers that doing so is a sign of not being good enough to handle things myself.

I fill in notes on the calendar, writing in tasks I might assign to Sam and Maggie, and flagging anything that Fiona might handle. I'm only halfway through the month when I realize that it's far too much for them. What was I thinking taking all of those orders?

That I don't know how to say no and want to keep everyone happy. That's what I was thinking.

Tears well in my eyes as I rest my head in my good hand. I'm good at troubleshooting, but this is too much. There are too many tasks and too many orders. And not nearly enough time. I hate the feeling of taking on more than I can handle because it feels like failure.

"Hey there, gorgeous."

When I turn, Logan's standing in the doorway of my office. He's wearing a different shirt and jeans, and his hair's been tamed since this morning. He studies my face, his brows pinching together with concern. "What's wrong?" he says, stepping closer. "What happened?"

"I'm completely screwed," I mutter. "This is a disaster."

"Tell me details," he says, glancing at the laptop.

I point to the calendar. "These are all of my orders through New Year's." I show him how I started assigning them to Maggie, Sam, and Fiona, based on their skills. "Even if they agree to take some of these, it's still too much," I tell him. "I'd still have to do some of this myself, and I'll be lucky to be moving at one-quarter speed." I collapse back in the chair. "But it's cool. I can go without sleep until January. Whatever."

He lifts a brow. "I think that's the opposite of the nice doctor's advice."

"I can't cancel these orders, Logan. Cancelling orders means lost revenue. And that means unhappy clients. And unhappy clients mean no repeat business."

He nods. "You can't do it all yourself, either." His voice is gentle, but firm. "You just need to find the balance."

I bark out a laugh. "Oh, is that all? I've been trying to find balance my whole life." Balance between my work and social life, my family's expectations and my own desires. So far, I'm failing.

"It's not easy," he says. "But it's a skill you can learn like anything else." When I don't respond, he nudges my shoulder. "What if I help you?"

"I can't ask you to do that."

"Then it's a good thing you don't have to." He leans against my desk and sets those fierce blue-green eyes on me. "I'm offering. Let me be useful. Otherwise, I'm going to sit up in that lake house all alone and be bored to tears until after Christmas. That's like three whole weeks."

"I thought you wanted to be alone in the quiet."

"Aye, I did. Until I met you."

Heat blooms in my chest and I feel my cheeks turning pink. There's nothing fake about the way his heated gaze pins me in place. Nothing pretend about how the smooth timbre of his voice lights me up and makes me think about how his big hands would feel sliding through my hair and over my shoulders as he places me exactly where he knows I want to be.

He eyes me carefully like he's staring right into my heart and seeing my deepest fears and worries. It's scary, because I've never felt so seen, and I'm not quite sure what to do. I like this feeling, even though it terrifies me.

In a blink, the moment passes, and he's stepped back across this invisible line between us. Once again, I've wasted too much time over-analyzing, and I've missed the moment.

"Come on," he says. "It'll be fun." He taps his fingers on his chest and beams, back in friendly teasing mode. "And really, when will you ever have another chance to have a guy as handsome and brilliant as me give you business advice?"

I swallow hard, pushing all the tempting thoughts of him aside. "Well, when you put it that way."

"I know, right? No-brainer." He gives me another nudge and sits on the corner of my desk. "Now walk me through the problems here. Let's see what we can do."

IN JUST AN HOUR, Logan's managed to convince me that I'm not entirely screwed.

Not entirely.

After color-coding all orders based on complexity, we've grouped them according to which ones need me to be involved. Spoiler alert: it's not as many as I thought. Typically, I do most orders myself, delegating only the simplest tasks to Sam and Maggie. My plan has always been to let them run the coffee bar while I work in the back, only bringing them in to bake and decorate when I needed extra help.

But now I see that's not the smartest way to run things. Especially when Maggie wants to do more with special orders. If she wants to do more decorating, I should let her. I should teach her more and help her hone her skills. That's a win-win. Plus, if I don't, then I'm just being a control freak and holding her back.

The perfectionist side of me wants to have a role in every order to make sure that it's…well…perfect.

But I see it's time to let that go.

"Don't let perfect be the enemy of the good," Logan says, and I roll my eyes, even though I know it's true. "Perfectionism will lead you straight to burnout. Ask me how I know."

"Fair enough, Obi-Wan."

He nods sagely and turns back to our list. "The next step is to talk to each person here and make sure they're up for doing these tasks. See if you can hire Fiona part-time through the holidays."

"Her aunt might help, too. She's an incredible baker. Her apple pie and pear preserves win at the state fair every year."

"There you go," he says. "And if you know what you want to focus on, hire people who can do all the other things that are sucking up your time. Like web design. Payroll. Ordering supplies."

Even though what he says seems so obvious, I've never put it into action. I've just handled everything myself because it seemed easier than training someone else.

The new calendar is still packed, but now it's feeling manageable. Once I confirm who can take the lead on which orders, I can add myself in to fill in any gaps. And this method doesn't require me to decorate cupcakes at midnight with a broken wrist.

"I don't know why this felt so daunting," I say. "Now it seems like an obvious solution that I should have seen months ago."

Logan shrugs. "You're in the habit of running the bee hive. It's hard to change that routine sometimes. But if you can keep assigning orders this way, it frees up much more of your time so you can focus on growth. And it gives your employees more experience, a bigger knowledge base, and it helps them feel more invested in the whole operation."

"I feel so much better already," I tell him. "I don't know how to repay you."

He shakes his head. "Don't thank me yet. Rule number one gets put into action tonight. It might be the hardest one to master."

"Care to explain?"

His smile turns roguish. "First let's get in touch with Fiona and nail down who's in charge of the next few orders. Then we can talk homework."

"Will there also be an exam later?" I say, teasing.

"Aye, if you play your cards right." His eyes flash with a devilish promise and I want to lock him in this office and keep him here forever.

"Thank you," I tell him.

He shrugs. "Of course."

"I mean for last night, too. You really didn't have to stay and do everything that you did."

He reaches over and brushes a loose strand of hair behind my ear. "I was more than happy to look after you, Gwen," he says. The way he says my name sends a shiver along my arms. His accent gives every word these rough edges and dark spaces that are entirely too inviting.

Stop, I scold myself. *Pretend boyfriend. Not real.*

But there's nothing pretend about the fiery look that he gives me, and nothing fake about the way my heart flutters in my chest like a bird.

Chapter Twelve

LOGAN

"My homework is a hayride?" Gwen says.

"We're learning about balance today, remember?"

She rolls her eyes, teasing, as the big dapple gray draft horse yanks the carrot out of my hand with a snort.

"You're welcome," I tell him. The black horse, a little taller and less ornery, nudges my hand with his velvety nose. "You already had yours," I say, stroking his cheek. He stomps his foot in the dirt and shoves his face into my chest, demanding pets.

"Check you out, horse whisperer," Gwen says. She looks gorgeous, dressed in slim dark jeans and a wool jacket, her pink scoop-neck sweater cut just low enough to give me the barest peek at her skin underneath. Up close, it's easy to see the faint spray of freckles on her cheeks and nose. I'm dying to know which other parts of her might have a dusting of freckles, too.

"We're just getting to know each other," I say, giving the horse one final pat. We're behind a big red barn in an apple orchard that seems to stretch for miles. The apples are long gone, but the the way the golden light plays along the rolling hills is enough to cause an ache in my chest. It's not so different from where my grandma lived in Skye—it was the place that felt most like home, and I haven't been there in ages.

"Let's grab a seat," she says, scratching the horse's ears. "There's a hay bale in back with your name on it." Her arm's still in the sling, but she seems to be in less pain tonight.

I can't remember the last time I sat on a hay bale—probably when I was about fifteen, in one of the barns on the estate. The last time I rode a horse was sometime back when I was in uni, when I was made of rubber and bounced right up after being tossed into the brambles.

We climb into the back of the wagon, where a young mom and dad sit with two girls who look about ten years old. Gwen and I sit along one of the sides, cups of hot apple cider in hand. One of the little girls holds a stuffed horse tight in the crook of her elbow.

"And so begins your holiday tour of Jasmine Falls," Gwen says. Her knee brushes mine and a little electric current zips along my skin. She smells like vanilla and cloves, and I lean closer as if pulled by a magnet. Seeing her today in her office, so overwhelmed and anxious, made me want to wrap her in my arms and pull her tight against me. But hugs don't solve every problem, and even though I don't know Gwen well, I know the stabbing fear of failure when I see it. She's surrounded by successes, but she's trained herself to look for the weaknesses, the failures—and I know a bit about that, too.

I also see a woman who'd rather die than ask for help. And I'd rather die than leave here without offering her what I've learned that might help her feel more confident in herself. She told me she built her successful business from nothing, and that's a huge feat. She doesn't give herself enough credit for the massive things she's accomplished, and if I can do one thing before I leave this town, it's to show her how to focus on her strengths instead of getting hung up on her weaknesses.

Growing isn't about addressing weaknesses—it took me a long time to learn that. It's about focusing on your strengths and finding ways to shine. Gwen shines pretty dang bright, and I wish she could see that as easily as I do.

A tired-looking dad climbs into the wagon with three young boys, and I scoot closer to Gwen—partly to be civil to the new folks, but mostly because she feels too far from me. When my thigh brushes hers, she doesn't move away.

"Hey, listen," she says, dropping her hand onto my forearm. "I need to apologize."

"What for?"

She bites her lip. "For this morning. I froze. I should have introduced you to my mom."

"Och, no apology needed. I felt bad that I overslept. I didn't mean to put you in an awkward position with your family."

"You didn't," she says, her gaze dropping to my lips. That one look heats me from head to toe and I really wish this wagon were empty so I could fold her into my arms.

"Yoo-hoo!" a voice calls from behind us. "Two more, Davey!"

Davey, our driver, turns and waves to a woman who's speed-walking towards us in a bright red cardigan and dark blue trousers. She looks to be in her sixties and has a perfectly styled platinum bob. Approaching the wagon, she shoves dark sunglasses up into her hair and waves. The woman with her, about the same age, is wearing tan pants and a bright green blouse and beams at us.

"I wouldn't dare leave you, Paula Sue," Davey says with a wink. "And Harriet, always nice to see you."

Now I recognize Paula Sue—the one with the bob. She's the one who told me about the hayride when she cornered me at lunch the other day.

"Well hi there, Gwen," Paula Sue says, reaching the steps. "And Mr. Fyfe, you decided to join us. I'm so glad."

"Wouldn't dare miss it," I say, and Paula Sue smiles as she introduces me to her friend Harriet.

I offer them both a hand as they climb into the back of the wagon and sit across from us.

"And how's the arm, honey?" Paula Sue says, motioning toward Gwen's sling. "I heard about that spill at the elementary school."

Gwen's cheeks turn pink. "It's fine. No big deal."

"I broke my arm once," Harriet says. "I was dancing on the roof of a VW bus with Jack McGinnis during a Rolling Stones concert down in Charleston."

Paula Sue snorts. "You did not."

"Did, too," Harriet says, lifting her chin. "He slipped when he tried to dip me and we both tumbled right off that thing and landed smack in the mud."

Next to me, Gwen shakes her head, trying not to laugh.

"It was the closest thing you could get to Woodstock down here," Harriet says, giving me a sly wink. "It was totally worth it."

"Can't take you anywhere," Paula Sue mutters.

"Well, this is one of the best times to visit Jasmine Falls," Harriet tells me. "We're famous for our holiday events, and people come from all over to see the lights."

"Gwen said it's really something," I say, and Gwen gives me a teasing smirk.

"Well, you have to come to the square this weekend," Harriet drawls. "The winter festival gets better every year, and this time I'm told we have a real reindeer."

"Is it Rudolph?" the little girl next to her says.

"I think it's a cousin," Harriet tells her with a wink.

The driver calls to the horses and we're off, plodding away from the barn and across the meadow toward the apple orchard. Tiny white fairy lights are strung all along the eaves of the barn and the adjacent buildings. Big evergreen boughs hang over the doors and windows, with little touches of red ribbon. It's a tasteful, rustic look that carries over into the orchard, where there are hundreds of lights blinking in the apple trees. Mason jars packed with tiny strands of lights are placed along the dirt road through the meadow. The kids are pointing at all the lights, tugging on their parents' sleeves, and asking when they're going to see Santa.

Harriet and Paula Sue are deep in a conversation about their last-minute plans for the New Year's Eve party in the town square, bickering over who's going to set up the floral arrangements.

Gwen nudges my arm and whispers, "Are you getting your fill of wholesome small-town fun yet?"

"Actually, I am."

She lifts a brow.

"I know it's goofy, but I love all the kitschy holiday things," I tell her. "Give me all the hayrides, all the Christmas tree lightings. The caroling and the ugly sweaters, the snow angels and the gingerbread houses. It all just reminds me of how the holidays used to be at my grandma's house." My voice catches in my throat and my chest stings at the thought. Christmas hasn't felt like Christmas in a decade. "I haven't done the small-town holiday thing in years. Not since my grandma died."

"Oh," she breathes. Her brows pull together and she says, "I'm sorry."

"It's okay," I tell her, but the truth is I haven't enjoyed the holidays since she passed. My family hardly sees each other now, and when they do it's just a big over-the-top black-tie party that I can't wait to escape. It's the opposite of the way things were in the small town where Granny lived. The opposite of connection and love. And isn't that really what holidays are about?

"Tell me something about her," Gwen says. Our hands are barely touching, but then she loops her pinky over mine like she's pulling a secret out of me.

I smile as we approach an area set up like a Christmas village, full of twinkling lights. It's like a stage set, with building facades made from sheets of plywood, but designed so it's hard to see the support structure in the back.

"She loved Christmas," I tell her. "She lived in this tiny town on the coast, up at the Isle of Skye. Even after my parents could afford to move her anywhere, she wanted to stay there because she said it was the only home she knew. When I was a kid, I used to spend a whole week with her at Christmas, when school was out. She spoiled me rotten with cookies and cocoa, and we did all kinds of stuff. Cut out handmade paper ornaments, knitted scarves, built gingerbread houses, and baked mince pies."

Gwen smiles. "I'm trying to imagine a twelve-year-old Logan knitting a scarf."

"Aye, I was quite good."

"I've no doubt."

"I loved being out there in the country," I tell her. "Christmas at my folks' was always full of big stuffy fancy events. My brother and sister were always sneaking out and getting into trouble, and my parents just fought over everything. It only got worse as I got older, and when Granny died, it was like everything I'd loved about Christmas died, too."

Gwen's eyes look glassy.

"Hey, it's okay." I give her a playful nudge. "I got more time with her than a lot of people get with their grandparents. I had her until I was eighteen."

She nods, and then says, "My grandma died three years ago. I still miss her all the time."

"We never stop missing them," I say, and she squeezes my

hand. "This time of year always reminds me of her. She'd have loved the way this town does Christmas."

"Grandma June loved the whole holiday scene here, too," Gwen says. "I mean *loved it*. She decked her whole house out and won the town decorating contest about every other year. Even talked me into helping her most years."

She smiles, and that's when it clicks. Gwen's not a Grinch, and she doesn't dislike the holidays at all. She's just had her heart broken, same as me. She just wears her little Grinch suit like a coat of armor—because it's easier to have everyone around her think she hates the holidays than to have them see through to the grief.

The little girls shriek as we come closer to the village, chattering like magpies. As we get closer, I see that the building facades are more elaborate than I thought. They're constructed like puppet stages, with a layer of plywood in the back, another in the front, and huge pieces of sheer fabric hung up like a kind of scrim in places where windows have been cut out. The sets are backlit, so you see the people in silhouette.

Since the people are dressed like elves, with big hats and exaggerated pointy ears, the effect is like seeing into the windows of Santa's workshop. The elves inside are busy hammering away at toy trains, wrapping gifts, and tinkering with big stuffed animals. Christmas carols play from hidden speakers, and there's the sound of elves working in the shop with tiny elf tools.

It's genius what they've done.

The kids love it.

I chuckle as the kids climb over each other and their parents, trying to get a better view as the elf silhouettes dance behind one of the scrims.

"Teenagers make great elves," Gwen whispers, her breath

warm against my ear. "I might have been an elf a few seasons, back when I had corduroy jeans and no bangs."

"Hang on a minute." I close my eyes and grin. "I want to take a moment to appreciate that fully. Can you describe the costume in detail?"

She swats me on the arm. "It was a great way to avoid my family drama for a few hours each night." She moves closer to my ear again and says, "Also, it's tradition for the elves to party pretty hard after the shift is over. What happens in the orchard stays in the orchard."

"Bet this is a great place to have a teenage party."

"Forbidden places are the best places," she says, her eyes flicking up to mine. "They might have called the cops on us one time back when I was about twenty and Harvey Jenkins dared me to ride the reindeer they borrowed from the petting zoo in Orangeburg. I couldn't confirm or deny."

"Naughty little elf," I tease.

"You have no idea." She gives me a wink. "That was a million years ago when I had time on my hands and no idea what to do with it. And was trying to rebel against my parents in some silly ways." She turns to me then, and those big blue eyes stare straight into my heart. "You ever want to just be bored? Some days I'd give anything to remember what that's like. To have hours on top of hours with nothing to do."

"Aye, maybe that needs to be your new goal."

She snorts. "Be a sloth? The cafe would sink in the red pretty fast."

I shrug. "Take enough time for yourself that you forget all the 'I should' for a while. The holidays are a good time to pause and re-evaluate."

"Except when you're in retail."

Fair point.

"What if I could help you with that, too?" I ask her.

She lifts a brow. "You want to remind me what boredom feels like?" Her tone is teasing, and I've decided I love it when she teases me. Her thigh's still pressed against mine, and I love that, too.

"No," I say, nudging her shoulder. "More like reminding you what taking time for you feels like. Because you deserve to feel happy and fulfilled. Wouldn't you agree?"

Her lips part just the tiniest bit. Her very full, very kissable lips.

"You make that sound so easy," she says.

"It's not, though, when we're taught to focus on things like productivity and quarterly earnings above all else. But you're in this for the long haul, right? Both you and your business will live longer if you take the time you need for yourself."

She narrows her eyes and gives me a sly look. "That's awfully presumptuous of you, telling me what I need."

"It certainly is," I say. "Maybe you'll forgive me for that when you're totally relaxed and haven't thought about work for a whole day—or if we really make progress, a whole weekend."

She sips her cider and stares at me like she's weighing all of this carefully. "You seem to think you know a lot about me, Lancelot."

I like her flirty tone. It's bright in the middle and dark at the corners, like the cute girl next door who has a little bit of rebel hiding just under the surface.

"I can suss out a few things," I whisper, leaning closer. "For example: you don't work a forty-hour week. It's more like seventy. You say you take days off, but you really don't, because you're always planning something related to your business, even when you're watching a movie in your pajamas. Now that you're older than twenty, you find it hard to connect with people, hence the so-called *dating* with the built-in timers. You've poured your heart into your business, and you're afraid that if you slack off even a little bit, you'll lose it all, despite how successful you are."

Her jaw tightens and she swallows hard. My aim on that last one might have been a little too true.

"It doesn't have to be like that," I tell her. "I think we could help each other find some balance and remember what it's like to make time for things we enjoy. You know, so we don't turn into a couple of thirty-something burnouts who forget what our friends' faces look like."

She purses her lips and I'm afraid I stepped over the line.

"SANTA!" the two girls squeal. The wagon comes to a stop and there's a flurry of movement around us as the kids vault out of the back and run towards a big guy in a red suit. Hay goes flying, cups of cider are rolling, and a small stuffed horse smacks me in the head as the last kid barrels past me and clambers over the side of the wagon. Even Paula Sue and Harriet climb out and head toward the spot where Santa sits in a big red Adirondack-style chair, surrounded by decorative trees and reindeer.

When the dust and bits of hay settle, Gwen and I are alone in the back of the wagon.

"Where did you come from?" she says at last. "I mean, really. How does someone like you end up in a place like this, with someone like me?"

"A chartered flight."

She gives me a long, calculating look. "I guess it would be unwise to ignore advice from a bazillionaire," she says, her tone teasing.

"I'm just a guy who narrowly escaped burnout."

"Okay," she says. "But I might be your biggest challenge yet."

I grin, offering my hand. "Challenge accepted, love."

She smiles as she takes my hand, and my heart hammers

against my ribs. I give her hand a firm shake and the tiniest squeeze, and her eyes flash a brighter blue.

"Now let's go see Santa," she says. "I have a bone to pick with him about last year."

When she pulls her hand away, I can't help but notice how perfectly it fits into mine, like two puzzle pieces locking together.

Chapter Thirteen

GWEN

"It looks like the Pillsbury dough boy exploded in here," I say. "Is everything okay?"

It's just after eight in the morning and the cafe is filled with the usual crowd. They're oblivious to the chaos that's unfolded behind them in the kitchen, and hopefully, we can keep it that way. Fiona and Maggie are busy making today's fresh cookies, and there's a fine dusting of flour covering everything in the room—including them.

Sam pokes his head through the kitchen door and shouts, "Hey, quick question!" Then he takes one look around and his eyes widen. "Nope," he says. "Never mind. It can wait."

"Totally fine!" Maggie says, beaming. There's a streak of frosting across her cheek and red fingerprints on her apron that I hope is food coloring. "We've got Jane's order of cupcakes boxed and ready for pickup."

"The flour's my fault," Fiona says, brushing her bangs from her eyes. "We put on an audiobook and the spicy scene took me by surprise."

Before I get the urge to start wiping everything clean, Fiona steers me toward the stack of boxes on a baker's rack by the back door. She opens one of the boxes to reveal the poinsettia cupcakes that she and Maggie made yesterday. It had taken everything in me (and okay, some prodding from Logan) not to come by here last night and check up on them. I'd begged him to drive me over here after the hayride, but he'd fixed me with that stern look of his and said, "You trust Maggie and Fiona, right? Let them handle this."

He was right, of course. I didn't want to be some cupcake overlord. But the perfectionist in me just wanted to make sure that Maggie and Fiona weren't struggling because I'd pushed my problem onto them. So we'd compromised and I'd texted Fiona for an update. She'd sent me photos of the cupcakes, with plenty of close-ups so I could see the details, and Logan was right. They were doing just fine without my scrutiny.

Today, the cupcakes looked even better in person. Were they decorated precisely the way I would have done them? No. But did they look amazing and delicious? Absolutely.

"Fantastic job, you two," I say, and Fiona grins.

Maggie gives me a thumbs-up from across the kitchen, where she's cutting out more snowflake cookies.

"I can't thank you enough for stepping in," I tell Fiona.

She shrugs. "Happy to help. I mean, I owe you one for basically becoming my art agent here."

"That reminds me. I need more paintings. I sold the last two over the weekend." I've been displaying Fiona's gorgeous bird paintings here for months now, and they always sell out. The one I have hanging in my bedroom is one of my favorite things I own.

"Will do," she says. "Now tell me about this hot Scot of yours. I want to hear all about your date."

"Not a date," I say, though the words feel like a lie. "And Logan's great. He's like the opposite of every guy I've met in the last millennium. It's too bad he's leaving in a few weeks."

"Awwwww," she says.

"He's sort of…coaching me on my business plans."

She raises a brow. "Please tell me that's code for something dirty."

"He thinks I need to make more time for myself and wants to teach me some strategies that he said saved him from burnout."

"And you said, *yes, thank you, please*?"

"He's full of good ideas. And it obviously worked for him, so it's worth a try, right? Who am I to turn down advice from someone who's a huge success?"

"Yes," she said. "And let the man take you out and enjoy yourself. Or keep you in. That's good, too." She grins. "Go have fun. Remind yourself of what real dates feel like. Although, this man might spoil you for all future dates—high chance of that."

I roll my eyes. "I know what real dates feel like."

"Do you, though? Do you remember? Because these last few months, the meetings you've described with these internet guys are not dates. Not by a long shot." She crosses her arms. "And speed dating doesn't count."

"Coffee is a date." As soon as the words are out of my mouth, I hear how lame that sounds.

"Nope. Coffee is a low-stakes meet and greet. Everyone knows that." She hollers, "Maggie, wouldn't you agree?"

"Yes," Maggie answers from the other side of the room. She stops rolling out the gingerbread dough long enough to give me a sad smile. "Sorry, Gwen, but everyone knows that coffee is like dipping a toe in. Either that or it's just the pre-game for a hookup."

"Ugh," I groan.

"Listen to the Gen Z-er," Fi says, nodding toward Maggie. "This man already fixed your website and made you dinner. And then he took care of you when you hurt your arm. He's not interested in a no-stakes hook-up."

"And high stakes is better?" I grumble. "He's leaving in three weeks. Why let myself get attached?"

"Why push a good guy away?" Fiona grabs my shoulders, mindful of the sling, and sets her big blue eyes on mine. "You, my friend, work too hard. You don't treat yourself. So rather than sit alone all through the holidays, why not do some fun things with a cool, interesting person who might remind you of what it's like to not be a workaholic?"

I sigh, knowing I have no room to argue. Workaholic is accurate.

"I like this plan," she says. "He's very cute and kissable. Brawn and brains, like Thor in the third movie. You deserve a hot winter fling."

"No flings," I argue. "Just a friend thing. He's helping me strategize, and I'm going to make sure he gets the total Jasmine Falls Christmas experience—because I can see how he loves the holidays." After what he said on the hayride yesterday, I realized how I could repay him for all of his help. It was clear that Christmas meant a lot to him because of his grandmother and how close they were. He'd talked about her with such deep love, that it had pulled at the corners of my heart, reminding me of how I treasured all the time I'd spent with Grandma June— especially at Christmas.

The idea of him being alone during the holidays, hiding out in my sister's lake house, was unacceptable. No, I'd make it my mission to make sure Logan Fyfe soaked up as much holiday cheer as he could this season.

She lifts a brow. "This is definitely not just a friend thing, because you loathe the holidays."

"It can *only* be a friend thing," I tell her. "And there are some things that I love about the holidays." I let it go at that because even Fiona doesn't know how hard it was to lose my Grandma June. Fiona moved away for a few years, and though she knows that I lived with my grandma for the last year before she died and took care of her, she doesn't know that losing her is what makes the holidays so hard.

She sighs. "I think if you feel something for this guy, you owe it to yourself to give it a chance, Gwen. You never know how things might align for you."

I laugh. "That's pretty woo-woo for you, Fi."

She shrugs. "If you'd told me a year ago that I'd end up with Alex Fox, I'd have laughed until I blacked out. But then something told me not to discount us quite so quickly. And now I can't imagine my life without him."

I consider that for a moment, but this isn't going to end like a fairy tale. Even though I love every minute Logan and I spend together, I have to keep reminding myself that this can't be anything serious.

"We're from totally different worlds," I protest. "He's part owner of like a dozen companies. He makes more in a day than I make in a year. He couldn't possibly be interested in me."

"So?" She shrugs. "You're amazing. Why wouldn't he be interested in you?"

"Fi, the man bought a distillery, for heaven's sake."

"Sounds like a man who knows what he likes." She lifts a brow, daring me to argue. "And he clearly likes you, babe, which means he has excellent taste."

Before I can say more, the kitchen doors burst open and my sister blows in like a hurricane.

"Gwen," she says, exasperated. "I need a favor. It's an emergency," she says, sounding out of breath. Her hair looks windblown and her blouse is wrinkled. Victoria never looks windblown or wrinkled.

I sit down at the prep table, worried that there might be an actual emergency. "What's the matter?"

Fiona heads back to her work table and starts piping the

snowflake cookies while Maggie rolls out more dough. Logan was right—having them both work on these orders was the right call.

"Mom's cake person canceled," Victoria says.

I wait for a moment, expecting more. "That's your emergency?"

Victoria frowns. "You know how important this party is to her. She's frantic."

"Which party?" Mom hosts so many, it's hard to keep up.

"The drop-in this Saturday," she says. "The one you keep saying you aren't going to. It has to be perfect."

I scoff. "They all have to be perfect." And right then, a bolt of something shoots through me, and I vow to stomp out my perfectionist tendency like a rhino stomping out a fire.

No way am I going to become my mother. Not in this lifetime.

How did I never see this connection before?

"I know, I know." Victoria huffs, pacing next to me. "But she's really in a bind. Every cake artist in a fifty-mile radius is booked solid and not taking any more orders before Christmas. Mom's beside herself. She's turning that weird shade of red like she did that time at Suzy's wedding." Two years ago, Mom had planned the reception for our cousin Suzy and then loaned Suzy her prized crystal punch bowl for the event. When the best man challenged another groomsman to a dance-off in the wee hours, they crashed into the refreshment table and launched the punch bowl into the air. It flew like it had been hurled from a catapult, and my mother's face froze when Beyoncé was drowned out by the only sound that could ever upstage her: an antique crystal punch bowl shattering against concrete. Mom had turned redder than a fire engine and sat practically catatonic while the groomsmen swept up the pieces and Aunt Lydia fanned her with a paper dinner plate.

"And what am I supposed to do about it?" I say. "I don't know anyone who'd take her on, either." Knowing my mother, she wants some extravagant cake sculpture that would be a feat for the most seasoned baker to produce. And this close to Christmas? Forget it.

Victoria's brows pinch together and she makes a desperate face.

I laugh. "You can't be serious."

"Please," she says. "She's going to drive me insane."

"Mom has never asked me to bake for one of her events," I say. "And don't think I've forgotten the way she turned her nose up at the truffles I brought to Thanksgiving that year." The woman had sniffed as if I'd brought her a platter of M&Ms and not creme-filled chocolate truffles that I'd spent an entire day making. Ever since then, I swore to never bake anything else for her. Ever.

"Listen," Victoria says. "I know there's some bad blood, but she's about to blow a gasket. And selfishly, I don't want her to drop dead a week before my wedding day. It would put a damper on things."

My sister has always been the peacemaker, but this feels like just another way of asking to be hurt. I know how this scenario plays out: I try to do something nice for Mom, and then she finds some way to throw it back in my face and act like I did something to slight her.

"Mom's made it clear that she doesn't think what I make is good enough to serve at her snooty little soirees," I tell her. "But now she's desperate enough to ask me?" I stare at her, already feeling the heat rise in my cheeks. And then it dawns on me. "You didn't ask her yet."

Victoria collapses onto a stool next to me and stares up at the ceiling like she's wishing the rapture would just hurry on up and make her poof right out of here.

"She already has a caterer," I say. "Surely they also do dessert."

"She doesn't like their cakes."

I bite back a laugh. "Of course, she doesn't." My mother never makes anything easy.

"I'm begging you," she says. "I'll do anything you want."

"What makes you think she's going to go for this?" I ask. "What makes you think she'll even let me through the door?"

Victoria bites her lip, and that's when I know.

"You don't want to tell her it's me," I grind out.

"Of course, we would *after*," she says, her tone lightening.

I laugh, gripping the countertop until my knuckles are white. My arm is starting to hurt, probably because all of the blood has left my limbs and gone straight to my pounding temples. "That's a whole new level, sis."

She grabs a pencil from the table and scribbles on a scrap of paper. When she slides the paper toward me, she says, "This is what she was going to pay the other baker."

"Holy bananas," I mutter. "Look at all those zeros." I did not get my thrifty nature from my mother. She's once again sparing no expense to impress her friends.

"So add thirty percent for a rush fee," Victoria says. "And then you deliver a delicious, gorgeous cake. The guests will love it, and shower Mom with compliments, and beg to know who she hired. And then you cash her check, and then we tell her you're the baker—surprise, Mom! And then you get what you've always wanted."

"And what's that?"

She gives me a tiny smile. "To watch Mom eat crow."

I do appreciate the diabolical glint in my sister's eye. She's had one foot in Mom's world and one here in the real one for a decade, but it's moments like these when I think Victoria might be more like me than she admits. She's always tried her best to avoid Mom's ire by being the good girl—but when it comes down to it, she doesn't appreciate being pushed around by Elaine Griffin, either. She just hates confrontation even more.

"Plus," she says, "You get orders from all her fancy friends for the next five years, because you know those ladies live to one-up each other." Her smile is triumphant. "Win-win."

"When's the party again?" I say.

"Saturday at eight."

Three days from now. I'd have to plan the design, then bake it tomorrow and decorate it on Friday. I hadn't tried piping anything since I broke my arm, but I might be able to do it.

"What kind of cake?"

She smiles. "You could do it in your sleep, Gwennie. Three-tier vanilla."

"Good, because this arm is complicating things." With Maggie's help, I could do it. She crushed it with the cupcakes, making poinsettias that looked almost real. "Can you show me some photos of what Mom showed the other baker?" Knowing Mom, she had a specific design in mind. I wouldn't be able to see what the other baker had planned, but it would help to at least see what Mom had looked at for inspiration.

"Absolutely," Vic says.

Chapter Fourteen

LOGAN

I do not need to be thinking of Gwen Griffin nonstop. That's what I'm doing, though. Every time my mind wanders, it takes me to her. She should be off-limits because she's so clearly rooted here. I'm just here for a short while, and she deserves more than a casual fling.

And that's all I can offer if I have no intention of staying.

I keep telling myself that over and over, sometimes out loud and standing in front of the mirror so I can give myself a strong hard stare.

Off-limits, Fyfe. You and Gwen want very different things.

But sometimes, that doesn't feel true.

Still, I can't stop thinking of how it felt to wake up with her leg draped over mine, her cheek resting against my chest. I can't stop thinking about her infectious laugh, how it lights me up and makes me want to pull her close every single time.

I'm in so much trouble.

My phone buzzes with a text and I check to see if it's Gwen, because (1) she's officially taken up residence in all parts of my brain, and (2) I told her to text me if she needed any help getting around. She insists on driving herself to the cafe each day, even though her arm's still in a sling. Determined to put my advice into action as soon as possible, she's putting in minimal hours at the cafe each day—but I still think it's too much. When I pressed her, she gave me an adorable huff and said, "The pain's not as bad as the boredom, Lancelot. And I have to make sure that my sweet little baristas don't burn the place down."

I was willing to concede on that one. But I still want her to give herself more time to rest. She's been doing everything herself for so long that it's become a hard habit to break.

But I'm going to try because I want her to reach her dreams, and burnout never made anyone live longer.

When my phone buzzes again, I see a text from Ma. She never texts me, so my brain goes straight to the catastrophic place.

You need to stop your gallivanting and come home, she writes. **Settle this.**

I grit my teeth, wondering how much she knows about Grandad's threats. Rory likely hasn't told her much because, at this stage, what good would it do? His goal is to keep everyone calm, which is just one more reason he should be taking over the operation.

My being there isn't going to change anything, I reply. Being home just means being harassed in person. I need to talk to Rory before I get tangled up in a row with Ma.

Have you no loyalty to this family? She prods. **No respect? Your father would be ashamed.**

Her words strike like a hot poker, and that's precisely what she wants. I take a deep breath and consider my response. Before I type, she texts again.

Stop behaving like a child, David. You can't hide from your problems. Every day you stay away, you're making this worse.

My face turns hot. She knows I hate being called by my grandfather's name—knows I hate being compared to him. But I refuse to let her see how her tactics get a rise out of me because it's just another way she manipulates. Rather than respond to her, I text Rory.

Any update? I ask him.

A moment later, my phone rings and I pick up the video call. Rory looks like he's been through the wringer. His eyes look tired, and that deep furrow in his brow makes me glad I haven't spent the last week at the estate.

"I don't know details, but the way Grandad's stomping around, I think we should be prepared for the worst," he says. "He's been meeting with his attorneys all week. Ma's afraid the company's in financial trouble. Like, the belly-up kind."

I swear under my breath. "You think that's it?" I've distanced myself from them for so long that I don't know anything about the current state of the company—except for what Rory's told me over the last couple of years. If anyone could suss out the deep, dark Fyfe secrets, it's Rory.

"Nothing would surprise me at this point, given his history." He drags his fingers along his stubbly beard and shrugs. "Hey, it might be that he's declaring bankruptcy and there's no family fortune to be written out of. Joke's on us."

"You think he wants to sell?"

Rory snorts. "Not inconceivable. But then the pressure's off you, right? Decision made."

I keep quiet because I know he's not going to like the solution I've come up with. Not entirely.

He runs a hand through his hair and rolls his eyes. "Grandad's staying tight-lipped and refuses to talk to anyone until you get here. But I heard the word *liquidate*, and that has me concerned. No one says *liquidate* when things are going well."

Rory sounds more agitated than I've ever heard him—he's the one who's always stood up for Grandad, trying to be the peacemaker and reminding us that he's an old man who's just afraid that everything he's built will be lost—as if that somehow makes up for his horrible behavior. But today is different, and Rory's not making excuses for him anymore. "For all I know, he's lost everything in bad investments and he's choosing now to tell us. It must be something way worse than before. I just hope we can all get out unscathed and not have to change our names."

Before, back when he hired the CEO who embezzled enough to pay off the national debt of a small country. Back when he ignored the warning signs and went against the advice of myself and Rory. Back when my father tried to pick up the pieces only to have them crush him under their weight.

I hated the way our grandfather had a stranglehold on everyone in our family. For years, we'd all bent over backward to please him—and my mother, too, for that matter—and what for? So we all wouldn't lose an inheritance? That seemed like a high price to pay for financial security.

My father paid the ultimate price. He had a severe heart attack that was one hundred percent because of the stress of working for our grandfather—and it put him into an early grave. I have no intention of letting a job do the same to me.

"He won't talk to me anymore," Rory says. "He says he'll only talk to you. Meanwhile, he's started using the bone china for shooting practice—had his valet toss the plates off the balcony—and finished off the 60-year Macallan. Last night he was so hammered he nearly fell down the stairs."

I pace by the kitchen window, staring out at the cool blue of the lake. "Great. So we've moved on to the sabotage phase." It's not that Grandad wants to hurt himself—no, he wants to burn everything down around him. It's his way or nothing at all. He thinks if he makes us all miserable enough, I'll come around.

Rory grumbles. "He's likely planning to sell so he can cut us all out of everything. And, you, know, burn the house down in a fit of rage."

"And Ma calls me a child."

Rory snorts.

"Fine," I groan. "Set up a phone call with him. I don't care what time. But you and I need to get on the same page first."

"Aye," Rory says. "So we do."

GWEN LIFTS a brow in that adorable stubborn way of hers and I can't help egging her on.

"Just ask me," I whisper.

She hates to ask for help, but I'm not letting her off this time.

We're standing in the gazebo in the town square, washed in the glow of a million colored Christmas lights. This town doesn't skimp on the holiday decorations. Every building on Main Street has winter-themed window decorations and garlands hanging from the rooftops. Strings of white lights stretch from light poles in a zig-zag pattern over the street, making it look like a carnival. The town square is filled with booths for holiday-themed games, and a few evergreens are filled with ornaments and fairy lights. I bet everyone in town came out to help with this, because how else would you hang this many strings of lights and garlands?

Gwen purses her lips and says, "Logan, would you be so kind as to come with me to my mother's ridiculous fancy-pants party? I could really use the backup."

"See, that wasn't so hard, was it?" I tease. But I know it's harder for her than she lets on.

"On the plus side, there will be a talented bartender and fancy cocktails with top-shelf booze," she says. "And if you tell a good joke, my dad will share his favorite scotch with you."

I shrug. "You don't have to sell it to me. If you're there, that's all the motivation I need."

She blinks at me for a moment and her cheeks turn a delightful shade of pink. She's wearing this powder-blue sweater that makes her eyes sparkle, plus killer knee-high boots and a short skirt that hugs her curves. Right now, I'd agree to anything she asked.

"There's one other thing," she says, biting her lip. "I'm baking a cake for the party and could also use a hand with delivery."

"That sounds great, but your face says otherwise."

She frowns. "Ordinarily this would never happen unless we were suddenly yanked into a parallel universe where my mother doesn't pick apart everything I do and make me feel completely incompetent. But the baker canceled, probably because she realized my mother's micromanaging would send her over the rainbow bridge. So Vic played the baby sister card because she knows my weakness, and here we are."

Her shoulders have that hard line again as if just thinking about it makes her anxious. "Plus, my mother was prepared to spend a pile of money on this fancy cake. Like, a pile big enough for me to roll around in."

"So that's a dream of yours, then? Roll around in a big pile of money?"

She snorts. "Obviously. What else does one do when given that chance?"

I give a dramatic shiver. "Do you know how filthy those bills are? They're like petri dishes."

She gives me a dramatic gasp. "A few germs are a small price to pay for living a rock star fantasy for a moment."

"It's not as fun as it seems."

"Spend a lot of time rolling around in piles of money, do you? Got bored with it?" She smiles and I'm completely undone.

Because now I'm thinking of Gwen rolling playfully in a bed made up with silken sheets (hold those grubby bills, thank you) and I'm not going to be able to pry that image from my mind for the rest of the day.

Maybe forever.

"Is that the only reason you want to do this?" I ask her. A favor for her sister that pays well is understandable, but Gwen's told me enough about her relationship with her mum that I wonder if this is setting herself up for more hurt. In the brief moment that I encountered her mother, I didn't pick up on an especially maternal or caring vibe. Granted I was wearing the clothes I slept in and had been caught half-asleep in her daughter's bed, but still. Gwen had her arm in a sling and was clearly out of sorts, and her mother hardly cared at all. In that moment, she'd seemed as ice-cold as my mum.

She sighs. "It's a ridiculous amount of money. But it's more than that. I know I'm good at what I do. Better than good. And I just want my mother to see that. So if she has to see it through the oohs and ahhs of her friends, that's fine by me. The few thousand in cash is just gravy."

I know exactly how she feels. For my whole life, I've felt like my family sees what they want when they look at me—but they don't see the real me. They see the version who's the buttoned-down heir to the Fyfe fortune, the David L. Fyfe III who can flash a bright smile and keep profits on the rise. They want this version who will be charming enough to make everyone forget about the scandal and smart enough to avoid any future ones. They don't like the version of me who openly sides with conservationists and people who live in small villages who'd like to not have their farms turned into luxury condos.

All of that makes for excruciating conversations at the family dinner table. On many issues, we'll never see eye-to-eye.

"Honestly," she says. "I just want to show her how wrong she is about me. Does that sound terrible?" Two tiny lines appear between her eyebrows as they knit together and suddenly I very much want to meet her mother again. "She's always acted like my career is some hobby or a flight of fancy, and not a real business with employees and write-offs and W-2s. It's like she's waiting for me to fail so she can tell me *I told you so.*" She sighs, sipping her cocoa. "I don't want to have this strained relationship with her, but she makes all of this so hard. Every time I want to chase the moon, I hear her in the back of my head, telling me all the reasons why it's a waste of time, why it's not good enough. Grandma June was the dreamer. She was the one who always told me to go for it." She smiles then, and says, "She always thought I was good enough to do whatever I could dream up."

My heart has cracked like an egg. Before I even think twice about it, I pull Gwen into a tight hug because I just can't help myself. She lets out a surprised "Oof!" when her chest smashes against mine, and holds her hurt arm out by her side. My arms are tight around her back, pulling her so close that I can feel her heart pounding through her wool coat. At first, she's stiff as a board, but then she relaxes against me, her good arm winding around my waist as she tucks her head under my chin.

"You know your mom's opinion has no bearing on how talented and amazing you are, right?" My voice comes out ragged and she pulls away, just far enough to look me in the eye.

She blinks at me for a moment, her big blue eyes glistening and I fear I've overstepped. Everyone has their Achilles heel, and hers isn't so hard to see.

She gives me a sad smile, one that says she doesn't quite believe me, but she wants to.

"It's a shame she can't see what an extraordinary woman you are," I tell her. "But that doesn't make it any less true."

She nods, and I wish she could see herself the way I see her.

Gwen's a force of nature. She's just been fooled into thinking that success means fitting someone else's definition of it and not her own.

"You know what it feels like to be constantly underestimated?" she says. "It's exhausting."

"Aye, I get it." It's why I'm so determined to get Rory at the helm of the company. Grandad makes a sport out of underestimating Rory, and I see how it wears him down. "But you don't have to prove yourself to her. And honestly, you'll never change her mind about anything. She has to do that herself."

She huffs, slipping out of my grasp, and I'm immediately cold. "But I *can* show her up at her fancy-pants party and enjoy the spoils that come when all of her friends want to hire me." She gives me a devilish smile and I want to see her shatter everyone's expectations. And I know that she will.

"That's the spirit," I tell her. "Show everyone why it's a mistake to underestimate you."

Before I can say another word, she stands up on her tiptoes and presses her lips to my cheek. She's so warm and soft, and as her hand tightens at my back, she pulls away just the slightest bit. Her eyes are wide, and her playful smile is gone. When her gaze drops to my lips, I feel like I'll combust, and then she leans closer and her lips press against mine. The kiss is slow and tantalizing, and when I feel the gentlest scrape of her teeth, it loosens something in my chest that I've been trying too hard to ignore.

My heart hammers in my ears and I squeeze her tighter against me. She's soft and warm and tastes so sweet, and all I can think is *yes, more, please.*

I slide my hand into her hair and keep her pace, even though it takes everything in me not to bury my face in her neck and leave a trail of kisses from her ear to her collarbone. She lets out a tiny sigh that nearly unravels me and I tug her closer, wanting to tease more of these delightful sounds out of her. Her hands move to the nape of my neck and slide into my hair and the world around us falls away.

Kissing her is even more amazing than I imagined, and I've imagined this a lot.

Just as I drop my hands to her waist, I hear someone behind us yell, "Look out! Runaway reindeer!"

Before I can fully register what's happening, another yell splits the air and Gwen pulls away like she's been touched by a live wire.

Honestly, I feel that way, too. And I never want it to end.

"Holy cow," she says, pushing me back toward the nearest tree.

I think she's referring to that kiss until I see an honest-to-goodness reindeer barreling toward us, head down, antlers looming, hooves pounding. She's wearing a jaunty little harness full of tinkling sleigh bells, but she's running like she's being chased by banshees.

Four men are running after her at full speed, and then a pack of dogs comes out of nowhere, barking like this is the best chase they've ever had.

As I shield Gwen's body with mine, the reindeer blows past us, the dogs right on her heels, their leashes dragging in the grass. Just as they pass, I feel something slam into my leg and my feet go out from under me. Gwen shouts as she crashes into my chest and I grab her shoulders to try to right us both.

But it's too late, and my balance is lost. There's a chorus of barking, an ear-splitting whistle, and the tickle of wind in my hair as I fall backward. The next thing I hear is a splash and Gwen's mouth forms a tiny O as she lands on top of me in a heap.

Chapter Fifteen

GWEN

The water in the koi pond is freezing. But it's still not enough to cool me off because this man is an incredible kisser, and he'd just barely gotten started when we were knocked over like a couple of bowling pins.

I've landed on top of Logan in a most unladylike position, straddling him with my good hand planted in the ice-cold water and the other tight against my chest. My knees are on either side of his waist, my face inches from his, and my skirt's rucked up high on my thighs.

He lifts a brow as he seems to note each of those details and says, "You all right, love?"

His hands are gripping my thighs and when I leave this world, I'd like it to be just like this—with a gorgeous man under me and staring at me like he wants to lick every inch of my body and can't quite decide where to start. Though I'd prefer we weren't in a fish pond.

"I think so," I mumble. Even though I can feel the water filling my boots and he's more than halfway submerged in a murky pond, I'm in no hurry to climb off of him. I should be ashamed of that fact, but the way his eyes are burning into mine makes me want to stay planted right here. Maybe for eternity.

"I feel like we got taken down by a torpedo," he says, his eyes dropping to my lips.

"It was a golden doodle. Are you hurt?"

He smirks as if to say he's not in a rush to get up, either. "Other than my pride being demolished by a dog in a Christmas sweater," he says, "I'm grand."

A whistle splits the air, loud enough to call a cab from a mile away. I cringe as a woman hollers, "Thelma! Louise! You get back here!"

I scramble to climb off of Logan because now we have an audience. My boots sink into the muddy bottom of the pond and I wobble for a moment, finding my balance. He's on his feet in a flash, catching me in his firm grip and helping me onto the grass.

There's another sharp whistle and a call, and then Paula Sue Hinson is standing in front of us, looking mortified. "Oh my goodness!" she says. "I am so sorry!" Decked out in Christmas plaid pencil pants and a bright red sweater set, she gives Logan a long look. He's soaked to the skin and his green button-down shirt and gray trousers are clinging to his muscular frame in a way that leaves little to the imagination. This image will be etched into my brain for the next hundred years.

"Gwen," Paula Sue says, her eyes wide. "Are y'all okay?"

"We're fine," I tell her, squeezing water from my skirt.

"Those dogs have lost their minds," she says with a *tsk*. "I took Thelma and Louise to the dog park today to get their zoomies in, and it just got them more wound up. They haven't taken off like that since Mr. Leonard's cow got into my petunias and now they're going to be little fireballs all night."

She turns to Logan, fussing with his shirt, and plucks a lily pad from the collar. "Sweetie, are you sure you're all right? That was quite the tumble."

"Aye, I'm fine. Promise." His voice comes out all rumbly and sweet and I have to tear my gaze away from him as he wrings out his shirt with those perfectly shaped hands of his. Hands that were, until moments ago, setting me on fire.

"You okay?" he says to me. "How's the arm?"

"No harm done," I say, and honestly I can't feel a thing, except my stupid heart pounding right out of my chest. I'm still seeing honest-to-god stars after that kiss and I really, really want to finish what we started.

Wincing, Logan pulls his cell phone from his front jeans pocket.

"Oh no," I say. "Is it drowned?"

He swipes a finger across the screen and it lights up with what looks like a string of missed calls. "Nah. It's waterproof."

"Because you often find yourself falling into ponds?" I tease.

"I can be clumsy. Drop one phone into one pool, and you never hear the end of it."

"Might be the universe telling you that a vacation poolside is no place for work calls."

He smirks and gives me a hungry look as he shoves it back into his pocket. "And you say you're no good at a work-life balance."

Paula Sue hollers again, and then the two dogs—one gray poodle and one golden doodle in matching red and green sweaters—are trotting towards her, tails wagging like they've done the best job ever. The poodle has the audacity to come sit at Logan's feet, tongue lolling. Logan leans down to scratch the dog's ears and mutters something in Gaelic that sounds like affectionate scolding.

Paula Sue grabs their leashes. "Have mercy," she says. "The council's never going to let us have another reindeer. I might never live this down. You wouldn't believe the hoops we had to jump through for that permit, either."

We turn towards a rumbling noise coming from the woods, where someone has driven a horse trailer to the tree line, no doubt trying to coax the poor creature out.

"Well, we've done enough damage for one night," Paula Sue says. "You two take care. I hope I'll see you at the holiday auction."

"Come on," I tell Logan, taking his hand. "Let's get out of here before you freeze to death."

We hardly say a word to each other as Logan drives us back to my sister's house. With the heat cranked up in the car, my sweater and skirt are nearly dry. Logan, though, is still soaking wet. He cuts off the engine and then turns to me.

"You want to come inside?" His voice is a rumble that tears me apart at the seams.

Yes. No. More than anything.

His eyes are wide in the moonlight, hopeful. I'm dying to pick up where we left off before we got knocked into that pond, but once we cross this line, there's no going back. What lies on the other side of that line is oh-so-tempting, but I know this needs to stop right here. I'm not looking for a fling, and that's all this could ever be. Logan's leaving in a couple of weeks, and as much as I love being with him, that's not going to change.

The smart thing to do would be to get out of this car and go to my house. Put on my pajamas, watch some TV to calm myself down, and forget that incredible kiss that will now be the one that all future kisses are measured against.

Before I can give that too much thought, Logan reaches across the console and brushes a lock of hair from my cheek, and that single touch is all it takes to light me up like a Christmas tree. I grab his collar and tug him closer until his lips crash against mine. He slides his hands into my hair and lets out a groan that nearly turns me inside out. In an instant, his kiss turns hungry and his lips are no longer gentle—and thank heaven for that. He's full of want and when his teeth catch my bottom lip and his hands slide into my hair, I'm certain I'll combust.

"Hang on," he mumbles, pulling away just an inch. His eyes burn into mine and his devilish smirk is back. He slides a thumb over my bottom lip and says, "I'm dying to get out of these clothes and there's no way I'm doing this in a tiny car like a contortionist because you deserve so much better than that, gorgeous."

I bark out a laugh, but he unleashes that tantalizing smile and then I reach for the door handle.

His hands grip my waist as he steers me toward the front door. We fumble our way into the house and he kicks the door shut behind us. I laugh as his scruffy jaw tickles my neck, and we're halfway across the living room when his shirt falls to the floor. He lifts me onto the kitchen island like I weigh nothing and then stares at me like he's deciding where to kiss me next. My heart's banging against my ribs and every second he's not touching me is an eternity. Stepping back, he reaches for my foot and slowly pulls it to his chest. This gives me a moment to study his tattoo, which covers most of his upper arm and part of his shoulder. Black and gray, it's a cluster of flowers and thistle with a songbird I don't recognize. My eyes drift over the chiseled muscles of his chest and torso until the heat of his hand snaps my gaze back to his face.

His gaze is locked on mine as he slides his hand up to my knee and unzips the boot. I say a silent thank-you to the universe as he drops it to the floor and plants a kiss on my ankle before moving on to the other boot. His fingers move achingly slow as he unzips it, and when the boot falls to the floor, he leaves a trail of kisses along my calf, working his way up to my knee and under the hem of my skirt.

His eyes are wide and dark with longing and I hook my legs around his waist to pull him closer. He makes that delicious growling sound again and slips his hands around my hips, just under the hem of my sweater. His stubbled jaw scrapes along my neck as he kisses and nips his way down to my collarbone and I'm done for.

When I reach for his belt, his phone buzzes in his pocket. I laugh, feeling the vibration against my hip, and he says, "God, I love that sound."

"Your buzzing phone?" I tease.

His deadly grin is back as he slides one hand into my hair and gives it a tug. "Nay. You. You make the most wonderful sounds."

He leans back into me and I slide my palms down his chest. The phone buzzes again and he mutters a curse under his breath.

"Do you need to get that?" I ask, my voice all breathy and ragged.

"Nope."

It buzzes again. "Are you sure?"

He sighs and pulls the phone from his pocket and glances at the screen. I catch a glimpse of a string of text messages and he shoves the phone across the kitchen island where it lands in the sink with a clatter.

"Okay, that was dramatic," I say with a laugh.

"My brother," he mutters, his lips moving back to my neck. "Not an emergency. He's been calling and texting all day."

"Is everything okay?"

As his lips graze my shoulder, he gives me a teasing nip that sends a bolt of heat straight to my core. "As okay as can be expected, I suppose."

"What does that mean?" I'm dizzy from these fiery touches but can't get past the feeling that something might be wrong— that he's shielding me from something important.

He catches my earlobe in his teeth. "He just pestering me, as usual. Trying to get me to come home early."

"Wait. What?" I pull back from him and catch his jaw in my hand so he can't avoid my gaze. "Are you?"

"Not right this second." He moves to kiss me again.

"Logan," I say, tightening my grip.

He grins and captures one of my fingers in his teeth. He's *so* not playing fair.

"Answer me. Are you leaving early?" The wedding's a little over a week away. We don't have enough time as it is. Even though I don't know precisely what's happening between us, I know there's never been another man like him, and I'm pretty sure there never will be.

"No, love. Rory's just being a pain in the ass, as usual. He acts like my being there is going to solve this problem for everyone, but that's just not true. And I'm tired of his interruptions." His hand slides higher up my thigh. "But do you really want to talk about my brother right now?"

His palm could melt ice, but I shove that thought aside and say, "Isn't this thing with him urgent?"

Pulling my hand to his mouth, he plants a kiss on the inside of my wrist. "If I tell you, can I keep doing this?"

"What, you can't multi-task?"

He lifts a brow as if to say he'll prove me wrong later. Then he rests his hands on either side of my thighs, not quite touching me.

"Remember how I said my family wanted me to step in and run the business?" When I nod, he goes on. "The part I left out is that if I don't agree to my grandfather's terms and sign a bloody contract by the end of the month, then he's writing my whole family out of his will."

"Seriously?" I ask. I can't even begin to imagine how much money that entails, but it's probably enough to justify skipping a wedding and getting on a plane.

"Now he's threatening to sell the family estate and sell the company. If he does that, we'd all be out an obscene amount of money," he says, his jaw tensing. "It's not that I need any of it—I'll be fine on my own. In the end, the whole family would be fine, because they already have more than they know what to do with. But losing the company means losing hundreds of millions that could do a lot of good in this world." He sighs, shaking his head. "Rory and I had this plan to overhaul the company and shift the focus to affordable housing and renewable energy. Make it future-proof. But if Grandad sells, that all goes out the window."

Hundreds of millions? I swallow hard. My internet snooping taught me a little about the Fyfe company, and Fiona was happy to dig up as much as she could. Logan Fyfe's world is so different from mine. Like, light-years from it.

"But now he's threatening to cut everyone else in the family out, too," Logan says, his voice gravelly. "He's trying to force me to do what he wants by turning them all against me."

"Oh," I breathe. Not what I was expecting, but I have the urge to fly across the ocean just to throw my shoe at his grandfather. My mother's tried plenty of ways to manipulate me, but she's never done something that cruel.

"I just want to separate myself from the family business," he says. "I want to do my own thing and not be thought of as just one more spoiled, entitled, cutthroat Fyfe. I had bigger dreams than working for a corporation, you know?"

I nod, wishing I could help him with his problem the way he's helped me with mine.

"Anyway, they're all furious at me now, because I haven't agreed," he says. "My grandfather and my mum seem to think they can scare me back into line. My brother and sister just don't want me to disappear—because they know how I get when I'm backed into a corner." He takes a step back, raking his hands through his hair. "The company's in big trouble, and they think

I'm the only one who can save it from going under. But working for that company is the last thing I want to do—and my grandfather knows it."

"I'm so sorry," I tell him. "That sounds awful."

"It's a bit of a predicament."

He steps closer again and I slide my hand over his scruffy jaw. "What do you want to do?" I ask him.

He shakes his head. "Sometimes what your head says and what your heart says are two different things." When he levels his gaze on me again I'm certain he's not just talking about business anymore.

"Hate when that happens," I say.

"How do you decide which to listen to?" He looks genuinely curious about my answer.

I study him for a long moment, watching his jaw tense and his brow furrow. "My head's kept me out of some dicey situations," I say at last. "But it's also left me with regrets. For example, if I'd followed my heart, I'd have been studying abroad in college and might never have set foot back here again."

"Ah," he says. His lip curves into a tiny smile.

"But then, I might not have the cafe. Or my grandmother's house, for that matter. Going away all those years ago could've set me on an entirely different path."

He nods, looking thoughtful. There's a flurry of mixed feelings swirling around in that head of his—that much is obvious. But it's equally clear that Logan Fyfe keeps his feelings close to the vest.

"I like to think that now my head and my heart temper one another," I say. "But I'm happier when I follow what's in my heart."

His eyes rest on mine again. "Aye, it's my heart that gets me into trouble."

"What's it telling you now?" I whisper.

He steps closer then, flush against the counter so my knees are on either side of his hips. His hand cups my jaw and his thumb traces over my bottom lip. In a blink, he's nuzzling my neck again, his lips moving from my ear to my collarbone. I don't ever want this to end, so I shove all those warning thoughts from my head and let my heart take the lead.

"Is this okay?" he rasps, his big hands resting on my hips.

"Mmm-hmm," is all I can manage. No one's ever made me feel so wanted. My skin's humming all over and all I can think is that I've been seriously missing out.

"What do you want me to do?" he asks, his voice a low rumble that sends goosebumps down my arms.

I make a small sound that's somewhere between a moan and a squeak. A million thoughts are rattling around in my brain right now, but the one that hits me hardest is *You are falling so, so hard.*

He pauses, flattening his hands on the countertop. His lips are right by my ear as he says, "Use your words, love. Tell me what you want."

Several answers come to mind, and some of them involve losing all of these clothes and letting him revisit that idea of multi-tasking right here on the kitchen island. But all of them seem like a solid way to get hurt because he's made it clear that whatever is happening is short-lived.

Because his life doesn't fit into this tiny town.

"I don't know," I whisper.

His scruffy cheek scrapes against my jaw and I'm pinned to this spot by his merciless mouth and this question that should be easy to answer. His thumb taps the side of my thigh, drawing my focus there. "Don't know or don't want to tell me?" he says.

When I don't answer, he draws himself back, just far enough so he can look me in the eye.

I open my mouth to speak, but none of the words in my head

sound just right. They just sound confusing and strange. I feel like I could love this man, and I'm not sure why that thought is so terrifying.

"Okay," he says, giving me a tender smile. "I can see you have lots of thoughts rolling around in there right now." He touches my temple and I lean into his hand, wanting to feel him everywhere again. "I think you need to decide what you want before we take this any further."

I blink at him as he steps backward and shoves his hands into his pockets.

"What?" My voice comes out like a squawk.

He lifts a brow. "Take the time you need, love," he says. "I'll wait for you." His voice is tender, yet firm. "But I need to hear the words."

For a moment, I freeze, thinking he wants me to come up with those words right now, while there's a hurricane of thoughts in my head. I'm still staring at him with my jaw hanging open as he pulls my boots from the floor and puts them back on my feet. He zips them carefully, but not as slowly as he did before. His hands aren't teasing anymore—they're set on a utilitarian task. My head's still reeling when he gently lifts me off the island and sets me on my feet. He grabs his shirt from the floor and slips it on, and my heart sinks as he buttons it.

"Come on," he says. "I'll walk you to your door." He kisses my forehead, then takes my hand and leads me out, and it's all I can do to put one foot in front of the other because this was not supposed to happen. I want to strip off these boots, drag him back to the island, and get back to the business of feeling his hands on every inch of my body—but I also want this to not be over in a couple of weeks. I can't make any of those words come out, though, because this man has completely short-circuited my brain.

"This is completely unnecessary, Logan," I say. "My house is ten yards away."

"Agree to disagree," he says, giving me that infernal smirk. He knows he's knocked me completely off-kilter, and he's not one bit remorseful about it.

"I feel like I'm being excused from the dinner table without dessert," I mutter.

"Not at all," he says, squeezing my hip. "We're just going to hit the pause button. I think you need to get clear on what you want. And when you do, I'll be here."

He keeps his hand on the small of my back as we cross the yard to my porch, and I'm still too stunned to say anything more. When I've unlocked the door, I turn towards him and he lifts my hand to his mouth. His lips graze my knuckles and he says, "Sweet dreams, love. I look forward to hearing your thoughts." His gaze could melt me right into the floorboards.

It's only when the door closes behind him, and I'm left in my dark living room, that I shout, "What the hell just happened?"

Chapter Sixteen

LOGAN

After spending the evening with Gwen Griffin, I've learned a few things.

First, I knew she despises asking for help, but it wasn't clear why until tonight. Now I see that she doesn't always know how to ask for what she wants. Somewhere along the way, someone must have taught her that it wasn't okay for her to ask for what she needed. Her feelings are locked down tight, and I'm dying to know how she feels about what's happening between us—but I'm not going to be another person who makes her feel uncomfortable about making her needs clear. I want her to know that her feelings are safe with me, and if that means I have to wait a thousand years for her to feel safe enough to make herself that vulnerable, then that's what I'll do.

That thought strikes me like a thunderbolt because my heart seems to think that leaving this town doesn't seem like an option anymore.

Second, she'll do anything for the people she loves. Including dropping everything to make a cake for her mother, which—based on what Gwen told me—will almost certainly backfire spectacularly. Gwen's exhausted and about five minutes from total burnout, but still she makes time to handle these little fires that everyone sets around her. Even though she has a broken arm, she's still determined to bake this extravagant cake for her sister's wedding—and she took on the one for her mom.

She's not used to being nurtured. I don't mean pampered or spoiled or looked after in a maternal way (though her mom seems about as maternal as those brown-headed cowbirds that leave their eggs in other birds' nests). I mean cared for in the sense that you'd look after anyone that you had deep-rooted feelings for—someone you long to see thrive. The way she acted when she broke her arm was my first clue—she'd been utterly shocked when I insisted on taking her to the doctor, taking her home, and seeing to it that she got into bed safely without slipping in the shower or being strangled by that overly large sweater. She's accustomed to people never making her a priority —and for some reason, she thinks that's acceptable.

She makes this purring sound when I kiss her that nearly burns me to the ground. I'd really, *really,* like to explore that further.

I've been telling myself all this time that I can't get attached to her because I had no intention of staying here. But the more time I spend with her, the more I think that might just be a story I'm telling myself—one that's not quite true anymore.

Because what if I didn't have to leave?

What if I could make her my biggest priority?

What if she let me?

IT'S JUST after eight in the morning when I drag myself out of bed and make myself some fried eggs and toast. I've only eaten half of it when Rory texts me.

You up for a video call? he types. **Grandad's finally agreed.**

I snort. Of course, the old badger wouldn't want to bother scheduling—this is just another of his power plays. He thinks he'll keep me off-kilter by not leaving me any time to prepare.

What he doesn't realize is I've been preparing for this for a long time. His manipulation won't work anymore.

Sure, I type. **Now's great.**

Strike while the iron's hot right? he replies.

I make myself another cup of tea and take a bite of toast as my phone rings with the video call from Rory's number. Not surprising, since Grandad still insists on using ledgers instead of spreadsheets. He hardly uses his computer and it's so old that running a video conference would likely cause it to explode.

"All right," Rory says in greeting. "I'm just getting set up here in Grandad's office. He'll be right back." His hair's mussed like he's been raking his hands through it. Onscreen, his face tilts sideways, and his thumbs cover the screen for a moment as he positions the phone on Grandad's desk.

"You go over anything with him?" I prop my phone up against a stack of books on the kitchen island and sit.

Angling the camera just right, he shakes his head. "Nah. He wanted to hear it from you." Satisfied with the position, he puts his hands on the big oak desk and leans close enough to the phone that I can see the permanent furrow in his brow. He's got the same blue-green eyes that I have, but Rory looks more like our father with each passing year. Rory got Dad's broad forehead and high cheekbones, plus his reddish beard. "You look good," he says, lifting a brow. "Wherever you are suits you."

"Aye, it does." More than he knows.

He smirks and I hear Grandad's gruff mumbling as the phone shakes. "All right, then," Rory says. "Here he is. I'm stepping out for a few."

Grandad sits in the big chair behind his desk, the same old leather chair with the pin-tucks that he's had for ages. With his ruddy cheeks and his heavy cable-knit sweater, he looks like a weathered old fisherman who's just come in from the cold.

"All right, Grandad?" I ask him in greeting.

"Aye," he grumbles. Never one for pleasantries, he stares at me with his steely gray eyes, his mouth a hard line. "Are you finally going to sign some papers, lad?"

"Figured we should discuss that."

"Let's have it, then." He speaks as if he knows what's coming.

"I'm just going to cut to the chase." I rest my elbows on the countertop and clasp my hands. "I'm not the one for this job," I say, matter-of-factly. "I can't take over the reins for you." I stop myself before I say *I'm sorry* because the truth is I'm not one bit sorry. It doesn't please me to be the source of strife, and I know this could cause a rift in the family. But I didn't ask for any of this, either. I don't want to run the company, and I don't want to be in charge of the Fyfe legacy. I just want to build my own life apart from all of that.

My legacy will be different.

All night, I thought of what I'd said to Gwen about following her heart, and I realized that I have to do the same thing. I can't control how my family reacts, or all the things that happen after. All I can control is my own decisions and actions. And I have to be okay with the fact that what I've decided could change everything between us.

I have to trust myself and put myself first. Just like I told Gwen.

His jaw tightens. "You'd give up your inheritance for this. Your share of the company." It's not a question. It's a threat—a way for him to reiterate precisely what I have to lose.

"I would if you insist on holding it over my head," I tell him calmly. I can feel that money slipping away, and I know it could do a lot of good if it were in a charitable trust. But I also know that I won't survive working for my grandfather, and I have no interest in trying to redeem his company after all of his ethical missteps.

The truth is, the company might not be salvageable. And I'm not willing to risk sinking with it.

But Rory thinks he can turn it around—he's not afraid of that risk. Rather, he sees this as an opportunity to right some wrongs—and that feeds his soul. For that reason, I'd love to see him succeed.

"I can't fix the company's problems for you," I say. "Or rather, I won't." That's the piece that fell into place for me a few days ago. Just as everyone in my family believes, I'm perfectly capable of fixing Fyfe Industries' problems—I could be the new clean face of it, I could hire new staff and put on the dog and pony show that the PR firm wants. I could polish things up and use my connections to do good, and I could slowly erode that image Fyfe has of being the cutthroat, heartless firm that cheats and steals—and leaves disaster in its wake.

But I'm tired of being his fixer. I don't want to spend the next ten years cleaning up my grandfather's messes. Deep down, I know that these are not my problems to solve. I won't devote my career, my life, to saving this company—even if it means disappointing my family. As much as I love them, I have to draw this line, because as long as I keep sacrificing what I want to suit them, they'll let me.

I have my own dreams and want to leave my own legacy. And that doesn't include Fyfe.

Grandad glares at me, his face unmoving.

"Rory's the one you need to run things," I tell him. "Not me. You've built a formidable company, and if you want to make it future-proof, you need Rory. We've put some ideas together for you, some outlines for ways he can bring in some new revenue streams. He's got solid ideas, and you should give them some thought." This idea might not stop him from cutting me off, but it might be just enough of an olive branch to stop him from punishing my siblings because of his anger at me.

He sits so still that I think the connection's frozen. Then his jaw tightens and his frown deepens as he barks, "Unacceptable."

I meet his stare. "Why?"

He snorts. "You're the eldest. It's your duty to take over, just like it was your father's."

"I'd argue that tradition is outdated. And isn't in anyone's best interest." And using my father? Not a great way to argue his point.

"You always did think you knew better," he grumbles. "Sometimes you do, but not on this. That lad's not ready to run things. He's made too many mistakes."

"We all make mistakes. It's how we learn to do better."

His eyes narrow and he leans back in his chair, crossing his arms over his chest. "So you're just going to run away, then? Turn your back on your family. Your legacy."

I dig my fingers into my thigh, willing myself to keep my voice cool and even. After all, I knew that jab was coming. "I'm not turning my back on anyone. Rory knows that I'm always willing to consult with him if need be." I take a deep breath, watching his face harden. "And I need you to understand that your legacy is not mine."

He's quiet for a moment, and then he pounds his fist on the desk so hard that the phone shakes. "I'd rather sell and have the company disappear entirely than have it crumble and ruin my name!"

I let out a heavy sigh because I know this comes from a place of fear—and he'll never admit it. He's afraid that Rory will change the company in ways he doesn't like. He's afraid that in a few years, the Fyfe name won't mean what it does now, or what it did fifty years ago. Change is the one thing that terrifies David Fyfe, even more than failure.

"If that's really what you want to do," I tell him, "then maybe you should."

He pounds the desk again and starts swearing in Gaelic as his face reddens. Then he leans close and growls, "You're a massive disappointment, and I was a fool to put any stock in you. You're dead to me."

A knot forms in my chest as I stare at him, surprised by the words. I'd expected him to be a giant unmoving mountain, but I hadn't expected him to go that far. He stands so abruptly that he knocks the big wooden chair backward and it clatters to the floor. The screen shakes as he swipes his arm across the desk and I see a blur of papers and books as the phone falls over. In a blink, the room tilts and I'm left with a view of the ornate ceiling as I hear heavy footfalls and more cursing, punctuated by a slamming door. Then there's Rory's voice in the distance, asking what all the clatter's about.

I listen hard, but can only catch a few words between them.

A few moments later, Rory's face fills the screen. "I see that went well," he says, arching a brow. He holds the phone up to his face as he sits on the corner of the desk.

"You have a Plan B?" I ask.

His brow lifts. "Aye. Always."

Chapter Seventeen

GWEN

It's a little after nine in the morning when Maggie and I resume decorating the cake for Mom's party. Yesterday we did the baking and assembly and put the base layer of buttercream frosting on. That means today is for making all the flowers and placing them on the cake to match the design that Maggie and I planned together. My arm still feels like it's being squeezed in a vise, and even with painkillers, it starts to hurt after only a half-hour of piping flowers. The dull throb makes me pace myself—which means Maggie's doing the bulk of the work today.

It's also been fifty-eight hours since Logan had me melting on the kitchen island, but I can't think about that today. We have a pile of buttercream flowers to finish making, which requires my full attention. I'm much slower than Maggie, but it's important that I still have a hand in this cake. It has to be absolutely perfect. And that means I don't have time to think about the kissing, the hip-squeezing, and Logan's seductive removal of knee-high boots.

Aside from a quick text yesterday confirming that he'd still help me deliver the cake today, I haven't spoken to him. Even after lying awake and analyzing everything we've said to each other and done together in the last several days, I still don't know exactly what to say to him.

"I've been watching this woman on YouTube who's amazeballs," Maggie says. She's been using her own toolkit with two dozen piping heads that are a variety of shapes—and different from what I have in the cafe.

"I didn't realize you were this into decorating."

"I wasn't at first," she says. "The traditional stuff doesn't interest me much, but look at this lady's work." She pulls up her Instagram page and scrolls through a stream of downright amazing photos. This woman she follows is a real artist with incredible designs. Her specialty seems to be flowers that look shockingly lifelike. I'm good, but I'm not this good.

Maggie shrugs. "Anyway, after you left yesterday, I practiced several designs based on the photos your mom had." She goes into the walk-in fridge and comes out with a tray of flowers, all piped in white. Some even have a little airbrushing on the tips of the petals, making them look more lifelike.

"These are stunning," I tell her. I'm amazed by the intricate details, and the different petal shapes. Maggie's made two dozen different flowers, all of them gorgeous. I'd be proud to have this kind of work done on any of our orders.

"Thanks," she says, her cheeks turning pink.

"You've been holding out on me. Big time."

"It's just something I've been trying out on the side," she says with a shrug. I can tell she's proud of them, though, and she should be. She shows me a design she's sketched out for the cake and gets more and more excited as she describes how she wants to group the flowers and add in some edible silver beads.

And then I feel like a real jerk when the next thought hits me like a brick: I've been ignoring her. I haven't talked to her enough about what she wants out of this job, and what she most wants to learn. All this time, I've had someone loaded with talent and drive right under my nose—and I was too preoccupied with my own goals to pay attention to her. For months, I should have been letting her take on more important orders and more detailed work. I should have been teaching her the skills I know, and letting her work by my side.

Yesterday, she helped me bake the cake because I couldn't lift the mixing bowls or transfer batter—or anything else that involved dexterity. Some things are just impossible to do one-handed, even with an alarming amount of cursing and willpower. It was important that I mix the ingredients since this cake has a delicate balance of flavors. Mom wanted vanilla, but I've been dying to make this matcha-pistachio cake that I know will wow her friends. Raspberry coulis and white chocolate buttercream make it the perfect showstopper. But too much matcha makes it bitter—and then that throws off the balance of the other flavors. This cake is a decadent three-tier *I Told You So* and it has to be flawless.

My pride meant that I couldn't hand this over to Maggie completely. A cake made entirely by my assistant would prove nothing to my mother. But now that my arm's throbbing again, I don't feel so prideful about collaboration. If I create the taste and she handles the design, I can live with that.

"How about I let you run with this one?" I ask her. "I'll go catch up on some work in the office, and you can grab me if you need an extra hand."

"Sure," she says. Her fingers move deftly as she conjures a giant carnation. "You got it."

After checking for new orders, I dig into my calendar, and for the first time in months, I don't feel overwhelmed. Fiona and her aunt are coming in this week to bake a couple of big orders, and Maggie's doing the decoration.

When my phone buzzes with a text, I ignore it, thinking it's

Logan. I haven't talked to him since Wednesday night when he kissed me senseless in his kitchen, and I still haven't quite found the words to explain how I'm feeling.

And I feel like I should be able to tell him—even if my thoughts are a tangled mess. I know I shouldn't get attached to him because he's leaving. There was never a question about that. But the more time I spend with him, the more I want to be with him, and I just don't see a way for that to work.

But I wish there was a way it could.

My phone buzzes again and I see it's a text from my sister.

Hey! Victoria writes. **Just checking in on the cake status.**

Great, I reply. **Finishing the decoration.**

Super, she writes. **Can we push delivery to 4:30 today? Mom will be out getting her hair done.**

Will do.

Perfect. It'll take at least an hour for Mom to get her hair sculpted just right, and the party isn't until eight o'clock. For Victoria's big sneaky plan to work, I'll deliver the cake while Mom's away, and then we'll reveal my identity as the secret baker afterward—preferably after payment has cleared the bank. Ideally, this will shock the pants off Mom, help her realize I'm an expert in my chosen field, and serve her up a heaping helping of crow.

When all of her friends are wowed by this amazing cake, the look on her face will be priceless. It's not that I'm dying for her approval—I just want her to see me as a professional who's forging my path and building a successful business. I want her to understand that this is not a hobby or some silly flight of fancy. It's something I know how to do well.

"This is gorgeous, Maggie. Mom's friends are going to lose their minds."

Aside from showing her a few of my techniques here and there, she's done this all on her own. And the result is breathtaking. The three-tiered cake is an asymmetrical design, with a cascade of flowers down one side. She's managed to get tinges of pink on the edges of the flower petals with some expert use of the piping tools, and again, I'm kicking myself for not seeing all of this sooner. The last several months would have been so much easier if I'd let her help this way.

"Thanks," she says with a big smile. "And thanks for shooting the videos."

"You bet. I'll start sharing them on our account too. You're about to get a lot more fans." It was her idea to shoot videos to share, and I made sure to take some great process shots of her piping the flowers.

She nods, still surveying the cake to no doubt make sure it's just as she wants it.

"One more thing," I tell her.

Her eyes flick to mine.

"I'm sorry it took me this long to see how talented you are. I've been distracted, but that's no excuse. You're extraordinary at what you do, and I'd love it if you did more decorating for us, and more for special events. If you want to."

Her brown eyes widen. "Really? I'd love that." She grins and clasps her hands together. "Oh my gosh, I have so many ideas."

That's not one bit surprising. "Good. I want to hear them all."

I'm just heading back to my office when I hear a knock on the back door of the cafe. Maggie shrugs because we're not expecting deliveries today. When I open it, Logan's there holding a paper bag against his chest. He's dressed in what has become his typical snug jeans and butter-soft button-up shirt with a brown motorcycle jacket. It's so unfair, the way he keeps wearing these fabrics that beg to be touched.

"Hi," I say, not thinking at all about sliding my fingers over that supple leather and luxury denim. Not imagining the feel of that at all.

He drags a hand through his hair as if he's nervous. "Haven't seen you in ages," he says. "I needed proof of life."

I try to ignore his weighted gaze. "You could have called or texted."

He gives me a playful smirk. "Aye, I could have."

"What's in the bag?"

"Lunch," he says. "I know how you sometimes forget to eat. Thought I might help with that."

Honestly, this man's urge to take care of me is astounding. And I'm realizing that I like it very much.

"I've been busy delegating," I tell him. "You know, taking your advice."

"Have you now?" His brow lifts in that teasing way that makes my heart flutter. "I can't wait to hear more about that."

"We're nearly done with Mom's cake. Maggie's killing it."

He peeks around my shoulder. "Can I see?"

"Let's see what's in the bag first, mister."

With a sly grin, he holds it toward me. "I hear it's your favorite."

Opening the bag, I'm hit by the familiar scent of curry from the Thai restaurant a few blocks from here. It is indeed my favorite.

"You hear correctly. Come on in, Lancelot."

He holds the door open for me as we step inside, and it feels like that invisible thread is back, pulling us closer. All I can think is that I want him to stay here, to keep bringing me lunches, to keep making me laugh. To keep me feeling safe.

It's a nice thought, the idea of him staying here. And for the first time, I wonder if it's so impossible.

Chapter Eighteen

LOGAN

"That's bloody gorgeous," I tell her. "It's a crime to cut something like that."

"We eat with our eyes first," she says, talking about food of course. That cake is stunning, but it's the farthest thing from my mind right now. I haven't been able to think straight since a couple of nights ago when Gwen nearly made me combust with that kiss. I've been replaying that in my mind ever since, and wonder if she has, too.

"I couldn't agree more," I reply, and bite back a smile when a faint blush rises in her cheeks.

Maggie comes in from the front of the cafe, cell phone in hand. "Let me shoot one more reel," she says, already swiping the screen. "This could get you so much new business. And we both know that your Insta needs some love."

"Hey," Gwen says. "You know social media is not my superpower."

"That's why you have me," Maggie says.

Gwen gives her a teasing smirk, but she doesn't disagree.

"It won't hurt to have him in the reel, either," Maggie says, cocking her head towards me. "Would you mind? You're liable to get us a thousand new followers just by standing next to the cake and looking like…well…like *you*."

"Aye, sure," I say, because apparently I can't say no to either of these women.

Gwen shoots me an apologetic look as Maggie positions me near the cake.

"Oh, I know!" Maggie chirps. "You can pretend to taste the frosting." She grabs a piping bag and a spatula from the work table. "You can't touch the real cake, because we've spent a million hours on it, and I'll have to murder you if you wreck it." She pipes a bit of frosting onto the spatula and hands it to me as if I should know exactly what to do.

"Logan," Gwen says with a laugh. "You don't have to—"

But then I lean close to the cake and give her a wink as I lick the spatula—and sweet Mother Mary, that frosting is the most delicious thing I've ever tasted.

Well. The second most delicious thing, because now I'm yanked back in time to the kitchen island, and the delightful taste of Gwen's neck as she purred against me and raked her hands through my hair.

Nothing will ever taste better than her. I'm officially ruined for anyone else.

Judging by the blush that's covering Gwen's cheeks, she's thinking of that moment, too. And I love watching her think about us.

"That's perfect!" Maggie says, a big grin on her face.

It's cheeky as can be, but I'll take her word for it. Even better, I'll take that heated look from Gwen that's enough to set this whole room ablaze.

"Get ready to break the internet," Maggie says. "Hope you're ready to be Jasmine Falls famous."

Gwen lifts a brow and I love that she's still speechless. Maggie flits back out to the front of the cafe, still chuckling as she taps on her phone.

"How about that lunch, gorgeous?"

"Uh-huh," she says.

"And then we can get this cake out the door."

"Yep," she says, still avoiding my gaze.

"You okay?" I ask, biting back a smile.

"You betcha."

I follow her to a work table in the corner where she proceeds to dig into the bag and spread out our meals. She steals another glance at me but doesn't say a word. It's clear my girl still has some tangled-up feelings that she's holding tight to her chest.

But just as I told her, I can wait. Because as I've found over and over, nothing worth having ever comes easy.

AT PRECISELY FOUR-THIRTY, Gwen and I pull into the driveway of her parents' house—it's a big brick Georgian in the historic part of Jasmine Falls, on a corner lot that's several blocks from the heart of downtown. I park where she tells me, leaving enough room for Sam to pull past us in the delivery van and park close to the back door by the garage.

As we climb out of the car, Victoria waves from the deck. Theo's pacing in the grass just a few feet from her, his phone pressed to his ear.

"Stunning house," I say. It's two stories with a sprawling yard and immaculate landscaping that was no doubt designed by professionals.

"If you're lucky my father will show you the musket ball that's lodged in the doorframe upstairs," Gwen says. "He loves to point that out at every party and joke about dodging bullets ever since."

"My heroes," Victoria says, coming to meet us. "You're right on time. Mom added a manicure, so we've got at least an hour and a half before she gets home."

"Let's get to it, then," Gwen says. She holds the back door open while Sam and I carry the cake into the house. We take it straight into the big dining room at the front, where the caterers will soon set up the rest of the food.

Once we have it situated on the table, Sam brings in a duffle bag full of extra supplies and then heads back to the cafe.

"This looks amazing," Victoria says, studying the flowers on the cake. "You've totally outdone yourself."

"And Maggie," Gwen says. "Hopefully it'll be a hit." The cake looks even better in this room, sitting on a big lace tablecloth under a crystal chandelier. With its cascade of cream-colored flowers and bits of edible silver, it looks festive and elegant without being over the top.

"Are you kidding?" Victoria says, leaning over to examine the flowers. "Everyone's going to love it." She pulls her phone from her pocket and snaps some photos of the cake. "Could we do some flowers like this on mine?"

"Of course," Gwen says. She walks around the table, examining the cake. "I see a couple of flowers that need some sprucing up. No biggie, though." She digs into the duffle bag and pulls out a few tools and an extra piping bag with icing. She told me on the way that they always pack a kit like this, just in case there are any mishaps with the delivery. Every now and then a flower gets brushed against a sleeve and she needs to do a little tidying. She even has a small box of extra flowers that can be placed on the cake as replacements.

She works slowly and deliberately, still favoring her injured arm. I try to help by holding some of the tools and she breathes a quiet, "Thank you." The cake looks perfect to me, but she keeps finding little spots to touch up. She looks completely at ease, in her element. I could watch her like this all day.

Theo comes inside and says, "Logan, man, I haven't even had a chance to say hi." He shakes my hand and grins, looking every bit as stiff as he did at St. Andrews. He looks more polished now, with his short blond hair and clean-shaven jaw.

"Good to see you," I tell him, but he's already looking away.

"Babe," he says to Victoria. "I have to skip the party tonight. A meeting came up."

"What meeting is that?" Victoria says, giving him a sharp look. "We've had this on the calendar for months."

"It's Steve and Carlos. I have to be there."

Her eyes narrow and she steers him a few steps away from us. "Is this about the Glenville property? I'm supposed to meet with them about that."

He snorts. "Babe, you're punching above your weight with those guys. Let me handle them. Besides, you've got this party to deal with. You couldn't have met them tonight."

Victoria glances at Gwen, who's focused on the cake but definitely listening, and then turns back to Theo. "I have a good relationship with them, and have spent countless hours—"

"Honey," Theo says with a chuckle. "Trust me. This one's not your expertise. It's mine."

Victoria stares at him like she has plenty more to say, but stays silent. Her lip quivers the slightest bit and then she says calmly, "Okay, then. Tell them I said hello."

My jaw tightens as Theo gives me an exaggerated head-shake. He was arrogant when I knew him, but never so dismissive. I may not know Victoria well, but I'm surprised she doesn't call him out on that nonsense. If he talked to Gwen that way, I'd lay him out without a second thought.

"And Logan," Theo says. He gives me an overly bright smile and it's all I can do to manage a stiff nod in return. "Dude, I have a stellar opportunity to tell you about. I know you're going to want to get in on this one—it's going to be huge." He tugs at the collar of his too-tight shirt and glances at Gwen before turning back to me. "I can't give you details here, but we'll get drinks this week and talk."

"Not sure I'm looking for any investments right now," I tell him, hoping to shut this down politely. I just learned everything I need to know about Theo, and I don't invest in people like him.

He grips my shoulder and says, "Dude, this one's a no-brainer. Development on the coast, only a few top-tier investors. A swanky place for high-rollers. Just your style. Don't tell me you don't even want to hear the pitch."

The fake swagger on him is nauseating. "Appreciate the thought," I tell him, certain that Theo has no idea about my style. "But real estate's not my thing."

"Don't tell me the great Logan Fyfe finally got burned," Theo crows. "No worries, man—this is big enough to make up for anything you took a beating for. You'd have to be nuts to turn this one down."

"Theo," Victoria says, keeping her voice low. "He said no."

"Why don't you worry about the cake and let us worry about investing," he says to her, and I feel my hands clench at my sides.

Victoria bites her lip and turns her attention to Gwen, who's still touching up flowers and glaring at Theo like she wants to stab him with her pointy icing tool.

Oblivious, Theo claps me on the back and says, "Let's see how you feel after a couple of drinks and a proposal. Trust me, you're going to be begging to get in on this one." He seems to think he can talk anyone into anything. Sadly, he's become the kind of person we used to make fun of in school—the sleazy guy full of bravado and half-truths who thinks swindling is a kind of investing.

Because only a swindler uses the kinds of tactics he's used in the last two minutes. Creating a spectacle like this? It's an amateur move. It's what you do when you're blowing smoke.

Victoria and Gwen share a strained look. I want to tell them it's fine, that they need not be embarrassed because of this nitwit. It's clear now why Theo invited me here—it wasn't out of friendship or nostalgia, or to celebrate his wedding. It was because he wanted me to write a big check and back some half-baked idea of his in the hopes that my money could work for him.

It's nothing I haven't seen before, but I never expected to see it from him.

He moves to kiss Victoria on the cheek and tells her, "I'll see you later tonight. Don't wait up." To me, he says, "I'll text you this week, my man," and doesn't wait for a response.

When he's out the door, Gwen steps away from the cake and turns to her sister. "You okay, Vic?"

Victoria's flushed from her cheeks to her collarbones. "Fine."

She's far from it, though, because she looks like she's ready to spit fire. And Gwen, too.

Gwen lifts a brow as if to say they'll discuss this later and then says, "Cake's all set."

Victoria gives her a tight smile and glances at her phone. "Fifteen minutes to spare, sis. You never cease to amaze me."

"We're out of here," Gwen says, steering me towards the door.

"You're coming back, right?" Victoria says.

Gwen lets out a groan and Victoria blocks the back door with her body. "When I tell everyone you made the cake," she says, "they're all going to want to talk to you—you'll be like the guest of honor. And it'll look weird if you're not here."

"Yes, fine," Gwen says. "But we're leaving after the cake's cut."

Victoria rolls her eyes and then turns to me. Her bright

smile's back like the last five minutes didn't happen. "You're coming, too, right?" When I confirm, she turns back to Gwen and grins. "Perfect. Everyone will want to meet the hot new guy, so you can avoid the painful small talk and be a wallflower all you want. Until I out you as the mystery cake genius, anyway. So go home and find something sparkly to wear and get ready to fill your calendar."

She practically shoves us out the door and Gwen grumbles something about leaving the country next Christmas. Once outside, she says, "My sister knows I loathe these parties more than anything else on earth. More than standing in line at the DMV. More than having a root canal. More than being audited by the IRS—it only happened the one time, but sweet baby cheeses, what a nightmare."

I give her a playful nudge as we head to the van. "I'll try to make it less awful for you than a tax audit."

She gives me a saucy smirk. "I'd expect nothing less, Lancelot."

I climb into the driver's side because I still don't want her driving with her injured arm. She can tease me all she wants about being a knight in shining armor, but I refuse to let her push herself too hard.

"You all right?" I ask her. That glare she gave Theo could have cleaved granite, and I know the way he acted with her sister has her simmering.

She lifts a brow. "She deserves better."

"Aye, agreed."

She's quiet for a moment, drumming her fingers on her thigh.

"Here's the thing, though." She heaves a heavy sigh. "It's her call. Not mine." Her eyes have turned a stormy gray-blue. "I always want Vic to turn to me when she needs me. But if I bag on her fiancé, I'll push her away forever. So even though he's a donkey's ass, I stay quiet and hope for the best. And when she needs me, I'll be here for her."

I nod, knowing that I'd do the same with Rory. "I'm sorry that's happening," I tell her. "But I get it. She's lucky to have you."

She gives me a tight smile. "Most people wouldn't understand my reasoning."

My heart aches for her because I can see how much she loves her sister. "You don't have to explain yourself," I tell her. "No justification needed."

Her smile turns warm. "And you're not most people," she says. "I like that about you." When she places her hand on my knee, my heart swells in my chest. "Now let's beat it," she says, "before my mother gets home."

Chapter Nineteen

GWEN

Twenty minutes into this party, I'm still keeping Logan at my side like a life preserver. Inside, the house is already hot and stuffy because fifty people are packed in like sardines. Just as I predicted, Logan draws every eye in the room, which is perfect because it means he and his dead-sexy brogue can do all the entertaining this evening.

He came dressed to kill. His navy suit fits him in a way that should be criminal. The tailored fabric accentuates his wide shoulders and muscular thighs, and I'm having a very hard time stopping my eyes from following the seams of that suit like a road map to ruin.

He makes an excellent distraction. The problem is, I'd like him to be much more.

These parties wreck me because Mom's friends are always full of questions about my work and my romantic life, and it feels like they're holding a measuring stick up to my sister and me.

Spoiler alert: Victoria always comes out on top.

Every year, I tell myself I shouldn't care about these comparisons. I'm happy for my sister. She has her dream job at a fancy real-estate firm, she's about to get married, and she and Theo live in a historic house that looks like a picture. It would be easier to hate her if she wasn't such a nice person. Truly, I'm proud of her—I just hate that Mom uses Victoria's successes to make me feel like I'm lagging behind.

Logan says something that makes the ladies around us titter with laughter and it takes another full minute to pry him away from them.

"So great to see you all," I tell them, steering him towards the living room.

"Your mom's friends are right cheeky," he says, tugging at his collar. "I was about to send up an emergency flare."

"They've probably all googled you by now, my friend. You'll be the number one person of interest in this town."

"Should I be worried?" he asks.

"Probably." I lead him past the bar, where the bartender is busy chatting with my old dentist, and grab two glasses of wine. "Full disclosure, this is one of my least favorite things on earth."

"Parties?" he says, taking a glass.

"Small talk with my mother's friends. Usually, I'm hiding outside in the treehouse by now."

Grabbing Logan's hand, I make a beeline for the kitchen and slip inside the butler's pantry where there's just enough room for us to lean against the butcher-block island. Once I shut the door behind us, I finally feel like I can breathe.

"You doing all right?" he says, brushing a lock of hair behind my ear.

"Better since you're here." He's the antidote to the whole situation beyond the pantry door.

"As parties go, I've been to far worse." He leans against the island so we're standing shoulder to shoulder and I feel a wave of heat move through me—my hands, my face, my chest. His woodsy scent fills the air and for a moment I feel anchored to the earth. Logan seems to always have this effect on me.

"I know schmoozing is required when you run a business," I say, "because how else am I going to network—but Mom's made me come to these parties ever since I was a teenager, and it was always the same. She raved to everyone about Victoria—her straight As, her scholarships, her pageants, every success that she had. And then she complained about me. If I had a dollar for every time she said *I wish Gwen could be more like Vicki,* I wouldn't have needed that small business loan." I take a big sip of wine, wishing I could let all of that go, just shed it like an old coat that no longer fits. "For years, these people have heard about every mistake of mine, every failure, and everything I did that was contrary to what Mom wanted. She constantly made me feel like a screw-up."

"Your past doesn't have to predict your future," he says. "Even though I have serious doubts that you've ever been a screw-up." He sips his wine, holding my gaze. "But in the end, does it matter what these people think of you? I mean, you chase the dream regardless, don't you? You do what you need to be happy."

"Where do you get this endless confidence?" I ask him.

With a small shrug, he says, "I believed it until it became real. You just have to know what you want. Then the rest gets easier."

He turns to face me, his eyes wide in the dim light, and my heart pounds in my chest. When his gaze drops to my lips, all I can think is how much I want to be introducing him to everyone as my boyfriend for real. No more faking.

"You asked me that before," I whisper. "What I wanted." I slide my fingers along his lapel and he inches closer. My chest tightens as I think back to that night at his kitchen island when he made it seem like it should be easy to put into words.

"Aye," he says. "So I did."

"I have some words for you."

He lifts a brow. "Let's hear them, gorgeous."

I take a deep breath, willing myself not to shut down again. He slides his hand over mine, and that's all I need to go on.

"I like you. More than I like—well, almost anybody."

"Those are good words."

"I have some more."

He gives me a sly grin. His body's not quite touching mine, which makes it seem too far away.

"I don't do flings," I tell him. "I don't want this to be temporary, and frankly that's scary to me. Because I don't see how this isn't temporary."

He nods. "What if it doesn't have to be?"

"I don't see how that's possible. You're leaving. I'm not."

Raising a hand to cup my jaw, he gives me a tiny smile that feels like a dare. "What if we just do what feels right to us? What if we don't have to have the answers right now?"

I stare into his eyes, feeling that familiar knot in my belly again.

"I know you like your plans and calendars," he says. "But maybe we could operate without a plan and see where this takes us."

"That sounds like you'd be okay if this was temporary," I say.

He moves closer, pinning me against the island, and now I feel him everywhere. Knees. Hips. Toes.

"I definitely wouldn't be okay." His hands move to my waist as he bends down to whisper in my ear. "Wrecked, yes. Okay, no. You've completely ruined me, love." I shiver as his lips move against my neck, as his scruffy jaw scrapes against my skin.

"How much longer do we have to stay here?" he says, kissing the corner of my mouth.

"In the pantry?" I giggle as his hands tighten on my hips.

"Around other people," he growls, and I'm not laughing anymore.

"I promised to stay until they cut the cake."

He groans, and the sound makes my whole body ache.

His lips are nearly touching mine when the door to the pantry swings open. We both freeze as Victoria says, "There you are, geez."

He pulls away and straightens his jacket, but keeps a possessive hand on my hip. I don't hate it.

"How'd you find us?" I ask Victoria.

She snorts like that's the most obvious question in the world. "This is where you always hide. Unless you're in the treehouse." She takes one look at my hot cheeks and then shifts her gaze to Logan and smirks. "Sorry to interrupt," she says to me, smoothing the front of her dress. It's a magenta fit-and-flare that's cinched so tight at the waist I wonder how she can breathe. She's trying to be bubbly, but I can tell she's still fuming over what Theo said earlier. I thought I was finally going to see her take his head off, and honestly, I was hoping that she would. Theo's the only person who gets away with saying things like that to Vic, and it makes no sense to me why she lets him. I've wanted to say that to her so many times, but I bite my tongue because her relationship with Theo is her business—she knows what she wants and never settles.

"We'll cut the cake soon," she says, "and I thought you might like to see everyone's reactions. You've already gotten a million compliments on your icing artistry. Just as I predicted, you're a huge hit."

"And Mom?" I ask.

"Still doesn't know," she says, "I had to play the ditzy blonde card, but I told her it came from a place an hour away that I forgot the name of. She was so busy worrying about the caterers that she dropped it."

I sigh, tugging at the hem of my dress.

"So if you two are done making out," Victoria says, "Come on out so you can be part of the big hurrah." She slips out of the pantry, leaving Logan staring at me with a mischievous smirk.

"Well, come on," he says, nudging my arm. "Let's go out there for your moment of glory. We can sneak back into the pantry later."

"Promise?"

The look in his eyes is smoldering. "Aye, be careful what you wish for. If I get you back in there, I might never let you out." He buttons his jacket, his eyes fixed on mine, and I kind of want to stay in this pantry with him forever.

Back in the dining room, my eighth-grade English teacher Ms. Deaton corners me by the punch bowl, her eyebrows waggling excitedly as she asks me all about my new business, my plans for next year, and this "handsome fella" who's with me.

Logan shakes her hand and introduces himself as my friend, and that will no doubt set the rumor mill on fire. With his chiseled jaw and artfully mussed hair, he looks like a hero from one of the comic books that Sam reads on his breaks. Factor in the gravelly voice and killer smile, and there's no way he's slipping under anyone's radar.

And the way he's looking at me? Friends don't stare at friends that way.

He plays the role of the mysterious handsome stranger well —and he's a good sport. Everyone here's been completely charmed by him, and he can't finish a sentence without someone first asking him where he's from, and then swooning when he tells them about the Isle of Skye. Even I'm hypnotized as I listen to him talk with such love about the place, and without even trying, I'm daydreaming about white cliffs, fields of thistle, and several other scenarios I have no business thinking of while standing in a room full of my mother's friends.

Logan's just telling Dr. Howell about the scotch distillery near his family's home when a group of women behind him catch my eye with their slices of cake and hoots of laughter.

A few feet away, Lee Anne Hardwick, head of the town council, stands next to Maxine Bell, head of the Arts Commission. They're both in their sixties and always look like they're dressed for a photo shoot, with perfectly tailored dresses and not a hair out of place. A couple of other ladies are with them, picking at their hors d'oeuvre as they all crack up at something Maxine says. Then Lee Anne takes a big bite of the matcha cake, and time stands still as her perfectly painted lips close around the fork. I hold my breath and what happens next is like a knife twisting deep in my gut.

Lee Anne's eye twitches and her lips pucker like she sucked on a lemon. And then she does the unthinkable—she spits out the bite of cake into a napkin and holds it under her plate. It's a furtive motion, one that plenty of people missed, but still—there's no mistaking what happened. She whispers something to Maxine and takes a big gulp from Maxine's punch cup and my heart stops beating right then and there. For her, it was a discreet move, but for me, she might as well have climbed up on the buffet table and smashed that cake under the heel of her chic open-toed shoe.

I step to my left, out of their line of sight. Logan's broad shoulders make for an excellent shield. If they look my way now, they'll be distracted by the Adonis in the room and won't notice me melting into the floorboards in a puddle of shame.

Logan says, "Right, Gwen?" as he chuckles at something my family dentist said.

"Yep," I squeak, "You bet," and stare over his shoulder as

Maxine takes a tiny bite of the cake and then frowns and wrinkles her nose.

Oh *no.*

This is terrible. Worse than that time in college when I had too many beers and threw up in my purse. Worse than the day in eighth grade when Victoria cut my bangs for picture day. Worse than that time in middle school when my dress got stuck in my pantyhose and I mooned everyone at the spring dance.

Logan gives me a quizzical look, but I can't worry about him right now—not when my future is going up in flames.

Maxine is our town's patron saint of the arts. She and Lee Anne are the closest thing we have to royalty around here, and with their stamp of approval, you're golden. They've turned people on to new local artists, and helped small business owners get a leg up—they're all the social proof you need to thrive in this town. If they give you a recommendation, then everyone wants to hire you and support your business. But the reverse is true, too: these ladies have no patience for mediocre, and not one minute to waste on anything they find distasteful. Lee Anne already hired me to make the desserts for an event happening in January—a huge deal—and I was floored when she chose me. She always books caterers and chefs who are the best of the best, usually from Atlanta or Charleston. Praise from her could give my business the boost that I so desperately need to grow.

And now, watching her spit out that cake makes me want to die.

She'll cancel. Simple as that. She'll call me first thing tomorrow, no doubt finding some words that might spare my feelings, and I'll never get hired for any special events in this town ever again. Happy news spreads fast here, but ugly news spreads like fire in a tinderbox.

So much for my business expansion.

Logan leans closer and touches my elbow, pulling me out of

my death spiral. "Everything okay?" he whispers. I can tell from his tone that he knows it isn't.

"I think I just saw my career die," I mumble, draining my wine glass.

His brow furrows with concern. "What do you mean?"

In that split second, I realize my only saving grace: Maxine and Lee Anne don't know yet that I baked the offending cake—and I have to keep it that way. I suck in a deep breath, trying to calm my racing heart. This isn't over. I can still save myself—I'll just ask Victoria not to tell anyone. We'll never tell Mom, and we'll take this secret to our graves. And no one, ever, will learn who made the weird cake at Elaine Griffin's party, which must have been some silly amateur baker's mistake.

You can do this. I repeat those words in my head like a mantra. Because I *can* do this—I can stop this train from careening off the cliff. But I have to act fast and find my sister.

Logan's fingers slide along my forearm—a nice tingly feeling that might have completely distracted me if I didn't have a ticking time bomb standing across the room draped in magenta silk and taffeta.

"They hate it," I whisper to him, just as Victoria taps a knife against a wine glass and calls for everyone's attention.

Logan's hand rests on my hip as he whispers, "I don't think that's true."

"Everyone, thank you so much for coming tonight," Vic says. She smiles sweetly and gives me a quick nod, and that's when I know that I'm now inside the train, on fire, hurtling towards the cliff.

"I trust everyone's enjoying the amazing food tonight," Vic says. "I just wanted to take a moment to thank our caterers, the Garden of Delights, for all of their hard work and delicious treats."

My knees go weak. I step closer to Victoria and made a tiny

chopping motion under my chin, willing her to comprehend. There are a dozen bodies between us, and if I want to say anything quietly to her, I'll have to shove my way through like a linebacker. Instead, I widen my eyes and bite my lip, contorting my face in that way that means SOS to most people, but Victoria doesn't get it. She lifts a brow and I make a more emphatic slicing gesture, edging closer. She goes on, undeterred.

I squeeze my way toward her, but a couple of Dad's golf buddies are blocking my path and this room suddenly feels more crowded than a Taylor Swift concert.

"Many of you have asked me about the gorgeous cake," Victoria says, and I wish the floor would just open up and swallow me because this—THIS—is how your career and reputation both combust at the same time in a town like ours. And this is how fate punches you in the gut and then dances gleefully on top of your limp body. If I could have any superhero ability, it would be to stop time—but because I'm no superhero and have no such power, my sister simply beams at me and says, "This cake was a special surprise for our mother, made by my incredibly talented sister Gwen, who is, by the way, expanding her business into making desserts for special events. I'm told this one is—correct me if I'm wrong, Sis—pistachio and matcha with raspberries and buttercream. If you haven't tried it yet, you'd better hurry before I finish it off myself."

There's some polite chuckling and whispers and I will myself not to look at Lee Anne and Maxine.

Or my mother.

Victoria points to me and then everyone whips their heads in my direction, and there's no way out of this now. I nod, squeaking out a "Yes, that's it," as if to say *Nope, nothing to see here!* Logan reaches over to squeeze my hand, giving me a warm smile. In five seconds, I'm either going to faint or hurl on my favorite peep-toe pumps.

Victoria continues her speech, and I hear chattering and laughter around us. Lee Anne Hardwick looks like someone just told her that a meteor was careening toward Earth and we all have about eight minutes to live. Maxine claps her hands sweetly, her expression unreadable. If she didn't like it, she had enough grace to pretend she had.

Ugh.

And then there's my mother. She's standing just a few feet from Victoria, smiling her polite smile as she talks to her guests and raises a glass to my sister—but her jaw tightens when she glances at me.

Too bad that meteor isn't headed our way.

IN THE NEXT TWENTY MINUTES, I become way too obsessed with cake: specifically, the ratio of partially uneaten slices to empty dessert plates. Some plates look licked clean. Others hold only the uneaten matcha layer. My unscientific analysis has left me exceedingly anxious, a little queasy, and one hundred percent eager to get out of here.

Victoria clinks her glass against mine just as Mom's friend Sheila Jenkins sidles up to me and says, "Gwen, that cake is delicious. I had two pieces."

Stunned, I say, "Thank you, Sheila."

"My daughter's getting married in May, and I'm sure she'd love to talk to you."

"I'd like that, too," I say, feeling my chest loosen the slightest bit.

Victoria beams. "She's doing my wedding cake, too. It's going to be amazing."

Sheila says, "We'll be in touch," and heads back toward her friends.

"See there," Vic says. "All that panic was for nothing. You blew their socks off."

Mom steps toward us just as Carlene Hendrix touches my elbow and says, Gwen, that's the best cake I've ever eaten. It's so daring."

"I'm so glad you liked it," I say, and that irritating voice in my head that always fixates on disaster seems a bit more distant. A few feet away, Logan gives me a reassuring wink.

Mom lifts a brow and purses her lips. She and Carlene have an unspoken rivalry about, well, everything.

"I'd love to have you do something for a fundraiser I'm hosting in the spring," Carlene says.

"I'd be delighted," I tell her.

As Carlene slips past me she turns to Mom and says, "Elaine, you've outdone yourself this time."

Mom's jaw tenses as she gives Carlene a polite smile and thanks her for coming.

"I'd say that's a hit, Mom," Victoria says.

My mother excuses herself and heads into the kitchen.

Victoria gives her an exasperated eye-roll as two other ladies I don't recognize walk over and ask her about her upcoming wedding. Across the room, Logan's been cornered by Lee Ann and Maxine, so I take that as a sign to go look for my mother and try to smooth things over.

I find her alone in the kitchen, sipping a glass of wine. Now that no one else is around, her face is stony. Dad comes in from the patio, where his golf buddies are smoking their cigars, and gives me a brief nod before heading toward the pantry.

"Great party, Mom," I tell her. "As usual. Everything looked perfect." Maybe she doesn't know that anyone spit the cake out into a napkin. Maybe she's only heard compliments.

"Yes," Mom says. "You made quite the scene tonight." Her voice is cool and even, like the evil queen in the fairy tales who has you right where she wants you. "First you pull that stunt with the cake, and then you show up late with a man I have no idea how to explain to people. Was it enjoyable, making a fool out of me?"

"Mom," I say, "That's a little dramatic, don't you think?" I try to keep my voice light, even though I'm exhausted by her theatrics. I should have anticipated that if I didn't introduce Logan to her immediately she'd take it as a slight.

Some things just never change.

The kitchen door swings open and Victoria buzzes in with Logan on her heels. "Mom," she says. "What did you think? Wasn't Gwen's cake amazing?"

My mother's gaze slips to the two of them and then settles back on me. Her scowl could cleave granite. On the other side of the kitchen, Dad picks through the cabinet where he keeps his favorite scotch, ignoring us.

"Mom, this is Logan," I tell her. "He's a friend of Theo's and is in town for the wedding. I didn't get a chance to introduce you when we got here because you were with your friends. I didn't want to be rude and interrupt you."

"It's a pleasure, Mrs. Griffin," Logan says, reaching for her hand. "You have such a lovely home and such delightful friends." He gives my mother a dashing smile that has no doubt been crafted precisely for disarming prickly people like her.

My mother sniffs as she shakes his hand. "Well, I just wish I'd met you myself before everyone started asking me about you. To hear everyone talk, you'd think the two of you are engaged. It seems everyone here knows more about you than I do."

"Aye, I should be so lucky," he says. "But Gwen's just been kind enough to show me around and make me feel welcome. It's clear she gets her hospitality and her kindness from you."

Lord have mercy. I shoot him a warning look—because really? Kindness?—and his lip ticks upward in a conspiratorial way. He's laying it on thick, but it's totally working because my mother's lips pull into a tiny smile. I roll my eyes, hoping I'm not as predictable as my mother.

Dad comes over and extends his hand toward Logan. "Roger," he says, giving him a hard stare. "Good to meet you."

Logan shakes his hand and says, "Likewise, Mr. Griffin."

"Sorry, Logan," I say. "You're now officially part of the Jasmine Falls rumor mill."

His smile widens. "That's okay. Being your maybe-fiancé would be the best rumor that ever spread about me." He gives me a devilish wink that makes my breath catch in my throat.

My cheeks turn hot. He's only joking, but the word *fiancé* sends those butterflies in my belly into overdrive—because it's so easy to picture. *Get a grip*, I tell myself. He's here for two more weeks, and then gone forever, back to a world I wouldn't begin to know how to fit into.

Thinking about that makes me ache all over like there's already a hole in my heart.

My mother arches a brow at him. "You don't have to worry about that, dear. No one would believe Gwen was engaged and hadn't told me."

Victoria stares at me as if she can see those butterflies dancing around in my belly. It's annoying how nothing ever gets past her. Except when it matters most, like ten minutes ago when I was sending her the signal to stop talking about the cake before she caused my complete destruction.

"Did you try the cake, Mom?" Victoria asks. "Wasn't it delicious?"

"I did not," she says.

"Well, everybody was raving about it," Victoria says. "Logan, would you get her a piece?"

Those butterflies in my belly turn into a tornado. I don't want her to taste the cake, because I know she'll hate it. And then all of this will be so much worse.

But Logan's already out the door.

"Mom," I say. "I'm sorry if you were embarrassed. That wasn't our intention."

"What were you thinking?" she says in an angry whisper. "Were you trying to humiliate me?" She turns to Victoria. "And you! I expect this sort of nonsense from Gwen, but not from you."

"Mom!" Victoria says, exasperated. "We just wanted to surprise you and do something nice for you. When I told Gwen your cake person canceled, she dropped everything to step in and help. And she brought you a cake better than anything that person you hired has ever made." Her tone is even, her voice cool. She's the one who can handle Mom without having an aneurysm.

I could have kissed my sister for saying that.

"I ordered vanilla," Mom says, her jaw tight.

"I wanted to make something special for you," I explain. "Something that would surprise and impress your friends." And that was the truth.

"Dad," Victoria says. "Tell her how awesome it was. I saw your buddies wolfing it down."

My father finds the bottle he's looking for and then says, "Gwendolyn, if you want to stay in business, you'll find it's best to deliver what people ask for. People have certain expectations and it's your job to make good on what you promise. People who have plans don't like surprises."

I grit my teeth and Victoria gives him an epic eye-roll as he goes back out to the patio.

"Ginny Howell is allergic to nuts," Mom says. "You could have killed her."

Victoria groans. "For heaven's sake, Mom, she's not *that*

allergic. She just breaks out into a little rash sometimes. Like I do after drinking malbec." She crosses her arms and huffs. "Besides, I put out a little sign next to it that said it contained nuts and dairy. You'd have seen that if you bothered to try it. And tell me it wasn't completely gorgeous."

Mom picks at an invisible spot on her dress and says, "It was pretty, yes."

Have mercy. My mother would rather be thrown into a volcano than give me an actual compliment. I cringe as Logan comes back inside with a slice of cake because still, after all the praise, that image of Lee Anne spitting a mouthful into a napkin is burned into my brain.

"I had to wrestle it away from a stodgy guy with a cane," he says. "But I'm pretty sure it was his second piece."

He smiles at me and my heart swells.

"You have to taste it," Victoria says. "It's one of her best." I love my sister for that, and as she speaks I'm overcome by a moment of bravery. Mom might love that cake or hate it, but I can't leave without knowing she tried it. Baking might be my superpower, but I know everyone has different tastes. (I mean, how else do you explain those vomit-flavored jellybeans that were so dang popular?) If my mom hates the flavor, then fine. At least we'd be basing our opinions on facts and taste-testing. But I refuse to let her hold this against me if she only goes by her friends' opinions and doesn't even bother to try it herself.

"Try it," I tell her. "If you don't like it, you can be as mad as you want to, and I'll send your payment back."

Logan gives me a reassuring smile and hands her a fork.

Victoria's mouth drops open. I know what she's thinking— and I did already have a plan for that money. But I'm not about to give my mother something else to complain about, and I'm certainly not going to let her think I tricked her just to get a big, fat check.

My mother stares at the slice of cake like it's a snake. "It's green," she says.

"It's all natural color," I counter. The matcha layer is a pale shade of green and looks even better than I'd hoped. The pistachio layers and the buttercream are warm, complementary tones, and the raspberry gives it a surprise pop of color. I cut a bite off with the fork and held it toward my mother. "Just taste it," I say.

She takes the fork and—amazingly—puts the whole bite of cake in her mouth.

Victoria stares at me and my heart twists into a knot.

My mother chews slowly, her expression unreadable. I pray to whatever deities are lingering nearby that the Griffin women share the same taste buds—it's only fair since we share the same thin brows, wide hips, and preference for Hemsworth over Evans.

My mother swallows and blinks at me. "It's not bad," she mutters. "But I would have preferred vanilla."

I'll take that as a win.

Mom stands and says, "I should get back to our guests." She straightens her dress, a navy satin sheath that fits like a glove, and dabs her lips with a napkin.

When she's out the door, Victoria digs into the abandoned slice of cake. "Rock star," she says, pointing her fork at me. "Help me with this. If I finish the whole thing, this dress is going to bust a critical seam." She licks her fork and pulls the plate closer. "Actually, never mind. I don't care."

A few feet away, Logan's leaning against the counter, hands shoved into his pockets. He gives me a warm smile that sends a tingle of electric current all the way down to my toes.

"Thanks, Vic," I tell her. "For everything you said."

"I meant every word." She winks at me, and something squeezes in my chest. "I did an unofficial poll if you're interested," she says. "I made the rounds asking folks what they thought of this new signature seasonal flavor of yours. I'd be happy to report my findings. I also posted a bunch of pictures on Instagram because you need all the help you can get there." She takes another big bite and says, "You're welcome."

"I owe you one," I tell her. She managed to rein Mom in and stop this failure from being a complete disaster.

"Bake one of these for my birthday and we'll call it even."

I glance over at Logan and say, "Meet you out at the car? I'm just going to tell Mom we're leaving."

"Sure," he says and steals a bite of cake.

Victoria's eyes widen as she jabs her fork at him. "That's a good way to lose a finger, my man."

He frowns. "I flew two thousand miles for you, remember?"

She arches a brow. "Okay, that's your one pass."

When I go out into the hall to grab my jacket, my mother intercepts me in the hallway.

"We're taking off," I tell her. "Talk to you later, okay?"

"Gwendolyn," she says, keeping her voice low. "A word." She steers me toward the end of the hallway, away from the guests. Satisfied that we're hidden, she says, "I hope that man is not who you plan to bring to your sister's wedding."

"What's that supposed to mean?" I say, too stunned to say anything more.

"Sweetheart." She glances toward the dining room as if to check that none of her friends are in earshot. "I only want the best for you, but you're out of your depth with that one."

"Out of my depth? Gee, thanks, Mom." I feel my cheeks burning with anger. Or is it embarrassment?

"That's not an insult, honey. I'm only saying that he's like a Kennedy. And you're, well…not."

I laugh. "A Kennedy? Come on, Mom. You've known the guy for five minutes. I know he's not—"

"I know how to use Google," she snaps, crossing her arms. "I'm a boomer, not an idiot. Don't you know who that man's family is?"

Her words sting, because of course I know all about his family and how very different our lives are.

"We'll be going now," I tell her. "Thank you for the invitation."

"Victoria told me who he was after we walked in on you," she pauses and looks at the ceiling, "that morning."

"Omigod. Good night, Mom."

"You know how people around here talk," she says, reaching for my arm. "I just don't want you to be hurt."

"And why would I be hurt?"

"I understand some relationships are…short-lived," she says, and at that moment, I know exactly what she means. She thinks I'm the Cinderella in this story, but there's no way I'm winning a prince. This is no fairy tale.

"That's not the kind of man you need," she says. "And parading around someone you're having a casual relationship with is a bit crass, don't you think?"

I roll my eyes so hard they hurt. "And you know the kind of man I need?"

"I just don't want you to embarrass yourself," she says.

My cheeks are hot enough to fry an egg and I feel like my whole head is on fire.

"Take it easy, Mom. I can take care of myself. My reputation is just fine. And so is yours." My heart feels like it's lodged itself in my throat, but I don't want her to know how badly her words hurt.

Jacket in hand, I stride out the front door and go around the yard to where the car is parked. Logan steps down from the deck, where he's been chatting with my dad.

"Goodnight, Dad," I say with a wave.

"Goodnight, dear," he calls as if he hadn't cut me off at the knees ten minutes before.

"Shall we?" I ask Logan. "I've had about all the festive I can take for one night."

He drops his hand to the small of my back and something flutters in my chest. When he opens the passenger door of his car for me, like a perfect gentleman, I bite my lip and will myself not to cry. We're headed back to the lake, on a dark road that winds through the woods. He's talking to me the whole way, but it's hard to focus on what he's saying because I can't get my mother's words out of my head.

Out of my depth, she said, as if it's plain as day to everyone.

As if I'm the one who's kidding herself.

Chapter Twenty

LOGAN

When Gwen knocks on my door, it's nearly eight o'clock in the evening. I haven't heard from her since the party at her mom's last night, which is unusual because we're in the habit of texting each other during the day. She was so quiet on the way home that I knew she was upset about something. But she clearly didn't want to talk about it and I didn't want to press her. Gwen locks herself up like a fortress when something hurts her, and even though I want to knock all those walls down and slip inside with her so she isn't alone, I know I have to give her space. She'll come to me when she's ready.

Now, she's holding a big paper bag with handles and looking like the cat that ate the cream. When she steps inside, she says, "Do you trust me?"

I shrug. "Of course."

She smiles, pulling something from the bag and tossing it into my arms. When I unfurl the fabric, I see that it's a Christmas sweater. A garish lime green one with pink flamingoes wearing Santa hats with little pom-poms on the tops.

"But I didn't get you anything," I quip.

"We're going to an ugly sweater party. It's tradition."

I hold the sweater up to my chest, halfway hoping it won't fit.

"It'll fit," she says, reading my mind. "I hand-picked it for you."

"And what about you?"

She smirks and unbuttons her wool coat to reveal a sweater with a blinding red and green zig-zag pattern that boasts an appliqué of a giant cat tangled in lights. She's paired it with bright green checkered pants that look like they've come back from Christmas 1974. Her red Doc Martens are the icing on the cake.

"Impressive," I tell her. I slip out of my button-down, leaving my tee shirt underneath, and hold my breath as I pull on the hideous flamingo sweater. It's so tacky, it's sort of cool.

"This is the one Christmas party I look forward to," she says. "Every year, Eli Bell hosts the Amazing Ugly Sweater party, and after we've had enough reindeer games and out-of-this-world eggnog, we all vote on the winner. Ghastly sweaters from Christmas Pasts are highly encouraged—but those of us who burned all the evidence of our past fashion mistakes are left to shop for new ones. Or borrow from the cache." She nods her approval and says, "Yours came from Eli's trunk, so you might be a shoo-in for the winner. Although he does tend to buy new ones every year because he's ridiculously competitive about it."

"Dare I ask what the winner gets?" I say.

She smiles again and it's like the sun coming out from behind a cloud. "It would be wrong to spoil the surprise."

When we pull up to Eli's house—a lovely farmhouse out from town—Gwen slips a headband from her purse and shoves it into her hair. It has fuzzy antlers and tiny bells on top that jingle when she shakes her head.

"You didn't mention accessories," I say. "Now I have zero chance of winning."

She pulls a hat from her bag and sticks it on my head—a beanie with flickering LED lights. "It would be unfair to leave you with an incomplete ensemble," she says.

"This use of color is criminal," I say, looking down at my sweater.

"You'll fit right in." And when she says it, I realize that I want to. I want to meet Gwen's friends and get along with her family. I know I'm supposed to leave soon, but I really don't want to anymore.

I've been feeling that way for days, but it still shocks me.

"Mom's party took three years off my life," she says. "This one will be fun. I promise."

"It wasn't that bad, was it?" I say, thinking specifically of that scalding kiss we shared in the pantry.

She huffs. "Complete disaster," she says, getting out of the car. "I should never have agreed to make that cake. And I was out of my mind to make the matcha."

"You *could* think about it that way," I tell her. "Or, you could consider that you made a bold move and took a risk. Not everyone's got enough guts to do that."

She looks stunning here in the moonlight, even in that ridiculous sweater. I'm trying desperately to focus more on her words than her full lips and the way that every time we're together, it just feels *right*.

So far, I'm unsuccessful. Ever since that night in my kitchen, all I can think about is her lips. And the way she used them to drive me out of my mind with want. Because in the last few days, everything I thought I wanted has fallen by the wayside. What I want most is Gwen.

"It was selfish," she says. "I should have just baked what she asked for. Plain vanilla, safe as you can get. Safe was what she wanted."

"Hey," I say giving her shoulder a nudge. "I'm proud of you.

Taking steps forward—even small steps—is better than not moving at all. You took a chance, and you made something amazing. Not everyone's going to love what you do. But they sure as heck can't call you boring." I shrug. "Plus, a lot of people did like it. It was a stunner."

"You're a little biased." She gives me a tiny smile, staring up at me through those long lashes. "But thank you." She seems more distant tonight, and I want to know why. This seems to be about more than just a cake.

Before I can ask her, she takes my hand and leads me up to the front porch of the house. There's a huge barn out back, and a dozen cars already parked in the yard. Between the barn and the house is a patio with a cozy seating area lit with strings of big outdoor lights.

"Eli's a metal artist," Gwen says. "He renovated that barn and made it into a forge." Next to it are two massive metal sculptures like the kind you'd put in a garden. "His grandmother Maxine heads up the arts council in town."

"Right, I met her last night. She's a cool lady."

When Gwen opens the front door, a wave of music and laughter washes over me. Fiona waves to us from across the room and makes a beeline for us, grinning from ear to ear.

"You're here!" Fiona squeals and her fuzzy Santa hat nearly topples from her head. "And you brought Logan. I'm so glad."

"Thanks for having me," I say.

"Wouldn't have it any other way." Fiona links one arm in Gwen's and one in mine and leads us into the kitchen. "We have fruit punch and eggnog and they're both high-octane," she says.

The house looks like the set of a Christmas movie. Lights are strung along the exposed beams, dotted in the potted plants, and even hanging from the windows like icicles. Every surface is covered in garlands and giant red bows, and in the corner is one of those massive silver Christmas trees from the 1950s that rotates like it's sitting on a record player.

"My grandparents had a tree just like that," I say.

"Pretty sure that's Maxine's," Fiona says. "Genuine vintage. Alex and I helped with the decorations."

"You've outdone yourself," Gwen says, scanning the room. "There's more holiday spirit here than the rest of South Carolina put together."

"It's been a while since I got to decorate a tree," Fiona says with a smirk. "I might have gone overboard."

In the den, there's an old Christmas movie playing on the big screen TV, the sound muted so you can hear the music from the stereo. Once Gwen explains the elf-on-the-shelf tradition, I see them set up in mini-tableaus all over the house. So far I've clocked two rappelling down the side of the punch bowl, two piled into a Barbie convertible with a mini-bottle of rum and a couple of stuffed reindeer, and one bungee-jumping from a limb of the Christmas tree with a group of dinosaurs watching.

This is not the kind of Christmas party I'd be at if I were in Skye right now.

And I love it.

Fiona leads us into the kitchen where two guys are refilling platters of finger food. "Logan, this is Alex and Eli. Guys, this is Logan."

"Thanks for the invite," I say to Eli. A broad-shouldered Black man, Eli towers over me. When he shakes my hand, his grip is firm and his eyes are warm. His bright red sweater looks electric against his dark skin and when he smiles, he lights up the room. Knitted into his sweater are little polar bears with scarves and martini glasses, and it seems to suit him perfectly.

"Heard you wanted the full Jasmine Falls experience," he says.

"You came to the right place," the other guy says with a nod.

"I'm Alex." He gives Fiona a quick kiss on the cheek and goes back to piling gingerbread cookies onto a platter.

"Nice sweater," I say.

Alex grins, pushing a spot on his chest to make the snowflakes light up around the snowman. He's as tall as Eli, with a brawny build and dark hair styled in a faux-hawk.

"He's oddly proud of his collection of these," Fiona says, giving him a playful nudge.

"That's one of my favorites," Eli says, nodding towards the sweater I'm wearing, one from his collection.

"Bonus points for the vintage ones," Alex says. "We had some of these before it was cool to have ugly holiday sweaters. And we have the photos to prove it."

"We should have a slide show of those," Gwen says. "I need to see that proof."

"Snacks are in the living room," Fiona says. "Win, Lose, or Draw starts in ten."

After we get our drinks, Gwen leads me back through the house, toward the porch. "They take their reindeer games seriously around here," she says. "We might need a safe word for when they break out Twister and the slip and slide."

"What exactly have I gotten myself into here?" I ask her.

"Hey, you wanted small-town fun, Lancelot," she says. "You got it."

AS IT TURNS OUT, I was a champion at Win, Lose, or Draw. Our clues were holiday-themed (of course), and Gwen and I were totally on the same wavelength through all of our movie and music references. Plus, she was great at drawing while I was stellar at blurting out lots of words that the rest of our team could arrange into actual book and movie titles. We were smashing the other team until the last round, when we got stuck on "Baby Please Come Home" (my fault, because my baby looked like a croissant with ears and sent everyone down the Yoda track) and the other team blew past us with a streak of classic movies from the 90s.

"We were so close," Gwen says. She leads me out onto the porch and I'm starting to feel like I'd follow her anywhere.

So much for not catching feelings.

This woman has my full attention, from the tips of her fuzzy antlers to the soles of her red velvet sneakers.

"I can't remember the last time I enjoyed a holiday party," I confess because it feels like about a million years. "I'm quite jealous of your friends."

She smiles, leaning against the porch rail. "Right? If only every holiday gathering was this much fun."

In truth, it's been years since I had a tight-knit bunch of friends to hang out with—the kind that made me feel like I could relax and be myself. In my family, parties meant milling around in a big cold drafty house while everyone stood around in stuffy suits and fancy dresses, trying to one-up each other with their recent acquisitions and mergers. Those parties weren't about community. They were just one more part of the Fyfe lifestyle that made me feel like I didn't belong.

I hadn't realized how much I missed that feeling of belonging until now. Being here in Jasmine Falls, with Gwen, has made me see other things that are missing from my life, too. In a few days, I'll be headed home—and with every day that passes here, that idea seems less appealing. When I chose this town for my getaway, I'd just been looking for a place to lay low and forget about my family for a minute. I hadn't expected to make friends and have fun—or to have any big epiphanies about how I wanted to spend my life. And I certainly hadn't expected to fall in love.

But that's absolutely what happened because now I'm having trouble picturing my life without Gwen.

"What are the chances your sister might sell me her lake house?" I ask.

Gwen coughs into her drink. "Being my neighbor is that much fun, is it?"

I shrug. "Yeah. It is."

She stares at me like she's just seen a yeti walk out of the woods behind us. "You're serious?" she says.

"I like it here. I like you." I lean closer and she fixes her big blue eyes on mine as I say, "What if I didn't have to leave?"

Her mouth drops open into a tiny O.

"Hey!" Fiona shouts, poking her head out the door. "You two are missing all the fun. Eli's setting up the limbo pole." She points at me and says, "Logan, how are you at limbo?"

I glance at Gwen and she still looks stunned. "Most days, I feel like it's my middle name," I say.

"Great," Fiona says, her eyes brightening. "Sadie's won three years running and I love her, but it's obnoxious." She stretches one arm over her side, and then the other. "I've been practicing," she says, looking determined. "But I could use some backup."

I can't decide if Gwen is relieved to be interrupted as Fiona ushers us back into the house. But I want to know how she feels about my question because I was only half-joking. As soon as the words were out of my mouth, I imagined what it would be like to move here—and the surprising thing?

It wasn't hard to imagine. Not at all.

Chapter Twenty-One

GWEN

Logan's surprisingly flexible for a tall person. But still, he's no match for Sadie at the limbo pole.

Sadie's our reigning champ because she's the only one out of all of us who practices yoga for more than an hour a month. To be fair, the pole isn't set very low because we're a bunch of people in our thirties who by now have had enough eggnog to fill a small pool. But what we lack in flexibility, we make up for in showmanship.

Eli and Alex didn't make it past the second round, but in their defense, they're the tallest people here and everyone knows that height is not your friend when you're under the limbo bar. They're also built like linebackers because of all their metalsmithing, and having a Hulk-like amount of upper body muscle doesn't help you maneuver under the pole, either. The only reason I made it to the third round was because my foot slipped in the grass when I was halfway under, dropping me the necessary two inches to get my nose under the bar.

Fiona and I were keeping up with Sadie until the last round. But then my chest bumped the bar and knocked it to the ground. Fiona slapped me a high-five and said, "If we weren't built like pin-ups, we'd have this thing in the bag," and Logan nearly choked on his eggnog.

But she's not wrong. And now Logan's blushing all the way to the tips of his ears and trying hard not to stare at my chest.

Fiona knocks the bar down on her next turn and Sadie dances over to easily glide under, as flexible as a noodle.

Cheers erupt all around us, and Sadie's fiancé James scoops her into his arms and dips her for a dramatic kiss.

After Sadie reclaims her crown (which is an actual paper crown made with aluminum foil and wrapping paper), she dances a victory lap around the backyard to applause and whistles.

Laughter fills the air and I love that these people are my family. They're the people who love me just as I am and don't make a sport of trying to change me.

Logan nudges my arm. "Thanks for another first, Gwen Griffin."

"First time under a limbo pole?" I ask him.

"This'll be etched in my memory forever." He gives me a look that I can't quite decipher, and I think back to him asking about the lake house. Was he serious? Surely he was joking. No one wants to move to Jasmine Falls after being here for five minutes. Especially men like Logan who sell apps for boatloads of money and have investment portfolios larger than this whole state's operating budget. My head's reeling and I can't think about all the things that might mean right now—or what I want it to mean.

My phone buzzes in my pocket, but I ignore it. Logan's watching my friends goof around, his hands shoved into his jean pockets, and he looks a little wistful.

"Hey, you okay?" I ask him.

He turns to me and gives me a tiny smile. "Thanks for bringing me here." He looks genuinely grateful, and I realize that for me, this was just a goofy party. A way to blow off some steam. For him, it seems to be a lot more.

My phone buzzes again with multiple texts, and I finally pull it from my pocket.

Are you okay? Victoria writes. **Don't worry. Let's talk about it later. I have some ideas.**

And then: **I know you're at the party, so just call me tomorrow.**

It sounds weird and ominous, and that's not something Victoria usually does. If it were an emergency with Mom or Dad, she'd say so. I unlock the phone and then see multiple texts from Maggie.

Hey, I just saw, she writes. **I'm so sorry! I'm already on it. Also, don't worry. We got this.**

But I *am* starting to worry, because what the heck is going on? And why are my sister and Maggie trying to keep me calm? I keep scrolling as my heart starts to race.

"Gwen?" Logan's voice cuts through the thoughts like a knife and I realize he's been talking this whole time. "Everything all right?"

"I don't know yet," I say, still scrolling.

He steps closer and lays his hand on my shoulder, and I'm grateful for the feeling of him rooting me to the earth.

I'll rock your social media, Maggie writes. **I'll post those videos we took last week. We'll bury this story.** **Heart emojis**

What's going on? I write back, feeling my throat tightening. **What's happened?**

Three dots appear and it's an eternity before Maggie replies with a link.

Holding my breath, I click the link. It sends me to the state paper's website—an article about holiday activities in Jasmine Falls. I quickly scan the article, scrolling down, down, until I see.

And then all the air whooshes right out of my lungs, and I let out a pitiful squeak.

"No," I say. "No, no!"

"What's going on?" Logan says.

"Gwen?" Fiona steps to my other side. "What's the matter, babe?"

I hold the phone out so they can see. "A write-up about the Bean," I sputter. "It's bad."

Fiona grabs the phone and reads, her lips forming a hard line. It's worse than bad. It's horrendous.

Logan joins her, reading over her shoulder. His jaw tenses.

Fiona snorts. "This woman's a doofus," she says. "Nobody reads this."

My chest tightens. "It's the state paper, Fi. Everyone reads it."

She rolls her eyes. "Yeah, but not this section." She's trying to make me feel better, but the truth is that this is a disaster. Everyone around here reads the Holiday Round-up because they're looking for fun small-town things to do in the winter, and looking for new businesses to try—or ignore.

And this article will turn people away. It's a piece about the town's holiday highlights: the hayride through the orchard, the caroling in the town square, the kid outside the town limits who strung up tens of thousands of lights and synced them to holiday pop songs. The writer did a round-up of shops in town selling local products, like the boutique that sells cute animal costumes, the bookstore that has a window tableau featuring "hidden gem" holiday books, and the Spare Time with its farm-to-table Christmas favorites.

And the Sentient Bean.

Each shop has just a couple of lines dedicated to an item or two that piqued the writer's interest. The Sentient Bean is praised for its kitschy decor and panned for the matcha cake— the only item the writer deigned to write about.

"Ah, it's not so bad," Logan says. "It's just one review."

"One review?" I cry. "She said it tasted like a freshly mowed lawn!"

Logan arches a brow. "Who is this person? A top food critic?"

Fiona huffs. "She wishes."

"Okay, so that's not a huge setback," Logan says. "Everyone gets bad reviews. Just makes you legit."

"She's a popular travel writer," I say, crossing my arms over my chest. "The sweetheart of Columbia." My cheeks feel hot. "Everyone reads it. The whole town will see this." The more I think about it, the worse it feels—like I'm being kicked when I'm down. "First Mom's party, and now this," I mutter.

Fiona frowns. "First off, Shelby Helms is hardly a sweetheart. She also has incredibly bland taste in restaurants, and everyone knows it. Her superpower is sniffing out nostalgia and charm and making every tiny town sound like Stars Hollow." She sighs, dropping her hand onto my shoulder. "That woman wouldn't know a good dessert if it landed in her face because she hasn't tasted natural sugar in thirty years."

"I knew I shouldn't have put that cake out for sale," I groan. "The one day I put out a crazy flavor, that's when a critic shows up. I should have done a taste test in the shop first." I collapse into one of the chairs in the backyard. "But it was so pretty, and I was so excited. Maggie and I had the leftover layers and I just wanted to put something new out there." I rested my forehead in my hand and mutter, "So stupid."

"Stop," Fiona says. "It wasn't stupid."

Logan squeezes my shoulder. "Don't let this get you down, love. It's one person's opinion. Making new products is always a risk," he says, and his voice is soothing even though the words are not. "Some people will love it, and some people will hate it. You can't let that stop you from trying."

I want the ground to swallow me up. "I feel sick." I think

back to Mom's party, to Lee Anne Hardwick spitting her bite of cake into a napkin and I want to crawl into a hole and never come out.

"Hey," Fiona says, kneeling in front of me. "This is nothing. That travel show that James and Sadie were filming—it airs in a few weeks, right?"

I nod. Thank goodness for the travel show—James Fielding is an excellent travel writer. And a handsome internet darling who people love to watch. The segment that he and Sadie filmed with me is bound to get us some attention. I just hope it won't come too late.

"Think of how many people will watch that," Fiona says. "It'll get way more views than some dumb web article from the state paper."

Logan says, "You're in a TV episode?"

"It's a travel show that James and Sadie did together for a big deal streaming service," Fiona tells him, and the pride in her voice warms me right up. "They're basically celebrities now—or they will be once that show drops. It's going to be outstanding."

"That's incredible," Logan says. "Why didn't you tell me about that?"

I shrug. Because I always fixate on the bad things more than the good?

"I'm going to head home," I say. Suddenly, all I want to do is climb under the big heavy covers on my bed and stay there for a day or two. This feels like a humiliating rookie mistake—something I wouldn't have done if I hadn't been so eager to prove Mom wrong about me. My friends are all being so supportive, but that irritating voice that lives down deep is telling me they're being nice because they're my friends—not because this isn't the result of a bad decision.

I turn to Logan and say, "I can call a rideshare so you can stay."

He snorts. "No way. I'm taking you home." His tone is so definitive that it makes the little hairs on my neck tingle. I do enjoy this man's authoritative side.

"If you insist."

"Aye, I do," he says, reaching for my hand.

That insistence of his is growing on me, too.

Fiona pulls me into a hug and says, "Don't rent space in your head to this woman." She squeezes me hard like a tight hug might force all the painful feelings right out of me, and I love her for that. "Shake it off, like Taylor says. I'll see you Wednesday."

In that second, a bolt of cold shoots through me and I'm reeling all over again.

Wednesday. Oh crap.

"Logan, lovely to see you again," Fiona says. "I hope we'll see you Wednesday, too."

Logan glances at me and seems to register the dread that has filled my body. "What's Wednesday?" he says.

A knot forms in my throat.

"The holiday auction," Fiona says. Behind her, Alex calls her name and she hollers, "Be right there!" She gives us a kiss and a wave and says, "Later, y'all," as if she hasn't just completely skewered me.

My limbs have stopped working. Logan opens the car door for me and I pour myself inside, already thinking of how I might back out of this auction. Can I? Would that just make this all worse?

"So what's the deal with this auction?" he says.

My heart's pounding so hard I can barely breathe. "I have to cancel. There's no way I can do it now."

"This is like a charity auction? Did you donate a cake?"

"I donated myself," I grumble. "But now I have to back out. I can't take any more humiliation."

"You mean like a date?" he says. His jaw tenses again as if

he's perturbed by that idea. Is that jealousy making his teeth clench?

I turn to face him and sigh. "Baking lessons."

He smiles and steals a glance at me, and that is definitely relief in his eyes. "Aye, that's brilliant."

That hollow feeling in my chest is back. I roll down the car window, needing to feel the cool air. "Except no one's going to want baking lessons from me now, after all of this. I'll have zero bids and be humiliated in front of everyone in town. Again." I rub my temples, where an ache blooms.

We pull into the driveway at the lake house and he puts the car in park. Then Logan turns to me and places his hand on my forearm.

"Hey," he says. "Look at me."

I shake my head, feeling the sting that comes right before tears start falling.

Sliding his thumb over my cheek, he says, "Gwen Griffin, you look me in the eye, love."

When I turn to face him, his eyes are wide in the dim light. "I know this hurts. But you are so much more than one cake. One event. You have to know that. You've taken on a huge task—and you're winning."

I let out a heavy sigh. I'm just so tired from everything: the injury, the holiday rush, the way everything's been upended in the last few weeks. And now Victoria's wedding is just days away and it feels like I'm in a nose-dive, spiraling towards the earth.

He lifts a brow and pins me with his gaze. "I know it doesn't always feel like you're winning, but you built this business from nothing, did you not?"

I nod. "Yeah."

"Just you, correct? No partners or investors."

"I had help from my friends."

"You hired employees. You bought a building. You've been steadily growing for how long?"

"Three years."

"If you don't have some rough days, then you're not doing it right."

I lean back against the headrest, feeling the calm take hold.

"Ask me how many of my businesses have failed," he says.

I turn back to him, surprised by the idea of Logan failing at anything. "How many?"

"Counting one crazy idea in uni…six."

"Seriously?" I study him for a moment, processing that idea.

"Failure isn't bad. It's just a part of the process." He reaches over to brush a lock of hair from my face and the warmth from his fingertip spreads along my cheek. "People here love you. One flavor that bombed isn't going to end your career."

"Lee Anne already emailed me about her order for the big holiday party. She told me she just wanted to double check that she'd ordered a strawberry-vanilla cake because she—quote—didn't want there to be any unfortunate mix-ups."

"So she's a worrier. That's okay, that's not your problem. She didn't cancel, right?"

I shrug and he gives me a gentle smile. "People can be fickle," he says, "But it's pretty clear from your mom's party that everyone in this town adores you. I'd wager that you could swap salt for sugar in the next cake, and you'd still have a pile of orders."

"Inaccurate. That last part anyway."

"Go to the auction," he says. "I'll come with you."

"Oh no. I'm canceling. I'm not going to be that person that gets no bids and makes them start dropping the price."

"That won't happen."

I shake my head again. "Nope. You don't know that."

"Let me rephrase." He leans closer, fixing me with his stare. "I won't let that happen."

I groan. "Can't let you do that. No pity bids."

"Who said anything about pity?" he says. "I want baking lessons."

I give him an unladylike snort. "I appreciate the offer, but I can't keep letting you ride to my rescue. I don't want to depend on someone that way."

"I know you don't, gorgeous." He sighs, bringing my hand to his lips. "But there's no use in punishing yourself, either. Help isn't always the same as rescue."

I stare at him for a long moment, a jumble of feelings swirling around inside me. I love that he cares enough to want to help me, but I hate that I can't seem to do these things on my own. I'm supposed to be able to fix my own problems and support myself, to run my business, and not fall on my face. I'm supposed to be able to do hard things without leaning on someone else.

And I'm not supposed to be falling for a man who's already told me he's leaving this place.

I'm not supposed to be falling in love.

Chapter Twenty-Two

GWEN

By the time Logan knocks on my door, I've tried on every combination of skirt and sweater that I own before landing on a teal wrap dress that cinches at the waist and makes my breasts look amazing. If I'm going to be humiliated at this auction, I'm at least going to look like a million bucks while it happens.

Logan knocks again, louder this time, and I quickly peel off the half-slip that's proving itself completely unnecessary by clinging to my thighs with enough static electricity to ignite a wildfire. I hurry to the door, stepping over the pile of discarded sheaths and slips, and cardigans left in my wake.

As I open the door I can't stop my eyeballs from taking a leisurely route from Logan's perfectly tousled hair, down the lines of his stylish navy blue suit to his big hands that rest on his hips. He gives me a sexy smirk that sends a zip of electric current straight down to my toes.

Mercy. It should be illegal to wear a suit tailored that well.

"Hi there, gorgeous," he says, his voice doing that sexy rumble thing again.

"Hi yourself. Nice suit, Lancelot."

He shrugs. "It's an important night for you. I wanted to make a good impression."

"Well, mission accomplished, sir."

His smile turns wicked and it takes every ounce of my willpower not to yank him inside by his lovely silk tie.

"Come on in," I tell him. "I just need a minute."

As he steps inside, I hurry to the bedroom and zip on my tan knee boots. Giving my hair one last finger-comb, I put on a little lipstick and grab my purse. In the front room, Logan's leaning against the kitchen island, nonchalantly eyeing the papers I left scattered there.

"Hey," he says. "This woman sounds a lot like you." Sometimes at night, when I can't sleep, I thumb through actual glossy magazines that let me geek out over kitchen renovations, local emerging chefs, and exquisite cakes that leave me drooling. This particular magazine has a profile of another cake artist down in Atlanta who, like me, started with a coffee shop and bakery and then quickly grew into a regional sensation. I have a vision board in my bedroom that's full of pages ripped from magazines like that one. One day, I want to be written up in a national magazine—just a little double-page spread that sings the praises of my newest cake flavor and swoon-worthy decorating skills—nothing too over-the-top.

But tonight, I'll settle for leaving the Cabin Fever Holiday Auction with my dignity intact.

"Yeah, she's amazing," I sigh. "I'd love to be her when I grow up."

"Sounds to me like you're hot on her heels," he says, and my heart flutters like a bird.

He offers his arm and leads me outside. "Ready to rock this auction? I did a little snooping today and I found quite a few things I might be interested in. You might need to explain goat yoga to me, though. Is that what I think it is?" He lifts a brow as if considering the mechanics of that. "They make it sound all relaxing, but the thought of those sharp little hooves…"

"It's actually a lot of fun," I tell him. "I tried it last year and I'm not great at yoga, so I mostly petted the goats and fed them greens. But I did leave feeling more relaxed."

"Would you do goat yoga with me, love?"

"Only because I owe you a few favors. Maybe their little hooves could re-align my chakras so I never have another matcha incident ever again."

He lifts a brow and places his big hands on my shoulders, stopping me in my tracks. "You need to stop beating yourself up, okay? No more." His eyes burn into mine. "I wouldn't listen to anyone else go on about you this way, and I won't listen while you do it, either."

I swallow hard. He's insisting again, but he's not wrong. All these things I think about myself, though—it doesn't feel like punishment. It feels like consequences for my decisions. Yet another thing I'm supposed to be able to deal with as an adult business owner.

"Tell me you understand," he says. He is voice is gentle, but firm.

"Fair enough," I say.

He kisses me on the temple. "Good."

***

THE GYM at Jasmine Falls High is packed. But it always is for the holiday auction. The stage is set up at one end of the basketball court with two dozen rows of chairs. A knot forms in my stomach as we walk inside, and I quickly pull Logan back into the lobby. The high school looks the same as it did when I graduated, just a bit brighter with a new coat of paint. It still has the old pine floors and the big mural painted with our beloved Freddie the Falcon.

By now everyone's had time to read that article in the state paper. It hurts to breathe and I've never wanted to disappear so badly in my life.

"Hey," Logan says, whispering close to my ear. "It's going to be fine." He slips his hand into mine, twining our fingers together, and it's about the sweetest gesture he could make.

I hate that I still feel like I'm going to hurl.

Tables are set up with snacks and drinks across the lobby. Lee Anne's standing by the punch bowl with a couple of other ladies from the Arts Commission, and seeing them there elbow to elbow makes me think again of Mom's party and how Lee Anne spit out my cake like it was garnished with ghost peppers.

"I feel sick," I mutter. This is definitely not going to be fine. We are a million light years from *fine*. My heart is racing and I'm sweating like it's the dog days of August. "What if I just leave?" I whisper, my throat closing as I force the words out. "If I'm not here, they can't auction me off, right?"

"I don't think that's an option," Logan says, his voice all smooth and sexy, like there's no catastrophe brewing here.

My eyes dart around the room and come to rest on Paula Sue Hinson, who's pouring herself some punch. She gives me an energetic wave and that escape plan goes right out the window.

"Right," I say. "That would just give them something else to talk about."

"Hey," Logan slides his hand along my forearm and sets those big blue-green eyes on mine. "You can do this. These people adore you." His voice is gentle, like he sees this storm brewing inside me and realizes it's more complex than just embarrassment over a bad decision about flavor. It's like he can see right into me, straight to the bottom of my heart where my deepest fear has taken root. Like he can somehow hear the voice inside my head—the one so insistent and loud, the one that tells me I might know how to fake it, but I'm not good enough to make it.

I shake my head, feeling dizzy and faint, but he steps closer and squeezes my hand.

"I can't do this," I mutter. "I'm out."

His hand cups my cheek and before my brain can even register what that means, he bends down and captures my lips with his. The kiss is tender and sweet, his lips gentle, but firm. His fingers slide along my jaw and then there's the scrape of his scruffy cheek. I lean into him, grabbing the lapels of his jacket, and my heart drops right to the floor.

When he finally pulls away, his eyes are wide and every thought has left my head except for this one: *I've never met a man who made me feel so safe and adored.*

He winks and whispers, "For good luck, even though you don't need it," but that did not feel like a good luck kiss—not even a little bit.

It felt like the kind of kiss that's full of longing and hope and all the delicious, dark things in between.

"Oh my god," I tell him. "You can't kiss me like that right before I go on stage."

"Why not?"

I fuss with the tie of my dress. "Because all I'll be able to think about is you."

He gives me that deadly smirk and says, "Good."

My mouth goes dry and every other thought falls right out of my brain.

Lord have mercy.

"There you are!" A voice from behind me shakes me out of my daze as Fiona grabs me by the elbow. "Everyone's about to line up backstage." Her eyes widen. "Are you okay? You look like you're going to puke."

I nod, still incapable of putting words or thoughts together, because good grief, that one little kiss has short-circuited my brain.

"Logan," she says, "So glad you came."

"Aye, I wouldn't miss it," he says, his gaze drifting back to mine.

"Alex is over there by the snacks if you want to sit with him and Eli," she tells him, oblivious to the fact that my brain is now broken. "You might need some backup—those red-hat ladies are total cougars. They come here straight from happy hour and they'll be all over you. But the boys can help you fend them off."

Logan gives a good-natured laugh and my eyes are still fixed on his mouth. Now I just want this auction to be over so I can feel his lips on me again.

"Can't get too annoyed with them though," Fiona says, "because they save up for these auctions and make a sport of out-bidding each other. Last year they paid for the library's whole renovation."

"Good luck out there." Logan places his hand on my forearm and says, "I'll see you in a while." He strides over to the snack table and Alex gives him a friendly wave. I try not to stare as he walks away, all confident swagger and taut muscle, and…good grief. When this man leaves, he's going to leave a Logan-shaped hole in my heart.

My head is still spinning from that kiss, but Fiona might as well have thrown ice water on me when she says, "It's almost time. You ready, babe?"

"As ready as I can get."

She waves to Alex and then smoothes down the front of her dress. It's a bright floral with a wide belt, and an A-line cut that's retro-chic. "Come on," she says, taking my hand. "Let's do this."

I follow her through the lobby and around to the back entrance to the gym, where all of the other participants are lined up. It usually only takes an hour or so to get through the bidding, but that feels like an eternity right now.

"The hot Scot is completely smitten with you," Fiona says with a smile.

"It's just a friendly thing. Casual." The words taste bitter as I say them.

She purses her lips. "Uh-huh."

"He's leaving in less than two weeks, Fi. There'll be an ocean between us."

She lifts a brow. "Guys like that will move heaven and earth to get what they want. You think an ocean's going to stop that man?"

I wish that were true.

Onstage, the emcee welcomes everyone and outlines the bidding rules, even though we all know them by heart. Nearly everyone from town is always here—if they're not donating, they're bidding.

Paula Sue Hinson appears with her clipboard, getting us all lined up in the proper order. She gives me a quick wave as she approaches.

The butterflies are back, swarming in my belly.

"What's going on with you?" Fiona says, narrowing her eyes. "What are you not telling me?"

"Nothing," I squeak.

She put her hands on her hips. "Spill."

"It's just that dumb web article panning the Bean, stuck in my head. I wanted to back out of this completely, but Logan convinced me not to, and I feel like I'm about to be a laughingstock because no one's going to bid on baking lessons from someone who makes cakes that taste like a cut lawn. And Logan kissed me and I think I'm falling for him, and I really don't want him to leave."

Her eyes are as big as saucers. "I knew it!" she cries. A few heads turn our way and she whispers, "I knew it."

Onstage, the auctioneer is joking with our beloved librarian Charlene Dickson, egging on the crowd as they bid on her costumed story hour. Charlene loves storytelling more than anything. A Type-A all the way, she takes it as a personal challenge to create real-life versions of famous characters in painstakingly accurate detail.

"I knew you caught the feelings," Fiona says, grinning. "You can't keep secrets from me."

I sigh. "We have a bigger immediate problem. Everyone's seen that web article by now. Lee Anne Hardwick wouldn't even look at me out in the lobby."

She rolls her eyes. "That'll be old news in five minutes. People around here are like goldfish." She snaps her fingers as if to reiterate how quickly a goldfish forgets, and I wish it were that simple.

Small towns have long memories.

I put my face in my hands. "I can't take another disaster right now."

"Hey." She squeezes my shoulder. "I love you to bits, but enough with the catastrophic thinking. You made a choice, and you went with what you thought was a good idea. We all make mistakes. You don't get to beat yourself up over this anymore. Got it?"

Heat blooms in my chest as she takes my face in her hands and stares me down with her bright blue eyes. "You are a force of nature and are a brilliant, amazing person. Nobody beats up on my bestie."

I nod, fighting back tears, because she's right—I have to stop being so hard on myself. "Thanks, Fi."

She nods and then the auctioneer calls the next person to the stage.

I let Fiona's words sink in as I take a deep breath and think of last year's auction—how everyone had been excited to bid on my cake decorating lesson. It wasn't the highest earner of the evening, not by far. But there were several bidders, and Janice Campbell (my fifth-grade art teacher) had won. She'd wanted to make a special cake for her granddaughter's thirteenth birthday and we had a blast together.

Sometimes I have to remind myself to focus on the good because my friends are right. It's here, all around me. I've just spent so much time fixating on the bad that the good gets overshadowed.

Fiona's up next, beaming while the auctioneer teases the bidders. Turns out several people want painting lessons from her, and in a blink, we're over five hundred dollars and the gavel crashes down.

I take another deep breath, tamping down those butterflies. Two minutes, and this will be over.

Fiona hurries offstage and makes a beeline for me. "Okay," she says, smacking me a high-five. "You got this, lady."

Ugh.

She has to give me a little shove to make my feet move. Paula Sue grabs my elbow and ushers me toward the stage as I hear the auctioneer say, "And next up is an exciting weekend baking lesson…"

The gym is packed. Logan's sitting between Alex and Eli, just two rows from the stage. Alex grins and offers a thumbs-up. Logan gives me a nod and an easy smile and I tamp down the tornado of butterflies in my belly. The bidding starts low and there's one raised hand in the back, then a pause and another closer to the front.

Ugh. It's Ellen Radcliffe. She makes a sport out of telling everyone how they're wrong about literally everything. She's a real-life energy vampire and a couple hours with her would leave me a shriveled husk of a human.

But two bids are not zero bids. *Look for the good.*

That thought leads my gaze right back to Logan because he's very, very good. When he gives me a reassuring wink, I can't help but smile. Grandma June told me once that you meet people when you need to—even the ones who are only in your life for a brief while. I still hate the thought of him leaving, but I'm awfully glad he's here.

"Going once," the auctioneer says, his voice low. "Are y'all gonna let the lovely Miss Ellen get this weekend of lessons for a steal? Seems criminal to me."

Ellen smiles her toothy smile that usually sends people running for the hills. I look over at Logan, who is doing exactly what I asked him to do and not rescue me. But still, I wish with all my might that he'll somehow understand what a dire situation this is because a weekend with Ellen Radcliffe will be insufferable. Logan lifts a brow and I try my hardest to send a telepathic message that Ellen is like a velociraptor in a cocktail dress and if he ever was inclined to get up on his big white horse and prove that I was wrong to refuse his aid, it's now.

At stage right, Fiona's biting her lip, furiously typing on her cell phone. With a sigh, I resign myself to the thought of spending a whole weekend listening to Ellen Radcliffe critique my baking skills and my life choices because nothing's off-limits in a town this small.

"This lady's getting a bargain," the auctioneer says. "Going twice."

Alex glances at Logan and then raises his hand and calls, "Two hundred."

Bless you, Alex. Ellen's a piranha, but she's also a bargain hunter. She leans forward in her chair and sets her steely eyes on him.

Logan turns to Alex, smirking playfully, and then his hand shoots in the air as he shouts, "Two-fifty."

On his other side, Eli shouts, "Three hundred!"

"Dude," Alex scolds.

"What?" Eli says. "I need all the help I can get in the kitchen."

The auctioneer teases them about who needs baking skills the most, playing them off each other. Fiona gives me an innocent shrug as she tucks her phone back into the pocket of her dress. The guys keep up their good-natured routine, upping the ante in fifty-dollar increments until Ellen scowls and sits back in her chair with her arms crossed tight over her chest.

The crowd loves it.

Alex grins at Logan and says, "Come on man, I want to learn to make something pretty for my fiancée. I get bonus points when I cook."

Logan shrugs as he quips, "Sorry, mate. I was never any good at sharing." Then he turns toward the stage and shouts, "Two thousand."

My jaw drops. Gasps and chuckles ripple through the crowd. Just offstage to my right, Fiona gives me a big smile, placing her hand over her heart. She no doubt texted Alex when she saw Ellen closing in, and I will love her forever for this.

Alex throws his hands up in mock defeat and then makes a gentlemanly bow toward Logan as the auctioneer cries, "Sold to the mystery man," and slams down the gavel.

Holy banana pancakes.

Chapter Twenty-Three

LOGAN

"Two thousand?" Gwen hollers. "Are you out of your mind?"

I shrug. "You're worth it."

Her mouth falls open and her eyes widen.

She's so cute when she blushes. No, scratch that. Not cute—completely gorgeous and one hundred percent irresistible. Even onstage, under those bright gymnasium lights, I could see the pink in her cheeks and it was driving me mad thinking of all the ways I could make her blush.

Based on the way she kept looking offstage like she was planning an escape route, she really didn't like being the center of attention. She preferred being the genius behind the scenes.

Noted.

On the drive over, she'd made me promise I'd only bid if no one else did—she'd put on a brave face when we got here, but I could tell she was still terrified of being embarrassed in front of her friends and people she cared about. I knew what it was like, to set a high bar for yourself and then feel like you got knocked down a few pegs in clear view of everyone. Each time one of my ventures failed, I had a sick feeling, too.

You get used to that feeling eventually, but it always stings.

She had a few bids, and I was trying hard to read her expression. My instinct, of course, was to bid higher because no one here was going to get my girl for a steal, even if it was friendly and for charity. I was trying to stick by my promise to stand down, but then Gwen looked like she was headed to the guillotine when that lady behind me tossed out the high bid. It was insultingly low and I just couldn't stand the idea of Gwen not getting the attention she deserved. And not being valued the way she should be. That would never fly.

Next to me, Alex had cringed and muttered something about *that miserable woman*, right about the time his phone blew up with text messages and he tilted his phone so Eli and I could see. Before I could even finish reading, he waved his hand in the air like he was signaling for a water rescue and hollered out a number that was still too low for Gwen but high enough to earn a pinched expression from that lady behind us.

Something came over me then and I whispered to Alex, "I think this crowd needs a little excitement, don't you?" He quirked a brow and gave me a devious smile, and just like that, it was on. The next thing I knew we were shouting out bids and tossing barbs at each other like we were old mates.

The crowd ate that up.

Alex's phone buzzed with another text, a little string of hearts from his girl, and I knew we'd done right.

Onstage, Gwen looked like she wasn't sure if she wanted to run over and kiss me or melt into the floor. I sure hoped it was the former because that quick kiss in the hallway had been just the tip of the iceberg. She'd looked so anxious out there that I just wanted to do something that would take her mind off of whatever had her so afraid. It was the first thing that popped into my mind—probably because I'd been thinking about kissing her again for days—and I couldn't help myself. I'd told myself it was just a friendly gesture, just something to get her through what was a difficult moment for her, but that was a big fat lie. As soon as I felt her lips against mine, my whole body lit up like a bleeding Christmas tree and I knew exactly what that meant.

I was in serious trouble.

The next thing I knew, I was shouting out a number that was higher than any other bid tonight.

I didn't always think these things through. I just knew that I couldn't stand to see Gwen hurt or embarrassed and if there was something I could do to make her happy, even for just one night, by heaven I was going to do it.

"I can't believe you did that," she says, leading me out the back door of the gym. "And Alex—I knew Fiona must have been texting him, but I didn't think you'd jump in like that. It was completely unnecessary." Her pace quickens, her bootheels clacking on the pavement.

"I stand by my decision," I tell her.

She shakes her head, avoiding my gaze as we make our way around to the front of the building where the car's parked.

"What's wrong?" I ask her. "I thought you wanted me to bid."

"Only if there were no others," she says. "You didn't have to do that. It was too much."

I shrug, trying to match my stride to hers. She seems in a hurry to get out of here and it makes me wonder if I misread her, if I went too far. "But I wanted to."

She stops then, shoving her hands into her coat pockets. "Why?"

She's so beautiful, standing there under the glow of the streetlights. The moon's high overhead and the air finally feels like winter. Her cheeks are pink from the cold, and I want to fold her into my arms and kiss her until we're both breathless.

"I told you," I say, reaching out to tuck a lock of hair behind her ear. "You're worth it."

Her eyes turn glassy and I feel something twist in my gut. If she starts crying, I'm a goner.

"I can't pay you back for that," she says, her voice cracking. "I mean, I can—and I will—it'll just take me a while. I don't have that much money—"

I scoff. "You don't have to pay me back, Gwen."

Her jaw tightens and she plants her hands on her hips. "Of course I do. It was way too much." She's indignant, and somehow that just makes me want her more.

I put my hand on her arm. "Consider it a gift. I don't want you to pay me back."

She shakes her head. "I can't accept that."

"Of course you can. It's for a good cause. And I get baking lessons from the best baker in the state—or the region, or the world, for all I know. Everybody wins."

She gives me a tiny smile, one that feels like the sun coming out from behind a storm cloud. "That's very sweet. But you overestimate me."

I step closer. "If anything, you are chronically underestimated around here. But I have a feeling that's about to change."

She arches a brow, her tone teasing. "Are you always so optimistic?"

Yes. No. Sometimes to a fault. "I know a good thing when I see it."

After staring at me for a long moment, she says, "You have to stop doing that."

"Doing what?"

"Being so supportive. And attractive." She waves her hand in the air between us. "And your relentless flirting."

I bite back a smile and close the space between us. "You don't think you deserve someone supportive in your life?"

"You know that's not what I meant." She looks at me through her thick lashes, her eyes dark in the dim light. "I think you're amazing, but you're leaving in a matter of days. We said we'd keep this casual, remember?"

"I think you're amazing, too. And kind, and brilliant, and tenacious, and the most gorgeous woman I've ever laid eyes on."

She looks up at me and puts her hands on her hips. "You can't say things like that to me, Lancelot. Not when you're leaving."

"What if I don't want casual?" I ask her, hoping that she feels the same.

"What else could this be?"

Everything. All I ever wanted.

I step closer so we're toe-to-toe, then slide my fingers along her jaw. "Whatever we want it to be."

She sighs, her brow furrowed, and I decide right then that I'm not leaving this spot until she tells me how she feels about us.

"What do you want, love? Whatever the answer is, you can tell me. But I have to hear it."

She stares at me for a moment, and then she smiles that real kind of smile that breaks me into pieces. "I don't want you to leave. I think I caught some feelings. Some big ones."

I grin, pulling her toward me. "Caught some feelings?"

She nods, sliding her hand beneath my jacket to wrap around my waist.

"I did a thing," I tell her. "I was going to make it a big grand gesture, but I can't keep quiet anymore."

"You? A grand gesture?" she teases. "I can't imagine."

"I signed a lease for a house," I say.

Her eyes widen. "Are you serious? Where?"

"Easiest decision I ever made. Your sister's my new landlord."

She shakes her head like she still doesn't believe me, so I pull the lease from my inside jacket pocket and show her my signature.

"Victoria wouldn't sell, but she agreed to rent the lake house to me until I find another place. I'm not keen on leaving, gorgeous." I slide my hand into her hair and savor the way she leans into my touch. "I want to stay here. With you."

When she looks at me, she has tears in her eyes. "Show-off," she says, and then bursts into giggles.

I shrug. "Grand gesture. Can't help myself."

Her gaze drops to my lips and I lean in and kiss her, sliding one hand along her cheek. Her lips are soft but hungry, and that electric current ripples along my skin again. She lets out a little sigh that nearly unravels me and I want to take her home with me and never let her go. Kissing Gwen sets my whole body on fire, and I might be unsure of lots of things right now, but I am not unsure about her.

This, here with her—this is everything.

She slides her hands into my hair and suddenly all I want to do is hoist her up, wrap her legs around my hips, and carry her back to the car. But we're out in the open, where anyone can see us, so I steer her backward until she's pinned against the wall of the school. She makes a humming noise that leaves me desperate to feel more of her skin against mine. When she catches my bottom lip in her teeth, I think my heart may explode with happiness because *this is real and we can stop pretending it isn't*. I know I should peel myself away from her and drive us home so we can be alone.

Instead, I tug her closer and deepen the kiss.

A whistle pierces the air from somewhere behind us, like a catcall. When I pull away, ready to give this gawker a lesson or two about interrupting world-shifting moments such as this one, I'm shocked to see the face staring back at me.

I'd recognize that lopsided smirk anywhere.

"Hi, brother," Rory says. "You can really disappear when you want to."

I'm equal parts annoyed and wary. "What the devil are you doing here?"

He nods to Gwen and then turns back to me. "You need to come back with me. Now. Grandad's in the hospital."

Chapter Twenty-Four

GWEN

My jaw falls open. Logan's body tenses and he steps to my side, keeping his hand on my lower back in a protective gesture. "What happened?" he asks.

"Heart attack," Rory says, his voice grim. "It's bad. They did surgery a few hours ago, and there were some complications."

Rory steps toward me and holds out his hand to shake. He's dressed in a crisp blue button-down shirt and wool trousers that likely cost more than my mortgage. "And you're Gwen," he says, his tone friendly. "Lovely to finally meet you. Logan's talked about you nonstop." He's shorter than Logan, and not as muscular, but he has the same brooding gaze, the same sharp jawline. His hair's a darker brown and swoops over his forehead in a way that makes me think of surly dukes in Regency romance novels.

"Good to meet you, too," I say, thinking I need to ask him to elaborate on *nonstop* later. "What a surprise."

Rory smiles. "Quite." Just like Logan, he has a firm handshake and an intense gaze that is completely disarming.

He turns to Logan. "Is there someplace we can talk? It's been a long flight."

Logan gives him a nod and then turns to me. "I'm sorry," he says, sliding his hand along my forearm. "I need to handle this."

"Of course," I say. "Let me know if I can help."

He kisses me on the temple and leads me toward the car, motioning for Rory to follow.

"So who'd you have to hire to find me here?" Logan asks him.

Rory smirks. "You saved me the trouble with those cute reels. It's not the way I imagined you going viral, brother."

I bite my lip, thinking of the photos Maggie posted of Logan with the cake. He gives me a little shrug and says, "Guess you got a bit more traffic after all."

AN HOUR LATER, I'm back at my house, stress-baking as I try to suss out what all of this means. When Logan drove me home (with Rory following close behind in a rental car), he told me that he'd been ignoring Rory's calls and texts for days. "But I'm glad he came," he said. "We need to get a plan together, and we might not have much time."

After assuring me that everything would be fine, Logan gave me a quick peck on the cheek and I headed across the yard to my house. By the time I got inside the front door, Rory had pulled into the driveway and was climbing out of the car. He looked stern as he strode into the house as if there was much more happening than a health scare.

My brain took that opportunity to start analyzing everything —every moment that had played out in the last few days. What would this mean for the Fyfe company? Logan couldn't possibly stay here now, could he? He'd have no choice but to go home. He might have signed a lease, but that money's nothing to him— and besides, Vic wouldn't hold him to that lease, anyway. Not when a family emergency like this pulls him away.

I want to believe what he said about falling hard and starting over here, but I know he feels a sense of loyalty to his family. There's no way he'll stay here with me when they need him most.

I was kidding myself to think this could be so easy.

Everything is falling apart, so I do the only thing I know to try and calm my racing thoughts.

I bake a practice cake for Vic's wedding and start making a boatload of buttercream flowers. Even though I've enlisted Maggie's help, I'm determined to make this cake for Victoria. My arm still hurts after a minimal amount of use, so I have to pace myself. Luckily, buttercream flowers keep just fine if you refrigerate them, so I can make them now. On the day of the wedding, Maggie will help me arrange them on the cake.

I've made about two dozen intricate flowers when my arm starts to ache again. The oven's made the kitchen like a furnace, so I walk out onto the deck to cool off and rest. I've only been out there a minute when I hear a yell from the house next door. When I look over, Logan runs out the door and onto the deck, shouting and ducking objects that are being hurled from inside the house.

"Cut it out, you eejit!" Logan hollers, bending down to pick up something by his feet. He's down the deck steps and in the grass now, chucking the small object back towards the open door.

"You're so bleeding' stubborn!" Rory shouts back. "Worse than the old goat!" He flies out onto the deck, setting off the motion lights. More objects whiz towards Logan, and once Rory steps into the light, I see that he's holding a big bowl of fruit and hurling oranges like they're baseballs.

Thunder cracks overhead just as I feel the first raindrops hit my skin. In a hot second it's pouring—this is one of those winter rainstorms that comes out of nowhere and pummels you with cold, right into your bones.

Logan curses as an orange bounces off his shoulder, and picks another off the ground, and throws it like a line drive. I cringe, waiting for the sound of it smashing through a window, but it seems Logan's aim is perfect.

Rory yelps and tosses a banana, yelling a string of Gaelic words that I can't decipher. When he reaches for a pineapple, I get my butt into gear and hurry down the steps of my deck and across the yard.

"Hey!" I yell. "What's the problem over here?"

They both freeze and stare at me like a couple of rabbits caught in a garden.

"Why are you two out here throwing fruit at each other like a couple of weirdos?" I'm standing between them now, and hoping they have the good sense to not start up again because that pineapple will certainly leave a mark.

Rory clutches the fruit bowl to his chest as Logan rakes a hand through his hair.

"He started it," Rory mutters.

"You bloody started it," Logan huffs.

A streak of lightning flashes close enough to illuminate the yard.

"Come on," Logan says, looping his arm in mine. "Before it gets any worse."

Inside the house, Rory's pacing in the kitchen, barefoot. I take a quick look around, hoping that nothing inside the house is broken because if so, Victoria will have their hides.

"Are you two finished?" I give them both a long look but don't see any injuries. Rory's clothes are mostly dry. Logan's tee shirt and suit pants, however, are now soaked and clinging to him in a way that is slowly melting my brain.

"I'm just going to grab a few towels from the hall closet," I say. "Try not to start another battle royale while I'm gone."

Logan snorts, glaring at his brother as thunder rolls overhead.

When I'm in the hallway, they start up again. Their voices are low but agitated. Quickly, I dig three towels out of the hall closet and realize that my thin tee shirt and flannel pajama pants are also completely soaked. Victoria always keeps spare robes around, so I dig through the back of the closet until I find a fluffy one and quickly wrap it around myself.

When I head back down the hallway, I hear Rory say, "You have the power of attorney. You have to make the decisions now."

Logan's response is muffled. I pause by the entrance to the kitchen, straining to hear him.

"Then don't do it for him," Rory says, sounding annoyed. "Do it for me. I need your help here."

There's another muffled protest from Logan.

"Then just bring her with us," Rory says, lowering his voice. "She seems delightfully bossy. I like that for you."

My cheeks burn as I realize they're talking about me. Rory's suggesting I go with them. The idea strikes me as completely bonkers, but then I imagine going to Scotland. With Logan. Meeting his family and seeing where he's from. Letting him show me around a place I've never been. It's not a terrible thought.

"Um, no," Logan says, and now his voice is clear as a bell. "Absolutely not."

His words are like a record scratch. He sounds appalled.

"Seems like the obvious answer," Rory says. "Leave tomorrow, and bring her along."

Tomorrow? My heart pounds in my chest. I was prepared for him to leave in ten days, after the wedding. But tomorrow?

"It's completely inappropriate," Logan says, his voice gravelly. "And it just makes all of this harder."

My brain stumbles over *inappropriate*—and then my chest tightens when I realize his meaning. I'm not the kind of woman he takes home to meet his family. He thinks I don't belong in their world.

My mom's words ring in my ears: *You're out of your depth, honey.*

And that's when the truth hits me like a train—the truth that I've been pushing away for these last couple of weeks. This moment shouldn't be a surprise. I knew it was coming. From the moment I met Logan, I knew he was leaving—despite the lease. He might have had small-town dreams, but my feet are firmly planted in reality. Whatever we had was always going to be temporary, because the world he lived in was light-years from mine. I knew it would end this way because it was the only way that it could. My mistake was letting a part of me hope it didn't have to.

I'd let myself believe he wanted us to be together no matter what, but that was just a fantasy. Now I see the truth, and everyone else sees it, too. He wants us to be together if it means he's a part of my world, in this place so different from his home. But he doesn't want me to be a part of his world because he knows I don't fit there. Everything he said about staying here and signing a lease? He was just caught up in the excitement and novelty of a new world to explore. He might have feelings for me, but that won't be enough for him to uproot himself and start over here.

Now that reality has hit him like a brick, he sees that I can't be a permanent part of his life.

The walls feel like they're closing in on me. This house is too small, this truth too heavy, and I can't stand to be around him one more minute.

"Found the towels!" I say it loudly before I enter the kitchen, so they won't realize I heard any of their words. I can't risk another awkward moment here, and I don't want Logan to leave here knowing I've been holding onto this ridiculous hope that we could be more than—whatever we are. When I come around the corner into the kitchen, I force myself to smile and toss a towel to each of them.

"I should get back home," I tell them, keeping my tone even. "I've got a cake in the oven."

"Sure you don't want to stick around for round two?" Rory says, teasing.

"Try not to break anything," I tell him. "Victoria's attached to her things, and you do not want to see her angry."

"It's still pouring," Logan says, his brows pinching together. "Just stay until it calms down out there." He gives me a pleading look, and it nearly unravels me.

I tear my gaze away because I'm afraid he can see right through my act. I don't want him to tell me that I'm right, and I don't want him to lie and tell me I'm wrong, either. "I won't melt," I say. But I feel like I might because I'm not ready for this man to be out of my life. I believed him when he said he wanted to stay here with me, but now I understand that he won't. Because as frustrated as he is with them, Logan won't turn his back on his family.

He's too loyal for that, and I wouldn't want him any other way.

Logan and Rory exchange a look, but before they can say anything, I'm out the door.

Once I've changed into dry clothes and taken the cake out of the oven, I'm back to making buttercream flowers and trying hard not to think about Logan Fyfe—and about what a big fat coward I am. I shouldn't have run out the way I did. I shouldn't have pretended I didn't hear him talking to Rory. I should have asked him point-blank what was happening and given him a chance to tell me what he needed to say.

But I didn't want to hear it. I don't want to feel that hurt.

I'm piping a rose as big as my hand when I hear a tapping at the sliding glass door that leads to the deck. Logan's standing outside, his hand held up in a silent wave.

"Come in," I shout, finishing the last petal of the rose. I set it down carefully as he comes inside and walks toward me.

"Hi, gorgeous," he says, his voice a low rumble. "You've been busy." He glances around the room, where the countertops and the kitchen island are covered in dozens of piped flowers.

I shrug. "The wedding's in two days. At this rate, it'll take me until then to finish."

He gives me a tiny smile and says, "Can we talk for a minute?"

A lump forms in my throat. This is it. But I have to be brave this time. No more running.

"Sure," I say, trying to sound normal, like I'm not about to have my heart stomped into the floorboards. I lead him over to the sofa, where he sits close to me, our knees nearly touching. His hair's still damp from the rain, sticking out in all directions like he's raked his hand through it a thousand times.

"First, I'm sorry that you caught a glimpse of Rory and me reenacting our teenage years." He sighs. "No one should have to see that."

"It's okay. I'd have turned the hose on you if it got any worse."

"Aye, that's fair." He gives me a sheepish smile and that sexy dimple is back. "I think you probably overheard what all that was about. So I wanted to explain."

"Oh." My breath comes out in a whoosh. "And here I thought I was being subtle."

He smiles again and my heart cracks right down the middle.

"Not exactly." He turns more toward me and our knees touch. He doesn't pull away and I don't either.

"I'm not good at hiding things," I mutter.

"I love that about you," he says, and immediately bites his lip as if that slipped out. He pauses, always so careful about choosing his words. "So I have to go back," he says, his eyes resting on mine. "I have to fix this thing with my family. It can't wait any longer."

"Because of your grandfather."

"He made me power of attorney for his financial affairs, including the business, and there are some decisions I have to make. Quickly." He sighs, sliding his thumb back and forth over his knee. "Plus it's looking like he won't come out of the coma he's in, and as much as I want to stay here, I have to go set things in order."

"I see." My heart's pounding and my head's starting to spin, and while I don't know exactly what I want for the two of us, I know that it isn't for him to go like this, abruptly, as though leaving me—us—is as easy as getting on a plane.

"Rory needs me," he says, dropping his hand to my knee. And that gesture feels a lot like goodbye.

"Okay," I say, keeping my voice calm and even. "I get it. This is how it ends."

He blinks at me for a moment, looking confused. "What's ending?"

"We knew this was temporary," I say. "I'm no Cinderella, and you're no Prince Charming."

He shakes his head. "What does that even mean, love?"

And the way he says *love*, it just about breaks me. I press on, though, because this has to be done.

"We come from totally different worlds, Logan. This couldn't be anything but a fun winter fling." I shrug. "But I don't regret anything we did. I like you—a lot—and as much as I hate for it to be over, we both knew where this was headed." With those words hanging in the air, it feels like my heart's been hollowed out with a melonballer. But this is what I get for breaking the only rule that matters—for falling for someone I can't have.

"What's all this talk about *over*?" he says. He stands up abruptly and starts to pace. "I meant every word I said last night. I want to be with you."

Tears spill down my cheeks as I shake my head.

He drags his hand through his hair and turns to me, his eyes wide. "I don't know exactly what to call what we have here, but I'm not ready for it to be over. Are you?"

"No," I say. "I'm not." And that's the scariest truth—the one I've been afraid to admit. I've never felt this way about anyone else, ever. I think I'm in love with him, despite all of my efforts not to fall.

He drops to his knees and rests his hands on my thighs. "Good." He wraps my hand in his and laces our fingers together. "I'm not leaving forever. I'm leaving for two days. Don't you know I'm completely in love with you?"

I stare at him, trying to process all of those words, which seem to be the opposite of everything I'd built up inside my head. "Wait. What?"

"This stopped being a fling for me a long time ago. And I think it did for you, too." He pauses, searching my eyes. "Tell me I'm right about that, love."

There's a tangle of emotions burning a hole in my chest, but I don't know where to begin. How do I put these jumbled thoughts into words and not say the wrong thing? I want him to stay, more than anything. But I'm afraid he'll regret it—he'll regret choosing me.

"Logan," I say, sliding my hand along his cheek. "You're completely overwhelmed right now. You act like a big stoic Viking, but I know you're emotionally exhausted from everything with your family. Plus you're doing all these things to help me, and starting a relationship under intense circumstances like these can't be a good idea."

It's a good argument, even if it's only half true.

He smirks. "So you admit that it's a relationship. You don't think of it as a fling, either."

"I can't let myself think of it as anything else. Not when your life is so clearly somewhere else, and mine is so clearly here." As soon as this stops being a fling, it starts to be heartache. And I don't think I can go through that again.

His brow lifts in challenge. "Seems to me that we just need to have a conversation about that."

"You make it sound so easy."

"Does it have to be difficult?"

"I'm just being realistic," I say, though it feels like more than that. Part of me still fears that when there's an ocean between us, he'll realize this can't work, and that I'm not enough to come back for. And I'd rather he realize that now before he carries my heart across an ocean.

He leans closer and levels his gaze on mine. "Tell me what you want, love."

It feels like my heart just cracked wide open again. There are so many things I want, and I know I just need to give myself permission to have them.

"I want you to come back," I tell him. "I want you to be right next door and watch goofy movies with me, and take me on hayrides and hang out with my friends. And schedule these baking lessons that you paid an obscene amount of money for."

He smiles and laces his fingers in mine. "That's what I want, too." When he brings my hand to his lips, he plants a soft kiss on my palm, then on the inside of my wrist. His scruffy jaw sends a tingle over my skin, and I realize I want that, too. I want all the butterflies, all the tingly feelings. I want everything with him.

"I'll be back for the wedding," he says. "This is the last thing I need to fix. I don't need to be away longer than it takes to have one big conversation. And fly across the ocean."

I open my mouth to ask how all of that is even possible—logistically, aeronautically—but then I remember: these aren't people who fly commercial. These are people who own a jet, or three.

"But what happens after? With your business. Your family."

He shrugs. "Rory will take over like he should have a long time ago. He's basically been running the business for years. He's severely underestimated, just like someone else I know." He gives me a tender smile. "We're leaving at a truly ungodly hour in the morning. Then I'll have a talk with my family, and then I'll come right back."

My head's reeling. I was prepared for a goodbye. Not for this. Once again, Logan Fyfe has turned everything upside down.

"You don't need to rush back here," I tell him. "Take your time with your family."

"Don't do that," he says, shaking his head. "Don't put yourself last like that. You don't get to do that with me." His eyes settle on mine, daring me to argue.

I stare at him for what feels like a full minute. I'm not even aware that I do things like this, but he calls me out every time. I'm definitely a fan of his authoritative side.

"Okay," I tell him. "In that case, hurry back, mister. We've got a lot left to do."

His grin turns wicked as he pulls me to my feet. "I think I want to see more of this bossy side of you," he says, his voice husky.

His eyes flick to mine and his gaze is smoldering. Then his hands are looped around my waist and he's pulling me tight against him, kissing me like he'll die if he doesn't. My whole body softens against his like it knows it belongs right here, with him. I sigh as I run my hands through his hair, still damp from the rain, and pull him closer. His kiss is somehow both tender and fierce and his hands tighten on my hips like he doesn't want to let me go.

My hands drop to his shoulders and slide along his solid chest and, mercy, every part of this man is just right, down to his big hammering heart. Never did I allow myself to think someone else could make my heart feel so light and my feet so grounded. But when all of my doubts fall away, I'm left feeling like my heart's split wide open—enough to let all these new feelings in.

And this time, there are plenty of cartwheels.

"This is not the end," he whispers, his lips against my ear. "Don't think for a minute that an ocean's going to keep me away from you." He kisses me again, more tenderly, the urgency gone. Now his lips move slowly, and when he gently catches my bottom lip in his teeth, he holds me against him like we have all the time in the world.

My heart swells as he squeezes me against him, and I finally feel like I believe him. After all, this is what love is: knowing what you want, and who you want to share it with, and taking a leap to get there.

Chapter Twenty-Five

LOGAN

For someone who spends entirely too much time fussing over his appearance, today Rory looks like he rolled down a hillside. He's dressed in dark jeans and a gray henley shirt, a casual look for him—but his hair is messier than usual and he's got several days of beard stubble.

Rory never grows a beard.

"I'm surprised you came," I tell him. "You know you could have called."

He sighs, picking at a bagel. "I couldn't stand it at the house," he says. "I would literally rather fly across the Atlantic twice than have to listen to everyone bicker for one more minute. Cait's running circles around the doctors and pacing a hole in the floor. Ma's in full-on honey badger mode and I'd just as soon induce my own medical coma that stay in the line of fire."

"I've changed my mind. I'd like to turn the plane around."

"Not bloody likely," he snorts. "I brought bungee cords and duct tape just in case."

"You did not," I grumble.

He doesn't respond but lifts a brow in a slightly evil way that makes me wonder.

"So are you going to tell me about the lovely Gwen?" Rory says, sipping his coffee.

"Nope." The last thing I need is for everyone in my family to know about Gwen. They'd likely find some way to use her against me because Fyfes can weaponize anything. Not Rory, because as tough as he acts sometimes, he doesn't have a bad-natured bone in his body. But my family can pry intel out of him, and I'm not willing to take that chance.

Someday, I'll tell him all about her. But not today.

"Kind of a long flight," he says, prodding. He laces his hands behind his head and leans back in the seat, propping his feet up on the table between us.

"Yep."

He grins, staring out the window. "Okay, brother. As you wish."

It's a little after nine in the morning, and we're somewhere over the Atlantic already. The ocean's a stormy gray-blue below, and I can't help but think that's a clear indication of what's coming.

I sip the coffee from my travel mug. "I'd rather we get a plan together. There's a lot we need to do when we get on the ground."

"Aye," he says. We're on the same page about the business decisions that need to be made—the ones I have to make—and the sooner we put those into action, the better. Based on the update we got from Cait late last night, Grandad's going downhill fast. I'll need to install Rory as CEO, get with the PR team to write a press release and handle a dozen other tasks before I can officially leave everything in Rory's hands and walk away—just like we've agreed.

As sad as it is for Grandad to be in this condition, it feels good to finally be able to hand Fyfe over to Rory and have a solid plan to move forward—one that doesn't keep me in a chokehold.

Being with Gwen made me realize that I want something different from my life. I want hayrides in orchards, town festivals, and ugly sweater parties. I want friends who like being with me because they like me—and not because they care about being seen with my family. More than that, I want to learn everything about Gwen Griffin, a little bit more every day. I want to be the taste-tester for her cakes, and cook her soup when she's sick, and watch silly movies while she's curled into my chest like a cat. There aren't many things I'm sure of in this life, but I'm certain about how it feels to be with her—like I've found where I belong.

I love her warm smile, her wild, contagious laugh—the way she calls me out on my nonsense and demands that I be honest with her. It's easy to picture all the ways we can be so good for each other, and it's now—as I sit on this plane, soaring over the ocean—that I realize I never want to be away from her again. *Love* doesn't feel like a strong enough word for what I feel for her. What I feel is tenacious, consuming, and as frightening as it is beautiful. As hard as I tried not to fall, I did, and I'm not one bit sorry for it. I've spent so many nights thinking about all of her soft curves and how they'll fit so well against my own rough edges, and I can't wait to explore all the other ways we might fit well together.

Last night she tried to push me away because of fear, and I wish I could make all of her uncertainty go away. She's got wounds just like the rest of us, and I know she has to work through whatever's making her believe that she's not good enough. Every time she looks doubtful, I want to fold her into my arms and tell her that she's more than enough—always will be—and that she makes me the luckiest man on this earth.

I wish I could pick up her broken pieces and put them back together, but that's something that only she can do.

I just want her to see that it's safe to let me stay.

I'll always keep her safe—if only she'll let me.

Chapter Twenty-Six

GWEN

Maggie kicks me out of the kitchen an hour before the rehearsal.

"Go on," she says. "We can finish the last touch-ups tomorrow. You have to go be glamourous."

"Glamorous is a stretch." I'll settle for not falling apart at the seams. Because looking at that house next door and knowing that he's gone? That's enough to split me in two.

Maggie and I have spent the whole day working on Victoria's cake, making sure that every detail is perfect. I've made more buttercream flowers in the last twenty-four hours than I have in the last five years, and Maggie has once again proven that piping is her superpower. I feel bad for ever doubting her drive, and grateful that Logan was around to give me the nudge that helped me see that.

Thinking of him now sparks a tiny ache in my chest. I've been checking my phone nonstop today, hoping to see a text from him. But there's nothing. Granted, he's probably somewhere over the Atlantic right now, and even fancy-pants private jets likely require you to put your phone in airplane mode for a safe flight. I'd halfway expected a friendly text before he left this morning, but there was none. Now the blank screen just reminds me that he's gone. And that niggling voice in the back of my brain is telling me that, despite what he said last night, there's a good chance it could be forever.

That voice keeps whispering that once he gets home and back to his real life, he's going to realize this was just a fun interlude. Not something worth coming back for.

I want to yank that little voice out of my head and throw it into a blender.

"This is the most gorgeous cake ever," Maggie says.

"Couldn't have done it without you," I tell her. "Truly."

The four-tiered cake looks like something from a magazine, and Maggie has documented this whole process with photos and videos that she's already sharing online. She's certain it'll bring us more business, and I'm feeling optimistic about that, too.

"Go on," she says, swatting me with a tea towel. "Go have fun. Sam and I will close up."

"Close early," I tell her. "Both of you should come celebrate with us at the party afterward."

"Will do," she says.

I check my phone once more as I leave, but there are still no missed calls or texts from Logan. Frustrated, I shove the phone back into my pocket. Rationally, I know that he's almost certainly fine. He hasn't crashed into the ocean, and he isn't clinging to a piece of scrap metal while treading water in his perfectly tailored pants. He's probably dealing with his family and trying not to blow a gasket.

All day, I've resisted the urge to text him. But I finally cave.

Hey, I type. **Just wanted to check in. Hope you had a good flight and things are okay.**

I keep it breezy, with no mention of my worry that he could be marooned somewhere in the icy Atlantic, getting side-eye from hungry sharks. By the time I get home and get dressed for the rehearsal, there's still no reply.

BECAUSE VICTORIA'S planned a simple wedding, the rehearsal is easy—though the wedding planner, Avery, is stern like a drill sergeant. She moves us from one side of the room to the other like chess pieces and stomps around in three-inch heels that could be murder weapons. We're at an apple orchard just a few miles outside of town, in a giant renovated barn that's used for special events. Tonight, it's decorated with about a million white fairy lights that make it look like something from a movie set. Inside, it's been tastefully draped with sheer white fabric and antique lace. Lanterns with flickering lights hang from the beams. Rustic and romantic, it's just what Victoria loves.

We move through the rehearsal quickly, because Avery's on a schedule and doesn't suffer any fools. I guess if you want to have the perfect wedding with no hiccups, you want a person like Avery.

"Okay, bride!" Avery yells. "You're up!" She hums a few bars of the wedding march and Victoria appears from the front doors of the barn. My breath catches as Vic walks down the aisle to where I'm standing with the rest of the wedding party.

Beautiful as always, she's wearing a navy sweater dress and tan boots. Her hair's in a loose bun and her lips are pursed in that way that means she's trying hard to hide how she's feeling. Her gaze lands on me for a moment and then flicks toward Avery. She looks pale and nervous, which is so unlike Victoria that it stops me cold. With a sigh, she squares her shoulders sets her jaw, and then walks toward Theo.

Theo smiles and then she's right by his side as Avery continues. I miss a few words because I'm trying to read my sister's expression—is it frustration? Doubt?—and my attention slips back to Avery when she snaps her fingers and drawls, "And then we have vows, blah, blah, kiss the bride, and cue the music out."

Avery's still shouting directions to the bridesmaids, but all I can think about is what has my sister looking more seasick than the last time we rode the spinning teacup ride at the state fair. She's avoiding my gaze, and then she's marching down the aisle again, and Avery's watching us like a hawk to make sure that we all remember how to link arms and keep a few steps behind each other as we promenade out.

As I'm walking next to my escort, there's a moment where the world seems to tilt and I imagine Logan here with me instead. It's not hard to picture him here in this very space, in one of his immaculate suits, his eyes fixed on me as I walk toward him.

Toward the altar. As if we're about to say our own vows.

I suck in a breath and this time, instead of pushing my feelings way down deep, I let them wash over me like a wave. I've pushed them all down for so long out of fear and shame, thinking that my feelings made me weak.

But I was wrong about that. And I don't want to pretend anymore that I didn't have some very strong feelings about Logan—about him being here, about how well we fit together, even about how I'm sometimes afraid of what could happen next.

I don't even want to ignore this burning in my chest that's here as I think about him leaving and now being so far away from me. I don't want to be this person who pushes her feelings aside anymore. I want to feel them all, the way I feel the chill of winter and the breeze in summer.

What I feel most now is an ache deep in my bones. If he doesn't come back, I don't know what I'll do.

When Avery's satisfied that we all know our parts, she rounds us up and rattles off her last reminders. Then she herds us all towards the parking area because she wants to do one last sweep of the barn and make sure everything is perfect before she locks it up tonight.

"I swear, that woman must have been a collie in a past life," one of the bridesmaids says. She's a friend of Victoria's from college, like most of the other bridesmaids. Across the parking lot, Victoria's climbing into a car with a couple of her friends. I start to walk over and make sure she's all right, but she laughs at something one of the women says and seems to have shaken off whatever she was feeling before. She's with her friends now, and I don't want to interrupt.

The other members of the wedding party are mostly Vic's friends from college. While they gather in the parking lot, I act like a true introvert and hurry off to my car. Everyone's headed to a restaurant in town to have dinner and drinks, but I'm skipping. Victoria could use a night to celebrate with her friends, and I could use some time curled on the sofa in my pajamas with a sample cake and *Bridgerton*.

All these feelings? I need to sit with them for a minute.

"Not so fast," a voice says from behind me.

I turn to find Fiona standing with her hand on her hip. "You're coming with us."

A jeep's parked behind her, with Sadie at the wheel. Sadie waves out the window and grins like the two of them have planned a caper.

"Girls' night," Fiona says, looping her arm in mine. She knows that Logan left because I've texted her about a million times today. She also knows that I'm going to spend the rest of the night over-analyzing the crap out of everything that's happened over the last couple of weeks because that's what I do when I'm alone.

And Logan's left me plenty to think about.

"Aaron's making holiday cocktails," Fiona says, referring to the bartender at the Wonky Donkey, our favorite dive. "And I for one, am curious about his new recipes."

"And quite thirsty," Sadie says.

Aaron is adorably surly—especially around the holidays. A couple of years older than us, he used to tease us mercilessly in high school. He turned out to be a big-hearted softie, though, under all those teasing barbs.

"We promise to get you home at a decent hour," Fiona says.

"No, we don't!" Sadie calls from the car.

Before I can argue, Fiona's herding me toward the passenger seat of Sadie's jeep and then climbing into the back. I send Victoria a quick text to let her know I'm skipping the dinner, but that she should call me later.

There's no response from her, either, which is highly unusual. At the very least, I expect a half-hearted jab at me for hiding out instead of doing shots with her on her last night as a single lady. She's with her friends, though, and I assume they've already given her a banner and a crown and heaved her into a car headed for the party.

"TRY THE SNOWBALL," Aaron says, pushing a blended drink towards us. Wearing a red checkered shirt and dark jeans, this is as festive as he gets. His dark hair is shaved short on the sides and styled high on top, and he's sporting a few days of beard stubble. With warm brown eyes and a muscular build, he's ruggedly handsome—and somehow still single.

Sharon's been trying to rope him into coming to her speed-dating events for months, but somehow he evades her.

It turns out Aaron's holiday cocktails are made from

amaretto, vodka, some secret spice blend, and low-level grinchiness. He's making them frozen, because it's back to sixty degrees outside.

Fiona lifts a brow and Sadie reaches for the straw. After taking a big sip, Sadie's eyes widen and she says, "Aaron, I've always hated eggnog until this moment. I think this might be a Christmas miracle."

I reach over with my straw to taste it and Sadie slides the glass out of my reach, muttering, "No way, missy."

"Guess you need to make that three," I tell Aaron.

One corner of his mouth lifts in a rakish smile. "Yes ma'am."

The Wonky Donkey leans heavy on the shabby and less on the chic, and that's why we love it—well, that and Aaron. Only the bravest tourists come inside during the peak season—there's a resin alligator over the bar that everyone thinks is taxidermy (which scares about forty percent of the tourists away), and then there's Aaron, who takes care of the other sixty percent with a gravelly drawl and a bristly attitude that's almost entirely fiction. Deep down, Aaron's a big cinnamon roll, but he dials his natural grumpiness up to eleven for the tourists because he likes running a little oasis for the locals and he has zero interest in playing tour guide and answering the endless questions from visitors.

When Aaron sets two more snowballs in front of us, he says, "Cheers, ladies." Down the bar, an older man calls to him for another round and he gives him a nod.

When Aaron's out of earshot, Fiona turns to me and says, "Now tell us everything."

I skip to the most important parts: Rory showing up after the auction, the fruit fight, the conversation I overheard in the kitchen, and what Logan said when he came over afterward.

"What if he doesn't come back?" I say. "That felt like a goodbye kiss."

Sadie and Fiona exchange a look that I can't quite decipher.

"What kind of kiss are we talking about?" Fiona says.

"On a scale of one to hot lava," Sadie says, leaning closer.

"Fires of Mordor?" I say with a sigh. My lips still feel a little swollen. With that one kiss, Logan Fyfe knocked every thought right out of my brain—except for my oh-so-naughty thoughts about him and all the things we might do together if he stayed. He'd even managed to silence that super annoying voice in the back of my mind that kept reminding me that we were from two far too different worlds and that he was way out of my league. For that one moment, it was just him and me, and those things didn't matter anymore. All that mattered was how my heart hammered in my chest when I was near him, and how the look in his eyes said he felt the same.

Even though he told me he loves me, part of me still worries that it won't be enough to bring him back. That I won't be enough.

"Why didn't he want me to go with him?" I say. That question's been bothering me ever since last night. When he told me he was leaving, I waited for him to ask me to go—I would have liked to have seen his home, but more than that, I'd have liked to have had the chance to be there to care for him the way he's done for me. "I know it's so hard for him to go back there—I just wanted to do something to help, even if it was to just be there with him. But when his brother suggested I go with them, Logan said no."

Sadie and Fiona exchange another pointed look.

"Did he give a reason?" Sadie asks.

The question strikes like a knife, because what he said was humiliating. "He just said it was inappropriate," I answer. "Nothing else." Just those few words were enough to make me doubt everything he'd told me afterward—because why would he think it was inappropriate for me to be there? Unless he didn't want his family to know about me.

"Maybe he's embarrassed," Sadie says. "You said his family had a lot of drama. Maybe he was afraid it would scare you off to be around them, or make you uncomfortable."

Fiona's brow furrows. "Maybe he knew he'd be really busy and you'd be stuck being interrogated by his mother. Maybe he's looking out for you." She shrugs. "Plus, death is really hard, even when the relationship is strained."

Sadie nods, sipping her drink. "I once dated a guy who asked me to go to his uncle's funeral. I went to be supportive and help him deal with a rough day, and then he ended up going to play basketball with his brothers and left me with his mom and sister, who hated me. I legit crawled out a window to get away."

"You did not," Fiona snorted.

"Tiny bathroom window," Sadie says. "All that yoga saved my life because I might never have contorted myself enough to get out otherwise. And those two would have buried me in the backyard if they'd had shovels."

Fiona reaches over and pats Sadie's hand.

"What?" Sadie asks.

"I'm just so glad you found James."

"Me too," Sadie says with a grin. "He hasn't once made me climb out a window."

They turn back to me when I check my phone and heave a big sigh. "He hasn't even texted since he left," I tell them. "That's a bad sign."

Fiona frowns. "Try not to obsess over it. There could be a good reason."

Aaron comes back to see if we need another round, which we definitely do.

"I didn't say *I love you*," I mutter. "He laid his heart bare and I didn't say it back to him. What if he doesn't come back because he thinks I don't feel the same?"

Sadie and Fiona both have the dopiest smiles on their faces.

"What?" I say.

"You love him," Sadie says.

"Of course I do!" I cry. "But I kept telling myself that it couldn't be real because we were so different, you know? And because this all happened so fast. And then I tried to push him away because I was too scared to tell him the truth. I was too scared of what it meant."

"Sounds like he called your bluff on that one," Fiona says, and Aaron lifts a brow.

Sadie smirks. "James calls my bluff every dang time." She gives a little shrug and says, "I love that about him. He doesn't let me get away with shutting down. It's hard sometimes, but it keeps us honest."

"I think I was afraid he'd hurt me if I told him how I really felt," I confess. "But it's scarier to think that might have been my last chance to tell him."

Aaron sets our fresh drinks in front of us and says, "Sometimes you have to do the scary thing. It's the only way to get what you want."

Sadie turns to Aaron. "That's a hundred percent true."

"I'd rather have fear than regrets," Aaron says. "My mom used to tell me that it's doing the scary things that help us grow."

The older man down the bar calls to Aaron again and he hollers, "For heaven's sake, Roy, you practically live here! Come pour your own draft."

Sadie gives him a surprised look.

"What?" Aaron says with a shrug. "He doesn't like the way I pour them, anyway."

Roy sheepishly walks over to the bar, nodding toward us as

he gets himself a clean glass. He looks like he's in his sixties, with short gray hair and deep-set creases around his eyes and mouth that come from laughter. "When I get old," he says, "I want to regret things I did. Not things I was too afraid to do." He pulls himself the perfect pint and then tips his ball cap at us as he heads to his chair.

Sadie nods. "What he said."

Fiona drops her arm around my shoulder and says, "Babe, I love you to bits, but you're great at standing in your own way."

"I'd really like to not do that anymore," I mutter.

"Wouldn't we all?" Sadie says.

"I think I know how you can start," Fiona says.

Chapter Twenty-Seven

LOGAN

When we land in Edinburgh, we go straight to the hospital. Rory calls Cait for an update once we're in the back of a car, and I hear enough of what she says to get the gist. Grandad's declined since she last texted us, and he likely doesn't have much time.

My chest feels heavy as we make the drive, which seems to take a bleeding eternity. Even though I'm not close to Grandad, the sense of loss hits me hard because it reminds me of my dad.

"He's in a private room where family can stay with him," Rory says, his voice matter-of-fact.

"How's Cait?" I tug at the collar of my shirt, already feeling the knot forming in my chest. This could be the last time I see my grandfather, and I know I should go in and talk to him, even if he can't hear me. But when I think of how he's treated me over these last months, trying to bully me into doing as he demanded, that knot twists tighter. I'm not ready to make peace yet, and forgiveness feels out of reach. So where does that leave me?

"All right," Rory says, sipping from a bottle of water. "She's prepared."

Our sister is nothing if not always prepared for any

circumstance. It doesn't stop her from feeling like she should be somehow doing more, though. She never sheds her surgeon hat completely—she's no doubt consulting the best specialists and handling everything to the letter. I'm glad my mum can lean on her because Cait's superpower is keeping people calm and focused.

It's nearly eleven p.m. by the time we get to the hospital. Grandad's in a special intensive care unit, in a private room. A nurse leads us down the hallway to where my mum and Cait are sitting in a couple of plush chairs outside the door.

Cait stands and pulls me into a hug. She's wearing her scrubs and white coat, so I wonder if she's spent the whole day here, on a shift. "I'm glad you're here," she says. Her green eyes look stormy like she's had an excruciating day.

"Good of you to come," Ma says, standing. She gives me a stiff hug, and for the first time feels tiny in my arms. Her tan wool trousers and cream cardigan make her look like she should be at a luncheon instead of a hospital. Her blue eyes look strained, the lines around them deep. Stone-faced, she's shoved all of her feelings down as far as they'll go.

Cait's filling Rory in on all the details, giving him the latest update from Grandad's doctor. Grandad's not expected to recover, and he's basically in hospice care until the inevitable comes. Cait's words wash over me, and while I understand what's happening, it doesn't seem real. But Rory's stern expression tells me that it's happening. This is the end. If I can't make peace with my grandfather, I can at least be honest about the feelings I'm having and take the first step toward forgiveness. Not because he deserves it, but because I do.

After all, I've seen how resentment and anger can destroy a man over time, and I don't want that to happen to me.

"You should go inside and talk to him," Cait says, resting her hand on my shoulder. "Both of you."

Rory nods toward the door, indicating that I should go first.

"I don't know what to say," I tell them. My head's reeling because suddenly the gravity of this has struck me. The sharp smell of antiseptic, the ridiculously cheery blue of the floor tile, the sophisticated-looking abstract painting on the wall. It all feels too real, like a super-saturated photograph—one that I don't want to look at too hard.

"I think you do," Cait says. Her eyes soften and she pushes a lock of red hair behind her ear. I imagine that if Gwen were here, she'd tell me the same. And I'd believe her.

That knot is back, twisting in my chest, and I know I have to go in and say goodbye. There won't be an apology, and I feel no need to explain my decisions anymore. I won't speculate about the reasons he might have had for doing these hurtful things over the years, because in the end, the reasons don't matter. Forgiveness might not come today, or in a week, or even a year. But I can let myself believe that it's possible if I choose it. And for now, that's enough.

WHEN RORY and I finally make it to my grandfather's house—a quick flight here from Edinburgh—it's nearly three in the morning. My mum grew up here, and I did too. But it never felt like a home.

Now Grandad lives here alone, but it's where we all still come together a couple of times a year. An imposing three-story, the house is built from fieldstone that's just as cold and impermeable as my grandfather. Stuffy and pristine, it's always felt more like a museum than a place where people live. Immaculate gardens surround it, and beyond are meadows prettier than any painting. You can see the ocean from the top floor, and smell the salty air from anywhere on the grounds. A curtain of ivy clings to the east side, making it look like something from a fairy tale. The rooms are huge, with tall ceilings and big windows, and most of them are full of antique furniture made from dark wood and plush fabrics.

It's a shame that a place full of such beauty can also house so much hurt.

These cold rooms remind me of being forced into a mold that doesn't fit. After my grandmother died a decade ago, Grandad kept the housekeeping and maintenance staff, so the house and the surrounding gardens always look picture-perfect.

Rory leads me into the study and heads to the bar. It's a dark, overly masculine room, filled with floor-to-ceiling built-in bookcases, leather chairs, and an oversized sofa. Stuffed pheasants are mounted on the wall opposite the fireplace, frozen in mid-flight.

"I'm completely knackered," Rory says. "But I'm having a drink anyway. I assume you'd like one, too."

"You assume correctly," I tell him because just being back here is already making me want to crawl out of my skin. A nice fifty-year-old scotch might take the edge off enough that I can sleep, but I'm already feeling like I want to get out of here as soon as possible—and back to Gwen.

When I check my phone, I see that the battery is nearly dead. Gwen never replied to the text I sent earlier today, but I figured it was because she had her hands full with the wedding rehearsal. I kept telling myself it was because of that, anyway, and not because she was shutting down. After considering that for a moment, I decide to text her again.

And then I see the red exclamation point above my last text to her. It was never delivered. I sigh, raking my hand through my hair. She's probably spent the whole day wondering why I didn't respond. I type out a quick message, and then hit send, waiting this time to see that it goes through.

Rory pours us both a drink and collapses next to me on the big leather couch. "I scheduled a meeting with our attorney for nine," he says, meaning just a few hours from now. "We just need to sign a few documents, and then the rest can wait."

I nod, sipping my scotch. In a few hours, Rory will be officially in charge.

"You know, he never signed the new will," Rory says. "I don't think he really wanted to cut us all out."

"It was a cruel way to bluff," I mutter. "He was willing to risk ripping the family apart just to get what he wanted."

He shrugs. "Aye, you'll get no argument from me there. But it's sad that he felt like he had to bully us into being loyal."

"He was a bully about a lot of things. And he had some twisted ideas about loyalty."

I turn to face him. "Do you think he had regrets?"

Rory sighs. "I imagine so."

The thought twists in my heart like a knife.

After a long moment, he says, "You're not staying here, are you?"

He means long-term, of course. After this long day passes.

I give him a small shrug. "You don't need me."

Rory smirks. "Debatable."

"Please tell me this isn't the part where you start talking about duty. Because even though he'll be gone soon, I still can't be a part of this business."

He lifts a brow. "I can tell you all about duty. Mainly about how it's your duty to live your one life in the way that means you spend your last moments feeling gratitude and not regret. It's your duty to love fiercely, and to keep learning, and to leave the world a little better than you found it."

I stare at him for a moment, my jaw slack.

He shrugs. "What? I can't work for a cutthroat tycoon and also have thoughts about our greater purpose?"

"I always saw the company as a crushing burden," I tell him. "But you like the challenge of reinventing it. Making it into a force of good."

He smiles. "Aye, you know I love a good challenge. And I think I'm entering my redemption era."

"I can't wait to see what you do with it." I sip my drink and lean back, feeling like I've been run over by a bicycle. It's a relief, though, to know that Rory's going to be in charge of the company, the legacy. I see now that he's been clear on what he wants for his future for a long time now—for far longer than I've given him credit. And now, I'm clear on what I want, too.

And right now, I feel like I can't get back to her fast enough.

Chapter Twenty-Eight

GWEN

Maggie does a little victory dance as I place the last buttercream rose onto Victoria's cake. We set it up in the barn a couple of hours ago, under Avery's careful supervision. That woman is determined that nothing will be out of place under her watch.

"It looks amazing," Maggie says.

"I couldn't have done it without your help," I tell her. "Thank you."

"You should go get changed," she says, checking her watch. "Tick tock, maid of honor."

We're an hour away from walking down the aisle when I go to check on Victoria. All of the bridesmaids are putting the final touches on their hair and makeup, and I'm as ready as I'm going to be. I haven't heard anything from Logan since early this afternoon when he texted me to tell me that his grandfather was in hospice care and that he'd be back as soon as possible.

His text was brief, but it had made my heart ache for him. From what he'd told me, his grandfather could be a hard man. But I know that doesn't make saying goodbye to someone any easier. I hated that he was having such a difficult day, and hated that I couldn't be there with him.

Victoria's in a separate building, a small cottage that she's using as a green room. It has a bedroom and living room, plus a small kitchen and bath. When I knock on the door, there's no answer, so I go ahead inside.

I find Victoria sprawled on her back on the bed, her head hanging off the end, wearing her gown and only one shoe. Her veil's hanging on a hook on the wall and her bouquet is lying on the dresser.

She blinks at me, upside down, as I walk into the room.

"Hey," I say. "Everything all right?" I feel a need to ask even though the answer is obviously *no*.

"I was getting dressed," she says, as if there was any doubt.

"I see that. You need a hand?"

She stares at me, eyes full of worry, and says, "I think I'm making a mistake."

"What do you mean?" I sit next to her on the bed and she rolls onto her side to face me. There's a deep furrow in her brow.

"I've had this knot in my chest all day," she mutters. "It's only getting worse."

"It's normal to be a little scared," I tell her.

She shakes her head, biting her lip. "This isn't just jitters, Gwennie. This whole week, I've been having some thoughts. Lots of thoughts." She pulls a flask from somewhere under all that tulle and satin and takes a big sip. When she notes my surprise, she says, "Compliments of my friend Roxy. She's been in two dozen weddings and says this thing's been borrowed every time."

"Tell me what's going on," I say, as she hands me the flask.

She heaves a deep breath and looks me in the eye. "I'm not sure I can."

"Why? You can tell me anything." I study her eyes, and then

realize—she means because of Mark. Because of how we ended things, right before our wedding. She thinks she's opening an old wound, but she's wrong.

"Hey," I tell her, taking her hand. "Anything."

Tears spring to her eyes and she fights hard to push them down. "Marrying Theo feels wrong," she says, shaking her head. "There's a lot I love about him, but there's a lot that I overlook. We're good together in some ways but in others..." Her voice trails off and she sighs. She doesn't need to tell me details, because I've seen the hurt in her eyes when Theo's dismissed her with careless words or tried to make her feel small. I never wanted to say anything negative about him, because I was afraid it would push them closer together. I had to believe that she'd make the right decision for herself. But every time he does that to her, I want to punch him in the face.

"I've just been going through the motions for so long now, I think I lost sight of what I really wanted," she says. "I don't think it's him." Tears spill down her cheeks and she says, "I want a spark, Gwennie. I want to feel crazy about the guy I marry. I want to feel like he's my complement, like he always has my back no matter what. I want to feel like I can't live without him —or rather, that I don't want to."

I nod, brushing a lock of hair from her face. That's exactly how I feel about Logan.

"I want that for you, too, babe."

"I'm not sure I ever felt a spark," she says, her brow furrowed. "I think I thought comfortable was good enough. I was afraid to admit that what we had wasn't right, so I tried hard to make it work between us." She slides her hands along the full skirt. "But I can't pretend anymore."

"You shouldn't have to," I tell her, taking her hand in mine. "And you deserve better than Theo."

Her eyes narrow. "I knew you didn't like him. Why didn't you ever tell me?"

I shrug. "Because it wasn't my call to make. And besides, would you have listened to me?"

She rolls her eyes. "Fine. Fair point."

"How do you want to handle this?" I ask her. "What can I do?"

"Well, the whole party's paid for, so I think we go ahead and enjoy it. Even if no one says *I do*." She stands and unzips the dress. "I'm going to change, and then I'm going to talk to Theo. We'll go from there."

"You know I've got your back," I tell her. "Whatever you need."

She pulls me into a bear hug that nearly knocks the wind out of me and says, "Thanks, Gwennie. I love you to the moon and back."

I hold my injured arm out to the side and squeeze her tight with the other. "Same." A huge wave of relief washes over me because my little sister's clear on what she wants—or at least on what she doesn't want. And for the first time in a long while, I feel that, too.

When she lets me go, she takes another sip from the flask and says, "Mom's going to murder me."

"She'll have to get through me first."

VICTORIA SQUEEZES my hand as we walk from the cottage to the barn.

"You got this," I tell her, and she lets out a heavy sigh.

"I think this is what they mean by do or die," she says. "I'm not a fan of this feeling."

We pause by the back of the barn. Just inside, fifty of her

friends and family are waiting. Victoria's face is stern, her big blue eyes dark. "Wait here," I tell her. "I'll be right back."

She heaves another deep breath and stares up at the sky.

When I slip inside the side door of the barn, it lets out a creak loud enough to split the building in half. I'm right next to where the bridesmaids are lined up and swallow hard when Theo's gaze meets mine. Every head turns toward me as I march toward him, and even though it's only a few yards, it feels like a mile. I try my best to arrange my face into an unreadable expression because I know everyone out there is studying it.

Theo arches a brow, his jaw set in a firm line. As much as I dislike the man, I don't want to be the one to deliver this message—but I'd do anything for my sister, and this is what she needs.

"Hey," I whisper to him, turning my face away from the crowd. "Vic needs to talk to you outside."

He blinks at me for a moment, as if he doesn't understand my words. And then his jaw tightens and I suspect he knows exactly what's coming. He brushes past me and strides past the bridesmaids and out the same door I came in.

"We just need a moment," I whisper to the officiant because I feel like I need to tell her something. She gives me a quick nod, her face revealing nothing as if she knows exactly what this interference means.

By the time I reach the door, I can hear Victoria's voice, low and calm. She's standing several yards away at the corner of the barn, and Theo must be right around the corner, near the front entrance. I hang back at the side door to give them some space, and then I hear Theo's voice, rumbling like distant thunder.

"And you're deciding this now?" Theo yells. "At the last possible minute?"

"I'm sorry about the timing," she says, her voice stern. "But I won't apologize for how I feel. Not anymore."

"This is a whole new level," he says. "Even for you."

"I didn't want to admit our relationship isn't working," she says. "But I can't pretend anymore."

"If this is about the Jenkins project," he drawls, "I was just trying to keep you from embarrassing yourself."

"Oh my god, Theo!" she yells. "Not everything is about your *job*! This is part of the problem, don't you see?"

I consider going back inside, but there's nowhere to hide in there, and everyone will be staring at me.

Victoria turns then and strides toward me, her brow furrowed.

In a blink, Theo comes around the corner, right on her heels. When he sees me, his eyes turn dark. "This is your doing," he says to me. "Guess you finally got what you wanted."

"Don't you dare," Victoria snaps at him. She plants her hands on her hips and stares him down with a look that could incinerate him. "You never take responsibility for anything you do," she says. "Never."

He brushes past her and barrels toward me, and for one brief moment I'm convinced he's about to put his hands on me and force me to throw my very first throat punch, but instead, he sidesteps me and reaches for the door handle.

But then he pauses and turns to Vic, straightening his jacket. "You know what?" he says, his voice low. "You tell them all. You blew this up, you can pick up the pieces."

Without another word, he shoves past her, jostling her shoulder, and storms off toward the parking area.

Victoria bites her lip. Part of me wants to chase Theo down and give him that throat punch after all.

"You okay?" I ask her.

"I will be." She pulls her hair back over her shoulders and says, "Tomorrow we'll talk about how I dodged a very big bullet. But first, the guests."

She gives me a quick nod and then swings the door open. I follow her inside as she strides up to where the officiant stands, holding her chin high. I've never been so proud of her.

"Hello everyone," she says, turning to the crowd. "Thank you all for coming. There's been a change of plans."

AN HOUR LATER, I'm sitting barefoot at a table with Victoria, watching Sadie and Fiona lead the last of Vic's friends in an enthusiastic line dance. The lights are low inside the barn, and outside the air's just chilly enough to cool off after all this goofy dancing that will definitely be on someone's social media later.

We're splitting a piece of the cake (which is delicious) and my sister looks more relaxed than she has in months. I'm so proud of her for doing the scary thing because it was so obviously the right move.

"All things considered," I say, licking my fork, "folks took this pretty well."

"Better than I expected," she agrees, taking a big bite of cake.

Theo's family had not taken the announcement well and had left shortly after, along with Theo's friends. There were less than a hundred people to begin with, and now only Victoria's closest friends and our family remained. Just as she asked, they'd stayed to eat the boatload of appetizers and enjoy the deejay and dance floor. Our parents had left just after Vic had explained what was happening, and Mom of course behaved as if Vic had just told her she was leaving her whole life behind to join the Coney Island School and learn how to breathe fire. If Mom had worn pearls, she would have clutched them. Instead, she'd shrieked and waved her arms around as if she were looking for a fainting couch. Dad had helped her to the car, promising to *discuss this later*, which probably meant heaving a big helping of guilt right into Vic's lap.

She can handle them, though. She always does.

"Any word from the hot Scot?" she says, going in for another bite.

"Not since this morning. He might be away for a long time." I steal another bite. "I'm trying not to think about it."

"Don't give up on him yet," Vic says, pointing her fork at me. "He did sign a lease, after all, and he knows I'll hold him to it."

I smile. "He'd pay you whether he came back or not. That's the kind of guy he is."

"True," she says. "But he's also desperately in love with you."

"I just worry that he's gone radio silent. Maybe he's reconsidering coming back. Or maybe something has happened with his family that means he has to stay."

"Listen." She reaches over and grabs my hand, squeezing it tight. "I need you to hear this." She's got her Very Serious Face on. "I don't have a crystal ball, but I can tell you one thing for certain. That man is not Mark. He's been nothing but honest with you, and he's in this for real—and I think you are, too. You need to take that little voice in your head that's no doubt screaming at you about all the ways this relationship could go sideways, and squash it like a bug. Believe me, if I could extract that voice from your head, I would have done it ages ago. But it has to be you, sis."

I give her a firm nod. "I know. I hear you."

"Good." She reaches for the last bite of cake just as Sadie and Fiona come over and grab us both.

"Come on," Sadie says. "Time to dance it out."

Rather than protest again, we follow them to the dance floor, our bare feet thumping on the floor as we shimmy under the twinkling lights. I'm loose-limbed from the adrenaline and the

Champagne, and when the music shifts to the next song, I tell them I'm going to get some air.

It's one of those chilly nights where the sky's a deep blue that seems to reach forever. The stars are bright overhead, the moon a pale sliver.

As I step outside, a realization hits me: not one person tonight looked at me like they expected me to fall apart. In all the time leading up to the wedding that didn't happen, no one asked "How are you doing?" in that sad way that's usually reserved for funerals and epic break-ups. No one looked at me like they had a magnifying glass—except for that one moment when my mother stared down her nose at my metallic silver shoes. No one asked about my ex, and not one person made mention of how I had an almost-wedding. No one made me feel like some fragile object they had to handle with care.

I didn't need Logan here with me—I never had.

But I wanted him here, more than anything.

Still staring up at that blanket of stars, I'm trying to do the math and figure out what time it is in Scotland when I hear a rustling in the grass behind me. Probably it's Victoria, wanting a break from the crowd. Somehow she's kept it together this entire evening, acting as if this whole day was a blessing in disguise.

There are so many moments that define us, and the most we can do is handle them with grace. And I definitely need to give myself more grace.

"Hey there, gorgeous."

I turn toward the sound and there's Logan, walking toward me in that slow, easy way of his. Like his footsteps aren't shifting the world on its axis. He's wearing that navy blue suit that fits him like a glove, loosening his tie like he's finally letting himself breathe.

"You're here," I say because I can't quite believe it. "How?"

"Private plane, an awesome pilot, and a swift tailwind." He shoves his hands into his pockets and says, "Sorry I'm late."

Heat blooms in my chest. "What if you're right on time?"

He smiles then, that lopsided grin that will always make my heart hammer against my ribs. "I like the sound of that."

"How are you?"

"Better now." He steps closer and pins me with his gaze. "It was a long day."

Placing my hand on his forearm, I say, "I'm so sorry about your grandfather."

He nods, giving me a sad smile. "Thank you. In the end, it was about as good as we could have hoped for. He went peacefully."

"How's your family?" I ask.

With a small shrug, he says, "All things considered, they're doing all right. Plus, I had a good talk with Rory, and he's got a solid plan for the company. One that doesn't include me." His gaze flicks back toward the barn, where light pours from the big open doors into the dark meadow. "Looks like I missed all the excitement."

Biting my lip, I say, "Um, yes. You could say that."

He lifts a brow. "What does that face mean? What happ—"

I grab his jaw and turn his face toward mine. "I promise I'll tell you all the details, but first I have some other words for you, okay?"

He blinks at me and then gives me a lazy smile that makes my heart do a barrel roll.

I want to see more of that sexy lazy smile. Preferably every morning and every night until the end of time.

"I'm so glad you came back," I tell him, matter-of-factly. Because this is a fact, after all. One of which I'm certain.

"Of course, I came back." He steps closer, so we're toe to toe.

His voice drops to a whisper as he says, "Did you think I wouldn't?"

This is the point where the old me would deny her fears, and her deepest feelings, and pretend they weren't tying her heart into knots. But I don't push those feelings down anymore. Now I know I need to feel these fears, recognize they're just my brain's way of protecting me, and take the leap toward what I want—and have some faith that I know how to get there. I take a deep breath, feeling that knot in my chest loosen just a tad. "I was afraid you'd get home and realize that I'm not what you want."

"Not even close." He slips a hand around my waist and fixes me with his piercing stare. Sliding his fingers along my cheek, he says, "I got there and realized you're everything I want."

I place my finger over his lips. "I'm not done yet. I have more words."

He smirks as he tightens his hands around me, pulling me tighter against his hips. I ignore all that hard muscle for the moment because these words need to be spoken.

"Second," I whisper. "I pushed you away. I shouldn't have done that."

He nods. "Okay. Bygones."

I smack his chest playfully. It's like a kitten batting at a tiger. "This is serious," I say, teasing. "I'm baring my soul here."

"Aye, I'm serious, too," he says. "Go on, then."

I rest my hands on his chest. "I was afraid to tell you how I feel because I thought you wouldn't feel the same."

He smiles. "And how do you feel?"

"Like I love you. Like I don't want you to leave again. Like you're the best thing that ever happened to me, and even though I don't entirely know how to take the next steps, I don't want to miss out on something incredible between us because it's scary."

He stares at me for a long moment.

"I'm done now," I tell him.

When slides his hands into my hair, I lean into him and feel my whole body relax—because yes, this is where it needs to be. Right next to him. "I don't want to leave you again, either," he says. "I love you to pieces, Gwen Griffin, and that's all I need to know."

My heart swells. "You completely blindsided me, you know. I didn't think what was happening between us could be real because it felt too good to be true. I didn't think I could get this lucky."

He gives me a devilish grin and says, "Aye, I'll see to it that you get lucky with me as often as you want, love."

I laugh as he squeezes me against his broad chest and tangles one hand in my hair. He tugs gently as his lip quirks up and he bends to kiss me. When his lips touch mine, it feels like striking a match somewhere deep inside my chest, and feeling that flame race along my skin is glorious. The butterflies are back, swirling like a hurricane, and I know it's because I'm exactly where want to be. Exactly where I need to be.

And no moment has ever felt more perfect.

Epilogue

GWEN

Six months later

I didn't think my hot Scot could get any more scorching, but I was wrong. When he ties an apron on over his thin tee shirt and well-worn jeans, I take a long moment to appreciate the way it accentuates his broad shoulders and tapered waist. It's a new apron I got just for him, a green one that's screen-printed with the words *I'm the Secret Ingredient.* He broke it in last weekend when we made three kinds of shortbread cookies and a lemon custard pie. The streaks of flour across the front remind me of how we very nearly burned the pie because Logan had insisted on deviating from the lesson long enough to hoist me up onto the kitchen island and kiss me senseless while it baked.

That's my guy, though—insistent when it matters.

"So, gorgeous, what are we making today?" he drawls. He's rolling his Rs with extra gusto today because he's learned it drives me completely wild—like a cat with catnip. It's one of the many things about him that I've decided make him completely irresistible. Other things that fall into that category include the way he makes me pesto when he knows I need comfort food, the way he pulls me tight against him when he crawls into bed, and the way he kisses the nape of my neck just before we fall asleep.

And the way he's staring at me now, with that mischievous glint in his eye—that's not bad, either.

The list of things I love about Logan Fyfe grows longer every day. And the list of ways we complement each other does, too.

"I thought we'd raise the bar today," I tell him. "I saw a recipe for a chocolate torte with ganache and raspberries that I'm dying to try."

"That bake-off show's going to be the death of me, isn't it?" he says.

"I think you're up to the challenge, Lancelot." I plant my hands on my hips and watch his eyes track the movement. "Aren't you?"

He gives me a delicious grin. "Aye, and what do I get when I win?"

"You get to name your prize." I give him an exaggerated wink and when I turn to get the recipe, he slips his fingers into the tie of my apron and pulls me close enough to nip at my neck, making me giggle as I squirm in his arms.

We fit together in the most perfect ways, but most of all, he makes me feel safe, valued, and loved beyond measure. We haven't spent a day apart since the night of Vic's almost-wedding. I've gone to Scotland with him once, for his grandfather's memorial, and he's still renting Vic's house next door. It's wild to think I have Theo to thank for bringing us together—despite all his jerk moves, he did manage to bring the perfect man into my life.

"We wrecked the kitchen last time," I say as he flattens his body against mine.

"And wasn't it delightful?" His voice is a deep rumble that vibrates along against my skin. His lips move against my ear, and it's the most delicious feeling in the world. They say the kitchen is the heart of a home, and for me, that's one hundred percent true.

I'll never, ever get tired of the way this man makes me feel so treasured. Or the way he's so wickedly distracting. And yeah, with him this house feels like a home again.

With one deft move, I slip from his grasp and wave the recipe card in front of him. Then I grab a wooden spoon from the counter and hold it against his chest, gently pushing him away while he gives me a hungry stare.

"Torte first," I tell him, giving him a saucy look. "I mean, we have to make sure you get your money's worth and learn to bake all the sweets you put on your list." I drag the spoon down his chest and he looks like the big bad wolf who wants to eat me up.

Later, I think with a smile.

"The auction folks will be very disappointed if you don't enjoy your lessons, Mr. Fyfe."

He leans back against the counter and smirks, shoving his hands into the apron pockets. "All right, then," he says and fixes me with a look that could spark a wildfire. "Tell me what to do, gorgeous."

I feel a blush reach all the way to the tips of my ears, because the last time he spoke those words, he then proceeded to put his lips on me in ways I'd never imagined—and had made me see honest-to-goodness stars.

Stars.

"Start by creaming the butter in the mixer and then add the sugar slowly," I say, because Logan really, *really* likes it when I give him directions. A complicated recipe like this one is full of directions, and it's going to take every ounce of his willpower to keep his hands off me until this cake's in the oven.

I grin at the thought because teasing him has become something I enjoy almost as much as he does.

"Aye," he says, turning on the mixer. "Can you read the full recipe to me, love? I like to know what I'm in for."

I take the recipe card from the counter and read out the ingredients to him as he tosses in the eggs. When I stop after the first couple of instructions, he turns off the mixer and says, "Go on, then. All the way to the end."

I shrug and turn the card over, reading aloud the next few lines that describe making the ganache filling, then the frosting. It's then that I see an additional note at the bottom of the card, written in a different handwriting.

You're the sweetness at the bottom of the pie, love. I'll savor you all of my days if you'll let me.

"Logan," I say, blinking back tears.

Before I can say more, he drops to one knee and takes my hand in his, keeping his eyes steady on mine. When he pulls a ring from the pocket of his apron, he flashes that roguish smile that will always make my heart pound. "What do you say, gorgeous? Want to marry me so I can be the luckiest man alive?"

Heat blooms in my chest as I slide my fingers into his hair. "How long have you had that ring in your apron pocket?"

"A while."

"How long have you been thinking about asking me that?"

He grins. "A long while."

"Then it's a good thing we had a baking lesson today," I tell him.

His brow lifts. "Is that a yes, love?"

"Absolutely," I say.

When he stands, he slides his hand into my hair and pulls me against him. His lips are firm and gentle as he kisses me. It's a kiss that's sweet, tender, and full of promise. I feel light enough to float away into the clouds, but then Logan's arms tighten around me, reminding me that he'll always be here to keep me grounded.

And that's the very best feeling of all.

Join My Newsletter

Like to be the first to hear about new releases and deals? Subscribe to Lucy's newsletter and always be the first to hear the good stuff.

As a bonus, you'll get a free Jasmine Falls novella, *You Got This, Maggie Monroe*, when you join. It's exclusively for newsletter subscribers.

Sign up at lucydayauthor.com.

Acknowledgments

Every time I finish writing a book, it feels like it took a lot of work—but also a dash of luck and a little magic, too.

First, to my friend Katie Pryal: you know you're my ride-or-die, and there's no one else I'd rather talk book projects with. Thank you for your insight, for your willingness to read a book a million times, and for always having my back. You're the best writing buddy I could have, and I sure am glad we crashed into each other all those years ago.

To my friends and family: thank you for encouraging and inspiring me. Your belief in me means the world—and I'm so grateful to have you in my life. You make me feel pretty dang lucky. And Camille Pagán, you get a special thank you because your words have helped more than you'll ever know.

To my readers: you're the best. Thank you for coming on these adventures with me—for not just reading my stories, but telling your friends about them and inspiring me to keep cooking up more love stories. You make it possible for me to do what I love, and for that I'm grateful every day.

Finally to Andrew: you cracked my heart wide open and made room for all these love stories. You bring the magic, and I can't wait to see where our story goes next.

About the Author

Born and raised in South Carolina, Lucy Day loves sweet tea, summer nights, and big-hearted love stories. She is winner of an IPPY Silver Medal for Romance (The Almost Lovebirds, 2023). She started writing in college and wrote her first novel after leaving her job at a web comic in St. Louis. Lucy is a bird nerd who can't live without strong coffee and wide open spaces. She's married to her best friend and when she isn't writing a new love story, she's out walking in the woods, dreaming up her next adventure.

To learn more, visit lucydayauthor.com.